THE LAST RESORT

THE LAST RESORT

by

Laurence Geller

Chauncer Press Books

An Imprint of Richard Altschuler & Associates, Inc.

New York

Distributed by University Press of New England

For information contact the publisher, Richard Altschuler & Associates, Inc., at 100 West 57th Street, New York, New York 10019, (212) 397-7233, or richard.altschuler@gmail.com.

Library of Congress Control Number: 2012906377
CIP data for this book are available from the Library of Congress

ISBN-13: 978-1-884092-84-8
ISBN-10: 1-884092-84-5

Chaucer Press Books is an imprint of
Richard Altschuler & Associates, Inc.

Printed in the United States of America

Distributed by University Press of New England
1 Court Street
Lebanon, New Hampshire 03766

To

Ana, Massimo, Naomi, Gemma, Gigi, Raffaello, Isla

You are my tomorrow

WHERE NO COUNSEL IS, THE PEOPLE FALL, BUT IN THE MULTITUDE OF COUNSELORS THERE IS SAFETY

Proverbs X1/14

Mossad's guiding ideology

Prologue

St. Paul de Vence

The Audley Resort, like a French Valhalla, looks down at the village of St. Paul de Vence and the Riviera coastline from its aerie in the hills of the Côte d'Azur. The village, once summer playground to Pablo Picasso, Henri Matisse, and James Baldwin, still serves as an attraction for rich tourists and famous artists. But the very rich and the very famous go to the Audley—if they can get a reservation.

To call the Resort a luxury hotel is to minimize it. Instead of individual bedrooms, guests are welcomed into a two-bedroom villa, totally secluded from its neighbors. There they will find hand-woven silk contemporary Tufenkian rugs and hand-crafted Grace Leo furnishings atop African hardwood floors; 3-D TVs, an endless stream of movies, iPod docking stations, Bose sound systems hidden in electrically opened recesses, and wireless high-speed Internet lend technology to each villa; and 600-plus thread-count pale yellow and cream striped Frette linens add comfort and style to each suite's subtle blend of modern and Art Deco design. Hiroshige prints or Jasper Johns watercolors and one of three editions of Jim Dine bronzes, cast uniquely for the Resort, stand in the reception area for each villa; and a black-bottomed infinity pool, sparkling like a field of diamonds in the Mediterranean sunshine, are the finishing touches. Absolute discretion and privacy are assured to all guests, and a personal butler attends to their every self-indulgence. Yet, should they choose to rouse themselves, they have the choice of a spa with wellness and beauty treatment centers cantilevered into tree-covered hills; a Jack Nicklaus-designed championship golf course; a Michelin three-star restaurant, under the direction of much acclaimed Chef Jorge Peres; or—for those who combine work with play—a conference center carpeted in hand-sewn lush Wilton, and cherry-paneled boardrooms featuring state-of-the-art telecommunications, touch-screens and leading-edge technology.

The Resort is surrounded by "*Les Residences*," luxury homes set in at least an acre of landscaped and wooded property, often used as a summer getaway for those who can afford the minimum price of Euros 10 million—and for an additional Euros 10,000 per day they can rent Elite, the 110-foot Azimuth luxury yacht moored at the Resort's marina, set fifty yards from the Audley's beach club, bar and restaurant. It is said that Jordan's King Abdullah owns one of the houses, and the movie stars Angelina Jolie and Brad Pitt another, though management discretion makes such rumors unverifiable.

The Audley Resort was the inspiration of Rolfe Ritter, founder and former chief executive of Kestrel Hotels, who bought the dormant Audley Hotels Group in 1993 and, less than a decade later, saved himself from the very brink of personal and financial disaster by selling both the Kestrel and Audley chains to the multinational conglomerate EUF. As EUF's deputy chairman, the Dutch-born Ritter persuaded his boss to let him realize his long, meticulously planned dream to create sister resorts by appealing to his vanity—"our shareholders will see you've built the very best in the world on land you already own"—one on the Riviera, the other on the coast of Southern California. The Audley Resort, St. Paul de Vence, was completed in 2005. One year later, its twin sister, the Audley Resort, San Diego Cliffs, opened to fanfare usually reserved for a Frank Gehry museum, and was quickly booked up a year in advance.

Ritter always selected his general managers carefully. For the Audley Resort, St. Paul de Vence, he had taken special care in anointing Bertrand Le Roi, GM of his Kestrel Hotel at Hyde Park Corner in London. The multilingual, diminutive, balding, rotund, impeccably dressed Le Roi had moved back to his native France with the aplomb and grace of a latter day Maurice Chevalier, becoming a minor celebrity among the most powerful people in the world.

*

"*Merde*!" screamed Le Roi in the privacy of his office. And again, "*Merde*!"

His assistant GM, Raymond Pelletier, alarmed by the shouts, rushed into the office. Le Roi rarely swore; only a disaster could have caused the outburst.

Le Roi stood transfixed by what he was watching on his monitor. The back of his neck was bright red; sweat ran down his cheeks.

"Sir . . ." Pelletier began.

"Look!" Without turning, Le Roi pointed at the screen. Pelletier moved closer. It took him a moment to recognize the Presidential Suite, another to make out the unmistakable features of Prince Jamail Al Saif, Saudi Arabia's Minister of Defense, and a horrendous third moment to realize the prince's guests were two pre-pubescent boys, and that what he was doing with them was unspeakable.

"We shouldn't be watching," Pelletier said when he had breath enough to talk. "The closed circuit isn't intended to intrude on our guests' privacy."

"Closed circuit?" Le Roi wheeled, apoplectic. "It's on the Internet, you idiot!"

"Oh, *mon Dieu*!" Indeed, Le Roi was staring at his computer screen, not at the closed-circuit monitor. Pelletier grasped the implications immediately. "The Resort. It's been humiliated. Defiled. No one will stay in that suite again."

Le Roi sighed noisily, and drew in a deep breath. Finally he said, "It is far more of a problem than a single suite. Our reputation for discretion, privacy and security is shattered. Our regular guests will scatter like leaves in the wind, never to return. Travel agents will shun us, the media will condemn us, no self-respecting guest will book us and our competitors will rejoice at our demise. Our Resort will never recover. We might as well shut the doors; we're finished, completely finished. I will be known as the clown that let this happen. I am finished! *Merde*! *Merde*! *Merde*!"

Mesmerized, Bertrand Le Roi watched messages scroll across the screen below the action: HE IGNORED OUR WARNING.

Le Roi's voice was shaky, his demeanor stricken. "That suite has the highest security. The prince's own security detail stand guard over it twenty-four hours a day. His people inspect every detail many times during the day. How in God's name did anyone get those cameras inside it?"

The two men looked at each other. Le Roi answered his own question. "Impossible," he whispered. "It's completely impossible."

Bali

In January, a fire, cause unknown, swept through the four-star Bali Oasis Resort on the Nusa Dua Peninsula, sending its panicked guests to the haven of the civic center in the nearby town of Denpasar. The following month, the five-star Putri Palace and the Sheraton Nusa Dua were also set ablaze. Clearly the fires were not coincidental, though the police could find no incendiary device to explain any of them. The American State Department suspected terrorists; Balinese officials blamed rivals in Jakarta. The Indonesian government replied that the Balinese hotel owners themselves had set the fires to claim the insurance money. The frightened hotel community, reacting with understandable panic, sent out confusing P.R. press releases that comforted no one.

Whoever the culprit, it looked like someone was out to destroy every leading hotel on Nusa Dua, a suspicion confirmed when, in early April, a massive explosion leveled one wing of the five-star Nusa Cliff Hotel, killing twenty-seven guests and thirty-four employees unlucky enough to be inside that part of the property at midday.

"Why not us?" wondered Sammi Chalabi, general manager of the Kestrel Resort, the crown jewel of all the hotels on the Peninsula. "We're clearly the most prominent property in Nusa Dua. Yet we've been untouched."

He was right about the Resort's prominence. Designed by the renowned Japanese architect Toshio Toshiro, who had been inspired by the gracious Balinese water palaces of the past, the Kestrel meandered over forty acres of winding rivers, waterfalls, koi-filled pools, and tropical gardens that hosted clouds of vividly-colored butterflies, which hovered above the flowers like pieces in an ever-changing kaleidoscope. Guests stayed in two-story bedroom wings and private villas strewn about the property, dined in one of four restaurants, and got married—for the Resort had quickly become the favorite honeymoon destination for Japan's upper classes—in one of two glittering wedding chapels set on meticulously landscaped and manicured remote promontories on the outskirts of the property. The Resort's ballroom, with its Dale Chihuly glass ceiling, could accommodate up to 1,500 guests for spectacular ceremonial dinners, making it the largest on the Nusa Dua Peninsula.

Rolfe Ritter had first spotted Chalabi working in the sales department at the Kestrel in Paris. Impressed, he had put the young Lebanese into the Kestrel Star Track advancement program; the Bali post followed after his rapid progression through a series of increasingly important assignments in the company's hotels, putting his fluency in six languages to good use. Chalabi, not yet forty, slim and elegant to a point of parody, had earned the admiration of his competitors, who elected him president of the Balinese Hotel Association. He felt it his responsibility to find the attackers—and to quiet their natural suspicions when the Kestrel remained unscathed. To his growing frustration, every avenue of investigation had led to a dead end.

Perhaps the Kestrel's turn had simply not yet come, Chalabi mused. All had been calm since the Nusa Cliff explosion, but still . . . . He entered Conference Room A where the Crisis Committee had assembled, and took his place at the head of the table.

"Reports?" he inquired.

Günthe Kutsche, the Resort's chief of security, was the first to speak. "We've quadrupled our manpower, instituted full property inspections, checked the backgrounds of all the nearly one thousand full-time and part-time staff members, begun car checks at all entrances, reviewed and double-checked the references of all new employees who have joined us in the past six months. Nothing suspicious to report."

"Same for my departments," added Robin Broadbent, head of the food and beverage division.

"And mine," said Hank Merritt, the Texan who commanded accounting and controls.

"What about you?" Chalabi asked Bill Petrie, the dour grey-haired Australian who ran the engineering department as if it were a nuclear submarine and sported a '60s-style military crewcut.

Petrie bristled. "Damn it, Sammi, if there was a problem, you'd have heard about it!"

Joan Chu, the Resort's unflappable rooms division manager, held up her hand, then quickly withdrew it.

"You were going to say . . . ?" Chalabi asked.

"Nothing. Just a feeling, an instinct."

The Chinese woman was too reticent by half, Chalabi thought. "In the absence of evidence, feelings and instincts are all we have to go on. Don't be shy, Joan. Tell the group."

"It's the Pakistanis, Mr. Chalabi. We have them staying with us all the time, so I generally wouldn't have noticed them, but I happened to be at the desk when they came in yesterday, and they didn't make reservations at any of the restaurants."

Chalabi raised his eyebrows. The Kestrel's internationally acclaimed restaurants were unsurpassed on the Peninsula. There were no eateries nearly as good within miles of the Resort. "How many were they?"

"Four. Two couples. And another strange thing: Neither of the women made appointments at the spa. Usually that's the first thing they do. It was odd enough for me to look up their records. Both couples had been guests here on three occasions already this year."

"When?" Chalabi asked.

"January, February and April."

"How long are they staying?" the general manager asked, a tremor in his voice.

"Four days. But they didn't seem to have much luggage. I'm sure it doesn't mean anything, but . . ."

If an alarm had gone off in the room, Sammi Chalabi could not have been more alert. He turned to his technology manager. "It could be a coincidence but it's the same months as the bombings. Pull up their information quickly, Gusti. Let's have a look at it."

The young Balinese I.T. expert switched on the computer in front of him and began typing. He stopped. Typed again. Stopped. "Strange," he muttered.

Chalabi moved to his side. "What is it?"

"It can't be!" The young man anguished.

"What can't be?"

"The data's disappeared."

"Impossible! What about the backup files?"

Gusti swung around slowly to face his boss. "That's just it, Mr. Chalabi. They've disappeared as well. All of the guest information for the past two weeks has just vanished, evaporated, gone. Every file for every guest in the hotel has been systematically and completely erased. The server's been wiped clean."

Silence paralyzed the room, as the stunned team members looked at each other.

"A disaster!" Joan Chu shouted, all reticence gone. "That means we've no idea who's in the hotel or where they're staying. No bills, no check-in or check-out dates, no credit card information, no accounts receivable, guest preference records, no security logs. Nothing."

"Pakistanis! Why in God's name didn't you say something to me before?" Chalabi seethed, his breathing labored. "I suppose we'll never find out who the mysterious foursome are."

"What about employee records? Reservation requests, Internet booking records, sales department data?" Kutsche asked. "We may be able to find out who made their reservations and when."

The young Balinese's fingers flew over the keyboard. "Gone! It's all gone."

Kutsche muttered, "Unless we get very lucky, we'll never find out who these people are. Even if we check with Customs and Immigration for the times Joan thinks they were here, I'll bet a month's pay they came in on false passports."

Gusti said, "The hotel's been damaged just as badly as if it was set on fire."

"How long will it take to recreate the records?" Chalabi's words came out with the speed of machine-gun fire.

Gusti turned back to his computer. "I don't think it can be done." He scratched his head. "No, it can't be done."

"What do you mean? Get the experts in. They can recreate anything from the server!"

"I've never seen anything like this, maybe it's a virus. Whatever it is, it has gobbled up every file; every single file," Gusti answered, his eyes fixed on the screen. "Everything's disappeared. Completely gone. Forever."

The general manager was close to tears. “What have we gotten ourselves into?” he moaned.

At that very moment, not four miles away, an explosion rocked the Regent Resort Nusa Dua, demolishing its convention center, killing forty-nine people and injuring over twice that amount.

Santa Monica

“Beth?”

“This is she.”

“Rolfe Ritter here, calling from New York.”

Beth Taylor’s hands trembled, whether out of anxiety or excitement, she could not tell. Maybe both. “Mr. Ritter! How can I help you?”

Rolfe was responsible for . . . well, her life, she reflected. It was he who provided her current job, general manager of the Kestrel Santa Monica; he who had faith in her when she had so little in herself; he who had inspired her still-increasing, albeit fragile, sense of self-worth.

“Only doctors can help,” he answered. Beth remembered hearing a rumor that Mrs. Ritter was sick. “No, I’m simply wondering how my ex-protégés are faring, and you’re on my list. Hotel running smoothly? Any problems with the new owners?”

“That’s very kind of you. I really haven’t had much to do with them. I suspect they’re more concerned with the Audleys than the Kestrels.” She could hear his intake of breath.

“The Kestrels are as important as the Audleys. Please don’t consider yourself a second-class citizen.”

“Oh, I don’t. Really. It’s just that . . .”

“Business good?” he interrupted.

“Close to capacity, 93 percent.”

“They won’t like ‘close.’”

“Well up over last year.”

“That’s because the former owner didn’t know the trade.”

She knew his self-deprecation masked enormous pride. Rolfe Ritter was unparalleled as the visionary and marketing-oriented taskmaster of the Audley, Kestrel, and Metropolitan chains, who only accepted excellence from himself and his team. Any response from her would be fatuous.

"How's Mrs. Ritter?"

A pause. Uh-oh, she thought. Forbidden territory.

"Doing as well as could be expected," he said at last. "Meanwhile, if you need advice, call me. The Kestrel Santa Monica still hosting the pre-awards dinner?"

"As always." She tried to be friendly. "Any predictions on who'll win the Oscars?"

"Not a clue." His voice was cold. Mistake.

"Thanks for calling," she said lamely.

"Keep up the good work. You know I'm fond of you, Beth. Do the company proud."

"I will, sir."

He had hung up.

*

Elizabeth Taylor's parents named her after the movie star, so their child insisted that she never be called by her full name—she wanted to be compared to no one. Beth was fine, or Lizzie or Liz, just never Elizabeth. Nevertheless, the thirty-four-year-old woman had matured into a beauty in her own right. True, her figure was less full than the idol's in her prime, the eyes not as luminous, her hair chestnut rather than black, but several of her male friends obviously preferred her looks to yesteryear's goddess; and her women friends, judging their looks against hers, found themselves wanting.

California-born Beth was the daughter of an actor and actress who never rose beyond regional theater, but who found steady employment in two-character shows such as "The Gin Game," "The Owl and the Pussycat," and "Two for the Seesaw." Their profession necessitated continuous changes of venue, and as Mr. Taylor joked, the itinerant couple knew the inside of every hotel between Wheeling and Walla Walla.

But they didn't know Beth. Between rehearsals and performances, her parents had little time for her, and so attributed her sullenness and anger to the constant changes in schools, rather than to something more deep-seated. "She'll grow out of it," they assured themselves when sitters or the administrators of the dozen-plus schools she had briefly attended complained about Beth's truancy, truculence, strange assortment of boyfriends, her hair—one day purple, another day green—her endlessly erratic behavior or her tantrums, which persisted long into adolescence.

Rolfe's call brought up myriad memories: the time she tore a fourth-grade classmate's hair from its roots, which was the first of three times she was expelled from different schools; the moment when, as a pre-adolescent, she took her first toke of a joint; the high of her first hit of cocaine and the pain of losing her virginity to the boy who supplied it; the cold of the streets in Milwaukee, where she had been deposited when she was old enough to be left at school; her pregnancy at eighteen; the long, lonely years of self-imposed estrangement from her parents; the birth of a daughter; the agony when the girl was torn from her arms by a social services do-gooder who gave the child up for adoption.

At least that had cleansed her. It had also soured her relationships with men—initially dating often but never consummating a relationship; always justifying her decision not to do it with reasons why her would-be lover was at fault; never acknowledging that the thought of making love repulsed her as, over time, her revulsion grew at the memory of her lovemaking sessions with her daughter's father. As the years went by, dates became increasingly infrequent and their inevitable conclusions became more painful and acrimonious, as her spurned would-be lovers were left in confused frustration.

Beth had grown up dreaming of all the wonderful things that happened in the hotels her parents couldn't afford to stay in, and, after a cross-country Greyhound Bus trip, she talked her way into a two-year course in tourism at Sacramento Community College, then to a job at the Kestrel Hotel in Union Square, San Francisco, as a front desk assistant. That Kestrel was Rolfe Ritter's first triumph, the flagship of the line, so he stayed there whenever he came to San Francisco, despite ownership of the newer, more luxurious nearby Audley Hotel. Though married to a woman of matchless desirability, he was still struck by Beth's grace and beauty, to say nothing of the ease with which she handled herself with the Kestrel's patrons; and she became a protégé, like Le Roi and Chalabi. Ten years after they first met, Rolfe promoted her to general manager at the Kestrel Santa Monica, a dazzling center-piece of the chain's Southern Californian coastal properties, situated on the beach. At night, the Santa Monica pier, with its sparkling Ferris Wheel, provide a backdrop to Fantu, the "beautiful people's" award-winning champagne and sushi restaurant, run by its eponymous celebrity chef who created the now-famous Caviar and Gold-Leaf Martini for the grand-opening celebration, and the location of many pre- and post-Oscar parties, where Beth previously attended to, among others, Elizabeth Taylor. Every time she walked through the lobby with its thirty-feet-high mummified palm trees filling its soaring atrium, or entertained at the rooftop poolside restaurant, she pinched herself to see if it was real; she really was the general manager of Santa Monica's centerpiece hotel.

She shut out her past, learned her trade, rationalized that she sacrificed personal relationships for professional success, and every day prayed she wouldn't be discovered as the fake she knew herself to be. At least Rolfe Ritter had been taken in, and she blessed him for it.

*

On the afternoon of his call, she was peremptorily summoned by Sheldon Lovell Jr., Kestrel's latest general counsel. "The FBI wants to talk to you," he told her, adding nothing but, "five o'clock. The Bob Hope Room. I'll be there to protect the company." Now she sat uncomfortably at Lovell's side in the meeting room named after the comedian, facing two huge, well-muscled men in gray suits—Fafner and Fasolt, she mentally dubbed them, after the giants in her parents' favorite opera, Richard Wagner's "Das Rheingold"—awed despite herself. No one was smiling. What could she possibly have done wrong?

Fafner, the older of the behemoths, began. "Is it true, Miss Taylor, that Chiang Shui-kan is a guest at this hotel?"

Beth hesitated. The man had registered under an alias. "Answer truthfully," Lovell instructed.

"Yes." Beth's heart raced.

"You know, of course, he's the Vice President of the Republic of China, perhaps better known to you—incorrectly—as Taiwan?"

Where was this leading? "I was aware of that, yes. He checked in under the name of Wong Hong-ren. Important people commonly use pseudonyms when they stay at the Kestrel Santa Monica."

"Do you know the purpose of his visit?"

"To spend time with his son who's studying film-making at the University of Southern California."

Fasolt looked up from his notes. "He stayed in the Douglas Fairbanks Suite?"

"Our best," Beth said with a flash of pride, then caught herself. Fasolt had used the past tense.

"Strange, then, that you do not provide it with adequate security."

Had something happened to Shui-kan? A knot of anxiety cramped Beth's neck. "On the contrary. Besides his own agents, who occupied the suites on either side of his, cameras in the corridor and in the foyer of the suite, linked to our own security room, operate 24/7. If something untoward occurred, we'd have seen it."

Fafner rose, put his fists on the table, and leaned toward Beth, breathing fire. "But something did occur. And you did not see it. Last night, the vice president's face came in contact with a rare and potent poison, a particularly virulent variation of Dioxin. He's now in critical condition at Cedars of Sinai Hospital in Los Angeles. If he survives, and I stress the 'if,' he will be horribly scarred forever."

Beth felt poisoned herself. She looked to Lovell for help, but he only put his hand on her arm and said nothing. "What do you mean, if he survives?" The silence that followed gave her time to think. "That's dreadful! But we at the Kestrel couldn't possibly have . . ."

Fafner interrupted in a voice so low Beth had to strain to hear it. "Miss Taylor, we found traces of the poison on the pillows on the bed Shui-kan slept in."

Electricity traversed Beth's spine like fire up a fuse. "Our pillows?"

"All four of them."

"How did it get there?"

Fafner sat back with a grim smile. "That's what my colleague and I are here to determine."

"Then look at the surveillance tapes," Beth cried. "Nobody could have slipped into that suite without being filmed."

"Ah, Miss Taylor. That's why you're here. Your security tapes have disappeared."

Beth began to shake. Lovell's grip on her arm tightened.

Fafner was implacable. "Yes, disappeared. How did that happen, Miss Taylor? Please explain."

Chapter 1
The Audley Resort, San Diego Cliffs

The second of "Rolfe's Twins," set on a cliff some twenty miles northeast of San Diego, had much in common with its sister in St. Paul de Vence. The size, facilities and amenities were almost identical, the décor Southern Californian but clearly inspired by its Mediterranean namesake. Here the two Tom Fazio courses boasted six oceanside fairways and greens between them, the Azimuth yacht was ten feet longer, the beach club featured caviar and sushi, and the award-winning, three-star restaurant 'C' was run by Jason Avington, the renowned British chef and TV personality, whom Ritter had persuaded to leave New York's fashionable La Belle Reve Restaurant with promises of a free hand and a no-questions-asked construction budget.

The adjoining residences went for a minimum of $15 million (the most recent had been sold to a biotech oligarch for $41 million), but the attention to detail—everything from the way fresh rose petals were patterned on the made-up beds each morning to the height of the hibiscus plants in the lobby—reminded everyone of the Audley St. Paul de Vence who was lucky enough to have stayed there.

General Manager Matthew Dirksen, thirty-nine, Cornell trained, Rolfe Ritter-tutored, treated the place like a royal baby. His first high-end hotel general manager's job had been at the 800-room Kestrel, on the Magnificent Mile, Chicago, a busy rooms factory with a tough and antagonistic union. It was here that Ritter spotted the lean, six-foot-two-inch, Indiana-born, high-school basketball star, and immediately saw his potential. He smoothed off his rough edges, advised him on the subtleties of dress, decorum and attention to detail, taught him to upsell and yield-manage his room rates, made him understand how to read the hotel's balance sheet—and not only the profit and loss accounts—stiffened his backbone for the labor negotiations, and pronounced him ready for his next career step, the most prestigious job in

Kestrel's North American universe, at the Audley San Diego Cliffs.

The rough edges needed considerable smoothing. Matt's mother, who had deified him, he later figured out, to make up for the loss of feeling for her husband, died when he was fourteen; and his father, an accountant in Chesterton, Indiana, had little to teach him beyond discipline and organization, both of which he reluctantly mastered. His height and natural athletic ability lead him naturally to excel at high school basketball. His father rarely attended games, and only when pressed by local peer pressure to see "an important one" would he grudgingly seat himself on the bleachers. Rarely venturing further than Chicago or Indianapolis as a teenager, Matt was self-taught in music and literature—his passions—and considered himself warm, where his father was cold, in relationships. He attracted many women, was attracted by some, but formed no lasting ties. Every serious relationship ended in tears. Maybe he couldn't find anyone to match his mother. He'd wait, he justified to himself; the peripatetic world of hotels meant short tenures if he was to rise in the business, and as such a wife and growing family would be a hindrance. He never believed that he retained a bit of his father's icy core, even when women themselves pointed it out to him.

Dirksen considered himself at the pinnacle of his profession; he'd come a long way, he reflected, from his first job as a busboy at Sand Creek Country Club in Chesterton.

To his amazement he had been selected by Ritter from seven shortlisted candidates for the post of general manager, and had overseen the Resort's debut two years ago. Now, as he strolled the footpath that ran from the *porte cochère* to the summit of the cliff, he believed he had fulfilled the mission his mentor had laid out for him: create the best resort in North America and perhaps the world.

When the teenage Dirksen carried his first tray of dishes through the swinging door from the kitchen to the Sand Creek country club's restaurant, he thought he had entered a world of luxury and opulence he could never have imagined. Now, twenty-five years later, he laughed at the memory. Luxury? The staff dining room at the Resort made Sand Creek's restaurant look shabby. At Ritter's instruction, he had traversed the globe visiting the top properties within the Audley brand, inspected any potential competitor's resorts, spent time shadowing Le Roi in St. Paul de Vence and compiled a best practices list of everything, every detail, no matter how big or small, that he thought would make his property the very best. He had methodically and relentlessly implemented every item on the list and was always searching for more ideas to further set his Resort far above all others.

Deep inside, he understood he was no more than an actor on a stage. Matt knew where he had come from and would never forget it. He would never be rich enough or grand enough to stay at a property such as his Resort. He belonged in the staff dining room, not in Jason Avington's gourmet restaurant.

His humility endeared him to the team he had carefully assembled to run the Resort. He would regularly eat with the property's associates, chatting in Spanish with the maids and gardeners, knowing not only their names but also their children's. No airs, no graces. Just doing his job as well as he expected them to do theirs. Matt Dirksen was always available to his staff, and he would often reach into his own pocket to help if circumstances didn't fit the Resort's policies. He had paid for more than one set of kids' braces, as well as medical treatments and, on one occasion, the funeral of a Mexican laundry attendant's teenage son, killed in a hit-and-run car accident.

He remembered himself still as the pimply teenager from Chesterton, and while his face had cleared and his clothes and manners were impeccable, he knew himself to be nothing more than a master of ceremonies, put at the Resort to please and entertain the blueblood guests and the newly rich who considered him another of their servants. He often repeated one of Rolfe Ritter's adages—"*Noveau riche* is better than no *riche* at all." The team at the hotel knew how he felt about his role as part of the team and revered him for his modesty, never considering the psychological underpinnings.

The sky, he reflected, looked as though God had only one color on His palette: the blue glittered. But there were man-made clouds on his personal horizon. Six weeks earlier, Fabrizio Battini, Chairman of Blenheim Partners, which in January had acquired the Kestrel Hotel Corporation from EUF, had arrived in person to tell

Matt that, from then on, he was to report to a senior vice president, Dieter Weiss, who, although new to the company, was now in charge of all Blenheim Partners Californian properties. Weiss and Matt had yet to meet, but that was about to change. Matt had been summoned to the Blenheim corporate offices in Los Angeles six days hence. The GM mistrusted corporations, especially those with Germans in senior positions. His grandfather had been blown to pieces by Panzer shrapnel in North Africa, and his father had never lost his hatred of "the Huns." Matt did not consciously share that hatred, but it lingered, he knew, in his bloodstream. Meanwhile, there was a far happier event to anticipate. Rolfe Ritter had asked if he and his wife could come for the weekend. Could they? Matt had arranged for the Imperial Suite to be repainted, the spotless carpet shampooed, the drapes dry-cleaned, and the limousine polished like fine armor. Ritter had insisted that Matt not personally meet the chartered Citation X when it landed, but rather provide transportation to the resort.

His cell phone beeped. "Twenty minutes out," Freddie Garcia, the resort's head chauffeur, told him.

Matt raced down the hill, arranged the pre-prepared executive committee under the bougainvillea-covered *porte cochère*, and stood them at attention in a line straight as any presidential guard, as the Resort's midnight-blue Bentley pulled up.

A human missile bounded out and grabbed his protégé in a hug. "Matt!" Rolfe exclaimed. "You've no idea how great it is to be here!" He took a step back. "And you, you handsome hotelier. You look terrific. And so does the place. Good job. Good job. It's just like I imagined it. Better. I'm proud of you."

Warmth more transporting than the summer air filled Matt's heart; he felt he had leave to unburden it. "I'll give you the nickel tour before dinner, then we can dine together or serve you in your suite. Your choice. But there's a matter I need to discuss with you."

"In the suite, please," Rolfe said. "You can join me there. Mrs. Ritter's tired after the plane ride. She'll want a nap. I don't think she's up to a lavish dinner. "

He moved down the reception line, introducing himself and shaking each committee member's hand. Matt smiled to himself, recognizing the practiced charm of the old pro—the best in the business, everyone said. He'd have replied that no one came close.

He was distracted by movement near the limousine. Freddie had gone to the passenger door and opened it for Mrs. Ritter—Momo, Matt remembered. He had met her once before when Rolfe and she had stayed at the Kestrel Chicago. He, the GM at the time, had been astonished not only by her beauty—her Eurasian black eyes, the sheen of her hair, her full lips, an imposingly tall figure that was both slim and voluptuous—but by the confident grace with which she moved and the musical modulation of her voice. Leave it to Rolfe Ritter to pick the "Jewel of the Orient," he recalled thinking.

Why had she taken so long to get out of the limo? he wondered. But then he saw her and knew the answer.

The woman who emerged could barely stand. She wore a woolen knit cap to cover her head; underneath it, her once remarkable face was puffy, as though reflected in a fun-house mirror. Her arms and hands were so swollen she could barely hold the walker Freddie had set before her. Matt had seen that look before, on his mother, whose brain tumor was treated with prednisone after the surgery and radiation. Sorrow for his past and pity for the Ritters engaged his soul. His father had borne the brunt of his mother's illness, and after she died he became even more remote; but he knew the pain himself: He had been robbed of his champion.

"Breast cancer," Rolfe said softly by Matt's side. "A double mastectomy, and a hell of a lot more on top of it. We had the surgery done at Sloan Kettering. That wasn't too bad but the radiation and chemotherapy have been hard for her to bear. She's very weak. That's why we thought a few days of luxury would be an elixir," he laughed, "so where else but the illustrious Audley San Diego Cliffs?"

Matt heard the agony behind the laughter. "I'm so terribly sorry," he said. "It must be tough for you."

Rolfe turned his head away. "Only if you aren't a fan of the Spanish Inquisition."

"Is there anything I can do for her?"

Rolfe regained his composure. "Absolutely nothing." He squeezed his wife's hand as she sat propped up by pillows in a wheelchair. "She's a real fighter, and not used to losing. If I were you, I wouldn't bet against her."

*

The setting sun filled the Imperial Suite with pink and gold hues. Matt remembered that his ex-boss's drink was a chardonnay, *Far Niente*, and filled Rolfe's glass with it.

Rolfe smiled gratefully. "An apropos name, isn't it? Means 'do nothing.' And '*no far niente*' means 'it doesn't matter.'" He waited for Matt to fill his own glass, and they toasted each other before he continued. "After the doctors told me how bad things were with Momo, the ugliness of everything that's gone on with the company didn't matter in comparison. At first, I simply didn't give a shit about anything or anyone except her. Now, though, I'm so pissed off with the way I hear things are going that I've taken a morbid interest in Blenheim Partners. Keeps my mind off my impotence." He sighed. "I tell you, Matt, there's nothing worse than having no control. I can get her the best doctors, the best medicines, proven and experimental, the best home care. But it's all stop-gap. This disease is going its own way, for good or ill, and all I can do is make her as comfortable as possible, boost her morale, then sit by and hope for the best."

Matt could not find words to console him. "I haven't seen you since Chicago, when you offered me this job," he said instead. "We were owned by EUF then. What happened? What ugliness do you mean?"

Rolfe seemed glad to get off the subject of his wife. "Everything started out well. I didn't like having a boss after all those years of independence, but Martin Treadway and I saw things the same way, and he let me build this and the St. Paul de Vence property. I thought things were going along just fine, but it didn't take me long to discover that Treadway has a short attention span and a gigantic ego. He lost interest in the hotels, only seemed to care about the next megadeal du jour. He started hanging out with the likes of Tony Blair and Bono, even traveled with a bodyguard like a rock star. I realized I meant nothing to him, that he'd offered me the deputy-chairmanship so I'd agree to the acquisition. All his seductive words about partnership and building a legacy were pure bullshit. My autonomy disappeared and the bean counters took control."

He held out his glass and Matt refilled it. "Two thousand five and six were good years for the industry, supply growth was nonexistent. I knew it was a great time to buy new properties. Everything for once was going the right way. I approached Treadway with a plan—facts, figures, statistics and opportunities; he sloughed me off. From that point on I had to make a damned appointment to even have a telephone conversation with him."

"And soon after EUF sold out to Blenheim?"

Rolfe leaned forward. "Right. You know how I found out? Treadway announced it at a board meeting—he'd sold the hotel division for 'a staggeringly high price.' It needed the board's approval, of course, but everyone had already been told about it, and the approval was a rubber stamp. Everyone, that is, except me."

Rolfe's fury was palpable. Matt had never met Sir Martin Treadway, but he could imagine the scene.

"I went ballistic," Rolfe went on. "Not a good move. I told the board that if it wanted to sell, we should have held an auction. At the very least I should have been given the chance to match Blenheim's bid, since I had created the business in the first place."

Momo spoke for the first time in a half hour. "Treadway laughed at him. Told Rolfe in front of the board that he had a short memory, that it was Rolfe who had lost the business, and that it was he, Treadway, who had rescued it. But it wasn't worth arguing the point, he said. Rolfe would be resigning from the company and the board of directors effective immediately. They didn't even allow him the dignity of waiting until the end of the meeting." Her voice was so soft Matt had to strain to hear it. But her outrage was as strong as her husband's.

"He thanked me for my service," Rolfe said. "Imagine that! As though I were the building's elevator man. That miserable son of a bitch wanted to humiliate me—probably was the only way he had left to get his jollies."

"Rolfe wanted to be done with the whole thing," Momo added. "But when Blenheim contacted him the next day, I persuaded him to find out what they wanted and would offer."

Rolfe finished his second glass of wine and waved away Matt's offer of a third. "And that's the strange thing. Seems they wanted me around—the prestige factor, institutional knowledge, transitional help, the usual. They offered me $3 million a year, plus a $10 million bonus if I stayed for five years. After Momo and I discussed the offer, I accepted, although not without serious misgivings.

"Not because Rolfe cared about the money," Momo said quickly, "but because he wanted to protect 'his' people from this man Battini's thinly-veiled threat of the Blenheim axe, he accepted. People like you, Matt, and Bernard Le Roi, Sammi Chalabi and Beth Taylor . . . he won't tell you this, but you're all very precious to him. And when he heard on the news about those awful fires and explosions in Bali, he became a raving lunatic until he managed to get a call through to Sammi . . ." She stopped, exhausted.

"Blenheim's chairman actually came out to see me," Matt said. "Fabrizio Battini."

"Oho!" Rolfe was clearly surprised. "What did you think of him?"

"A pompous popinjay. I wondered how he could be running a multi-billion dollar enterprise; he seemed like a business lightweight to me. But what do I know about titans of industry?"

"You're being too kind," Rolfe laughed. "You might add oily, glib and untrustworthy. I wonder the same thing. What did he want?"

"To tell me I had a new boss, fellow named Dieter Weiss. I'm to meet him next week in Los Angeles. Do you know him?"

"No. I only met Battini and a landfill of lawyers. If you want, I can have him checked out."

"Would you?" Matt was as grateful as an eight-year-old offered a new bicycle. "I'd be even more in your debt than I am now."

*

Momo was asleep in the bedroom. Matt and Rolfe were finishing their light supper of smoked Scottish salmon omelets and a mixed green salad. Flames from the fireplace cast flickering shadows across the room and the faces of the two ex-colleagues. Matt felt an intimacy grow between them, as though now that they were no longer boss and employee, they could talk as friends.

"Months later, why did you suddenly quit Blenheim? Was it because of Momo?"

"In other words, why did I leave you and the rest of my team in deep shit? Partly because of Momo, of course, but also . . ." He paused.

"Go on."

Rolfe pushed his virtually uneaten supper away. "You're the only one besides Momo I'll have discussed this with, so be very careful with whom you share it, if at all."

Matt flushed. "Rolfe, I swear . . ."

"I trust you and the old gang, but you're with Blenheim now, so promise me you'll be cautious. I say this for your own good."

Ominous, Matt thought, remembering his conversation with Battini. "I promise."

"As soon as Kestrel changed hands, I suggested to your friend Fabrizio that we spin off our downscale brand, Metropolitan. I told him it didn't really fit in the long term with Kestrel and Audley. We could use the money, I said, to build more hotels like the twin sisters and buy more hotels to convert to the Kestrel and Audley brands."

Matt shrugged. "Makes sense."

"But I couldn't get an okay on any new hotel—indeed, on any new deal whatsoever. I couldn't even get permission to build a ten-suite addition in D.C."

"Was he stonewalling you?"

"I still have scars from butting up against it. What's more, I began getting orders from Blenheim executives: Install so and so as house manager in the Audley St. Paul de Vence; put in thus and such as the new comptroller in Bali; a different head engineer in Santa Monica; a new chief of security; a new head of technology—Jesus, a new head housekeeper! Granted, these requests were spread over all the hotels, but it rankled. What was wrong with the people my GMs had hired? The hotels were operating smoothly, profits were going up over the previous year at a greater pace than we had budgeted for, forward bookings were stronger than ever. Why change?"

Apprehension coiled around Matt's gut. "They got at me, too. I received e-mails from a department called Human Capital Development, whatever the hell that is, telling me to hire new people I'd never heard of. No one promoted from within the company. My controller, who came with me from Chicago, was replaced. I screamed and screamed, but nobody cared. 'Give him a bonus and send him on his way,' they said. So a different guy—their guy—comes in and barely talks to me, preferring to report to 'corporate.' I can't even see my own figures until after they're sent to Los Angeles."

This was one of the matters he wanted to talk to Rolfe about. Plainly he had his mentor's attention, but decided it wasn't the moment to elaborate. Rolfe had his own history to recount.

"Not long ago we were primarily a decentralized organization, relying on great GMs like you. Today Kestrel's a rigidly controlled corporate monolith. That might work if you're manufacturing a single product like breakfast cereal or paper clips, but with luxury hotels it's a disaster. I'll grant you that limited service hotels can operate in a more standardized way—after all, they're more or less identical—but I'll never believe anything but that high-end hotels are organisms that can flourish only if their own individual environments are taken into consideration. That means the local GMs must be given their head so their flair, culture and personality are imprinted on every aspect of the guest experience and the operation. So what does the company get? An autocratic CFO with a regiment of comptrollers counter-signing every purchase order and paying all bills centrally: four general counsels located in Los Angeles who wouldn't know local laws if they fell over them; regional vice presidents who are in charge of all the hotels in their district and are so overwhelmed they barely can find their way to an individual property's front desk. They in turn are to report to a few senior vice presidents of operations, all brand-spanking new to the company, and who are so removed from the hotels themselves that they just know what they're fed by the VPs and have a steady diet of major league suck-up. The GMs—the people who know their properties like the inside of their hands—are no more than order-obeying functionaries." He stood, waved his arms. "Can you blame me for being pissed off? I struggled for decades to build a great culture, one that bred excellence in every way. We built a family of the very best professionals ever assembled in our industry, and in months this gang has turned the whole organization to shit!"

Dieter Weiss, Matt thought, taken in by Rolfe's rage. A man who's never even been to the Audley San Diego Cliffs is going to be telling me what to do. It was as though his dispassionate father had made actuarial judgments without every studying the books. He felt sick.

Rolfe began to pace, his agitation like a wasp's trapped in a bottle. "When Battini told me about the changes, I barely held my temper. But by then I knew about Momo's health and figured the fight wasn't worth it. It was their money, their company. Intellectually I knew it could and should be their culture. So I shut up and vowed to protect the old gang, yourself included, as best I could." Rolfe stopped pacing. Matt could see his fatigue and frustration. He shrugged. "Didn't do a very good job, did I?"

They were at the crux of the conversation at last. Matt added a log to the fire and poured them both a 1948 Grand Armagnac in large Baccarat snifters. "In that case, why did you . . ."

Rolfe finished the younger man's question for him. "Quit? I didn't."

"But I received the memo like everyone else."

"You mean the one from Battini: 'Due to his wife's health problems, Rolfe Ritter has regretfully resigned from Blenheim Partners, effective immediately. Dimitri Netski has been appointed as chief executive officer.' I will become non-executive chairman." He sat heavily. "I know the damn thing by heart!"

"Yes, that memo," Matt said quietly, stunned by Battini's hypocrisy.

"The first time I saw the bloody thing was when one of the GMs sent it to me. I called Battini. He gave me some bullshit that he'd been led to believe that was my decision. 'Heads will roll for this mistake,' he promised. Yeah! If you believe him, I have some swampland in Florida for sale where you can build a new Kestrel." Rolfe didn't mention that Battini had told him that only if he stayed out of company affairs, would he keep his full compensation package.

Matt refilled the snifters. “Did you hear what happened at the St. Paul de Vence property?”

Rolfe stared at him, eyes bright. “You mean the Saudi prince?”

So Rolfe knew! “Yes.”

“Seems Le Roi disobeyed his instructions and talked to a friend of his at the *Sûreté*. Battini was apoplectic when he found out, told Le Roi he should have handled it internally, and threatened to can him on the spot if he said one more word to anyone. That’s when Bertrand called me, asking if I could help. There wasn’t a thing I could do. He’s still there, hanging on by his fingertips, afraid to say or do anything to rile his boss. But he’s mad as hell, and I don’t know if he’ll be able to control himself.”

“Maybe he’s being overly obsessive,” Matt said. “He wasn’t the only one in trouble.”

“You mean Sammi Chalabi in Bali?”

“No. I was thinking of someone else.”

“Just to finish on Sammi. All his records went missing. They fired his head of security, both the I.T. manager and the rooms division manager, but he was promoted because his hotel was the only one that hadn’t been burned or bombed.”

Matt didn’t know Sammi Chalabi, but at least Battini had rewarded him. “Maybe they notice good work.” His own work was impeccable, he felt. The upcoming meeting with Weiss didn’t seem so threatening.

Rolfe took care of that notion. “Yes, they made him GM at the Kestrel in Lima. Same as making him GM of the Kestrel Siberia, if there was one. They were getting him out of town fast as they could.” He sipped the Armagnac. ”Who’s the someone else?”

“Beth Taylor.”

Rolfe’s eyes widened. “That was recent and strictly hush-hush. Not long after I’d checked in on her to see if she’d had any Le Roi or Chalabi type problems, she called me in great confidence, needing guidance I couldn’t really give her. How’d you hear about it?”

"Beth and I talk sometimes, though we only meet at general manager conferences," he blushed at his lie, hoping that Rolfe Ritter wouldn't notice. "We're the young kids on the Blenheim block, so we compare notes. She told me the weird story about the Vice President of Taiwan. Every day she expects a call from corporate telling her she's history."

"Did you tell anyone else?" Rolfe asked quickly.

"Le Roi. I thought if he knew others had worse problems than him, he'd stop obsessing about the Prince."

Rolfe sat quietly, thinking. At a cry from the bedroom, he rose, quietly opened the door, then closed it. "Still asleep. Poor darling's wiped out." He sat again. "There've been other changes—changes in GMs for no apparent reason. Sarah Wang in Hong Kong was let go for not meeting a budget she had neither seen nor agreed to. Stephan Prager in Zurich was given a choice of running the Leipzig Metropolitan, a cesspool, or taking early retirement—the man's in his forties! And Gidon Lahav? Transferred to Melbourne, this after he made the Kestrel Jerusalem the best hotel in Israel and had bought a new house for himself near the King David Hotel when assured he would stay."

"All your appointees?" Matt asked, knowing the answer.

"Every last one of them."

"Any changes in their personnel?"

"No idea," Rolfe sighed. "No, they're after me even though I'm no longer part of the company."

"Why?"

"I wish I knew. The people who have been transferred or let go are loyal to me, I understand that. But they're all professionals. Their welfare depends on how they do their jobs, not on what they feel about me. They've been moved on flimsy evidence or no evidence at all. Each of the hotels was profitable, more so than last year. Each was ahead of budgeted expectations."

Matt looked hard at his ex-boss. "Are you telling me I'm next?" Precisely the question he wanted to ask when Rolfe arrived.

"I don't know for sure. But I'd be careful. Strange things are going on at Blenheim Partners, though I'm damned if I can figure them out."

The answer didn't help. Matt thought of the future. If Blenheim let him go, he'd find another position, although there was no job in the world like his present one. He realized Rolfe hadn't chosen the Audley San Diego Cliffs merely for a vacation, but to warn him, and he felt immeasurably grateful.

That same cry from behind the door interrupted their conversation. "I'd best be with her when she wakes up," Rolfe said, standing. In the firelight, he looked like an old man. "You say your meeting with this Dieter Weiss is next week?"

"Yes."

"Let me know what happens if you want. Meanwhile, my advice is to say yes to everything and smile. You'll keep your job, at least, if not your integrity. This way if you decide to leave, it will be your choice and timing, not Blenheim's."

*

"I'm sorry we're leaving sooner than planned," Rolfe said the next morning as he stood at the open door to the Bentley. His face was drawn and there were dark circles under his eyes. "Momo had an awful night. I'm taking her back to the hospital in New York."

"I'm sorry." Matt winced inwardly at the inadequacy of his words. "If there's anything I can do . . ."

"Pray." Rolfe clasped his protégé's hand. "I thought about our conversation last night, about your feeling that Le Roi was being obsessive. I may be guilty of the same thing. I'm yesterday's news, without voice or influence, the kiss of death to anyone who was on my team. It's not my company any more, it's Blenheim's. You're all better off if I keep out of things. Besides, I have to focus on my wife. We took too long to find each other. I'm damned if I'll let her go without a hell of a fight."

"Mr. Ritter, Rolfe, this company is your creation. It's in your blood. It's your culture that makes our hotels great. Your guys will always think of it in that way. If you step away, they all will miss you. More importantly to me, I'll miss you."

Rolfe managed a smile. "If you need advice from time to time, or just a sounding board, I'm your man."

He joined Momo in the Bentley. Matt watched the car pull away and vowed to leave his ex-boss in peace. He would handle

Blenheim on his own. As an adolescent, he'd learned to tackle problems by himself, and it had served him well. Time to stop leaning on Rolfe or anyone else for support. But his stomach knotted at the thought. The sun glanced off the cedars lining the driveway; four guests were laughing at the doorway; two parrots traded pleasantries in the distance. The air was cool. It was a perfect day.

And he was alone.

Chapter 2
Los Angeles

Dieter Weiss looked like a walking slum, and his clothes matched his appearance. Large, virtually square head topped by salt-and-pepper hair cropped by a lawn mower, hair-filled Dumbo ears, darting rat's eyes, feral teeth. How such a man reached so high a position in the Blenheim firmament was a mystery, but there he was, sitting stolidly behind an incongruously pristine desk in a large, personality-less office, acknowledging Matt's arrival with a grunt but no handshake. Probably Battini's hatchet man, Matt figured. His apprehension, steadily rising throughout the drive to Los Angeles, threatened to explode.

Weiss grunted again. Matt cleared his throat, waiting for his new boss to say something. Did the man speak English?

"Changes are needed," Weiss said at last, his eyes anywhere but on Matt's. "Yes, much needed."

"At the Audley San Diego Cliffs?" Matt was stunned. The Resort was as spotless as a wedding gown. Besides, how would he have reached that conclusion? This man had never seen the place.

"Well, of course. Why else do you think I brought you here?" Evidently Dieter did speak fluent English, albeit with a slight German accent. "Brought" was "bwought" and "grounds" was "gwounds" on his tongue.

"I'm afraid I don't understand," Matt said. "The Resort's virtually new. We have a maintenance department unrivaled anywhere in the company, technicians and engineers, scores of gardeners and landscapers, two teams of fulltime painters, an in-house carpentry shop. Not a single guest has complained about . . ."

"Dirksen, let me finish." Weiss's brusque admonition startled Matt. "Not the grounds and not the rooms. Mr. Battini says they're adequate for now. But the Resort has been poorly marketed, and its internal systems are seriously flawed."

Adequate! "But Mr. Weiss, we're running at 82 percent occupancy for the year, while the best of our competitors are in the low 70s. Our average room rate is nearly 30 percent higher than the competition and our guest satisfaction scores are through the roof. The Resort's internal audit results were lauded as being amongst the best in the company. As for our operating systems, why only six months ago . . ."

Weiss stood abruptly. He was a short man, fifty-ish, at five feet-six inches almost as wide as he was tall. His rumpled trousers were stained. "Follow," he said. It was an order. He led Matt from the office, limping. Matt wondered if it was a war wound until he realized Weiss had been born after Hitler's death.

They entered a small boardroom. Here, too, the furnishings were generic—long table, modern chairs, a credenza, a bar, fluorescent lighting; save for the bar, the room was as appropriate for a third-degree as for a policy conference.

"Meet Mr. Netski," Weiss said. "He has good news for you." He gripped Matt's arm. "The information is for you alone. You're not to discuss it with anyone, particularly not the other GMs. Do you understand?"

Standing in the shadows at the far end of the room was a man so thin and still he could have been a lamp. Matt had missed him on first appraisal of the room. Now he stepped forward, hand extended. Matt shook it. Dry and cold.

The six-feet-tall Netski was immaculately dressed in a bespoke charcoal gray Saville Row suit, handmade, DN-initialed cream Egyptian cotton shirt, Hermes tie, Gucci shoes so highly polished it was difficult to tell the color. His long, slicked back, black hair was set in a sea of gel. Either a manikin or a robot, Matt thought, noting the wafer-thin gold Patek Phillipe watch, but the man's smile broke the effect. Indeed, he seemed pleasant until Matt noticed the eyes: pale blue—almost white—lifeless as arctic ice.

"What did you think of my emails?" he asked abruptly.

Oh, God, the man was Blenheim's chief executive! Matt had Googled him; Netski was a Czech with a Russian father who had spent most of his professional life in the Far East as marketing manager for an Asian conglomerate. He had joined Blenheim in 2003. The e-mails, which had arrived as a storm when Dimitri Netski assumed control of Kestrel and were quickly forgotten, had stressed marketing and teamwork: "Blenheim Partners wants the Kestrel, Audley and Metropolitan Chains to be the World's Lodging Brands. All three of our brands must be world beaters. There is no place for anyone who does not play his part to achieve our goal." "A smile is the hotelier's greatest asset." "Impeccable hotels require impeccable behavior." Motivation like this, Matt thought when he read them, belongs on a high-school football field, or in the trash. "They were an inspiration," he now answered, remembering Rolfe's advice.

Netski beamed. "Congratulations are in order."

"For what?"

"The Summit organizers have said yes to the Audley San Diego Cliffs!"

Matt reeled. Over a year ago, he had made a passionate pitch to the State Department proposing that the G8 hold their annual summit meeting at the Resort. After a site visit by State's staffers, some of whom seemed more interested in lunch than an inspection of the back of the house, he had heard nothing from their representatives about it. It was a political decision, he realized; the last G8 meeting held in America, in Sea Island, Georgia, was plagued by protesters. Although the United States was hardly popular among foreign governments, the G8 rotation made it the host country for this upcoming summit. Even as Matt made his presentation, he figured the odds against a yes were one chance in a hundred. Matt had presumed they'd want the venue to be as far away from the politically active West Coast as possible. He had no idea that the corporate office was involved; Blenheim must have used every ounce of their influence. Now he rejoiced. God, the summit was worth at least $5 million of business! He imagined the public relations value beyond measure.

"You were a superb salesman," Weiss said. "I could have told you by phone, but such important news is best conveyed in person. The organizers had a favorable impression of you personally, which apparently helped sway their decision."

So the meeting was to let Weiss tell him he was a hero! Matt figured the German's manner was inbred—too many cousins intermarrying since the Middle Ages—and nothing personal. He'd tell

Rolfe, knowing how pleased his mentor would be. All that apprehension for nothing.

"That's why we need a new invigorated marketing campaign—the Resort as the world's choice, as America's finest. This event will showcase the Audley brand and, by association, the entire Kestrel company," Netski said, his left hand smoothing back his long, slick, black hair. "This is a once in a lifetime opportunity. We need to take full advantage of it."

True, Matt thought. I am sure it will be a great advertisement for Blenheim partners and make their investors look good. Dimitri Netski will no doubt take all the credit for the Resort's hard work and have his photo plastered throughout the media.

"It's why we need to update the back-of-house systems," he went on. "The Conference Center will have to be completely renovated. We'll need to install state-of-the-art electronics and a variety of new and unequalled equipment. Anyway, these upgrades are conditions of our selection."

Weiss put an arm around Matt's shoulders. "We'll be bringing in a new director of engineering, more experienced than the man you have today. Given the amount of our capital we'll have to spend, he'll be reporting directly to me on all the improvements. You'll have to let your own man go. He's not to be transferred. In these circumstances it is my philosophy that it is inappropriate for people to continue to serve anywhere in our organization. Best thing is to get rid of him quickly and quietly; avoids bitterness and internal conflict. I'm sure you won't mind. We both know it's the right thing under the circumstances."

The hairs on Dirksen's neck stood on end while the German's arm felt like a lasso. Weiss stood for everything Matt hated: imperiousness, coldness, unwarranted exercise of power. Matt's present engineer was tops in his field, and to fire him was a travesty of fairness. Just smile and say yes, he remembered, feeling like a traitor, but realizing he should bring up nothing controversial and agree to everything, at least for the moment. "No, that's fine," he said. "The Summit's in November, less than ten months away. Your engineer will have to move quickly."

*

Rolfe was in his New York City apartment when Matt reached him. "But that's splendid!" he said when his protégé told him about the G8 summit. "Makes all our fears seem like paranoia."

"I know, I know. But Rolfe . . ."

"Something's wrong?"

"It's a feeling I can't shake." Indeed, he'd been queasy since the Los Angeles meeting. He paused.

"Go on," Rolfe said.

"They hustled me out of there as if I were a pedophile uncle. The charm offensive finished as if someone had thrown a switch. No celebration, no further discussion. Just the announcement that my engineer's out and they're sending in their own guy to install state-of-the-art systems. I don't get it? Our systems are only two years old! They were over-specified at your instructions and their backups are just as good. The summit inspection team never mentioned upgrades to me. Maybe I'm paranoid, but something's fishy."

"Charm's hardly their strong point. It sounds like those guys are over-excited by being anointed. It's a big win for the company. As for the new engineer, he'll probably decide no more work is necessary, and all this nonsense will fade away. Jesus, Matt. It sounds as if having you on the property is also a condition of the deal. If you want to get some color, call the guy at State who did the property tour with you and get background for the request. In the meantime take a deep breath and relax. You're safe for now. The Summit will make your professional career like nothing else can. Once it's over, you'll be swimming in offers if you decide you can't live with Blenheim anymore."

Rolfe's right, Matt thought. He'd make sure the Summit ran so smoothly it would set a standard no other resort could match. After it was over, if he didn't like his bosses, he'd quit.

"Keep your thoughts to yourself and be careful whom you talk to in the company," Rolfe said. "If you need to chat, call me."

"Will do. Thanks. Give my best to your wife."

Rolfe sighed. "She'll need it. But she's fine."

Rolfe's tone of voice told Matt he was lying. They hung up. The queasy feeling in Matt's stomach intensified.

Chapter 3
Santa Monica

Beth Taylor had a queasy stomach as well. When she felt threatened, as she did now, she ached to run away, as she had often done when a teenager. More urgently, she bit her lip to keep away the craving for the drugs that had been part of her past. Her self-denial made her defensive and, therefore, testy.

Her day had started so well with a regular dawn run along the beach path from the pier in Santa Monica to the end of Venice. Exhilarated, she had returned to the comfort of her third-floor taupe and oatmeal colored apartment, with its overstuffed furnishings and her most prized possession, a signed Warhol lithograph of Queen Elizabeth II, which hung resplendently above the fireplace. Below it, to one side, was a picture of her parents in their most vibrant prime. Reconciled with them just months before her father's death from emphysema, caused by a lifetime of smoking three packs a day, her mother now lived with Beth's aunt in a retirement home in her native Baltimore—paid for by the hotel manager—where she still entertained the other residents, albeit from the confines of her wheelchair. Sitting on the balcony with a cappuccino she had picked up from the Starbucks on the next corner, Beth had read the *L.A. Times* and allowed the sun's early morning rays to permeate her body. Energized, she had come into the office ready to conquer the world. Then her new boss unexpectedly arrived.

"I don't need a baby sitter!" she argued, her temper barely under control. "I've been over it a dozen times. We couldn't have stopped the attack on Chiang Shui-Kan."

The unpleasant, overweight man, tie askew and hair unkempt, who had barged into her office first thing that morning, drummed his nail-bitten fingers impatiently on Beth's desk. "Our own security people concur with the finding of the Secret Service and the FBI. Shui-Kan was nearly killed because of lax internal security and procedures at this hotel. You and you alone are responsible for this property, and you alone bear complete responsibility for this terrible event. The man's back in Taiwan now. His face is so scarred there's no chance he'll resume his political career."

Beth fought to remember this loathsome man's name. Ah. Dieter Weiss. She started to protest, but he held up his hand. Despite his slovenliness, there was power in his gestures, command in his voice. "The only reason you haven't been fired is that Blenheim's general counsel feels such an act might be an admission of liability and leave ourselves open to a lawsuit."

Again she tried to interrupt; again he held up his hand. He sneered at her. "If it were my decision, I'd tell the lawyers to go to hell, you'd be out of here in a minute, and I'd make sure you never worked in a hotel again."

Well, then, "fuck you" came to the tip of Beth's tongue, but she swallowed the response. "Anyway," he continued, "Mr. Netski and I have decided to appoint a managing director for the Kestrel Santa Monica. You will remain general manager—we don't want to alarm the staff since you'll be staying on—and you'll continue to be responsible for the hotel's day to day activities. Mr. Lee will oversee strategy and new business development."

Beth felt as she had in parochial school when reprimanded unjustly by a malevolent nun. "Mr. Lee?" she asked.

"Jimmy Lee. The new M.D. Shanghai born, Stanford MBA, excellent connections in China." Weiss recited his achievements as though bestowing an award. "He'll make the hotel the stopping-off place for Asian visitors and help the company develop the expanding Chinese market visiting the States." He glared at her. "You will obey his instructions as if they were coming from me."

"That's exactly what I'll do," Beth said, carefully keeping her tone free of irony. She relived the endless and frustrating dealings with the bureaucrats who had "helped" with her daughter's adoption. Dealing with Weiss was equally pleasant.

"By the way, you'll not discuss this, or anything else that happens in the hotel, with any other GM—indeed, with anyone you know. Otherwise, general counsel or no, you're—how do you Americans so quaintly put it?—you're history."

*

At least Jimmy Lee was handsome. Well dressed, too, Beth thought, when he was ushered into her windowless basement office. She appraised him as openly as he was studying her. His Chinese face gleamed as though it had been sandpapered to remove any line or blemish, his eyes bespoke openness and honesty, and his body was slim and lithe beneath his Ralph Lauren suit and his Dunhill tie.

"Aren't you a little young to be a managing director?" she asked, motioning him to sit.

He had the grace to look uncomfortable. "Twenty-eight. I admit it's awkward for you to be reporting to me when you're . . ."

"Six years older," interrupted Beth, stung by the age difference. "Actually, I've no problem with it, so long as you leave me freedom to do my work."

Lee was eager to oblige. "Absolutely. My primary job is to build bridges to Asia. I'll be on the road more than I'm here, and as long as you avoid any more poisonings or other disasters, your independence is assured."

That's a relief, Beth thought, picturing an almost endless Golden Gate Bridge stretching from Santa Monica to Shanghai, and wondering how such a nice, well-mannered man got a job with Blenheim. Patently, his connections played a large part. "I'm sure we'll get along famously," she said. "Any instructions at the moment?"

He grinned. "Simply to carry on as you've been doing." His cell phone rang. He pulled it from his inside jacket pocket with the grace of a karate master. "Yes, sir," he said. "Yes, with Ms. Taylor. Yes, we're having a pleasant meeting. She's most charming." He paused. "Of course, Mr. Weiss. Noon, you say? I'll be in your office at quarter to."

"That was Mr. Weiss," he told Beth, who had overheard him with rising concern. "At noon, I'm to be at a meeting at corporate."

"And in Mr. Weiss's office at quarter to. Don't let me detain you."

They both stood. Beth held out her hand. Lee bowed and clasped it in the Japanese fashion. "I trust we'll be friends," he said.

"I trust so. When will you be back?"

"I don't know." He seemed stricken. "It depends on what Mr. Weiss has planned for me." He released her hand, turned like a soldier on parade, and left, closing the door gently behind him.

Beth sat behind her desk and stared at the door. He's a marionette, she thought. His strings run all the way to the corporate offices in Century City. The smooth face, polished manner, his just-what-she-wanted-to-hear words had been scripted in corporate headquarters. Another toady. I'm being set up, she realized, and a stab of adrenalin made her stomach contract. But for what? She would not be working for Jimmy Lee, but for Dieter Weiss; that much was clear. Still, the Santa Monica Kestrel was doing splendidly; corporate could only be pleased.

Weiss's warning and Lee's blithe reference to more poisonings reverberated in her memory. Chiang Shui-Kan had been attacked in her hotel. No matter how much she protested, they could do what they liked with her career. You and you alone are responsible. Lee's instructions to her would be coming from Dieter Weiss.

Unease rose in her like helium until she felt lightheaded. She looked at the picture of Rolfe Ritter and the other GMs taken at the last general managers' meeting he attended. Standing directly behind her at the time was Matthew Dirksen. She grew sad as she stared at the photo. She vividly remembered that day in Boston, now well over a year ago. They had previously met at other general managers' get-togethers and, whenever they'd chatted, Matt was always interested in her hotel and her operational challenges. He seemed a nice man, certainly attractive but professionally distant, didn't patronize her, nor hit on her like so many of the other GMs would do, and he was happy to offer advice when asked. She enjoyed comparing notes with him on the several occasions they talked afterwards. The tables at the final dinner of that particular meeting had been arranged so that GMs in a particular geographic area could get to know their colleagues in a social atmosphere and, Rolfe had said, foster closer and more productive cooperation. When Beth arrived at the table, she found her namecard next to Matt Dirksen. As the dinner progressed, and the wines paired with each of the six courses flowed copiously, she and Dirksen found themselves completely absorbed in each other, as the eight other

GMs at the table gave up trying to be part of their conversation. Time sped and she had been both astonished and disappointed when Rolfe announced the formal adjournment. He then immediately followed up with his traditional invitation to host drinks at the hotel's bar, for those who didn't want to retire for the night.

She was equally surprised when Matt said, "I'm enjoying myself too much to get in the middle of that Bacchanalian scrum. I like the Piano Bar at the Four Seasons; let's have our drink there."

Beth had readily agreed and one drink quickly led to more, as she realized she was increasingly attracted to this man in a most unprofessional way. Looking at her watch, she gasped "Good Lord, it's past two in the morning. I have a seven-thirty a.m. plane."

As she started to stand, Matt put his hand over hers and said, "I don't want this evening to end. I can't remember when I've enjoyed myself as much. How about dinner in L.A. next week?"

Sobering up instantly, her heart pounded as she replied, "Matt, we can't. We're colleagues, we have to maintain a professional relationship."

Matt reached out and clasped her other hand. "To hell with a professional distance. I know you feel the same way as I do. Wednesday at Crustacean in Beverly Hills? Eight o'clock?"

Much to Beth's surprise, she heard herself saying, "I can't wait."

*

The Wednesday dinner was followed by another and another, as Beth quickly realized how much she reveled in his company. That first tantalizing, chaste kiss outside the Crustacean was followed by deeper kisses and increasingly passionate embraces. She found herself missing him when they were apart and longing for more time when they were together. Beth could sense Matt's growing physical needs and his frustration at her constant avoidance of the subject of when. Beth Taylor wouldn't—couldn't—explain her inhibitions to Matt. She wasn't sure she understood them herself. For the first time in years, she was determined to cast aside her rules and overwhelm her inhibitions if and when the moment felt right. So far the moment hadn't been right.

"Beth, this is ridiculous. I'm on fire and I know you are too. What are we waiting for?" Matt would plead with increasing frequency.

"Give me time," she would plead, "a little more time." However, Beth knew that she was running out of time.

*

Unable to sleep, Beth stared into the darkness. Her mind was full of Matt. She yearned to curl up naked in his arms, to run her fingers gently over his body, to feel him deep inside of her. She shivered. Not with excitement but with another feeling you couldn't pinpoint. Was it fear? Revulsion? Maybe both? She tried to push the hollow feeling away. He was the one, she rationalized. Matt would be the man with whom she would end her years of self-imposed celibacy. Her body shuddered at the thought. She breathed deeply, forcing herself to think rationally. There was no other alternative, if she didn't make love with Matt, she would lose him.

The decision made, she prepared her plans as meticulously as a military operation and invited Matt to dinner at her Santa Monica apartment. Remembering Matt saying that he liked simple meals, she had prepared Vichyssoise, grilled Dover Sole with sugar-snap peas, raspberries with calvados-flavored whipped cream, and put two bottles of a crisp Chablis on ice. Setting aromatic candles throughout her comfortably furnished apartment and lighting the logs in the chocolate-granite fireplace, she set the lights on low and, accompanied by the tones of Antonio Carlos Jobim's Brazilian jazz, she was finally ready. Smoothing her emerald-green, off-the-shoulder silk dress down with her hands, she gulped, trying in vain to repress her nervousness.

When Beth opened the door, Matt gasped at her beauty, the apartment's soft glows silhouetting the curves of her body. He enveloped her in a hug, kissing her gently on the lips.

"Mmm, you smell nice," he murmured. "Taste pretty good too."

Gently separating herself from his embrace, she led him by the hand to the sofa and served them both wine in Baccarat glasses, which sparkled in the flickering candlelight.

*

The flawless meal over, Waterford snifters of Grand Armagnac in hand, Beth's head was nestled against Matt's neck as they sat in front of the crackling fire. She felt Matt's hand stroke her hair, and turned her face to him. He kissed her gently at first, then with increased urgency. Please, she thought, please let me . . . His hand moved to her breasts.

No! She felt her body clench and broke from his embrace. Standing, inhaling deeply and taking his hand in hers, she guided him to the bedroom. His desire was manifest in the heat of his flesh and his ragged breath, and she longed to respond. She had rehearsed this moment time and again in her mind, vowed to please him, willed herself into compliance with the act of love.

They embraced. She could feel his engorged penis against her. "Yes," she breathed, but the word, the wish, choked her and she knew she was dry, lifeless, worthless as a lover, an incomplete woman.

Matt pulled the silk strips of Beth's dress over her shoulders. She sat on the bed, helping him remove her dress entirely, and saw the wanton lust ignite his eyes at the sight of her full breasts. "Matt!" she cried in terror, but he took her moan as excited acquiescence and reached beneath her black lace thong to find her core. She spasmed, closed her legs, pushed at his body with clenched fists; but he had pulled off his clothes and now eased on top of her, using his leg to pry hers open.

Her mind flew back to a different lover, a taker, a savage. She twisted from under him and bit into the pillow beneath her head.

"What is it? What's wrong?" Matt panted, rolling to his side.

She kept her face hidden but couldn't stifle her sobs. "I can't, Matt. I want to, but I can't."

"What do you mean, can't?"

"Don't make me explain. Please."

Matt leaned against the headboard, his penis flaccid against his thigh. "I don't understand. The months together, the buildup, the meal, the seduction. What happened to you?"

"I wanted to. I want to . . ." Her sobs were unrestrained.

"I don't get it. If you want to, then . . ."

Beth stood and put on the robe lying at the foot of the bed. "I'm so sorry, Matt. Please forgive me. I need more time."

"More time? Why?" His tone mixed bewilderment and rage.

She looked at him, her eyes rimmed with tears. "You're special. I want with all my heart to make love to you. It's just . . ."

"Just that you're afraid I'll screw you and never see you again? That I'm that kind of bastard?"

"No. No, it's not that at all. It's about me, not you, but I can't explain. I know you're good and kind, and I . . ." Again her tears flowed. "Leave me. Forgive me." She wanted to add "love me" but the words wouldn't come.

Matt got dressed and went to the door, potential sympathy stymied by his own need. "I don't get it and frankly don't want to know. You're acting like a silly teenager. What a god-damned tease."

"Matt," she wailed.

He pulled the door open. "Too bad," he said. "It could have been wonderful."

*

Beth Taylor recalled Matt's coldness at the last call she had made to him—reserved, careful, a matter of information, not a plea for help—after Chiang's accident. "I'm sorry to hear about this. My advice is to tighten security, and move on. What's past is past," he had said enigmatically.

Now she wondered if a managing director had been installed there as well. She had to talk to someone. Matt was a true pro and would understand that this was strictly a professional matter. Beth's emotions confused her. She wanted to see him, needed to see him. She would feel him out discreetly; if his situation at the San Diego Cliffs hadn't changed, she'd go no further. She could separate business from personal matters and so could he. This would be strictly business.

She picked up the phone, and trying in vain to calm her racing heart, dialed his number. When his secretary put her through, he seemed unperturbed by her call, and asked what he could do for her.

"You could meet me for a talk," she said. "It's important, strictly business."

He sighed, "When? Where?"

She tried to read his voice. Was he going through the same set of feelings she was? Well, she'd find out soon enough.

They agreed that the coming Wednesday afternoon would work, and she suggested the Ritz Carlton Laguna Niguel for their meeting.

"Neutral territory," he said humorlessly. "Anyway, I need to scout it out. Just been refurbished, a Tanya Franco design. I hear it's not only stunning but, more importantly, very successful. Maybe it'll give both of us a few ideas."

Chapter 4
Los Angeles

"I know you'll be upgrading many of your systems, however you will have to install new electronics systems capacity," Tim Matheson said in a tone that brooked no argument.

Matt stared at him. "Why? The Audley's virtually new and has state-of-the-art systems as it is."

The two men were sitting with Dieter Weiss and Jimmy Lee in the Kestrel Hotels and Resorts cavernous walnut paneled boardroom. Matheson, the eighteen-year-veteran State Department official responsible for the Summit, leaned back in his chair. Matt had met him both in Washington and when the State Department team had toured and inspected the Resort during the selection process. Then he'd liked him, now he wasn't so sure.

"Do you know how many countries will be attending? How much simultaneous translation capacity will be required? How many segregated communication lines to multiple locales across the world are necessary? How many different nations' security services will be involved? Their needs? Can you even imagine what the media's requirements are going to be? My dear Dirksen, no hotel or resort, no matter how new, how sophisticated, could possibly accommodate all of this without special electronics and significant systems upgrades."

He was right, of course, Matt reflected. The scope of the Summit was just now becoming apparent. He had seriously underestimated the task ahead. His naiveté made him feel foolish, as he realized how much he'd underpriced his bid. "Who'll pay?" he asked bluntly.

"Why, you will." There were no wrinkles in Matheson's grey, single-breasted suit, no spots on his inevitable red tie, no scuffs on his black, wing-tipped shoes with the immaculately tied waxed laces. It was as though the man had been poured into his clothes on arrival. His nonchalance about the cost spoke of many high-level negotiations.

"Impossible!" Matt roared. "We're already way over budget. These extra capital expenditures will destroy us!"

"Blenheim has agreed to provide and pay for all the extra equipment. The publicity for the Resort and our Audley brand is worth every penny," Weiss interjected smoothly. "So, don't be surprised when tons of equipment from Germany and an army of installation experts arrive on your front lawn."

"Why does everything have to come from abroad? Use the same American suppliers with whom we built the Resort, save shipping costs and make life easy—particularly when it comes to post-installation problems and warranties," Dirksen argued.

Lee smiled contemptuously. "Mr. Weiss will take full responsibility for all matters relating to the Summit, including those decisions pertaining to the specification, ordering and installation of the equipment. He and I will liaise with Mr. Matheson directly, leaving you free to run the Resort without complications. Indeed, we've agreed with Mr. Matheson that, if necessary, one or both of us will relocate to the property to ensure that everything went as efficiently as we promised. You've been invited to this meeting to ensure there'll be no misunderstanding of our respective roles."

Shit! Just what I need. Matt thought. These two Blenheim clowns getting in everyone's way, mine in particular.

Did Matheson wink at him? "What we agreed during the contract discussions, Mr. Dirksen, was that Mr. Weiss and Mr. Lee would be responsible for arranging the planning and installation of the physical upgrades that are a condition of our agreement to award your Resort the opportunity of hosting the G8 Summit. However at no time did I agree, nor would I, that we would liaise with Mr. Weiss or Mr. Lee on anything else regarding the functioning of the Summit. There is no need for them to be on the property, I assure you, until the equipment arrives, if at all. Indeed, one of the most influential factors in our decision was our extremely favorable impression of the Resort's management team, and particularly you, Mr. Dirksen. Your presentation was outstanding but it was our confidence in your ability to execute the plans that swayed the State Department in the Resort's favor. As I told Mr. Weiss at the outset of our discussions, he had to commit to you remaining in place for the duration of the preparation and execution of the Summit."

He turned on Weiss like a prosecuting attorney. "Again, should you wish to change this arrangement it is your prerogative. In that case, naturally, we'll be obliged to reconsider our decision. Does that satisfactorily describe our arrangements? Is that agreement satisfactory, Mr. Weiss?"

The German clenched his fists so hard the whites of his knuckles shone through the skin. "Madness," he seethed, obviously trying not to lose his temper. "An operation of this scope mustn't be held hostage by a single general manager."

"Satisfactory," said Jimmy Lee, placing a restraining hand on his boss's forearm.

"Excellent," Matheson said. "Perhaps you'll accompany me to the elevator, Mr. Dirksen. I have a plane to catch, but we'll have a few minutes to chat until my car arrives."

Matt was sure now. The State Department representative was a godsend. "I'm beyond grateful," he said as the elevator doors closed behind them. "You saved my butt in there."

Matheson grinned. "Let me know what I can do to keep that pair off your back. You've got your hands full enough without those two control freaks driving you mad."

As the Lincoln Town Car receded into the distance, Matt regretted not having pointed out that Dieter Weiss was his boss, not Tim Matheson.

Chapter 5
San Diego Cliffs

Netski's like my father, Matt realized with a shock on his drive back to San Diego. Precise, no-nonsense, ungiving, with the emotional warmth of a polar cap. I'm used to such a man, he thought, but there was little comfort in the knowledge. All his life, and particularly after his mother died, he had turned to his father for support, grudgingly receiving it in words—support was his father's job—but never in vibrations from the heart. His father, David Dirksen—an independent accountant specializing in the construction industry—praised him for his high-school triumphs on the basketball court, encouraged his career, and expressed gratification more, his son sadly felt, as a sense of duty than as an expression of joy, as Matt rose in the Kestrel hierarchy. However, the two men saw each other rarely (David Dirksen had never visited the Audley San Diego Cliffs, despite several ignored heartfelt invitations from Matt who, despite never having met with the success of any of his entreaties and unconsciously realizing the futility of his efforts, couldn't stop himself from seeking his father's respect and admiration). When they met in Chesterton, their talk was of global problems, not personal ones. Matt never knew about his father's romantic affairs, presuming there were some; the older Dirksen never knew of his, having never enquired.

Now he remembered an incident when he was ten. He had fallen from a tree in the yard and gashed his knee. Howling, he sought out his mother, who ministered what he needed—comfort and a bandage. Once the pain had stopped, the wound became a badge of honor—look how daring he was!—and he rushed to the study to show it to his father. David Dirksen barely looked up from the sheaves of ledger papers on his battered wooden desk. "Not now," he said, hardly looking up from the blue, bound ledger. "I've got the Iverson accounts to finish." How small Matt considered himself. How insignificant! The feeling left him only when he went away to college—even then, not entirely, he thought wryly. Netski had made him feel the same way.

Matt regarded Rolfe Ritter as his surrogate father. It was Rolfe who motivated, encouraged, praised, and told him when he was wrong and how to get it right; who made Matt perform well beyond the up and coming hotel man's wildest expectations; and, above all, who made Mathew Dirksen believe in himself for the first time in his life. It was Rolfe he called immediately after Netski had told him about the Summit; his father, Matt figured, wouldn't read about it in *The Los Angeles Times*. Certainly the news wouldn't be reported in the *Chesterton Chronicle*. He doubted his father would understand the import of this event, or even care, in the unlikely event he heard about the Resort's selection.

Elated, he shared the news with his Executive Committee as soon as he got back to the Resort, announcing it at a hastily called meeting in his conference room.

Stunned silence. Then a hubbub as everyone started to talk at once.

Matt waited until the noise died down. "I'm as excited as you," he said. "But we're in for a tough ten months. Staging an event like this is going to take all our energy at the best of times. However, we aren't just going to do it as well as Sea Island, or even better. We are going to put on the best ever Summit, an event so perfect, so far ahead of anything that has ever been dreamed of, let alone attempted, that we will have redefined the term excellence. The standard we will set will be so high that I doubt any Resort anywhere will have the guts to even attempt to meet it in the future. Remember, Rolfe Ritter wanted this property to be the very best in the world. We think it is already that, but this is our opportunity to make that statement a globally publicized reality. This is our time to shine and that we will do.

"We'll have to worry not only about our own added security, but all the needs of each country's own security team, the meeting planners, the protocol departments of each government, the State Department, the Secret Service, the FBI, dietary requirements, media facilities, secure communications networks—Jesus, it'll be like setting up a mini White House. And on top of everything, part of the deal is that Blenheim's about to install new mechanical and electrical systems, to say nothing of, heaven knows, what other new technology. Many of you met Tim Matheson, The State Department guy who led the tour. He seems like a good guy and was very complimentary of us. I invited him for a planning meeting in the next couple of weeks and I'm sure he'll guide us through the various, inevitable hoops and pitfalls. He was responsible for Sea Island and knows what he's doing. If we keep him on our side, at least we won't have to reinvent the wheel. After the meeting, I'll host a dinner for you to get to know him. Best behavior please. He did tell me that every other management team he has been involved with underestimated the work and chaos involved. I can promise you one thing, we won't be like them. However, running this property and keeping our guests more than just satisfied in the meantime, coping with physical improvements and, on top of it, planning for the best Summit event ever delivered anywhere is going to tax our resources to the limit. We can and will do it and we will end up as the professional envy of every other Resort team anywhere."

He paused to let the scope of it set in, knowing that the workload for each member of his team had just more than doubled. "In short, we've less than a year to stage an event where the spotlight of the entire world will be on us. But let me make one thing clear: In the meantime we're running the best resort in North America, and we're not going to let our Summit preparations interfere with our service delivery and profitability, not for one moment. Our guests pay handsomely for the best, and we're going to continue to give it to them. Understand?"

Nods all around. Anyone who cared about his job would relish the challenge no matter the workload and how overwhelming the stress, Matt knew, and he was surrounded by the best. He smiled, feeling galvanized, alive. "I'm setting up a Summit Committee to coordinate all our preparations. Pete," he turned to his house manager, Pete Wilson, "you'll be the committee chairman and report to me. The rooming requirements alone promise to be a diplomatic nightmare. Okay?"

The thirty-five-year-old New Yorker shrugged. "Do I have a choice?"

Matt could see he was delighted. “No.” He turned to Ben Winnick, his food and beverage manager, who had started out as a junior line chef at the Kestrel in Maui. “What you have to do is get the food and beverage requirements of everyone sorted out. You’ll have to draw on resources from Audley and Kestrel properties all over the world. You may even have to get hold of an army field kitchen or two to help you cope. It’s one hell of a task.”

Winnick wore a grin as wide as his face. “Unlimited budget?”

“Even if you had one, you’d outspend it.” The room echoed with knowing chuckles. “Jack, get hold of the State Department and figure out a liaison with the Secret Service. Put together a plan.”

Jack Turner, the Resort’s director of security, had worked with Matt in Chicago. When Matt asked him to come West his comment was, “If you hadn’t taken me with you, I’d have had to shoot you.”

“Gina, coordinate with Blenheim on finances. Keep them abreast of what we’re spending, and if they balk, let me handle it. Remind them that Mr. Netski wants this to be a worldwide advertisement for the Audley and Kestrel brands. Tell them advertising is expensive and this will cost them big time.”

Gina Walsh, the thin, forty-year-old director of finance, with mousy hair set in a perpetual bun and black horn-rimmed glasses, had come from the Audley in New York. “How do I budget for all of these new systems?” she asked.

“Damned if I know. Blenheim’s sending in their own man to set them up. Dieter Weiss is handling the whole matter personally, let him budget them. It’s his problem as far as I’m concerned. Send an e-mail to Mr. Weiss and see if he wants us to carry his budget as a line item in ours.”

He noticed the horrified expression on Bill Jamieson’s face. In his zeal, Matt had forgotten the price: a new director of engineering. Jamieson had given up a twenty-year career with the project management company that had supervised the development of the Resort when Matt prevailed on him to take the job running what he had built. He had performed superbly.

“We’ll talk as soon as the meeting’s over,” Matt said, dreading that conversation. He looked around the room. “Pete, I want the first draft of a plan and timetable on my desk one week from today.

The rest of you, Pete'll need daily memos on progress. Keep 'em brief please, less than one page—no e-mailitis and no social media gossiping!" He felt suddenly hollow, exhausted. "Bill, why don't we have that chat now?"

*

"But why?" Jamieson's face was red with bewilderment.

Matt felt sick. "All I can tell you is they want you out. It's unfair, a miscarriage of justice. If I can do anything . . ."

"How about letting me stay as this new guy's assistant?"

"Impossible. They're adamant."

"A job at a different Audley?"

Matt had asked. "They don't want you anywhere."

"They're treating me like a criminal!"

Matt thought of Sammi Chalabi and Bertrand Le Roi. "Agreed. But don't make waves, Blenheim can destroy you. Believe me, if it wasn't for the Summit, I . . ." He quickly restrained his involuntary thoughts. "Forget I said that, anyway I'll give you golden references, try to get you any job you want outside the chain. And you'll get a year's severance even if I have to take it out of my own salary."

Jamieson avoided Matt's eyes. "Thanks."

Matt stood. "I know how you feel, I really do. I know it's unfair and the whole thing sucks. All I can say is thank you for everything you've done here. Without you, it would have been a lesser property. Good luck, Bill, you're going to be fine."

The men shook hands. The chief engineer avoided meeting Matt's eyes. "Maybe someday you can tell me why the fuck this is happening," Jamieson exploded, and stormed out.

When I find out, I'll tell you, Matt said to himself, unable to catch the nagging thought flashing through his mind.

Chapter 6
The Ritz Carlton, Laguna Niguel

She looks wonderful, Matt thought. But then she always did. Beth Taylor sat across from him at one of the sleek Sommeliers' Tables at Eno—the opulent Macassa wood-paneled wine and steak room with the central, iridescent, glass wine tower at the Ritz Carlton—and found himself distracted from their conversation, important as it was, by the radiance of her hair and the glow in her bright, enquiring green eyes. Startled, he realized that he wasn't seeing the general manager of the Kestrel in Santa Monica, he was seeing the enigmatic woman who had harshly spurned him.

Dirksen had enjoyed a succession of affairs as he rose in the hotel business, some serious, most not. But work always took precedence over relationships, and the women would leave, impatient for more, frustrated with his always putting his job above their time together. Or he would back away when too much of a demand was made on him. The one woman he thought he had truly loved was a Cuban-born oncologist in Miami, who had simply left his clothes in a garbage bag in front of her apartment with a note telling him to call her when he'd left the hotel business. Devastated, he'd applied for a transfer from his position as the general manager of a 200-room Metropolitan Hotel in Coral Gables to anywhere but South Florida, just to get away from the nearness of her, en route realizing she had neither the sympathy nor the empathy to truly engage him long-term. It was her way or the highway, and he'd chosen the latter.

Matt's attraction for Beth had been overwhelming. The cruelty of his letdown had been devastating. He had known it was stupid to date someone in the company. However, he rationalized that they were both smart adults and, given her circumstances were similar to his, she would understand the vagaries of his schedule. Anyway, he rationalized that she worked a hundred miles away, a safe distance if he needed to escape.

When they had first met, he had assumed she was probably already taken (albeit she wore no wedding ring) and there was no hint in her manner that she wanted anything from him other than professional interaction. As their relationship had turned from the professional to the very personal, he had allowed himself to wonder if she could be the one for him. The brutal letdown in her Santa Monica apartment had rid him of his daydreams and had become the stuff of his nightmares. Beth was a colleague and therefore off limits. He should have left it like that. Besides, she was flawed like the rest of them. Worse, she had probably seen his faults all too quickly and far too clearly, and that was the root cause of her killing his passions.

"When that man left my office, I needed a shower," she said, referring to Dieter Weiss. "And Jimmy Lee. That boy's my boss? Nonsense! Every time I see him, I get the feeling he was sent to spy on me, but I've no idea what he's trying to find out."

They had discussed the seemingly random, recent personnel moves, each as mystified by their meaning as the other, both carefully avoiding any mention of their past relationship. Now she had moved to her personal concerns.

"He made me squirm. My guess is that he's just Netski's hatchet man."

Beth leaned forward. "Do you know Netski?"

"Met him once. Suave son-of-a-bitch, slick as Pennzoil."

She wore a medallion around her neck, gold against her blue dress. His heart jumped. She is still irresistible, he realized.

"Are you staring at my breasts?" she asked, immediately regretting her impulsive comment, realizing that she should have kept away from any non-business subjects.

He blushed. "At the medallion. I can't help it if . . ."

"It's a gold Roman coin. After that terrible evening, I needed some shopping therapy and bought it as a . . ."

"As a what?" he asked, knowing he should keep quiet.

"It doesn't matter." She had bought it as a reminder of her past. The past she wouldn't let him touch—no one could. She had thought Matt might have been the man to bridge the past and the present, but that wasn't to be. No, the past was definitely off limits to everyone. Even a professional colleague. Especially the one sitting opposite her. Taylor wished that included herself and that she could forget her past forever. The step from the streets to the heights was an accomplishment only she could savor. Her heart had been seared by the father of her child and her episode with Matt, and proven that she was incapable of a full relationship with a man. No more men, she vowed. Now, every time she caught herself thinking about a man, any man, in more than a casual sense, she chastised herself and banished the unwitting male from her life with brutal finality. That included the very handsome and desirable man sitting opposite her on the bar stool.

She was smiling in that way where the corners of the mouth turn up but the light in the eyes is extinguished. He would probe no further. Time to get back to safer ground. "Tell me about this Jimmy Lee."

"We're converting our second biggest suite into an office complex for him. Waste of money, far as I'm concerned. The suite sells for three grand a night. Can you imagine Rolfe Ritter doing that? He'd take a cubicle in the boiler room rather than lose a penny of revenue."

He smiled ruefully. "Nothing but the second best for Mr. Lee."

Beth's eyes lit up as she momentarily relaxed and chuckled. "The weird thing is, he's installing brand new wiring and electrical panels for Lord knows what technology. Maybe the Kestrel Santa Monica's an offshoot of NASA. We've had power surges and circuit overloads so often that the emergency generators are on their last legs."

Matt thought of the new systems with miles of rewiring about to be installed at the Audley San Diego Cliffs. Were the two projects connected, he wondered. If so, how and why?

Beth ran a hand through her hair, the worry apparent in her graceful gesture. "Anything similar happening down your way? Needless electronics? New employees at the behest of Blenheim?"

He decided not to mention changes requested to accommodate the G8 meeting. The news wasn't public yet, and there was no reason she should know. He had already decided to help her in any way he could, a triumph of optimism over pragmatism—amazing what the turn of a head, a hand through that luxuriant hair, glowing eyes and superb breasts could do—but it would not help her to share this information. He had no compunctions about going against Weiss's orders (how different if they had been Rolfe's!); the fact that they were meeting was evidence of that. Still, he felt possessive about the Summit. It was his treasure and he would horde it for as long as he could.

"As a matter of fact, corporate sent me a personal assistant. Said I've been overworked and my current assistant wasn't up to the task. Claimed the new one would help me immensely. Her name's Olivia Wade. Veddy British, veddy posh, oh so proper, multi-lingual, quite terrific."

She looked at him closely. "Sounds as if you like her."

"Personally? Good God, no. She's as efficient and off-putting as an electrified fence." Truth was, though, that Olivia was attractive, and he realized with some dismay that had she not been so good looking, he might not have accepted her so readily. He warned himself to be careful with Beth.

Beth frowned. "She doesn't know you're meeting me?"

"No. Only that I'm having drinks with a client at the Ritz Carlton."

Her frown deepened. "Was it wise to tell her that much?"

He recognized her anxiety and the accuracy of her question. He'd been foolish. "No. Won't happen again. I'll grab a wine list and menu, write a memo to corporate on the concept and cover my ass." An urge to hold her hand filled his heart, and he acted on it. She looked at him, startled, and pulled away. "I'm sorry, I shouldn't have," he said, feeling the heat rise in his face. "You're really worried, aren't you?"

"Not worried so much as . . . creeped out. I just don't like it, Matt. That awful Weiss. The charmboy Asian. The unnecessary changes. It doesn't feel like 'my' hotel anymore."

He thought of Le Roi, Chalabi and the others. If she was "creeped out," they must be downright terrified. "Damn!"

"What's wrong?" she asked.

"I haven't been reading the signals. I'm in trouble, too. It's just that I was so excited about the . . ." He broke off.

"The G8 summit?"

Shock sent pinpricks up his arms. "How did you know about that?"

"Jimmy Lee told me. Said that if we shaped up the Kestrel, Santa Monica, we'd be in line for a similar assignment. Maybe a Pacific Rim conference." She shrugged. "I just think he was trying to make me jealous."

So the secret was shared. Lee wouldn't have told her without an okay from the Weiss/Netski tandem. What kind of strategy was going on? He'd heard about bosses who pitted employees against each other, the competition a spur to productivity, but in this case the other signs spoke of something more ominous. Rolfe Ritter's genius was to make his top hotels idiosyncratic, original, suited to their locations (even the "sisters" weren't twins, just similar in their environments—and separated by 6,000 miles). Did Blenheim plan to make both the Audleys and Kestrels homogeneous chains? Standardize them? You'd be in one in Peoria or Hawaii and not know the difference? Introduce those "synergies and economies of scale" that had ruined too many great hotels and resorts in the past? He wouldn't stand for it! For as long as he was GM of the Audley San Diego Cliffs, he would preserve Rolfe's vision and obey Rolfe's original instructions to make the hotel an icon, a true original, a trophy in every sense of the word. Unlike Jimmy Lee, he wouldn't settle for second best. That had never been the Ritter way and it would never be his. Rolfe Ritter had demanded greatness of him and he would damned well deliver it, whatever it took.

"Look," he said, "What happened between us shouldn't affect our professional relationship. We're adults and can keep the past in the past. Besides two heads are better than one so we'd better keep talking to each other about this. If there are more unexplained changes, get in touch. I'll do the same. It's possible we are just being paranoid. However, it doesn't mean there's not a problem. We may be up against a common enemy, and we'll need allies."

"Yes," she answered, trying to mask her sadness. "Let's be uncommon friends."

Uncommon friends. The prospect excited him. They stood. He had an inclination to hug her, but restrained it. If she had been wearing a KEEP AWAY sign, her body language could not have been clearer. He smiled at her. "When shall we see each other again? Professionally, I mean."

"When there's more trouble. It's probably not a good idea if we're together too much. Let's be careful."

He started to protest, but she had already turned toward the door. He watched the ease of her walk, the grace of her figure. In an instant every emotion he had carefully cast aside returned. Careful? Yes. He'd obey her signs, though every fiber pleaded with him to catch up to her. She could, he thought, be the most dangerous enemy of them all.

*

"You spoke to the manager on duty and he told you Dirksen was having drinks with a woman?" Weiss confirmed.

"Yes."

"A tall, well dressed, striking redhead?"

"Yes, Olivia Wade acknowledged."

Weiss sighed. "Well, we both know who she is, don't we?"

Chapter 7
San Diego / St. Paul de Vence

It was past midnight when Matt picked up the phone to listen yet again to Bertrand Le Roi's concerns.

"You know about my problem with the Saudi Prince, the Bali explosions, the Taiwanese nearly murdered in Santa Monica. But did you hear that Gidon Lahav at the Kestrel Jerusalem's been replaced by some guy who's meant to be from Marriott named Leon Barken? Lahav's now the GM at—get this—the Kestrel Melbourne!"

Matt shivered, though he wasn't cold. He carefully kept his voice neutral. "I heard. I still don't believe it."

"It's true. There's no record of Barken's existence before he went to Jerusalem. Certainly no one I know at Marriott has ever heard of him. The house manager told Gidon there are dirty tricks almost daily at the hotel—room buggings, hidden cameras installed by Barken's own contractors, guests checking in and out without folios, passports disappearing, phone lines to Barken's office that don't go through the switchboard. It feels like a throwback to the days of Savak in Teheran or the KGB in Moscow."

"Aren't you being overly melodramatic?" Matt cradled the phone in one hand and an open bottle of Perrier in the other. From the comfort of his well-worn, chocolate-leather club-chair in his townhouse in La Jolla, his mind wandered and he imagined he could see the flickering flares of the fire pits and gas-lit torches set throughout the Resort's grounds. The thought normally relaxed him. Not tonight. Le Roi's rants had set his mind working over-time.

"It's not melodrama. There's something very strange going on."

"So there's a rogue GM in Jerusalem. Maybe he's in business for himself. It wouldn't be the first time, won't be the last." Even as he spoke, Matt realized how weak his clichéd rejoinder was.

"He works for Blenheim! They put him there! And what about the Australian Ambassador in Buenos Aires, killed by a runaway car, not one minute after he walked out of the Kestrel's staff entrance. Or the European Community Finance Ministers meeting at our property in Zurich, cancelled in midstream because of food poisoning. Or the assassination of the oil minister in Kazakhstan as he was on his way to our hotel's grand opening party? Or the Minister of Economic Affairs for Argentine dying of a heart attack in the steam room of our Buenos Aires property's spa. The man had no previous heart problems, and the medical examiner found a mysterious hypothermic needle entry between two toes but couldn't link it to the heart attack. Some happy ending to that massage! Have you forgotten the incident at the Kestrel in Rome where the Mayor of Mexico City had just visited the Pope in the Vatican and then died of an overdose of 100 percent pure cocaine during an encounter with a high-priced call girl? She still hasn't been located, and who gets hold of pure coke anyway? Do you want me to go on? All in or near our hotels, Matt. Coincidence? I don't think so!"

"You're connecting dots that don't exist," Matt said, more confidently than he felt. "We're a global company. You could theoretically link any incident anywhere to us."

"Then what about Jack Turner?"

"A tragic accident. That's all it was, Bertand, an accident." Turner, director of security for the Audley San Diego Cliffs, had run off the road on his way home and smashed his hips, both legs and four ribs on top of a punctured lung and serious concussion. Dieter Weiss had immediately sent the new corporate head of security, Brad Marshall, to be in charge of the Resort's security until after the Summit. Marshall seemed coldly competent, and knew he would return to corporate once Turner mended. Matt stopped himself from mentioning Weiss's intention to replace Ben Winnick, his food and beverage director. Matt had argued to keep Winnick on, and the German had relented, but not without the chilling comment that this would be Matt's first and last act of disobedience.

"Your old controller suddenly gets promoted to a better job in New York and the new one reports to Los Angeles, not you. Dots, *mon ami*? I'd say skyrockets."

Le Roi was only echoing Matt's fears. These were no coincidences, but whatever Blenheim's purposes, they had given him the most prestigious assignment imaginable, and he didn't want to lose it. He felt he owed the glory to Rolfe, and in managing the summit would be repaying his mentor's vision and trust. Maybe he could even get his father's attention.

"Let's have these talks more often," he said noncommittally.

"Listen, my dear Dirksen," Le Roi said. "I'm convinced something sinister's happening, something to do with the company that owns us. One way or another, I intend to find out what and why. We owe it to Rolfe and to ourselves. Whether you want to help is up to you. We need never speak about this again. But you'd be well advised to stay alert. They've made three major changes in personnel in San Diego already. At least let me know if they make more."

"Of course," Matt said, relieved that the conversation was ending.

Neither of the two GMs noticed the barely audible click as they put down their phones.

Chapter 8
Santa Monica

"Sit down, please."

Goggle-eyed, Beth looked around Jimmy Lee's palatial new offices. Three different sets of double-screened computers, one with English characters, another with Chinese, and the third a bilingual Bloomberg filled with moving numbers, news flashes and graphs; a 60 inch plasma TV tuned to CNN; furniture so sleek you could ice skate on it; Mazini gooseneck chrome lamps hanging over chairs and tables like praying mantises; Rothko paintings, black on black, white on white, on rosewood walls. This was the first time she had been in his office; heretofore, his communication had been voice messages, phone calls or e-mails.

She sat in front of his desk. Her chair was lower than his behind it. "We have a problem," he said.

"We do?"

"Yes. I understand that Mr. Weiss told you to obey all instructions to the letter. Do you remember his saying that?"

Her mouth went dry. "That's right."

"And one of his instructions was that there would be no sharing of information among the GMs?"

"It was."

He bore in on her. "In which case, would you mind telling me what you and Matt Dirksen were discussing at the Ritz Carlton Laguna Niguel?"

Oh, God! How did he know? She sat silently, stupefied.

"Movies? The weather? The Lakers?"

Would he fire her? She had worked hard for this position. No other job would be as good. He could disgrace her, drive her out of the business, post her to some God-forsaken Eastern European country—Kestrel was in the process of opening hotels in Croatia and every country ending with a "stan," projects started before Blenheim took over. She berated herself for calling Matt in the first place, for being attracted, despite herself, by his charm, his smile, the soothing tone of his voice, his gorgeousness. Jimmy Lee could only know she had been with him if he had ratted on her. What a fool she was. All men were betrayers. Matt Dirksen was no different.

Lee stared at her with angry eyes, no longer the polite Asian. This man is my jailer, she realized with a flash of horror. Fight!

"Mr. Dirksen and I were looking at Eno, their new wine and steak room. We wanted to see if there were any innovations we could incorporate into our respective properties."

"So you spent over two hours discussing the décor?"

"Yes, and the electronic interactive wine list, the staff, the silver, the plates and glasses. They serve flights of wine, cheeses, chocolates, olives, superb prosciutto . . ."

The Grand Inquisitor could not have been more disbelieving. "Not a word about Blenheim?"

"Of course. We agreed that Blenheim was doing a splendid job, that the innovations and new blood were what our resorts needed, that Mr. Netski seemed the ideal dynamic chief executive." She was blathering, she knew, her words as unconvincing as Charles Manson protesting his innocence.

"I'm delighted to hear it," Lee said, with an overlay of sarcasm so marked he stumbled on it. "Tell me, Ms. Taylor. Where do your loyalties lie?"

"With the Kestrel, Santa Monica."

'Which has recently been acquired by . . .?"

"Blenheim Partners."

"Thus loyalty to the Kestrel Santa Monica means loyalty to Blenheim, does it not?"

He wasn't going to fire her—she was sure of it. "It does, Mr. Lee."

"Excellent. Make sure that loyalty does not waver." He opened a drawer and took out a manila envelope. "You have ignored Mr. Weiss's instructions. You will not do so again."

"I promise," Beth said, feeling her tension-filled shoulders relax.

"You understand that this is your first and last warning."

"I do."

He stood languidly, walked to her side of the desk, and handed her the envelope. "I believe you. Do you know why?"

"Because it's the truth!"

"No, Ms. Taylor. You are, I think, an accomplished liar."

"Then . . . ?"

"Open the envelope and you'll see why."

Fear, which had lain coiled like a snake in the pit of her stomach, now struck. Hands shaking, Beth did as she was told.

Inside the envelope was a single photograph. Beth's scream reverberated throughout the suite.

Jimmy Lee smiled down at her. "Here's what I want you to do." He told her.

It was horrible, beyond any request she could have imagined. Yet she sat dazed and miserable, her head filled with the blackness of her assignment, and nodded.

"Let me hear you say it," Lee commanded.

"Whatever you want, Mr. Lee."

The smile broadened. "Excellent."

Chapter 9
Santa Monica

Beth Taylor stared into the mirror above the basin in her apartment's bathroom, loathing what she saw behind her red-rimmed eyes. Her mind slipped back two decades and she saw herself as the young woman gone wrong. Alcohol, drugs and unfriendly streets were part of her itinerant past. Until now she had succeeded in creating a new Beth Taylor, the sophisticated, successful female executive thriving in the chauvinistic, male-dominated hotel industry. That all ended when Jimmy Lee forced her to relive every foul, humiliating moment of her long-repressed past and making her far worse than a common whore.

Matt Dirksen is a good man. I've already hurt him enough she kept repeating to herself, knowing it didn't matter. She had no choice. Whatever she felt didn't matter. The real Beth Taylor would do as instructed by her Chinese overlord.

Chapter 10
Bel Air

Four men sat in deep armchairs on the Mexican-style pergola of Dimitri Netski's Bel Air home, talking softly. The house, invisible from the tree-lined avenue that fronted it, was bathed in the mellow glow of the late afternoon sun. Silver shards danced on the surface of the black, infinity-edged pool. The men paid no attention to the light or to the songs of birds in the trees. Sunglasses shielded their hard eyes from each other's scrutiny, but by the hierarchical placement of the chairs, high to low, all were told where they fit in the Blenheim firmament.

"So far so good," Netski said from on high. Our people are mostly in place and we're gradually getting rid of Ritter's hoteliers." He spat the word as though it was a curse. "A few months more and they'll all be gone, from receptionists to managers. There's no reason to stray from the course we charted."

"Good job." Fabrizio Battini sipped from his freshly picked mint-laced iced tea and looked up at his boss. "It was sheer good luck that Dirksen was working on the Summit business before we got involved."

"And better luck we were able to lubricate the right people to choose the resort," Weiss added.

Netski stretched languidly. "It's amazing how hard cash and blackmail make a potent cocktail."

"You're keeping Dirksen on, of course, until after the Summit? Battini asked.

"Regrettably, there's no choice in the matter. When I tried to maneuver around the issue, an officious prick from the State Department called Matheson put a stop to it. No Dirksen, no Summit."

"And that Taylor woman who met with Dirksen?"

Netski turned to Jimmy Lee, lowest in the order. "Is she behaving?"

"Now she is. After she saw the photograph, she's so subservient that before I sneeze she brings me Kleenex."

Dieter Weiss laughed. "I'll bet she is. That information cost us a lot of dough, but it was worth it." His forehead glistened; the underarms of his Hawaiian shirt were dark with sweat. "We're fortunate that Ritter's wife has cancer and that egomaniac is now completely obsessed with looking after her. He could have made things much harder."

"I'm concerned about Dirksen," Netski said, glancing at the German. "I don't like him, don't trust him. Le Roi called him, you know. The Frenchman's still obsessed about the incident with his prince at his precious resort, and is poking into a few incidents he's found out about, as well as some of the personnel changes we've made. Dirksen was far too sympathetic for my liking. Your job is to make sure he causes no trouble until after November. You'd best watch him closely."

"I've had an idea," Jimmy Lee said tentatively. "Indeed, I suggested it to Beth the other day, and she naturally agreed. I've encouraged her to see as much of Matthew Dirksen as possible. What do you think?"

The implications of the notion hung in the air like poison gas. The men looked at Netski for a response. He stood and put a hand on Lee's shoulder. "Clever," he said at last. His chuckle had no mirth in it. "Very clever."

"That leaves the Le Roi problem." Battini's glass was nearly empty, the others hadn't touched theirs.

"Problem?" Netski asked.

"Not only did he speak to Dirksen, he spoke to Gidon Lahav in Melbourne and also called Ritter asking for advice."

"So?"

"Ritter told him that he was being paranoid. His wife was very sick that day and he didn't want more problems to worry about."

"How is she now?" Weiss asked.

"The same. But if she gets better, Ritter might listen more attentively."

"Then let's hope she doesn't."

"Indeed. Meanwhile, Le Roi's gone back to the *Sûreté*. They refuse to reopen the investigation."

Netski's fingers gripped Lee's arm. "I don't like it. Not one bit." He stared into the sun, then chuckled again. "I'll deal with the French authorities. Can you help us with our over-curious French resort general manager, Mr. Lee?"

The Chinese shrugged. "I believe so."

Netski sat back down and raised his glass. "Then *au revoir*, *Monsieur* Le Roi."

Chapter 11
New York City

International Herald Tribune, Nice Bureau, Côte d'Azur:

"Bertrand Le Roi, legendary general manager of the exclusive Audley Resort in St. Paul de Vence, one of the Resort's marketing directors, three U.S. travel agents and six crew members were killed yesterday due to an explosion of unknown origin aboard the Resort's luxury yacht, Elite. There were no survivors.

Le Roi's career . . ."

TO: Corporate Officers and General Managers
FROM: Dimitri Netski, Chief Executive Officer
SUBJECT: Sad Loss of an Esteemed Colleague

It is with great regret that I announce the tragic, accidental death of our much respected colleague, Bertrand Le Roi, general manager of the Audley Resort, St. Paul de Vence. Le Roi was a great professional whose loyalty both to Blenheim Partners and myself, personally, spoke to the generosity of his heart and vision.

We are fortunate in Mr. Le Roi's replacement: Rupert Fellowes, formerly of Waltham & Sons, a London-based private equity company, where he was responsible for real estate operations. It is a testament to our reputation that we can attract senior executives of Rupert's caliber. I know you will all welcome him by giving him all your assistance as he takes over the challenge of making the Audley Resort—Saint Paul de Vence—even greater than it was under Mr. Le Roi.

*

Someone had mailed Rolfe Ritter the press release anonymously from the general post office in Los Angeles. He read it quickly then stared into space. After five minutes he wordlessly handed the release to Momo.

Her eyes widened as she scanned the paper, “My God!” she exclaimed. “Whoever was behind those incidents at the hotels must be behind this tragedy. It means Bertrand must have been getting too close.”

Anger suffused Rolfe Ritter’s face, his eyes inflamed with rage. He tore the press release from his shocked wife’s grasp, crumpled it into a tight ball and flung it against the closed window of their library. Looking unblinkingly at his wife, he said, “My well-honed instinct says it’s Blenheim. Those motherfuckers. They’re behind it. They murdered him.”

Chapter 12
San Diego / Melbourne, Australia

The insistent ringing of the bedside phone woke Gidon Lahav, the new general manager of the Kestrel Melbourne.

"Gidon, it's Matt. Matt Dirksen in San Diego. Sorry to wake you."

"Matt. Good to hear from you." The men had met at several GM sessions across the years and maintained a cordial friendship. Still, this midnight call was unusual. "How can I help you?"

"Sorry to call so late, but I need to talk. I don't like using my home phone and this is the first time I could get off property. Did you get Netski's release about Bertrand Le Roi? Did you see the *Herald Tribune* piece about the 'accident'?"

Off property to call? Instantly alert, Lahav reached for his robe. "Let me take this in the study. The phone's secure there—I checked it myself. Habit. Too long living in Israel, I suppose. Besides, I don't want to disturb Shulamit." He padded to the study, worry rising. So Dirksen had been disturbed by the press release as well. He picked up the extension.

"How are things in Melbourne?" Matt asked.

"I miss Jerusalem, but a hotel's a hotel. Shulamit hates it here. She's away from her family, friends, the home she just spent two years building and furnishing. I keep telling her it's too early to tell what life's like here, but she wants me to quit, and get a job in Israel." It had only been two months since his abrupt transfer from the Kestrel Jerusalem. "About the release . . ."

"It stinks to high heaven," Matt interrupted. "Or am I being paranoid?"

"If so, we belong in the same psych ward. I spoke to Bertrand before I left Jerusalem. He told me the Blenheim people were all over him to say nothing about the Saudi Prince, but he was damned if he wouldn't tell what he knew to the police. He told me he had high level contacts in the *Sûreté* and he was trying to pressure them to reopen the investigation."

"So he went to them . . ."

"And now he's dead. An accident."

"A spasm in the long arm of coincidence. I don't buy 'accident' for a second," Matt growled.

It was good to talk, Lahav reflected, even to someone who was not a close friend. He'd harbored the same doubts as Dirksen. To air them was a release, though it accentuated his fears. "What do we do about it?" he asked.

Dirksen didn't answer directly. "Any news from Jerusalem?"

"Only that the hotel's gone to hell, margins have dropped like a lead weight and profits have fallen down the toilet. Barken's brought in a new controller and head of security who've never worked in hotels before; he's systematically fired my entire executive committee, anyone who disagrees with him is let go; and he entertains all kinds of odd people lavishly without any of them bringing a single shekel's worth of new business. There's been no attempt to upgrade anything. Some of the expensive artwork in the public areas have magically disappeared, the restaurant's become a joke, you can shoot a cannon through the place without hitting any diners. It kills me. All that hard work, my years of sweat . . ."

"What's been Blenheim's response?"

"That's the amazing part. No one seems to care." He thought he'd swallowed his bitterness. Now it left him trembling.

"Why don't you say something?"

"To whom? Netski? The Australian prime minister? They've got me isolated here. There's nobody I can talk to." He paused. There were people. "Actually, I still have friends in Jerusalem. Maybe I'll make a call or two."

"Mossad?" Dirksen asked.

Lahav gasped. "Never use that name on the telephone. God knows, you didn't hear it from me. Forget I said anything."

"Sorry. But if your friends are powerful, I have a feeling we'll need them."

"We?"

"Every GM Ritter appointed, the dwindling few of us still with a job." Matt hesitated, as though considering his words. "Don't be naïve Gidon, that press release from Netski. It wasn't a condolence note. It was sent to us as a warning."

Chapter 13
San Diego / Lima, Peru

"After Nusa Dua, managing this property's about as exciting as watching paint dry," Sammi Chalabi said, responding to Matt Dirksen's casual enquiry about how he was enjoying his new job at the Lima Kestrel. "Lima's not a growth city, so apparently Blenheim's not about to invest another penny in the hotel. There hasn't been a room renovation for ten years. Our technology's as up to date as an abacus. The meeting room carpet's so thin you can read a newspaper through it. As far as our company is concerned, this place is irrelevant and I'm the quintessential invisible man."

"And when you complain?" Matt asked.

"Netski won't return my calls. I even tried that fellow Weiss, although technically he has nothing to do with this place. Did you hear the comment that if Netski abruptly stopped walking, Dieter Weiss would disappear up his boss's well-kissed posterior? The last call I made to the corporate office was six weeks ago. That hasn't been returned as of yet. I don't even have a regional vice president to bitch to. The only contact I have is with some new accounting vice president in Los Angeles, who only wants to know when I can get the company's blocked funds released. I'm exiled here. Fed up. I'd quit except you and I both know that would make me look like I was responsible for Bali."

"Don't quit," Matt said hurriedly. "There are only a few of us old-timers left and we need to stick together. Gidon Lahav's not leaving, for example."

"And he's further away from headquarters than I am." Chalabi chuckled. "Lucky man."

"Did you get the release about Le Roi?"

"Yeah. Sad, isn't it?"

"A tragedy," Matt acknowledged, deciding not to reveal his conviction that Le Roi was murdered, which could reflect his own terror that the call to him from Le Roi might have added to the motive. Sammi was as headstrong as Bertrand, and if he decided to investigate, particularly since he'd gone to the police about the explosions in Bali, he could be killed as well. "What do you hear from your old property?"

"My replacement, Henry Tchou, came from some unknown marketing company in Singapore. All he knows about hotels is that he sometimes stays in them. Spent his first two weeks trying to find out what 'incentive travel' meant. He thought it was something you won in a lottery."

Matt roared. Incentive travel was a lucrative and vital business from the big insurance companies, car dealers, and the like that wanted to reward and motivate their key agents, salespeople and business partners, by inviting them to lavish meetings and parties. Cost made little difference; only the best would satisfy.

"The hotel's losing that business," Sammi continued. "The place is going downhill like it was caught in an avalanche. Tchou's canned all the key people and brought in incompetents. He doesn't spend time with prospective customers or with the guests. Profits are plummeting. He tells anyone who asks that it's because he's cleaning up the expensive mess I left behind. Some general manager! The competitive hotels' GMs tell me they're sending complimentary letters about him to our corporate office. He's so good for their business they want to be sure he stays."

Matt hung up, deeply disturbed. Blenheim was ignoring the profitability of their hotels and resorts, starving them of capital—except at the Audley San Diego Cliffs. Why? They'd paid a giant price for the company. Since they were a private equity firm, surely making profits was their lifeblood. Yet, seemingly willfully they were allowing their signature properties to disintegrate and with it the financial strength of the organization. Matt couldn't fathom it.

He wished he could call Beth for another meeting, but when he'd tried once before, her assistant told him she wasn't available to him and had given him the impression that she wouldn't be. The news hurt. She had called him, promised they'd meet again if there were trouble—and trouble was upon them, he felt—but now, silence. Did she hate him that much? Did she think being with him was too dangerous? Well, damn it, if he was willing to risk it, why wouldn't she? A sudden feeling of jealousy ran through his mind. "Did she have someone else?"

Chapter 14
Los Angeles

"Have you picked up your e-mails?" Dieter Weiss yelled, barging into his boss's office.

Dimitri Netski, immaculate in gray, pinstriped Armani slacks, an open-necked, monogrammed shirt, Ferragamo-shod feet resting on his paperless desk, glanced at his lieutenant with scorn. The German looked like he'd been dragged backwards through a hedge. "Not yet," he said. "Calm down, Dieter, and next time knock before you enter."

"I've just sent you recordings of phone calls our disobedient prima donna made earlier today. We installed listening devices on the home, office and cell phones of the remaining Ritter-appointed GMs. Anyway, I forwarded you Dirksen's calls to Lahav and Chalabi. Curiously, Lahav installed an anti-bugging system on his home phone; however it was child's play for our people to get around it," Weiss said, ignoring the contempt in Netski's tone. "You'd do well to listen."

Sighing as if pandering to an errant child, Netski unwound his long legs from the desk, swiveled his chair to face the computer monitor on his credenza, and clicked on the e-mail Weiss had sent.

As Matthew Dirksen's disembodied voice filled the office, Netski produced the rictus of a smile and his eyes went cold as a Siberian midnight. "Stupid, stupid man," he said. "It is time for him to be disobedient no more." He pressed a preset call button on his desktop phone, waited, and as soon as the call was answered said, "Implement the first phase of the Dirksen contingency plan you and I discussed."

Chapter 15
San Diego

A month had gone by. Matt had just about given up the prospect of talking to Beth when, on a late Friday afternoon, she called.

"Beth!" His delight was so transparent he hoped it wouldn't frighten her off. "I'd given up on you."

"I know," she said. "My fault. I can't tell you how many times I picked up the phone. You know why I didn't dial the number."

"Well, at least today you dialed it." He winced at his own feeble humor. What was happening to him? "I hoped that after our meeting, you'd want to see me again. At least professionally. God knows, I wanted to see you; there's lots to discuss."

"That's just it. I felt that with Lee looking over my shoulder, and Dieter Weiss over his, that meeting together would jeopardize us both."

He stood, carrying the phone, and paced his office. "Then why the change of heart?"

A pause. "This is difficult for me," she said at last. "I've relived that evening a thousand times and still can't believe what happened."

He pressed the receiver to his ear, and consciously heard only the sound of her voice and the implication of her words. "Go on."

"It's simple. I thought of being with you again, and suddenly I didn't care about the consequences. You do feel it too, don't you?"

"Oh, God, yes! I haven't stopped thinking about you, Beth. This call has made me happier than . . ."

"Shush. The Hotel Del Coronado. Monday. The restaurant and bar's called 1500 Ocean. Five o'clock?"

He ridiculously wrote the time on his calendar. As if he'd forget! He felt buoyant, light-headed. "Whatever you say, boss."

"Be on time," Beth said sternly, and hung up.

*

Three floors above Beth Taylor's office, Jimmy Lee's thin smile replaced his normally impassive look, as he too hung up the phone.

Chapter 16
San Diego

The lunch service had just finished at the Resort's Beach Club when Pete Wilson sat down with Dirksen to discuss the Summit. Both men hung their jackets over the backs of their coral-lacquered rattan chairs, breathed in the exotic blend of salt air, hibiscus, oleander, lavender and bougainvillea, and watched as the Elite docked and disgorged its passengers.

"What have you got for me?" Matt asked, without preamble.

"Good news. Business is terrific. We're booked solidly until the Summit. Your idea of pushing rates until people start screaming is working. We're already up more than a hundred bucks per room over the same time last year, and no one's said a word. That extra revenue's dropping like a brick to the bottom line."

Matt drank iced tea. "Push it up another fifty, stick the food and beverage prices up another 20 percent, and see what happens."

"Got it. But that's not the point I wanted to make. Business is so good I'm having difficulty displacing all the reservations we have on the books for the period of the Summit."

"No choice. Arrange it. And without letting our guests know why they're being bumped."

Wilson winced. "It gets more complicated. Our new director of engineering, that fellow McGregor . . ."

"I know you don't like him, but you've got to live with him. He knows his stuff. His areas are tighter than an aircraft carrier's."

"He pisses me off. It's not just me he ignores, but also you."

"If I can live with it, so can you. What about him?

"Yesterday he told me that Dieter Weiss has ordered all the new systems mandated by the State Department from Germany and that the manufacturers will be sending teams of installers from their plants."

"So?"

"It means that when they're ready to switch equipment and systems, all the power will be off and our Conference Center will be out of business during the transition and testing period. We'll have to cancel all the meetings booked for that period of time. But we've had that business on our books since we opened. It's not just about loss of profits but about our guests. Some of our best and most loyal customers will be displaced. I feel like we're deliberately screwing them over and they'll be pissed. Rightly so. God knows how we'll deal with it. I'm beginning to wonder if this damned Summit is worth all the aggravation and costs."

Matt felt his impatience rise. "Suck it up and get on with it."

The resident manager was clearly exasperated. "It's so goddamned ridiculous. What in heaven's name is wrong with the systems we have?"

Matt glared at his colleague. "You're wasting energy whining. This was a condition of the deal in the first place."

"Shit, Matt, it's . . ."

"Enough! This is a business, not some high school debating society. You promised me an amended budget by last Saturday. Where is it?"

Chapter 17
Interstate 5

Traffic light. The red Saab 9-3 convertible purred south along I-5 effortlessly. Normally a long drive with the top down on a cloudless day would relax the driver, as the wind flowed through her long, red hair and the warmth of the sun permeated her body. Today, as the off ramp to Laguna Niguel passed unnoticed, Beth Taylor's haunting fear increased proportionately to the decreasing distance to her destination.

The landmarked red, wooden dome of the Hotel Del Coronado in sight, Beth pulled the car over and removed a manila envelope from the glove compartment. Studying the 8 x 10, glossy, color photograph carefully, she brought it to her lips and gently kissed it. Angling the mirror towards her, Beth slowly brushed her hair, trying to dispel her self-loathing. It's just your job. That's all this is, a job, one that you have to do well, she rationalized. Glancing at the black and white photo for reassurance, she reluctantly accepted that she didn't have a choice. She methodically touched up her makeup, her racing heart gradually slowing, her determination increasing. She was ready.

Smiling at the photograph and at herself in the mirror, she replaced the envelope in the glove compartment and pulled the car out into the light traffic for the two minute journey.

Chapter 18
Coronado Island / Santa Monica

The crowds of tourists just descended from the seemingly endless line of tour busses that flowed like water through the manicured grounds, shops, restaurants and beaches of the iconic Hotel Del Coronado. This was where Tony Curtis and Jack Lemmon had pursued Marilyn Monroe in "Some Like It Hot"—a piece of good fortune for this hotel, Matt reflected, while enjoying the warmth of the round fire pit and sipping the Verbena tea he had ordered for himself and Beth—which added to the place's attraction for the nearly fifty years since the movie's release.

He spotted her walking across the Windsor Lawn, her red hair streaming in the warm sea breeze. He stood and held out his arms to her, but she adroitly avoided his embrace and simply sat across from him at the restaurant's table, head averted. "I'm feeling suddenly embarrassed," she said.

"Me too." He gently lifted her chin so he could look into her eyes. They were full of tears. "Crying? Why?"

Annoyed with herself for allowing the emotion of the moment to crack her resolve, she poured herself some tea. "I don't know. Tears of relief, I guess, at having the guts to come here." But it was more, she knew, even beyond the fact of Jimmy Lee and his odious blackmail. Her past was still locked in her soul, a dark, dead-end street. Today it would stay there. Today was all business.

The man opposite her now was not like the others with whom she'd had brief, always unsatisfactory, but never consummated relationships. However, he was a real man and a very attractive one. She had tried so hard with him, come closer than with the line of others that had preceded him, but she couldn't bring herself to cross that final hurdle. As she had done so often in the past with so many things, she had pushed the painful and embarrassing memories of her failed seduction of him in her apartment deep into the hidden recesses of her unconscious mind. Now they surfaced and, when added to Jimmy Lee's odious instructions, they made an ugly combination and overwhelmed her. And now, just as she had banished her feelings for Matt to some distant and remote place, her Chinese overlord was forcing her to confront her demons in a full frontal assault. To succeed, she knew she had no choice but to suppress her imagined or real emotions for Matt Dirksen. She was suddenly afraid that she would let down her guard and this man would explore her past and loathe what he discovered. Her present . . . well, she loathed herself.

The intensity of her feelings matched his, though he had no way of guessing the true meaning of her tears. He felt proud, as though he'd won a great victory. "When I drove down here," he said, "I thought that if we both got fired for seeing each other, we could start our own hotel."

She laughed wryly. "With two general managers, no staff and no money."

"Maybe we could get Rolfe to back us?" he joked, suddenly realizing there was more than a scintilla of seriousness in his comment.

"Anyway, I feel safe just seeing you. Weiss isn't going to can you before the Summit, and Jimmy Lee's been hands-off for the past weeks. Maybe I've passed some sort of test. Every day I don't have to see him is a bonus."

Her optimism was belied by her demeanor. Again she avoided his eyes, concentrating instead on her hands, which were trembling slightly.

"Did you get the release about Bertrand Le Roi?" he asked.

"Yes. Poor man."

"That's what you think? 'Poor man'?"

"I'm sorry, I seem callous. He must have been a friend of yours, so forgive me. The truth is, I barely knew him, so his death has no resonance for me. 'Poor man' sums it up."

"He's the main reason I kept trying to call you. Beth, I think he might have been murdered."

Her eyes, opened wide, staring at him with incredulity. "Is there evidence?"

"No. But he went to the *Sûreté* about the Saudi Prince—you know, the pederast."

She clicked her tongue. This conversation, freed from the personal, strictly business, was strangely liberating, though she would have to report it. “I didn’t know. My, my, so the rumor’s true? Another debauched Saudi prince. There’s a surprise! Shocking, but so what?”

“It’s not funny. My bet is that going to the French authorities got him killed.” He took her hand. It felt warm and fragile.

“Dieter Weiss is a monster,” she said gravely. “And Jimmy Lee’s not only very weird and treats me like I’m lower than whale shit in his pecking order, he’s evil. Did I tell you I’m not allowed to bring guests to Fantu if he’s eating there? I was eating with a guest when he came in and sent the *maître d’* to tell me Mr. Lee thought I should depart as soon as possible. You have no idea how humiliating that was. But are you’re implying they are murderers? Impossible. Why?”

He felt emboldened by her presence. “That’s what I intend to find out.”

She gasped. “Matt, be careful. Don’t get involved. Please. You’ve got so much to lose. I couldn’t stand it if I . . .” She stopped and slipped her hand away.

“If you what?”

“If anything happened to you.”

“I’ll be careful. Just a few discreet questions, to friends only. I’m trying to see if there’s a pattern.”

She was looking at him with such profound concern that he was all the more sure he was right in asking her to meet him. Her mouth was slightly open and she was breathing hard. He thought he had never known anyone so alluring. “Let me help you,” she said.

“No!” The word exploded. “Stay clear. I’d insist that we not meet again, only”—he smiled ruefully—“only I’m not strong enough to resist you. I was hurt and angry after that evening in your apartment. Right now, I don’t want to talk about the hotels or Blenheim from now on unless there’s a crisis in Santa Monica. I want to talk about you and us, about how precious my world seems now that you’re back in it.”

She closed her eyes and forced herself to relax. It’s time she concluded; it’s now or never. Drawing a deep breath, she stood and came over to him, enfolding him with her arms, her breasts soft against his back. Traitor, she thought, even as she moved closer, her heart pounding rapidly, her body taking over her mind. It felt good, he felt good. I can do this! She was surprised how easy it was. Besides, I have no choice, I'm acting under instructions, ones I can't disobey.

He rose, turned, and kissed her fiercely, imbued with the familiarity and passion that had fed his fantasies. They parted to catch their breath. When they moved to kiss again, for a fleeting moment he hesitated. But their lips touched and her tongue sought his, and he was lost.

*

The "Do Not Disturb" sign hung on the corridor side of the door to Room 347.

This time Beth took the lead. She was different, she knew, avid and available, yet more careful, more controlled, as though she had steeled herself not to disappoint him. She undressed him slowly, gently rebuffing his attempts to reciprocate, until he stood before her, his pulsating erection hard to her touch.

She guided him to the bed then slithered out of her dress, all the while massaging him with the tips of her long fingers. He groaned with pleasure. She knelt between his legs and enveloped him with her mouth, her tongue gently exploring, while simultaneously caressing his nipples. She could feel his body writhe in exquisite pleasure.

"Agh . . . ."

She felt herself on a different plane, separated from her own actions, imagining herself a courtesan in an ancient house of lust, there to provide maximum stimulation, quintessential bliss.

He tried to pull her on top of him. "Not yet, be patient," she whispered, allowing him to knead her breasts while she played with the underside of his scrotum and licked the tip of his throbbing penis.

"Beth, Beth, I'm com . . ."

"Not yet." She moved her mouth to his lips and felt his hungry tongue invade her. His hands spread her legs and he reached for her vagina. She grew wet, open and to her astonishment, tendrils of pure delight coursed through her body, pleasure unknown to her for eons. What was happening, she wondered? I'm terrified when sex is love, responsive when it's impersonal, a duty. The conundrum disappeared when he penetrated her, chasing away everything but sensation. Deeper and deeper he plunged, her legs wrapped tightly around him, her body arching in blissful response. She briefly succumbed to joy, as she gave herself to this man, in the instant before the familiar tightness seized her and her muscles contracted not from abandon but from fear.

"Oh, my God!" he shouted, as he came, his body shuddering. "That was fantastic. Unbelievable." He kissed her gently, moved his head to her chest, and stroked her flowing hair. She pulled away. Bathed in sweat and Beth's body juices, he lay on his side and looked at her.

She averted her eyes.

"What's wrong?" he asked.

"Nothing."

"That can't be true. Not after what we've just done together. We were so close, so in tune . . ."

"It's just that . . ."

He waited for her to go on.

The photo in her glove compartment blazed in her mind. "Just that this is difficult for me."

"Seems to me you're an expert. I have a witness to that effect." He joked as he lifted off the single, damp sheet covering them and pointed to his now limp penis.

"Please, Matt. I can't explain, or I could, and I will, but not now."

He could feel her fear, her sadness. "There's no rush."

Now she could look at him. "Thank you." She rolled him on his back, put her head on his shoulder and gently kissed the lower part of his neck.

He caressed her breasts lightly, thinking that he had to be careful with her, that she was fragile. "To be continued," he said. "On the mainland."

She was silent for a while, and when she spoke again her voice was strong. "Yes. I'd like that."

*

While Beth's Saab sped northward on I-5, its driver was lost in a melee of thoughts. On the one hand she had accomplished her mission and Jimmy Lee would be satisfied. On the other hand she realized she was worse than a whore; at least a prostitute was honest about her profession. Nothing I did today was honest, she concluded.

The miles passed by quickly as Beth replayed every minute of her time with Matt. As she pulled into her apartment's garage, she smiled to herself and thought: I wonder if a prostitute enjoys the emotionless sex as much as I did?

Chapter 19
Santa Monica

The pink hues of the Pacific sunset suffused Jimmy Lee's office the following afternoon. Beth, ignoring them, sat in front of his desk, her hands tightly clasped, her lower lip sore from biting it. She had told the unsmiling Chinese about Matt's suspicions and his determination to investigate further, but nothing about that first kiss, its passionate aftermath, and a welling up of desire, quickly repressed, she thought dormant inside her forever.

"He likes you?" Lee asked. "He finds you attractive?"

"I think so."

"He wants to see you again?"

"Yes."

"Did you do what I instructed?" he asked, his glaze as hard as granite.

Beth flushed and looked down at her hands folded on her lap.

"Did you? I repeat, did you?" His voice raised an octave.

"Yes," she whispered.

"I can't hear you?"

You son of a bitch! You want the gory details. Well screw you. You're going to get them and let's see if you get a hard-on, she thought. Beth described in great specificity every minute of their lovemaking, enjoying watching her Chinese master squirm.

"Do you need any more information?" she asked sweetly.

Jimmy Lee cleared his throat twice before responding. "That seems adequate, for the moment," he said, failing in his attempt to add menace.

"What should I do next?" she asked demurely.

"Go on with the meetings. Tactfully, of course, in public. Intimacy between you should be saved for bedrooms. For example, Room number 347 at the Hotel Del Coronado."

Her skin crawled at the realization that she had not told Lee the room number. She had been followed by one of Lee's acolytes, and he was reminding her that she was nothing but a pawn. Guilt suddenly overwhelmed her, as she struggled in vain to suppress the implications of her betrayal of both Matt and herself.

"I'm ashamed of what I did at the Del. Please, Jimmy," she cried, unable to maintain her stoic facade. "Don't make me do it again. Don't make me hate myself."

"Remember the reason. The question isn't whether you hate yourself, but how much you love your daughter. The daughter you abandoned. The daughter in the photograph."

Her chest ached with her desperation. "I've done exactly what you asked. Met him. Made him want me. Made love to him. Passed your messages on to him as if they were my own. Made him want me even more. Told you what he said. It's too hard. All too hard. Let Britney go. Let me go. I beg you—let us both be free."

"You're a smart woman. You know the answer, don't you?"

"How long must I do this?"

"Only 'til after the Summit."

"That's when you'll let me see her?"

"That's what we agreed."

"And you won't do anything to her? You'll let her alone?"

He smiled, evidently relishing her pleas. "Unless you break your word, or disobey instructions, your daughter is safe with us."

Chapter 20
New York

"I just had an odd conversation with young Dirksen," Rolfe Ritter said, striding into the brightly-lit kitchen of their Manhattan apartment, oblivious of the pain etched in his wife's face.

"What did he say?" Momo's strained whisper jolted her husband, as if he had been shocked by an electric cattle prod.

"Darling, what's wrong," he said, rushing over to the kitchen table and sitting next to her.

"I . . . I can't go on. I feel so weak, so ill. My head feels like it's ready to explode. Every day I have less energy. I'm dying and we both know it. I just want it to be over." She cupped her face in her hands, her body wracked in sobs.

Rolfe enveloped his wife in his arms and brought their bodies so tightly together he could feel her racing heart. "Don't be so silly, my darling. Mitch Sheinkop warned that you'd feel terrible from the cumulative effects of the chemo."

"It's all a waste of time. I'm sorry Rolfe, I just can't go on. It's time, my precious, and we both know it."

"Don't talk that way. Depression's normal. You're strong, we've been through so much, and we'll get through this together." Rolfe gulped, trying to hold back his own tears.

"I can't take this anymore. I want to die with some dignity. Help me finish it. Find a way. You can do it. Please, Rolfe, please."

"Never. You're going to live and we're going to get old together. Stop talking like that and think of all the wonderful lovemaking we have ahead. In fact, I'm feeling horny right now. Wanna fuck, lady?"

Momo smiled weakly, clasped his hand and kissed the nape of his neck. He felt the warmth of her tears on his skin. He gently caressed her cheek, endlessly repeating the whispered words, "I love you more every moment. All will be well. I promise."

Finally, she levered herself upright against his body and, with red-rimmed eyes looking into his, smiled wanly. "All right, all right. I'll stay alive just so you don't suffer from DSB."

He chuckled at the long-shared codeword for his wanting to make love: "Medicinal reasons," he would say. "DSB—Deadly Semen Backup."

Momo composed herself and slowly pulled herself upright, her face the color of aged parchment. "You came here burbling about Matt Dirksen? What did he say?"

"He's normally very measured with me. Very careful what he says. This time was different. He started by saying he was calling from a public phone at a gas station and then announced he was convinced Le Roi's death was no accident. He told me Gidon Lahav felt the same way and they were both digging into it."

Momo was aghast. "My God! If your suspicions are even partly correct, they could both be playing with fire."

"I warned him not to meddle. Leave it to the authorities. If there was something going on, they'd find it."

"You of all people know that's bullshit. Nonetheless, if you're right about Blenheim, and we both know that's a big if, then amateurs like Gidon and Matt will put themselves in danger."

Rolfe sighed, "I tried to talk him out of playing private detective. He agreed to think about things. He said he would, but it felt like he was only paying lip service to me. It's unlike Dirksen."

"What are you going to do about it, if anything?" Momo asked.

"First, I'm calling Mitch Sheinkop and ask him what he can do to help you. Then, then . . ."

"Then what?"

"Then, I'm going to make a few calls and see if I have any friends left inside the company."

Chapter 21
Waikiki Beach, Hawaii / San Diego

"Where in God's name is Gidon?" Matt Dirksen asked himself the same question for the umpteenth time as he paced through the soaring atrium lobby of the Hyatt Regency, Waikiki Beach. The Israeli was due at eight a.m.; it was now eleven. There'd been no e-mail from him, no phone call, no text message, no word at the front desk, no delay on the flight from Sydney to Honolulu, no traffic jams between here and the airport—nothing to account for his absence. Calls to his home had gone unanswered.

Lahav had called his cell phone two days earlier at three a.m. Pacific time. "I've followed up on our conversation," he'd said abruptly, not even giving his name. "My friends are concerned."

"What friends?" Matt asked groggily, then realized whom Lahav meant. "Oh."

"We have to talk," Lahav said. The urgency in his voice had Matt fully awake. "Not on the phone. Face to face."

"Jesus, Gidon, the Summit's only five months away. I can't fly to Melbourne."

"You won't have to. I'll meet you Saturday at the Hyatt in Waikiki. Breakfast."

"How will I explain my absence to Blenheim?"

Gidon laughed. "Wink, then tell 'em you've got a heavy date. They'll be so shocked, a monk like you, that they'll believe you need to schlep all the way to Hawaii just to get laid. It'll give us the weekend to talk."

Matt frowned. "It's that pressing?"

"More than pressing. Life or death."

Matt's brain was automatically rearranging his schedule as he reached for his blackberry. "I'll be there."

*

Dirksen continued to call Lahav's home; no answer. He called Sammi Chalabi and Beth Taylor; neither had heard from the

Israeli. Impotent and nearly mad with worry, he finally booked a late afternoon flight to Los Angeles. Maybe there'd be news from Gidon at his home or at the Resort.

There was an e-mail message waiting for him when he got home after midnight and logged on.

> TO: Corporate Officers and General Managers
> FROM: Dimitri Netski, Chief Executive Officer
> SUBJECT: Second Tragedy Sorrows Blenheim
>
> It is with heavy heart that I announce the death of our dear colleague, Gidon Lahav, in a motor accident on the road from Melbourne to Sydney. Lahav, recently promoted to the post of GM at the Kestrel Melbourne, had already made significant improvements in the hotel's bookings and profit margins. Our deepest sympathies go to his wife, Shulamit.
>
> No replacement for Mr. Lahav has yet been chosen. I will inform you all when he or she is selected.

*

Matt barely made it to his bathroom before he threw up. He retched until there was nothing left, then propped himself up against the tub and stared catatonically at the white-tiled floor. This time surely there could be no doubt. Lahav had been murdered. For what? Obviously for what he needed to tell Matt. Perhaps Mossad had found something that a secret someone would commit murder to hide. It had to be Blenheim. It was so obvious. Why couldn't others see it? He had no idea what that secret was, how vast and how powerful, but the extent of Blenheim's determination was terrifying, and he shivered uncontrollably.

For one thing was absolutely clear: Blenheim knew Lahav was going to meet him. And that meant his own life was theirs to take, whenever they willed it.

Well, fuck them! He was still alive, and would continue Lahav's search for that secret as long as they let him.

He staggered into the bedroom, reached for the phone, not caring if it was tapped. Again he tried Lahav's home. This time someone answered.

"Shulamit? It's Matt. Matt Dirksen."

"Mr. Dirksen. Matt." Her voice was flat, as though all emotion had been erased from it hours ago.

"I'm so terribly sorry about Gidon." How awkward his words sounded; he had met her only once at a GM meeting.

"It's terrible. I can't bear . . ." A sob cut off her voice.

"This is a bad time for me to call, I know, but I've got to ask you a few questions."

"He was a gentle, good man. A kind man. They say carjackers or muggers shot him when he stopped for gas on the road to Sydney."

So much for Netski's version of history. Some motor accident. More like a planned murder, Matt thought.

"Do you know why he was going there?" Dirksen gently asked.

"To fly to Waikiki." He heard a sharp intake of breath. "Oh God, he said he was going to meet you!"

"That's right."

"Are you there now?"

"No. I came back to San Diego. Shulamit, did Gidon say anything to you about me or about our conversation?"

She paused, evidently struggling to remember. "Three nights ago, he'd been on the phone with someone from Israel and was clearly upset when he came into the bedroom. He said he had to call you right away."

"He did. That's when we agreed to meet in Hawaii. But he didn't tell me anything more; said we had to meet in person." He spoke slowly now, emphasizing each word. "Do you know the name of the person he talked to in Israel?"

She started crying again; his heart bled for her. Finally she said, "I'm sorry, Matt. I've no idea. But my brain's . . . fuzzy . . . right now. I still can't believe Gidon's gone. I'll call you if I remember anything."

*

His heart pounded so hard that he fumbled with his cell phone's keypad. Matt reached Sammi Chalabi's office and held his breath. No one answered. Terror mounting, he tried Chalabi's cell phone. A recorded voicemail told him to leave a message. He dialed the Lima Kestrel's main number and asked to be put through to the house manager.

Come on, come on. Pick up the goddamned phone!

"Carlos Morales speaking."

At least someone's alive, he thought morbidly.

"This is Matt Dirksen. I'm the GM at the Audley San Diego Cliffs."

"Yes, of course. I've heard many wonderful things about your hotel. How may I help you?"

"I've been trying to get hold of Mr. Chalabi with no luck. Do you know how I can reach him?"

"That's a question many of us have asked. Including the police."

Matt fought for breath. "What do you mean?"

"He was kidnapped yesterday evening by Shining Path. At midnight, the local daily newspaper received a call demanding the release of all the political prisoners in Peru's prisons in exchange for Mr. Chalabi's life." Morales's voice, until now controlled by his professionalism, broke. "They also want the release of four prominent Palestinian prisoners jailed by the Israelis. The story is splashed all over today's front pages."

Matt had heard about Shining Path, a terrorist group known for their savagery, which for years had bedeviled the Peruvian government. Morales's news was, Matt thought, a death sentence for his colleague. "What are your police doing about it?" he barely whispered.

"Looking for him. But it's the government's position that it will not negotiate with terrorists, so it's unlikely they'll find him. Off the record, the police told our people that Mr. Chalabi, as a Lebanese citizen, might be connected to some terrorist organization himself. They suggested he was involved with the explosions in Bali."

"Garbage!"

"I'm sure. But the police intimated that Shining Path may be linked with Al Qaeda in Mr. Chalabi's kidnapping. All of the TV newscasts are leading with that story."

Ever since the 9/11 attacks, Matt thought that the world had gone mad. Now he was sure of it. Sammi Chalabi was the gentlest of men. He winced when he remembered that Shulamit had used the same word to describe Lahav; it was preposterous to think of him as a terrorist. "If the police won't do anything, what about Blenheim?"

"They're deeply concerned. However, the Peruvian government threatened to withhold the hotel's operating license and not release the hotel's long-blocked foreign currency funds if we negotiate a financial deal with Shining Path. So, again, the answer is 'nothing.'"

Matt felt that a knife had skewered his soul. "So there's no way to help him?"

"It's terrible, Mr. Dirksen." All hint of composure had collapsed. "Mr. Chalabi is a good man and a fine boss. It's going to be a very long week."

An alarm went off in Matt's skull. "What do you mean?"

"Shining Path has given the government one week to comply with their demands, or they will behead Mr. Chalabi."

Chapter 22
Santa Monica

The walls of her office closing in on her, Beth Taylor uncharacteristically brushed past her assistant muttering about her need for fresh air.

She found it on the beach's boardwalk in front of the hotel, gulped it to calm herself, and started to walk south toward Venice Beach.

Damn Jimmy Lee! She paced forcefully, oblivious of the inline skaters, bikers and runners swirling around her.

With each stride came increasing clarity. The problem's not Jimmy Lee. It's Matt Dirksen.

She couldn't respond to his lovemaking when she was attracted to him, wanted him. But at the Del Coronado, when he was nothing more than an . . . an assignment, then she could climax in abandonment as though she was an erotic fountain, without restraint, without fear. Alan Campbell, her daughter's father, used to make her come like that, and he was a bastard, a selfish bastard for whom lovemaking was just about how quickly he could come, no thought for her. That should have been her clue. When he betrayed her, he betrayed her sexual self. She'd become an effigy of a woman, a hollow, terrified creature at her core.

Then what had happened at the Del? Had Matt become literally a prick, an instrument of pleasure no more human than a vibrator? She'd heard whores couldn't enjoy sex. Maybe that was wrong? Maybe they enjoyed sex because it was business, the way she had? Was it just business? Could I have felt fulfilled, she asked herself, if it was just an assignment? Could I feel fulfilled if it was love?

She turned off Ocean Front Walk onto North Venice Boulevard, made a sharp right and strode along Grand Canal, her mind in turmoil. Self-disgust permeated her; she felt filthy, the slime so ingrained that not even all the ocean's waters could wash it off.

A new thought intruded. I love Matt Dirksen! Maybe Jimmy Lee has given me a precious gift instead of a sordid punishment? Maybe with Matt I can feel real pleasure? Make love with him? Yes! Willingly! Thrillingly! My God! The next time we make love, I'll . . .

The thoughts disappeared—as though someone had shut off the radio at the climax of a symphony—replaced by new ones. How can I continue to betray Matt? How can I not? Jimmy Lee has my daughter. I can't abandon Britney a second time.

Beth Taylor slumped on the nearest bench, shrouding her face with her hands. Her sobs went unheeded by the passersby.

Chapter 23
New York

"I don't believe it," Rolfe Ritter exclaimed, dropping the phone's receiver from his hand.

"What don't you believe? What is it? Who was on the phone?" Momo asked, shocked by her husband's appearance, all color having instantly drained from his face.

"That was David Michels, the house manager at the New York Audley," Ritter said, his voice flat, vacant eyes staring into space.

"I remember him, nice man, bald as an egg, plays tennis every day. You took him from being a bellman at the Detroit property and put him at the front desk in the Kestrel in Lower Manhattan. When the Audley was built you gave him a shot as front desk manager. I didn't know he'd been promoted. Snap out of it Rolfe, what did he say?"

Rolfe Ritter slumped into the overstuffed armchair, slowly shaking his head from side to side. "He told me that Gidon Lahav had been killed in a carjacking in Australia."

"Oh, my God! You warned that he and Matt Dirksen could be in danger if they meddled in this mess. It can't be a coincidence, can it? Poor Shulamit. All her family's in Israel. She's on her own. What can we do for her? What should we do about Gidon's death? More importantly, what can we do? Who can we talk to?"

"That's not all. Sammi Chalabi's been kidnapped and if the kidnapper's demands aren't met, they will behead him within a week." He buried his head in his hands, his breath heavy.

"Then it's only money. If Blenheim won't pay, we can," Momo said triumphantly.

Her husband sighed, "If only it were that easy."

*

The bottle of Far Niente Chardonnay sat half empty in the silver wine cooler perched on the coffee table in the Ritters' library.

Rolfe finally spoke after a half hour of heavy silence. "Dirksen is in grave danger. Those bastards are killing off what's left of the old hands I put into the company. I have to protect him, stop him from interfering. They'll kill him, I know they will."

"He'll listen to you, but you'd better see him personally. You'll have to go to San Diego," Momo said.

"Bullshit! You know I can't, I won't leave you."

"You'll only be gone overnight. I'll be fine."

"I'm not going, not with your next treatment the day after tomorrow. Pass me the phone."

Knowing better than to argue with her husband when his mind was made up, she handed him the cordless phone as he searched for Matt Dirksen's numbers in his navy blue, suede-covered address book. He dialed a number, waited, hung up and dialed again. "No answer in his office," he muttered, looking in the book again and dialing a different number. Hanging up, he dialed a third number, then put down the phone in frustration. "No answer from his cell phone or his home. Shit! Now I'm really worried."

Chapter 24
San Diego

Pete Wilson, frustrated and furious, stomped around his office, barely resisting the temptation to throw the crystal model of the hotel at the door, which the corporate security supremo, Brad Marshall, had recently exited. Damn the man, he thought. What a prick!

There was no answer at Matt's office or on his cell phone, and his boss wasn't responding to e-mails on his Blackberry—just when Wilson needed him. It wasn't enough that Marshall barely communicated with anyone on Matt's team, giving the impression they were the very lowest form of existence in his world, the real world; or that he had summarily dismissed all of Jack Turner's security team, replacing them with his own people. It was the way he had marched in to Pete's office and ordered him to temporarily close down five of the larger villas, while the Secret Service came to place even more miles of wiring for the communications network that would eventually be installed.

"If you don't like it, take it up with Mr. Netski," Marshall said when Pete refused.

Fat chance. Only Matt could do that. And even that was a maybe.

Then there was the issue of the personnel files. Only yesterday Vern Simmons, the Resort's normally calm director of human capital, had come to see Pete in Matt's absence, angrily complaining that Marshall had taken a number of the files so the Secret Service could begin the security clearance process.

"So what's your point?" Pete had asked. "Obviously, there have to be clearances."

"The point is that I talked to two new men whose files Marshall had grabbed. I happened to look at those two files by chance before Marshall took the whole pile. Turns out their histories are different from the information in their files. When I challenged

Marshall with this, he told me I was an amateur and had misunderstood the men's broken English. So I figured I should talk with them again. But when I went to find them, I found they'd been fired hours before."

Remembering, Pete slammed the model on his desk. Shit, Matt. Where the hell are you?

Chapter 25
San Diego

He had to warn Beth. It seemed too much of a reach to think that Blenheim was not involved in Chalabi's kidnapping. There were many fine hotels in Lima, but it was hard to believe the terrorists had chosen the Kestrel and Sammi randomly. Shit! If it was Blenheim, he thought, that means I could be next—or Beth. They had to talk, to plan. It was imperative he see her. His heart raced in anticipation.

Deliberately having ignored the insistent and persistent ringing of his home and cell phones, Matt waited for dark, then went to his garage, pressed the automatic door opener, and tried to relax. It was dark inside the garage, but he saw that the BMW listed to one side. Damn! A flat. He opened the trunk to retrieve a jack and his spare tire.

The baseball bat that smashed across his back and shoulders slammed Matt into the opened trunk cover. Blood gushed from the wound on his forehead. The bat struck again, and he toppled to the concrete floor. He started to scream. A heavy boot smashed into his kidney, cutting off all sound. Two pairs of hands jerked him upright and pushed him face first against the garage's shelving. Boxes and tools tumbled on him as the bat slammed behind his knees; he buckled, but one pair of hands propped him while the other pulled a sack over his head. Claustrophobia overwhelming him, he lashed out with his fist and made contact with the side of an assailant's head. A guttural voice shouted, "What the fuck?" and the bat smashed into the side of his head.

Oblivion.

*

He was roused by the sound of the surf. His head throbbed mercilessly; his eyes slowly opened. Darkness. Firm hands on either side pinned him to the seat. He tasted blood, his blood, and inhaled the stink of the fetid Hessian sack. Bile rose in his throat. "Where am I?" he screamed. A punch in his side silenced him. He vomited helplessly.

"Fucking pig. He threw up on me!"

Coarse laughter. The car doors opened. He was dragged out of his seat by powerful arms. His knees gave way and he sank to the ground. Sand. He was on a beach.

"Pull him up," he heard the man with the coarse laughter say with a Texas accent, no hint of amusement now in his voice.

He was lifted up and pulled backwards, his heels scarring the sand, one shoe coming off un-noticed. No energy left, his head bounced up and down on his shoulders. The surf grew louder. Were they going to drown him? He was beyond fear, reduced to accepting what would come.

A fist slammed into his gut, but he was not allowed to fall. The fist rammed into his solar plexus once more. He vomited again, gasped for air. There was none. Again and again the relentless fist hammered home.

Pain. Only pain.

The assault stopped. He felt a man's breath through the sack. "Listen carefully, motherfucker." The Texan. "This is your one and only warning. Stop interfering in matters that aren't your goddamned fucking business. Do you hear me?"

He tried to answer. No words came. The fist rammed into his side. He nodded.

"You've caused enough pain to your friends. Got it?"

Again, he could only nod.

"Two of them are dead because of you. If you keep nosing around, your pretty, redheaded girlfriend will be next. Are you listening, motherfucker?"

He fainted. The voice screaming in his ear brought him back. "I said, are you listening, you son-of-a-bitch?"

He tasted blood. He forced out a painful grunt.

"Good. Now hear this, Dirksen. You're out of your fucking depth. So do what you're fucking told and keep your fucking trap shut. Understand?"

"Ssss."

"We left you a package to think about. Remember, we know everything about you, everything you say and do. Every fucking thing." The Texan's voice dropped. "And just in case you give a motherfucking damn, only you can save Sammi Chalabi's life."

A thunderous kidney punch sent white-hot pain through Matt's body. Suddenly free of his captors' grip, he crumbled into the sand, the surf lapping onto his legs.

Chapter 26
La Jolla

Every inch of his body hurt. Opening his eyes was agony. He closed them quickly. Images of the Texan's club-fists flashed across his mind, but he forced them away. He was home now, having retrieved his cell phone after ten minutes of searching the sand for it. Despite its smashed screen, the phone still worked and he had called a cab. Shoeless, he managed to climb up the cliff's steep, dirt road to the paved street, waited endlessly for the taxi to arrive, fumbled with his house key in his swollen and bruised fingers, and somehow opened his front door. Half a dozen Tylenols, swallowed through cut and swollen lips, had done little to ease the pain, and he lay fully clothed on his bed, aware only of how badly he'd been hurt.

An hour later, after he convinced himself he could move, he staggered to the shower. The simple act of removing his foul-smelling, ripped clothes made him scream in pain, as did the steaming, hot shower water that felt as if golfball-sized hailstones were ferociously smashing into his body.

Still, the water helped, and he made his way back to the bedroom. On the dresser lay the large envelope tossed near his body by his tormentors. He stared at it in the steel grey light of dawn flooding through his windows, until fear and uncertainty propelled him to pick it up.

Sand still stuck to its edges. Naked, he sat heavily on his bed, worked open the flap, and shook out the contents. Photocopied papers spilled onto the blanket.

He picked them up reluctantly, his heart racing. When he finished reading, he let them fall from his fingers and stared catatonically into an abyss.

Chapter 27
London

Annabelle's on Berkeley Square was humming. Lithe young women dragged middle-aged men to the dance floor at the far end of the basement venue. Crystal champagne flowed ceaselessly, accompanied by Servuga caviar and buckwheat pancakes.

Ignored by the late-night crowd, four men huddled at a corner table. Low-wattage, warm, white lights recessed in the arched ceiling cast macabre shadows on their faces. Their three long-legged, short-skirted Russian companions danced with each other, oblivious to the entreaties of hovering unattached males. They would return when summoned.

Dimitri Netski poured himself a generous shot of Johnny Walker Blue Label and glared at Dieter Weiss. "How could you let this happen?" he hissed. "Dirksen's out of control!"

The German blanched. "How was I to know he'd play private detective?"

"It's your business to know." His rage encompassed Fabrizio Battini and Jimmy Lee, both doing their best to pretend they weren't at the table.

"I'm sorry," Weiss began.

"Sorry doesn't do it. We've had to pay off the goddamned Melbourne police so they wouldn't investigate Lahav's death, and fix matters in Peru so no one'd know if Al Qaeda, Shining Path or the man in the fucking moon kidnapped Chalabi. Then you pull a stupid stunt and have Dirksen beaten up in his garage by a couple of your two-bit thugs. Are you out of your fucking mind?"

"They shut the garage door after them and finished the job at the beach," Weiss muttered.

Netski leapt. "The fucking beach. Where any late-night dog walker could have seen them."

"I wanted to give him a warning."

"Oh, brilliant! What if he goes to the police? What would he have said if he'd been hospitalized? Don't you ever use your fucking brains, or is it all about your petty, sadistic pleasures?"

"He won't go to the police," Weiss said. "I left him a package."

"Which contained?" Battini ventured.

"Enough shit about his father that he'll do what we say."

"Why didn't I know about it?" Netski asked.

"I have my own way of finding things out. Besides, my plan worked. Dirksen called me this morning to ask for a few days off. Said he had family business in Indiana. Surprise, surprise."

"Did he say anything to Beth Taylor?" Battini asked Jimmy Lee.

The Asian grinned. "Not a word. She hasn't heard from him in over a week, well before he went to Hawaii."

"You sure she's not lying?" Netski asked, his anger waning.

"Positive. The woman's doing exactly what I say. When I tell her to screw Dirksen's brains out—she will. And tell me the exact diameter of his dick or the weight of his balls to the ounce."

"That might be vital information," Netski laughed. "She has two jobs now. Report everything he says to you and douse his suspicions. She should be fucking Dirksen's brains out so often that he gets addicted. Taylor's got to control him and know everything he's thinking, even if it's only to get a Coke. I want that son of a bitch completely addicted to the whore's pussy. If he doesn't call her daily, she's to call him. He's got no one else to talk to now. The Ritter gang is dead, dispersed or kidnapped. Anyone we missed will be too frightened to say anything." He emptied his glass and refilled it. "The Summit's in five months. Is everything else going smoothly?"

Weiss wiped sweat from his forehead. "Brad Marshall's taking care of security checks and procedures with the FBI and the Secret Service. Not a hiccup."

"And the new electronic systems?"

"All organized and planned."

"Is the property prepared?"

“Our chief engineer, Keith McGregor’s, all over the planning, scope documents, installation and scheduling.

Netski glanced at Weiss. “At least some things are going well.”

The German reddened. “Damn it . . .”

“Relax,” Netski said, raising a hand. The four Russian women stopped dancing. “Enough shop talk, my friends. We’re away from Los Angeles. Let’s finish off the scotch, have the caviar—and, of course, for three of us, the ladies.”

Chapter 28
Chesterton, Indiana

"Jesus Christ, Dad! Why in God's name did you do it?"

The two men were in the Dirksen living room, Matt pacing furiously, his father's thin frame wilting in a couch under his son's barrage. The old man's colorless face looked haggard, his thin grey hair hanging limply over his eyes, his jeans and frayed denim shirt too large for the body they covered. The papers from the damning envelope that had been left beside Matt's battered body on the beach lay in his father's liver-spotted, heavily-veined hands. He'd read the first page, then stopped reading. He already knew what they contained, Matt realized, with a throb of sorrow.

"What a mess. What a goddamned mess."

David Dirksen did not respond, staring listlessly at the floor. Nothing was changed since Matt had gone off to Cornell Hotel School. Stains still scarred the carpet; the couch and armchairs had not been recovered; the shabby wallpaper was eerily familiar. Even the books were the same; not one new title had been added. It was as if the place had been in a time warp for almost two decades. This was the room in which he'd told his parents he wanted to become a great hotel manager. He remembered his father's blank stare as if it was yesterday. Had Matt's mother remained alive, the room—the house—would have been refurbished, warm, full of her laughter, welcoming. But here was only his father, or the ghost of him, as unconcerned about the room's appearance as his own. Matt felt a rush of fury. It was as though David Dirksen had attacked him deliberately—now, when the events at the Resort were threatening to overwhelm him, with the pain from his battered body even worse than it had felt in La Jolla. And here was his father, as limp and useless as a crippled dog.

Every damned word in the papers was true. His father made no denial; his condemned man's eyes were proof enough. What was in the papers could send his father to jail, and Matt vowed not to let that happen. He wasn't there to judge the man; he was his father's son, and whatever had happened, whatever his father had done, he had to help. Still, the house made him feel old, irrelevant, ineffectual. "You're just like your father," his mother had said to him in those rare instances when he didn't work hard enough at his homework or refused to mow the lawn. The words hurt, but maybe she saw something in him that only now he could identify. Damn the man!

He stared out the window at the uncut lawn, remembering how his father had rough-and-tumbled with him and his friends on it, during those days when it was carefully manicured; the laughs they had together; the strengths of mind his father had passed on. All of us are fallible, Matt knew. He felt his anger and frustration seep out of him, replaced by sadness and guilt at the pain he was causing. He sat next to his father and rested his palm on top of the old man's hands. "Tell me what happened. It'll be all right, I promise."

"I'm so ashamed," his father whispered. "So sorry."

"It's okay, Dad. Just tell me the story."

David raised his head and for the first time looked at Matt squarely. "As you and Amanda were growing up, we were doing fine. My practice was small, but we made enough to live reasonably well. My biggest client was Armstrong Cement—you know, not ten miles down the road. Your sister was seventeen and you fourteen when the plant closed. I cut costs at the office, but nonetheless we were hurting."

"How come you never said anything?" Matt asked.

"Chesterton's a small town and appearances mean a lot. Besides, your mother was sick by then and I didn't want to worry her." His voice grew stronger. "We had counted on you and your sister going to the University of Indiana. State school, cheap fees, subsidized costs for state residents. But Amanda was accepted at Trinity College in Connecticut—I hadn't even known she'd applied—and your mother was dead set on her going. Small school, proximity to New York and Boston, an escape from the local yokels like me and your mom. Thirty thousand per annum. But the joy in your mother's and 'Manda's faces was worth it. I knew I had to find the money four years running. Your mother died when Amanda was a freshman. Although I stopped going to her church after she died, it seemed essential for me to fulfill her wishes for you both, to carry on by myself. Then you decided to go to Cornell. You promised to work and take student loans and you did. I knew it would be still another $15,000 or so a year to find."

"Why didn't you tell me you couldn't afford it? I was a big boy. I'd have understood."

His father sighed, "I didn't, couldn't. It wasn't fair short-changing you after 'Manda. So, off you went to Ithaca to conquer the world."

"Is that when . . . ?" Matt knew the answer.

"Yes. I was doing the books for the Sand Creek Country Club, handling everything, the banking, the lot. It was easy to take money and fake entries so the bank statements reconciled and the cash balanced. I was convinced something would come up, another big client, something. I'd be able to put the money back, with nobody the wiser." He shook his head.

"But nothing did come up, did it?"

"Never did, I guess it never does. I grew more and more desperate, took more and more."

"And then?"

"I couldn't look at myself in the mirror. Years of faked entries, with interest I must have owed the club close to quarter of a million bucks. I went to the club's president, Jack Hulse. Remember him?"

"Yes. A florid man with a neon smile."

"Right. Anyway, I confessed everything. I'd known him since junior high, we were real friends. I promised him I'd pay everything back with full interest and, after he cooled down, he agreed; and provided I'd stick to a strict schedule and begin payments immediately, he wouldn't reveal the fraud."

"I sold everything I could, traded in the Caddy for that small, rust-bucket Chevy, took every bookkeeping job that came along, no matter how small, worked as a night auditor at the Holiday Inn in Hammond. You and 'Manda were out of school by that time. I needed nothing for myself; ate so many cans of the cheapest tuna that I began to stink like a fish. Everything I earned went to Hulse—every damned nickel—until we were square."

Relief flooded Matt like a warm bath. "Then there's no problem?"

"I wish it were that simple. Jack died last year. He didn't tell anyone about our arrangement. I have all the books and records, of course, but who'd believe a thief, expert at doctoring documents? If those papers get out I'm ruined. No one would hire me again. What would I use for money? The house is already mortgaged to the hilt."

"I'll give you everything you'd need!" Matt cried.

"You have no idea how many times I'd thought of asking," David admitted. He bowed his head. "No. A man must pay for his own sins. I'll get by without help. So long as those papers remain private, I doubt anyone will notice. If not . . ." He shrugged. "I hear the food's good at the state prison in LaPorte County; I hope canned tuna's not on the menu."

He stood suddenly, fury in his expression, moving back from Matt like a cornered animal. "How did you get the papers?"

That wasn't the right question, Matt thought. How did they get them?

*

Sleepless, lying on the single bed of his childhood, Matt felt the walls closing in on him. How little parents confide in their children! He felt excluded from his father's life—one of secrets and pain and desperation. Would he really go to prison rather than let Matt help him? Matt believed so. He could have helped, he considered. Financially, even emotionally, if his father had opened the door to his troubles. Only now did the distance between them seem comprehensible. His father's coldness was a defense against fear, against revelation, against disgrace. Guilt washed over him. He promised himself he would help financially whether his father liked it or not, and would narrow that distance in the years ahead.

As he closed his eyes, he could see himself as a sophomore at Cornell, needing money to keep going. A job waiting tables at the Finger Lakes Tavern and Grill in the outskirts of Ithaca provided the answer. He gulped as the long-repressed memory of his humiliation emblazoned itself once more in his mind. Shocked when he realized that the three seasoned waiters working the room were pocketing the tips and not sharing them with the new boy, he determined not to be taken advantage of and started doing the same. Three nights later, as his shift ended, the manager had walked up to him and coldly said, “Dirksen, empty your pockets.”

“Why?” he asked.

“Do as I say or I’ll call the police immediately.”

“I don’t understand,” he stammered, noticing his three smirking colleagues standing behind his accuser, as he slowly emptied his pockets with shaking hands.

The manager pointed to the pile of crumpled notes and coins that lay on the table’s scarred laminate surface. “Look at the coins, Dirksen. You’ll find two quarters with a hole drilled through each and four one-dollar bills with your name written in black ink on their top left-hand corners. How would I know that?”

“I don’t know,” he whispered, instinctively knowing the answer.

“Well, I do; you fucking no-good thief! I’ve been wondering why the amount of tips we share have gone down, so I planted the notes and coins and you took them. You’re not so high and mighty now, are you? Your type makes me sick. Think you can take what you want just because you’re a fancy Cornell student up the hill? I’m keeping the wages we owe you and putting them in the tip pool. Now get the fuck out of here and think yourself lucky that I’m not going to press charges.”

The long-sublimated, overpowering wave of embarrassment, guilt and shame he had felt all those years ago overwhelmed him again, as he struggled to cast aside the all-too-vivid memory. Who was he to judge his father? He was no better than a common thief. He too had been found out. He was his father’s son.

He needed Beth. After their wonderful lovemaking at the Hotel Del Coronado, he tried to call her several times, left messages, spoke to her apologetic assistant, who told him how busy Beth had been. Finally she had returned his calls, apologized and explained that she was torn with conflict, as they were professional colleagues, and that both of their careers could suffer as a result of their burgeoning relationship. She had pleaded with him to give her time to sort out her emotions. Almost childlike in his pleasure at finally talking to Beth, he had reluctantly told her to take all the time she needed, as he would be waiting and was living in anticipation of their next encounter.

After his abortive Hawaiian trip, he had hung back from calling her for reasons of her safety. He hadn't called her after his remorseless beating, despite knowing it was as much a warning to her as to him. Look what happened to Bertrand, Gidon and Sammi. And she was precious; he had to protect her now.

*

Beth called him that morning. "I've been worried sick," she said.

Her voice was balm, erasing the shock of her call. "How did you know I was here?"

"I couldn't reach your cell phone . . ."

"I left it home," he interrupted, not telling her it had been broken in the beating.

". . . so I called Olivia Wade. She told me you'd gone to your father's. Is he all right?"

"He's fine. I needed a few days off, and I hadn't seen him in a while, that's all."

"You left without telling me?" she said jokingly.

"I've been waiting so long for your call that my phone has cobwebs," he responded, more lightly than he felt.

Beth's silence hung ominously in the ether.

"I'll be back tomorrow. I figured you could live that long without knowing where I was," he quipped, unable to restrain his sarcasm.

To his amazement, she began to cry.

"What's wrong?" he asked gently.

"I missed you."

Her words came out as a sob. "But that's wonderful!" he cried. "I missed you too. That's nothing to cry about."

"You don't understand. I don't want to miss you." She took a breath. "The Del Coronado scared me. The feelings I had . . ."

"Feelings I share!"

"My feelings were too strong, too dangerous. And now . . ."

"Dangerous?" he interrupted. "Why should natural feelings be dangerous? They're between us, a man and a woman. It's happened to others before. We're not hurting anyone."

She longed to tell him about the photograph, about what Jimmy Lee had made her promise, and then flee, get as far away from him as possible. But she was held here, held by that photograph, and her assignment from Lee seemed to her as precarious as a high wire act over a chasm. She would have to make love again to a man she was beginning to love so she could continue to betray him. "We should meet," she said, hating herself for abandoning her baby and now for her treachery to this good and kind man.

He hesitated, torn. "When you told me you needed time, I waited and waited for the call that didn't come. After I heard about Gidon's death, his murder, I knew I had to speak to you, to warn you."

"Why didn't you?"

Uncertain, he hesitated.

"Why, Matt? What aren't you telling me?"

"The reason I didn't call you, the reason I stayed away, is because I didn't want to worry you."

"Worry me?" Her voice was a whisper. "What's happened?"

He told her everything, only leaving out the nature of the threat Netski held over him—the attack, the package, the fact that Blenheim knew about them, even his guilty foreboding that when it came to Bertrand, Sammi and Gidon, he'd become The Angel of Death. Several times she tried to interrupt, but he rushed ahead, releasing his fears and sorrows, as though in the grip of mania.

Much of it she'd known or sensed already. What he said merely exacerbated her terror. The noose was tight around her throat.

Finally, she got through to him. "Matt! Don't tell me anymore."

"Why not?"

"Please don't ask. Please. I beg you."

The urgency in her voice stopped him at last. "What's going on?" He could hear her inhale and waited silently.

"I'm frightened. Terrified," she said hoarsely. "I can't tell you why. There's too much at stake. They've got something on me too. Don't trust anyone, even me, especially me. Don't tell me anything more. Promise. Just go back to the resort, do your job, get through the Summit, get out and never look back."

His brain seemed densely packed with cotton. He understood nothing. "What do you know? What aren't you telling me? Beth, talk to me. I need to see you!"

He was entrapped, she knew, just as Jimmy Lee had ordered. "Yes," she said flatly, then "No! Not now. Not ever. You're a wonderful man and I do have feelings for you. But swear you'll stop calling and don't try to see me. I'm doing this for both of us. Believe me, please!"

He heard a click. The phone went quiet. Her sobs echoed long after the connection was broken.

Chapter 29
New York

"Rolfe," Momo called from the bathroom. "I can't get out of the tub."

He ran to her side. Momo lay in bathwater up to her neck, a frightened look in her eyes. "I tried to pull myself up, but I slipped," she said ruefully. "Jesus. I don't have the strength of a baby."

"Let me help you."

He placed his arms beneath hers and raised her up, heedless of the water drenching his clothes, aware instead of the cherished softness of her body, the fresh perfume of her flesh and the surprising lightness of her frame. She leaned against him. He dried her with the luxuriant towel she loved, wrapped her in it, and laid her on the bed while he searched for her nightgown.

"I can put it on myself," she told him, sitting up. "Dr. Sheinkop says I'll get my strength back when this round of chemo's over."

"And Mitch Sheinkop's infallible," he said, too much cheer in his voice.

She pulled the nightgown over her head then stopped, the cotton hiding her face. "There are days," she mumbled, "when I wish this were all over. Today is one of them."

He uncovered her face and stared fiercely at her. "Stop that nonsense. We've been through this before. I'm selfish. Don't deprive me."

"You're the reason I'm still alive," she admitted. "If I didn't love you so much . . ." She hugged him tightly.

The phone rang.

"It'll pick up," he said.

"No, answer it. Maybe it's Mitch."

He lifted the receiver quickly. "Rolfe? It's Matt Dirksen. I hope this isn't a bad time."

Rolfe covered the mouthpiece with his hand. "Matt Dirksen," he whispered. "Should I tell him to call back?"

Momo shook her head. "Don't be ridiculous, you've been worried sick about him not answering his phone."

"What can I do for you, Matt?"

"Save my sanity."

There was such intensity in Matt's voice that Rolfe's brain, thinking only of Momo, switched gears. "What's up?"

"I think Blenheim's murdering your people."

Rolfe felt relieved that Matt shared his own concerns. He had tried to push the idea away in the interests of Momo's care, but had been unsuccessful. Now, his own feelings expressed by Dirksen pumped alarm into his veins. "Where are you?"

"Indiana. In my father's house. Blenheim's discovered damaging evidence about him. They're using it to pressure me. That's a euphemism for blackmail! That and a beating the other day to press their point."

Concerned, but relieved that his protégé was safe, Rolfe sat on the bed next to Momo and held the receiver so that she too could hear. "A beating?"

"Brutal! They wanted to make sure I didn't investigate the deaths of the GMs. And they've got something on Beth Taylor, too. I've no idea what the hell it is but she begged me not to speak to her again." Matt paused, his breathing audible. "I've got no one to turn to here, so I thought that maybe you . . ."

It was a simple decision. "Of course. Can you come to New York?"

"I can be there tomorrow."

Rolfe gave him the address.

"I don't know how to thank you," Matt said. "Without you . . ." His voice broke.

Rolfe smiled. "My pleasure. Momo would love to see you. It'll do her good."

*

"Thank Heavens he's alive" Momo said.

Rolfe expressed both of their thoughts "But for how long?"

Chapter 30
San Diego

"I can't find him," Olivia Wade said, forcing herself not to wilt under Dieter Weiss's withering tirade.

"Why not?"

"His cell phone isn't answering. I'm looking at my screen now. The tracker device I installed shows the phone's at his home. It hasn't been moved in three days. No calls have been answered in days."

"What about the locational monitor you stuck into the seams of his briefcase?"

"I'm looking at the briefcase now; it's by his office desk."

"What did his father say?"

Olivia gritted her teeth. "Mr. Dirksen said he was going to visit an old friend for a couple of days, then come back to San Diego. He didn't say where his friends lived or who they were. The old man seemed pretty much out of it."

The broadside continued. "Listen carefully, you stupid woman. You're paid plenty to keep track of him." Weiss's voice rose an octave. "No excuses. You'll damned well find him and don't lose him again. I want to know where that interfering son-of-a-bitch is twenty-four hours a day. *Verstehen*?"

"Yes, sir. I assure you I do."

"Good. That Taylor woman's in Santa Monica, I presume?"

"I'll just check." Olivia typed in commands and code words. A detailed map appeared on her monitor, a red flashing circle moving slowly across the screen. "Yes, there she is. Checking the beach facilities, I'd guess. I've checked the voice-activated tapes of her phone calls as you'd instructed. Mr. Dirksen hasn't spoken to her ever since she begged him not to contact her."

Weiss's fury erupted as it had when he had heard the tape of that call and screamed at Jimmy Lee. "How dare that fucking whore disobey your instructions and tell Dirksen not to contact her again?"

The German realized it was pointless berating the Wade woman again and forced himself to concentrate. Certainly it was time for Taylor and Dirksen to renew acquaintances, Weiss concluded. The beds at the Ritz Carlton, Laguna Niguel, are particularly soft. Perhaps their next encounter should be videotaped? Not only would he enjoy watching their couplings, but knowing it could be on the Internet in minutes would add more pressure to those two dumb general managers. He'd call Jimmy Lee. But all he said to the terrified Olivia Wade was "Call me as soon as you have located Dirksen. Don't you dare screw up again."

Chapter 31
New York City

Rolfe's aged, Matt thought. It's what happens when you visit Hell. He was sitting with Momo and his mentor in the sun-filled living room of the Ritters' thirty-fifth-floor apartment, overlooking the Metropolitan Museum and Central Park. Light oatmeal-colored grass paper covered the walls; there was a limestone fireplace complementing the limestone slabs and silk rugs on the floor, a Henry Moore bronze on its mantle. The onyx coffee table with a gold-lacquered flat bowl on its center seemed to float above the floor. A Chagall, a Miro, and a Botero composed the art, all of which could have graced the museum across Fifth Avenue.

He allowed himself to relax into an overstuffed armchair. The breakfast cup filled with cappuccino, powdered chocolate on top of the foamed milk, smelled wonderful. Smoked Scottish salmon sandwiches slaked his hunger. He was with the man he respected above all others and for the moment felt safe.

"Bring us up to date, Rolfe said gently.

Momo, skeletally gaunt and pale, her legs curled under her, bald head hidden by a yellow bandanna, sat next to her husband on the loveseat opposite Matt. Both, barefoot, clad in jeans and tee-shirts, allowed the younger man to tell the story in his own way, only interrupting if a point needed clarification.

Matt left out nothing. The facts were as vivid in his mind as his own fear. When he described Dimitri Netski and the unswerving obedience he demanded throughout Blenheim, the Ritters looked at each other as though expecting exactly that. When he described Bertrand's death, Sammi's kidnapping, and his conversation with Gidon Lahav's widow, he began to tremble.

"Did Shulamit ever call back?" Rolfe asked.

"No, but I didn't expect her to."

"What about Sammi? Have there been further demands?"

"None. It's been a week and . . ."

His self-control crumbled. He bowed his head and covered his eyes with open palms. "It's my fault," he sobbed. "If I hadn't contacted them . . . Dear God, what have I done?"

"You're not to blame," Rolfe said crisply. "Whatever happened to them would have happened anyway. What about your Miss Taylor?"

As unemotionally as possible, Matt described his growing feelings toward Beth, their intimacy, and the strange, sudden way she had ended the relationship. Rolfe listened without comment. "And you?" he asked.

Matt described the attack on the road and the horrifying beating on the beach. Rolfe walked over to him and put an arm around his shoulder. "I'm so deeply sorry."

Matt glanced at him, surprised by his mentor's show of emotion. "As you can see, I've recovered. The bruising makes it look worse than it is."

"It's just that I had a similar incident many years ago in Berlin. My nightmares are as fresh today as they were immediately after it happened." He shook his head. "I seem to attract violence."

He sat back down on the loveseat. Momo took his hand and kissed it. "Get out," she said to Matt. "Leave the Resort. Disappear. In time, Rolfe will be able to get you another job."

Matt had thought of it. He shook his head. "I can't."

"It's good advice," Rolfe said.

"Maybe. But I'd be leaving Beth alone—they've got something on her, though God knows what—and my obligation's to the Summit, to the Resort, your Resort. As I see it, my interfering's caused the death of two friends, the kidnapping of another, the loss of a relationship with an incredible woman, and a sword of Damocles poised inches above my father's head."

"What's this about your father?"

Matt explained. "Now you understand. I can't run. Not now."

"So Blenheim's won," Rolfe said, sadness and resignation evident in his words.

"Yes. I'll go back to the Resort, say nothing, and wait for the end of the Summit."

Momo smiled at him. "You'll be careful?"

"The good soldier Dirksen." He stood. "I'm sorry to burden you with this, but you've taken my paranoia seriously, and that's a great comfort. I'll fly back tomorrow."

"Where will you stay?" Momo asked.

"The Kestrel, I suppose." He managed a grin. "They give Audley GMs special rates."

"Are you nuts?" Rolfe stood also and put a restraining hand on Matt's arms. "Ten minutes after you've checked in, everyone in the company will know where you are. What will you say you're doing in town? Visiting your closest friends, the Ritters?"

Matt sat back down. "You're right. I hadn't thought it through."

"You're staying with us," Momo said. "The guest room's already made up for you."

I'd be safe, Matt thought. Safe and with the only true friends I have. For one night at least, he could sleep.

*

Matt woke at dawn, showered, dressed, and folded the sheets, pillowcases and towels at the foot of the bed. Once a hotelier, always a hotelier, he chuckled. The Ritters would have a host of servants, but he couldn't leave the room for them to clean up.

Momo and Rolfe, already dressed, were drinking coffee in the kitchen. Rolfe gave a cup to Matt.

"We've been talking about you," Rolfe said. "I wish we agreed you were paranoid. If it weren't for the beating and the papers about your father, maybe—and I stress, maybe—we could rationalize everything else as coincidence and paranoid imagination. Unfortunately for us all, you're as sane as Momo's Doctor Sheinkop. There's a cancer in my company, and you've diagnosed it."

"It's not your company anymore," Momo reminded him.

"You and Netski might think so, but it's part of my DNA, my bloodstream. Always will be."

"Then can you help me?" Matt asked, loathing himself for the question.

"Not really. Until Momo beats this damned cancer, she's my day and night."

Momo pounded on the kitchen table. "Bullshit! You built the company. You don't have to see everything you created destroyed by a bunch of slick foreigners."

Rolfe laughed. "Have you forgotten I'm Dutch and English? You're sleeping with a slick foreigner."

She tried to restrain her own laughter. "No more Japanese tail 'til you help this American."

"All right, all right," Rolfe acquiesced. "I'll make some more calls, maybe there are still a few people who owe me, see what I can find out. In the meantime, young man, get your bony ass back to the Resort and go to work with a vengeance. Put the grovel-ometer on full, suck up, smile, be nice, show Netski and his pals you're enjoying everything about your job and can't wait to strut your stuff at the Summit. In short, be the consummate professional I trained you to be."

"But you'll need an ally inside the company," Momo said, serious now.

"Who?"

"There's only person. Beth."

"Beth? She won't talk to me."

Momo chuckled. "You don't know women very well. She's not only trying to protect herself, but you as well. If everything's as you described, she's looking for an ally herself. Right now, I'll bet she's very alone and very frightened."

Matt felt a surge of elation. "You don't know how much I hope you're right!"

Rolfe poured fresh coffee for the three of them. "You told us Beth comes from theater people. I hope she's a good actress."

"Why?"

"Because if my guess is right, she's been told to tell them everything you're doing. There's no other explanation for her standoffishness. And she'll keep talking. The only change is now she'll be telling them only what you want them to know."

Pain shot through Matt's gut. "That means she's been betraying me. Christ! She'd be sleeping with me because they told her to?"

Momo grabbed his hand and squeezed. "Listen carefully. You'd know if she weren't sincere. She obviously cares for you, but there's some awful hammer at her head held by those miserable bastards. She told you as much. Now she thinks she can protect you by pushing you away."

"Now listen to me carefully," Rolfe said. "Once you've persuaded her to become the Mata Hari of your generation . . ."

Matt looked blankly at Rolfe.

"You are young. She was a double agent in World War One, and that's what Beth will be. But you've got to be careful, both of you. If these guys are as dangerous as they seem, then you're playing with your lives."

"What should I do?" a chastened Matt whispered.

"Get separate and unlisted telephone lines in your homes. And another cell phone for both of you. Only you, Beth and Momo and me should know the numbers. Buy the cheap deals with limited minutes. Throw them away at irregular intervals. Take the Sim cards out and dump them separately. Get new hotmail e-mail addresses—again, only the four of us should know what they are. Change those irregularly as well. And even after all that, be wary. Talk and communicate in some sort of code. Assume everything you write or type is being read, and also assume you and she are being watched and listened to at all times."

This is real life, Matt thought, dazed at the implications. Rolfe's belief that Beth had been reporting his words back to Lee sickened him. What was real, what play acting? Was that why she had cried so hard at the Coronado? Is that why she'd begged him not to see her again? Because she'd betrayed him and was now feeling guilty?

"Think the worst of everybody, you'll still be disappointed," Rolfe went on somberly. He wrote on the pad beside the kitchen phone. "Here are our cell phone numbers and e-mail addresses. Use them only if essential. The longer those creeps don't know we're involved, the safer you'll be. Momo and I will also get new numbers, e-mail and social media addresses and let you know what those are."

"Beth was right about one thing," Momo added quietly. "You mustn't trust anyone. Not even her."

Think the worst of everybody and you'll still be disappointed. Yes, Matt reflected. And think the best, then you'll want to drive a dagger through your heart.

*

Matt flew back to California that afternoon. Meanwhile, Rolfe took Momo to Sloane Kettering for chemotherapy. Momo dreaded these sessions and their pernicious aftermaths, he knew. Still, they were her only chance.

"Shit!" he exclaimed suddenly, minutes after they sat in the back seat of the limo. "I'm a bloody moron."

"What have you done?" Momo asked, jolted out of her morbid thoughts.

"Remember I told you I had a bad feeling when I first met Fabrizio Battini after Blenheim took over from EUF?"

"Of course."

"I contacted Longstreet Investigations. Sid Longstreet's long retired but his son, Mark, is running the business now with no loss of expertise. Anyway, I asked Mark to dig into Blenheim and Battini. His report arrived at home in Monte Carlo the day we found out you had cancer and left for New York. Naturally, I forgot about the report. Never even opened up the damn thing."

"So it's still in Monte Carlo?"

"Bound to be. I'll call Mark while you're getting your treatment and have him e-mail it to me."

*

They read the report the next morning. Momo put the papers down thoughtfully. "We need a lawyer."

Rolfe went to the phone. "I'll get Ron Falkman over here immediately."

Chapter 32
New York City

Although he had recently turned eighty, Ron Falkman's unblemished face and full, wiry, white hair made him look fifteen years younger. He wore hand-tailored slacks and sports jacket, a crocodile belt with a monogrammed buckle, and Loeb loafers. "Buy the best," he had told Rolfe years ago, and he lived up to his own mandate. Still working-out at five each morning, he wore no glasses, sported professionally-manicured nails, and carried himself in a manner that left no doubt that he was the best at what he did.

He had taken on no new clients for five years, but worked just as hard for his old ones, Rolfe Ritter included. To those privileged few he was lawyer, mentor, friend, psychiatrist, priest, rabbi, business advisor, marriage counselor and chief strategist for their busy lives. A religious Jew and Talmudic scholar, advisor to presidents of the United States and prime ministers of Israel, the five-foot-eight-inch lawyer ("a Jewish six feet," he would chortle) had taken up golf at age sixty-eight, and at seventy-six had become a member of Augusta National. When he sent a bill, it would be one line—the amount owed, having no bearing on the hours he put in. Those who did not pay immediately lost a lot more than a lawyer.

Rolfe paid. He owed Falkman his career and trusted him more than any man he had ever known. "A complex man for complex clients," he described him to Momo, "to be called upon in emergencies."

This was an emergency. Rolfe and Momo had long-finished their lunch of Salade Nicoise and focaccia bread; the lawyer's salad remained untouched. Rather, he used the Ritters' dining-room table to lay out the Longstreet Investigations' report of Battini and Blenheim. "Mmmm," he said. "Very interesting. Things aren't always as they seem."

Rolfe had kept his eyes on Momo, who seemed to be getting tired, but Falkman's words commanded his attention. "What do you mean?"

"Blenheim's losing money. Swagger or no, I bet they're in the red, big time."

Rolfe grinned. "Astonishing!"

"I thought you'd be pleased." Falkman took a bite of his salad at last. "Let's start with what we know. Blenheim Partners' shareholders appear to be a series of trusts based in all the netherworld's favorite places: Switzerland, Holland, Lichtenstein, Guernsey, the Isle of Man, the Cayman Islands, Belize, Hong Kong and Singapore. Even Liberia. They don't seem to employ anyone in those places. For the most part, all Longstreet could find were registrations addressed at lawyers' offices. Not particularly unusual, just a far more extensive scale than one would normally see.

"You've been to the Los Angeles headquarters of Kestrel; they've kept your old offices. Based in New York, Blenheim has posh Fifth Avenue offices and seems to have an odd investment strategy—and I use 'strategy' loosely. For example, they've poured money in a startup security firm run by what looks like an ex-CIA man with extensive Russian connections. According to their latest IRS filings, they've lost almost their entire investment. Real cash losses, not soft losses and write-offs."

"Legitimate?" Rolfe asked.

"Sure looks like it."

"So they made a lousy investment. As you know better than anybody, I've done that too many times to count." He shrugged self-deprecatingly. "What about Battini?"

Falkman gave him a Cheshire cat smile. "He's an odd one, isn't he? From time to time these characters surface in New York. Multi-lingual, mostly European, smooth as silk, sophisticated, cultivated, educated, well dressed, live the good life—fancy addresses in Manhattan and the Hamptons. They claim to represent important foreign clients looking for investments, then run around the world looking for investors. Sometimes they make money, sometimes they don't. Usually, they just fade away."

Rolfe was astonished. "So Battini's just a broker?"

"Not really, Rolfe. More of a front man, I'd guess. It's cute. He pays his Wall Street friends big advisory fees for working on deals for Blenheim Partners, deals they never seem to finalize. But the brokers don't mind. They get their fees, deal or no deal."

"What does he get out of that?" Momo asked.

"Respectability, access, his name out there as a player."

Another bite of salad. At that rate, Rolfe thought, he'll be here until midnight.

The lawyer seemed to be enjoying himself. "According to Longstreet's investigation of the IATA airline ticketing system, Battini travels abroad extensively—London, Hong Kong, Beijing, and, curiously, half a dozen trips to Moscow. In the summer, the South of France; winter, Palm Beach and St. Barts. He lives lavishly in a rented Park Avenue apartment where he entertains his young boyfriends. Fits my profile, doesn't he?"

"But you think the whole thing's kosher?" Momo asked.

Falkman beamed. "I didn't say that, did I? Beware of premature evaluation." He waited in vain for a laugh. "My instincts are that it's not kosher, though there's no hard evidence. If I had to guess, I'd say that Blenheim is a front for Arab or Russian money that wasn't made legitimately. Based on an old man's instincts, I'd bet on the Russian connection."

"Shit!" Rolfe exclaimed, remembering his own encounters with Russian money. "The Mafia?"

"Not necessarily. Remember, after the fall of the Soviet Union, fortunes were made through privatizations and all sorts of odd business dealings with the ruling party. Some of the deals got violent. Well, it's still going on. This time it's Putin's and Medvedev's buddies, not Yeltsin's, who've made obscene amounts of money. They have to legitimize it, so when their turn comes to be out of favor with the next tsar and his cronies, their money is in hard currency, and it's safe."

Momo was horrified. "So buying Kestrel was just a money-laundering scheme?"

"I doubt it. Too big, too well known. So far, their investment pattern's been random—small stuff here and there. Then, wham! Out of the blue they swoop in to buy a giant and highly visible company like Kestrel. That doesn't fit the profile. What's more, they paid for Kestrel without borrowing a penny. Normally, such a large investment by private investors is loaded with as much debt as can be borrowed. If it works, they make higher returns because the debt is cheaper to them than the value of their own cash. If it doesn't, they've laid off the bulk of the risk on the banks, so their downside is limited. It's even stranger because any normal deal would be structured with debt, even internal debt—money they lent themselves from one holding company to another, for tax purposes."

"Then what's their motive?" Rolfe asked, fascinated. "They buy Kestrel, pay cash, take losses when they don't have to, pay unnecessary taxes—the whole thing doesn't make sense."

"Especially not after what Dirksen told you. Why go after your people? Why the changes to the hotels, the explosions, the killings, the kidnapping? Why ruin your own business?"

"Mystifying," Rolfe said. "I don't even understand why Treadway dealt with those people. Not his style."

Falkman laughed. "That's the one easy question to answer. My dear boy, will you never learn? Blenheim was recommended to EUF and to the very pompous and self-centered Sir Martin Treadway by a London-based boutique investment bank. You know the sort: Some Wall Street biggies figure they can make more money than their already obscene compensation packages by going off on their own. The Kestrel sale was quite a coup for a startup bank, and they must have offered a 'can't refuse' deal.

"Treadway obviously had enough of the hotel business, didn't want to run the risk of a downturn like 2001, already had benefited from the notoriety of owning the world's most luxurious chain of hotels and, on top of everything, you were becoming a real pain in the ass. *Et voila*! Blenheim shows up. Puts an irresistible number on the table. EUF pockets a huge profit, and Kestrel's theirs."

"I know the damned press release by heart, the one where Treadway announced the sale," Rolfe said. "Usual stuff—reinvest the proceeds in higher yielding assets, that kind of bullshit. Trouble is, he hasn't done it and the company stock's flat as a road in Kansas. I ought to know. The Ritter family has a bunch of shares and stock options that are so deep under water you need a scuba diver to even find them.

"But none of this explains why they're so eager to sabotage their own business, why they'd resort to murder. Or why, if they're dead set against the company succeeding, they agreed to host the Summit, which could well swing their business around."

Falkman gathered up Longstreet's report and put it in his briefcase. "Rolfe, are you still in touch with your late Uncle Mike's replacement in the British Counter-Intelligence Service?"

"You mean Kenneth Palmer at MI6? I was, until I got fired from Kestrel. He kept asking for favors: information on this person; put one of his staff on the payroll at some godforsaken hotel; occasional room bugging. The usual. I guess he's still around. Why?"

"Get hold of him. Tell him the whole Blenheim story and see what he can find out. I'll contact some people I know at the Justice Department and I'll get a high-level introduction to the FBI. With the G8 Summit involved, they'll have to take me seriously."

Rolfe shuddered at memories of his mishandling by the Feebs, but knew the lawyer was right. Every avenue of information would help.

"One last thing," Falkman concluded. "Keep Matt Dirksen sane. He's got to be lonely as hell, and he's a newborn at this type of thing. If you can help get Beth Taylor back on his side, that'll ease his situation. But don't let either of them take risks. Until we know what's going on, view everything as dangerous." He took Momo's hand and kissed it. "Feel better. And thanks for the salad. It was spectacular."

Chapter 33
San Diego

"For Christ's sake, Pete, this is madness!" Matt tossed a spreadsheet full of numbers on the conference room table.

Pete Wilson returned his boss's stare, unruffled. "Sorry, but this is what the entire event is going to cost us."

The balance of the Summit Committee seated around the table avoided Matt's angry eyes.

"We're damn well paying the G8 for the privilege of hosting this goddamned extravaganza. Look at food and beverage, for instance. Ben, are we feeding a couple of Third World countries?"

Ben Winnick squirmed uncomfortably in his chair. "The State Department suggested we hold a 'Feast of Nations.'"

Matt's glare was withering. "You know that's crap. Those bozos could never have thought up such madness. This is some goddamned orgasm you dreamed up, and you found the ultimate putz willing to say yes."

The food and beverage manager's sheepish look was confirmation enough.

"Perhaps you didn't consider that we have to expand and floodlight the Great Lawn to accommodate eight hundred people, set up a mobile finishing kitchen a quarter of a mile from the main kitchen, import chefs from our hotels in each of the member nations, have four locations for each station—that's thirty-two stations, each staffed by our associates dressed in local costume—set up eight wine tasting areas to showcase each of the nations' wines, bring in four portable stages so that indigenous dancers can perform, hire ridiculously expensive set designers and lighting consultants to stage that nonsense, and set up an acoustical system good enough for a fucking rock concert—and you want fireworks every half hour, each time displaying the colors of one of the eight country's flags."

"The costs are in front of you," Winnick whispered.

"So I see. I also see that we originally quoted State a fixed price for the whole event, meaning Blenheim will have to swallow most of the costs. Do you want to tell Dieter Weiss, or do I have to do the dirty work?"

"Weiss knows," Pete Wilson said.

"What?"

"Yessir. When I tried negotiating with Tim Matheson's staff after they made their wishes known, they said they'd already cleared the costs with Dieter Weiss, and that the original deal stood."

Matt sat back wearily. "Without checking with me?"

"You were away. We didn't know how to reach you."

"And you couldn't have waited 'til I got back?"

Wilson shrugged. "Weiss told us to get going. I got the clear impression that costs didn't matter."

"Even though the government is robbing us blind? That we should charge several hundred-thousand more dollars to pay for even half of this goddamned shindig?"

'Their only issue is a smooth Summit. That's what I've been told. That's what Mr. Weiss told me to tell you. 'It's all on Dirksen's shoulders.' Those were his precise words."

And if I fuck up, Matt thought, what then? He didn't allow himself to speculate, though he felt a spasm of triumph. It's all on Dirksen's shoulders. His mind flashed to the image of his father's house, and of the stooped, defeated man who lived in it. He had surmounted his upbringing, maybe even his DNA. If anyone could handle the myriad problems he was facing, and the greater ones to come, it was he. Anyway, he had no choice. That was the crux of the issue, he realized, every way he turned he was faced with no choices.

Chapter 34
San Francisco

The Kestrel San Francisco was not only Ritter's flagship hotel, but his first and enduring love, a symbol of his struggles, the first step in his quest to ascend to the top of the hotel world, more precious to him than all the Audleys combined. Over time, though, the queen had aged and her crown had become tarnished. One of Rolfe's final acts as Deputy Chairman of EUF had been to develop and execute a complete master plan for the renovation of the hotel, to coincide with San Francisco's reemergence from the recession that had hit the city in the aftermath of the "tech wreck," the global economic slowdown, and the pernicious effects of 9/11 on travel and tourism.

From its majestic perch overlooking Union Square, the crown of the Kestrel Hotels once again sparkled. The long reception counter had been replaced by individual desks, recessed lighting glowed where chandeliers had once blatantly blazed. New Fung Kit-designed carpets, furnishings, and her personally selected art added dramatic glamour. A mezzanine restaurant looking down on the lobby had been met with critical acclaim—its wine list the envy of all in the city—and had instantly earned Michelin's coveted three stars as a reward. A wine tasting room, modeled after the neighboring Napa Valley's winemakers tasting rooms, had been opened on Post Street, while next to it a bakery sold all the fresh baked goods the hotel's team of bakers and *pâtissiers* produced to the general public—the morning line always stretching around the block. The newly created Clock Bar, opening on to the Square, had instantly become the city's favored watering hole. The refurbished high-tech bedrooms, replete with completely new bathrooms, had been met with unparalleled high levels of guest satisfaction; the meeting rooms had been upgraded, replete with the latest technology and multimedia equipment; and a new ballroom, added between the hotel's two towers, was larger and more sumptuous than the existing Grand Ballroom, home of the city's most prestigious social events ever, since Rolfe had first bought the property.

All of this was lost on the four men eating at the Penthouse Suite's walnut dining table, as were the panoramic views over the city and bay. Picking randomly at a crystal bowl of seedless grapes in front of him, Dimitri Netski was interested only in the Summit to come.

"Everything's on schedule: All the stuff you've ordered will be coming to the Resort from Germany. Right, Jimmy?"

The Chinese nodded.

"The installation team's been assembled and will be on site before the equipment arrives to prepare new facilities to house everything. And McGregor has cleared out the Engineering Department and installed our people?"

"Brad Marshall's arranging security clearances for them. I reviewed the entire process with Tim Matheson at last week's meeting. He seemed very satisfied," Dieter Weiss answered. Unlike the others' ties, Weiss's tie was pulled down, the top two buttons of his shirt open.

"He damned well should be. The government's getting a Rolls Royce event for Chevy prices," Netski grumbled.

"Matheson knows we'll get millions of bucks worth of publicity out of it and is playing us like a Stradivarius," Weiss muttered.

"Are the rest of the staff being brought to the Summit our own selected people?" Fabrizio Battini asked.

"Don't be ridiculous," Weiss snapped. "Hundreds of extra staff are needed. Only the senior people will be ours." He helped himself to a grape. "What a stupid question."

The Italian blanched. "Don't talk to me like that. I'm chairman of the company!"

"Chairman?" Weiss said quietly. "You're a fucking puppet, nothing but a rent-a-suit. Why don't you go back to your room and fuck the toy-boy you've hidden there."

Battini turned to Netski, who was patently enjoying himself. "I don't have to take abuse from him," he blustered. "I'm finished with this. I'm out."

"The abuse you'll take will come from me. And I assure you it's abuse you don't want." The Russian pointed a finger between Battini's eyes. "You'll be out when I say you're out. Now do as Dieter says, and when you're finished, you'll take your money and disappear. Money—that's what you're in it for, isn't it?"

The words struck Battini like bullets. He sank back in his chair.

"Dieter, from now on keep your big mouth shut," Netski said calmly. "Any other business?"

"What about Dirksen? Is he behaving?" Jimmy Lee asked.

Weiss was back on safe ground. "The lessons have sunk in. Our blue-eyed hotelier is doing what he should. Works eighteen hours a day, goes home, watches television. Few personal calls, none even to his father, only the daily calls from Beth Taylor."

"Sounds too good to be true," Netski said.

"It's true all right."

"I'll take your word for it. What about Beth Taylor?" Netski plucked another grape.

"Under control," Lee answered. "Docile as a lap dog, reports verbatim every one of Dirksen's words. We check the transcripts of their calls."

"Then it's time," Netski drawled, "for her to become a bitch in heat."

Chapter 35
San Diego

"That was some meal you served us tonight, chef," Tim Matheson said.

"My pleasure. The Resort's management team is one bloody tough audience, but I love to show off to people like them who understand food and booze," the thirty-five-year-old said, his grating Cockney accent seeming out of place in the lush atmosphere of C's private dining room.

"Jason's weekly TV program is filmed in this kitchen, and now has been picked up and syndicated throughout this country in addition to the U.K. He's quite the star," Matt explained to the State Department official.

"Got to tone down my bleedin' language for you Yanks," Jason Avington complained, his infectious grin showing how much he enjoyed being a celebrity. "If you don't need any more food, then I'm going to join the rest of your team at the bar and leave you two effing old farts to save the bloody free world."

"Quite the character," Matheson said as the door closed behind the chef.

"Amazing fellow. Brilliant chef, constantly innovating. Has a brigade of youngsters in the kitchen who would follow him to hell and back, and a three-month waiting list to get in here, despite the astronomical cost. The longer the waiting list, the more he bumps up the prices." Matt refilled their glasses from the bottle of eighty-three-year-old port.

"Matt, I appreciated meeting all of your team. That's quite a group you've surrounded yourself with. You seem to have everything under control for the Summit, and the coordination with us, the Secret Service and the FBI is outstanding."

"I sense a 'but' in your voice," Matt said.

"It's nothing, really. I suppose coming from government I don't understand the ins and outs of corporate life."

"What do you mean?"

"This is off the record, okay?"

Dirksen was fully alert, the soporific effects of the meal suddenly gone. He nodded.

"Take security for an example. Brad Marshall wasn't here tonight, the only no-show. I understand he's a corporate officer and feels above it all, but shouldn't he be an integrated part of your team?"

Matt shrugged. "I agree, Tim, but what the hell can I do about it? I'm just a hotel manager and do what I'm told. What else?"

"A week or so ago, I had a meeting in your Century City's offices with Weiss and Lee which worried me. They updated me on the progress of the equipment procurement. It's all coming from Germany and seems under control. However, when I asked what role the Resort's team would have in the installation, Mr. Lee got irate. 'None. Why should they?' Frankly I'm perplexed to know how you can run a property like this without you coordinating something as potentially disruptive as new systems."

"You met Keith McGregor tonight; he's the director of engineering. He seems to be the only one that corporate discusses these things with. But he's damned good and I don't doubt he'll keep things organized."

"That's a copout if I ever heard one." Matheson laughed. "But it's your business, I'm only making a comment. There's one more thing . . ."

"Go on."

"Weiss and Lee would like nothing better than to have everything to do with the Summit running through their hands and not yours. I get the sense they'd be happier if you weren't around. Nothing was said, just an old political hand's instincts and paranoia coming through. What's the problem?"

Matt shifted uncomfortably in his chair. "I really don't know if that's the situation or not. They didn't appoint me, but inherited me, so I guess that makes them uncomfortable. I know it seems an odd situation, but so far it's functioning and I'm not complaining. Tim, I appreciate you raising this with me. If there's a problem, I promise I'll let you know before it gets out of hand."

Tim Matheson smiled benignly at the younger man. “I have no doubts you’ll pull it off superbly. I know none of this is my business, it’s just that this is the biggest and most important Summit ever staged, with more heads of state and muckity-mucks than have ever been assembled in one place and . . .”

Matt laughed as he interrupted. “And your nuts are on the line?”

“You’ve got the idea. But it’s two sets of nuts riding on this—mine and yours!”

Particularly mine, more than you’ll ever know, Matt thought.

Chapter 36
New York

The reflected lights of the city shimmering on Central Park's Reservoir went unseen by the three people engrossed in conversation on the balcony of the Ritters' apartment.

Momo, covered by a fur wrap, wearing her ever-present turban, sat with her feet up on an ottoman, between her husband and Ron Falkman.

"So you met with the FBI and what happened?" she asked.

"The whole episode was very bizarre," Falkman admitted. "Through a good friend of mine's introduction, I met two agents in my office and went through the whole situation on a no-names basis. I didn't give them the Longstreet report, although I quoted liberally from it. The two agents seemed completely engrossed and asked endless questions. They promised to get back to me quickly and indeed they did."

"And?" Rolfe asked.

"And a few days later, the older of the two guys called me, asked more questions, and then explained that he and his superior were very concerned, and the matter was being 'pushed upstairs' with a recommendation for a full-blown investigation."

"Thank heavens we aren't nuts!" Rolfe said.

"Wait, there's more," Falkman cautioned.

"I thought you said . . ."

"I told you what happened, but then it gets bizarre. Three days later, I received a call from the same agent telling me the investigation had been shut down on orders from 'on high', and he'd been castigated for taking this matter seriously."

"What the hell!" Rolfe jumped from his seat.

"Hold your horses," Falkman said. "He then told me that was the official version. Unofficially, he said that in twenty years in the Bureau he had never seen an order like that. He and his superior both felt someone had put the fix in, maybe politically, maybe something else."

"Meaning?" Momo asked.

"Meaning that maybe someone on high was bribed, blackmailed—or God knows what."

"Holy shit!" Rolfe exclaimed. "What in heaven's name have we got ourselves into?"

Chapter 37
San Diego

This defines torment, Matt thought. I must speak to Beth, save Beth, but I don't know how.

He had taken Rolfe Ritter's advice and obtained additional phone lines, e-mail addresses and new cell phones for both him and Beth, so they could communicate with each other. But what good was that if calls on established phones—to say nothing of sending any kind of e-mail or instant message to set up a system—risked compromising her, his father, Sammi? He felt like a dog on an electrified leash: to venture beyond its perimeters meant a swift, possibly fatal, shock.

Day or night, as his mind drifted to her, he would reach for his new cell phone to call Beth, needing to talk. The result was always the same: too terrified to risk a single call, even one of love, he never called. Days turned to weeks without communication between them.

*

Preparations for the Summit were distraction enough to fill his days, but the nights were agony. When he closed his eyes, he saw Bertrand disappear in a fireball a mile off the French Riviera's coast; Gidon's brains splattered onto an Australian highway; Sammi's headless body delivered to the Peruvian police by Shining Path; his father's last days spent friendless in jail; Beth killed or maimed or kidnapped—what was the hold Blenheim had on her? A night's sleep was impossible. Even when he dozed off he'd awake in a claustrophobic panic with the smell of that fetid hessian sack and his body aching from the vivid memory of his vicious beating. He took to driving toward Santa Monica then turning back just as he exited the freeway, his brain full of needles, his exhausted body that of a cancer-wracked old man.

On this night he spotted a sign: SUNRISE DINER: Comfort Food 24-7.

Matt figured that without coffee he might not make it back to the Resort. He walked in.

A waitress in a stained uniform greeted him cheerfully, evidently pleased to have someone to break the loneliness of the night. Oblivious to the pervasive smell of years of cooked fat, he ordered black coffee and a slice of carrot cake for its sugar, signaling, to the waitress's disappointment, that he wanted to be left alone when she brought his order.

He took a bite of the cake, a sip of the coffee, folded his hands on the table to cushion his head, and closed his eyes.

The jangling of the bell above the diner entrance roused him. He had no idea how long he had slept, but the waitress had disappeared. The newcomer was a woman, indistinct in the stark neon light, walking quickly toward him. He blinked her into focus, then blinked again.

"Aren't you going to offer a girl a cup of coffee?" Beth Taylor said.

He gave a small cry and tried to stand but couldn't, brought down by the heat that suffused his body and his mind.

She sat across from him. "The strong, silent type. I like that. Although I hate to see a man cry."

Indeed, he was conscious of tears in his eyes and on his cheeks. He took her hands as if they were made of the finest porcelain and gently kissed them. They were warm.

"How did you find me?" he asked, his eyes taking in the blush of her skin, the fierce delight in her eyes.

"You were followed."

Was there something wrong with the wiring in his brain? He stared at her, mystified.

"Followed? What are you talking about?"

"Blenheim. They've had you followed every time you've left the Resort. This is the first time you stopped. They called me, and here I am."

It was too much to comprehend. He felt a surge of anger—was she playing with him? "Explain."

"I will, but not here. I'm supposed to take you back to my place and seduce you." She stood. "Follow me home. It's an assignment I've been looking forward to for weeks, even if their eyes and ears are around."

As they walked to their cars, Beth realized it was no lie—she had been fantasizing about Matt since their Del Coronado encounter. Between her daughter and Matt, she had thought of nothing else.

Chapter 38
Santa Monica

Matt kissed her, caressed her hair, her face, her breasts—the same familiar and intoxicating taste and smell that had tantalized his memories and fed his fantasies, yet he felt no desire, no love, only sadness. Although he had refused to admit the truth, he realized he had been a naïve optimist. Rolfe was correct: The beautiful, passionate woman stretched naked on the bed—inviting, alluring, welcoming, all he had been dreaming of for months—was working for Blenheim, for Jimmy Lee and Dieter Weiss. The unrestrained intimacy he thought they'd shared at the Del Coronado seemed to him but a fragment of a fantasy, one he would never recapture. For her, it had been an act. Whatever had remained of his innocence had been shattered. He pulled away.

She stared at him in fear. "What's wrong?"

"Sorry," he said. "I can't."

"Is it something I . . .?"

"Yes, it's something. How can I make love to a woman I don't trust?" Rage consumed him. "It isn't my cock you want to fuck, it's my brain!"

"No!" she cried, her wail eerie in the room. "I love you!"

They were words he had once longed to hear. "Sure you do." His voice held such loathing she flinched. "Only you love Blenheim more."

She began to cry, great sobs that racked her body. "Matt," was all she could say. "Matt. Matt, Matt, Matt," repeated like a mantra, like grief.

Silently, he rose and began to dress. He wanted to comfort her, to murder her. Her agony was convincing, but then again her parents were actors; she had surely inherited their genes. "I wonder," he said, as cruelly as he could, "what it would be like to make love with you if you weren't under orders."

Her head snapped back as though he had struck her. "Don't say that."

"Why? I enjoyed myself at the Del Coronado. You seemed to like it too. A little bonus, I suppose. There's no law saying you shouldn't have fun in the workplace."

From her knees, she slapped him in the face with all the force she could muster. When she moved to strike again, he caught her wrists and held them tightly. His cheek stung from the blow, but his heart sang with a strange peace. There was an explanation, an answer; there had to be. "You betrayed me," he said quietly.

"Yes."

"You would have gone on betraying me."

"Yes."

"You did it for Blenheim."

"Yes. Jimmy Lee's orders."

"Then what am I supposed to think?"

Her voice was subdued but steady. "That I don't want to lose you, lose everything. Jimmy Lee told me to make love to you so you'd tell me what you're doing, whether you're still snooping around, what you've found out; they want me to keep you in line."

The confirmation rocked him. He could barely breathe. "The first time, too?"

"The first time, yes, and I told him what you told me. Lee still knows nothing of our previous relationship, how I screwed that up. But the awful thing was that I fell in love with you at the Crustacean all those months ago. It took me long after that amazing afternoon at the Del Coronado to realize it. I fell in love with you so deeply that all I can think about is you, you and me, so much that I was thrilled to bring you here, make love with you again. What does it matter if it's what that bastard Lee wants? I want to be held tight in your arms, feel you deep inside of me, kiss every inch of your body—not because of any other reason than I love you completely and unconditionally. Surely that's enough?"

Dizzy, Matt grasped the headboard for support. He wondered what was true. Were his own feelings mocking him? Which of her words could he believe, and which were scripted by the men he was starting to loathe?

"I couldn't help myself." Beth was sobbing now. "It was weak, wrong. But oh, Matt—if you only knew . . ."

"Knew what?"

"Don't ask," she said. "Please, please. Let it go. Get through the Summit. Quit and we'll get away. So far away that they'll never find us. Until then, we mustn't, daren't see or talk to each other. Even that's a risk. I'll have disobeyed orders and have to face the consequences. Just do the Summit, keep me away and at least I'll know you're safe."

He released her hands. "I'd hoped you'd be with me," he said quietly. "Rolfe said I should ask you to help. But you've already made your choice—you're working for them. And you're right; it's fine with me if we don't see each other again."

She recoiled. "Yes. Better that way."

He moved away. "I'll find out what this is all about without you," he went on. "I can't give up. I owe it to Bertrand and Gidon. I owe it to Sammi."

"Don't you get it? Bertrand and Gidon are dead," she screamed. "And the only way to save Sammi is to do what Netski says. You owe them nothing. You owe me my, my . . ." She crumpled to the bed, her sobs intensifying.

His heart was as cold as the look in his eyes. "I don't think I owe you anything. Not now. You told me the reason you asked me to come with you. At least I owe you for that."

"Never again! Never again, I promise. That's why you must leave. Why I can't see you."

He looked at her closely. She had hidden her face in a pillow like a little girl and her body trembled.

"What is it?" he asked gently.

"Nothing."

"Tell me."

She lay motionless. "If you can't trust me, then you're right, I shouldn't have brought you here. Don't worry. I won't try to see you again."

He turned. Beth's apartment echoed with the sound of the door slamming.

She hesitated, then followed and flung open the door. "Wait, Matt. Wait. Don't leave," her breathless wails echoing down the corridor. "They've got my daughter."

*

"Her name is Britney," Beth said. "She was born seventeen years ago. I put her up for adoption. Jimmy Lee showed me her picture—I've no idea how he got it, or how he found out I had a daughter in the first place. The moment I saw it I knew it was she. The red hair gave her away, that and the smile that lit my soul. I was barely nineteen when I got pregnant. Long story, a schoolgirl infatuation that got out of hand. The father was thirty-three, married, two kids of his own, told me he was going to leave his wife. I was needy enough to believe him. When I told him I was pregnant, I thought he'd be happy, and that he'd get a divorce so we could have our baby together. He got furious, insisted I get an abortion, said he couldn't leave his wife just then. I knew 'just then' meant not ever. Two weeks later, I called him and lied. I told him it was all taken care of and he didn't have to worry. That was the last time I spoke to him. He can rot in hell, far as I'm concerned. After I gave the baby up, I had a rough time of it, a wild ride. Too many drugs, too much booze. It wasn't until I reached rock bottom that I resolved to get cleaned up, start a new life. I went to community college, took courses in hotel management and . . ."

Matt was sitting on the couch, Beth in one of the armchairs. She told her story calmly, dispassionately, though he could tell she was trying to cover her guilt and humiliation. "When Jimmy put that photo in front of me, I screamed, and then I melted. In an instant I was in love with her all over again. I'd tried to keep her with me, but I couldn't swing it financially, emotionally. The baby didn't sleep, wouldn't eat, I was a wreck. The social workers kept pressuring me with their threats; it was horrible. So finally I gave in, put her up for adoption, and cried for weeks after her new parents took her away. For a while they let me visit—strictly forbidden by the adoption agency, of course—but Cherri and Jim, who are wonderful people, didn't mind telling Britney I was her

Aunt Beth. Finally, though, Cherri asked me to stop coming. My love for Britney was so transparent, so ardent, that she was afraid the girl would have mixed loyalties, even figure out I was more to her than an aunt. I agreed it was the best course for Britney. But now that I've seen that picture, I know that I need to dance at her wedding, play with her children, see her happy. Most of all, I need her to be safe."

"So the deal was seduce me, spy on me, control me and Jimmy would keep her safe?" Matt could barely get the words out. Was she telling the truth this time, or was it another of her dramas, invented to draw him in? His heart raged at Blenheim. They were ruthless, remorseless—but for what reason? "I'll stop investigating," he said. "It's not worth jeopardizing your daughter."

Beth went over to him and put her finger on his lips. "Matt, you're very special. Do what you have to do. I won't try to stop you, I won't give you away, I'll lie, tell them you pushed me away, lost interest, have someone else—I'll think of something. But I can't help you. I can't . . . won't risk harming her, losing her again. I need you to understand. Please."

"Quit," he said. "Get out. You'll get another job in a second. I'll hire a private investigator. He'll find your Britney."

Her composure broke. "I wish I could. They need me to report on you. Make sure you're behaving. That son of a bitch Jimmy made it clear that quitting wasn't an option."

"Then I'll go on. I've got to find out what's going on. It's connected with the Summit, I'm sure, but I'm damned if I know how."

"If you must, you must" she said. "Go on. If you need me to make up stories, I will. But whatever you do, promise me you'll tread lightly and, for God's sake, be careful. I am petrified by all of this."

*

They went to bed at 4 a.m., holding each other for comfort, not sex. Matt fell asleep immediately. Beth woke him just as the first gray light of dawn brightened the sky. "I want to make love," she murmured.

He was instantly aroused. “Next time,” he said. “Not now.”

But she would not let him go, gently took his penis in her mouth while the long fingers of her hand lightly caressed his scrotum and its surrounds, the other hand gently massaging the nipple of his right breast; and he succumbed.

*

“Matt, wake up.”

Sunlight streamed through the windows. “Again?” he groaned. “You’ve got to be kidding.”

“No. Not that.” She propped herself up on one elbow, her face resting in the palm of her hand. “I haven’t slept a moment.” Her expression was troubled, her eyes red-rimmed and puffy. He realized she’d been crying. “What you’re doing is courageous. You were right in going to the Ritters; there’s no one else for you, for us to trust. Battini, Netski, Weiss, Lee. These people are pure evil. Whatever they’re up to, they have to be stopped.”

“I know. Let me tell Rolfe what they have over you. He’s got resources, connections. He’ll think of something.”

“I’ve made a decision,” she said firmly. “They’ll never let Britney come back to me. Why would they take that risk? The only way to save her is to find her. The only way to find her is to find out what those bastards are planning.” She took a deep breath and her words came in a rush. “I’m terrified for me, terrified for Britney, terrified for you. I’ll help you in any way I can; there’s no choice for either of us. Tell me what to do.”

Chapter 39
New York

Momo Ritter's full-length, ruby, silk robe was loosely tied as she slowly walked into the apartment's conservatory. Dawn brought shards of light through the glass roof, spaying kaleidoscopic patterns of ever-moving shadows on her husband.

"So that's where you are. I thought you'd left me for another woman."

"Good morning to you, too," Rolfe said, laughing. "Who'd have a washed-up, unemployed sixty-year-old like me. I probably ought to join the AARP and get cheap deals on insurance, rental cars, public transport and movie tickets."

"That'll be the day. The thought of you on public transportation is perfect. I'd sell tickets to that event," Momo quipped, automatically stroking her bald head. "Is that why you couldn't sleep?" she asked, pointing to the sheets of yellow-lined paper spread over the table.

"Yes, too much information swirling around my mind, so I decided to try to make sense of it all by writing it down. I'm not doing well; maybe two brains are better than one."

"Well, this brain needs coffee to start working. You're the hotelier; go make it for us both."

Ten minutes later Momo was cradling a large Rosenthal porcelain breakfast cup of steaming cappuccino, seated opposite her husband, with her legs curled beneath her.

"Do you remember I said I would reach out to the few friends I had left inside the hotels to see if I could learn anything?" Noting his wife's acknowledgement, he continued. "I decided not to put any of my old gang—of the few general managers left—at any further risk by asking them to snoop around, so I went to the source of all information at the properties, the line employees. Many of them had been with me for decades and are still loyal friends."

“Judging by the hundreds of Xmas cards we received last year, I’d agree with that,” Momo said.

“Over the past few weeks I’ve been getting odd snippets here and there. I’m sure I’m missing something but I can’t seem to work out if there’s a pattern or an answer.”

“Give me some examples,” Momo said, her curiosity aroused.

“Rolfe scanned his notes and asked, “Do you remember Bob Duggan?”

“You mean the concierge at Union Square? ‘Mr. Fix It’? Been there forever and a day.”

“Yep. I bet his files are worth a fortune in blackmail value. Probably the richest man in the city by now. Anyway, I asked him if there was anything unusual with the Netski crowd when and if they came to the hotel. His response was quintessential Bob: ‘You want me to find dirt on them, boss’?”

“And . . .?” Momo interrupted.

“Netski, Battini, Lee and Weiss had a meeting in the Penthouse Suite recently.” Weiss instructed Bob to get him a pair of hookers for the night. Gave detailed specifications, wanted the very best, and, of course, insisted that the hotel pay for them. Nothing unusual about that; the man’s a shit and a cheap one at that. Bob pulled a favor from the girls and asked them to make sure the German drank too much, got completely worn-out, and then snoop around when Weiss was snoring. One of the girls looked through his briefcase and reported that Weiss had a passport in a different name with his photo on it, and tickets booked to and from Moscow for the next week in the name on the passport.”

“Did she give Bob the name?”

“Sure did,” Rolfe answered, triumphantly brandishing a yellow stick-it note.

“Anything else?”

“A handwritten note addressed to DW, I guess that’s Dieter Weiss, saying that BT is doing her job and D is under control. It was signed J.”

“I suppose J could be Jimmy, as in Jimmy Lee?” Momo asked.

Rolfe shrugged. “Maybe. I’ve no idea what the hell that means. I speculated that BT is Beth Taylor and, if so, then maybe

D is Dirksen, but that may be too simple. Rick also told me that he had the maids look for anything unusual in each of the men's rooms. The only interesting thing he reported to me was a leather cigar carrying case, full of cocaine, in Battini's washkit, plus some unusual sex toys in a closet drawer. The fact that there was a teenage boy obviously staying with Battini in a one-bedroomed suite was a matter of little consequence in Rick's mind."

"Battini's such a class act!" Momo muttered.

"I also called Alena Bartova, who runs the Room Service Department at the Audley in New York. By the way, she had heard you weren't well and asked about you. Netski often stays in the Presidential Suite and I thought perhaps she'd hear something. The next time the great man showed up, she decided to deliver Dimitri Netski's dinner order herself. The fact was, the order was for two, and there were two bottles of Crystal pink champagne to top off the caviar and tiger prawns, but only Netski and a pair of woman's high heels were in the Suite's sitting-room. According to Alena, the shoes were alligator, Christian Louboutins that cost about three-and-a-half grand. No cheap hooker for Netski. Naturally the bedroom door was shut.

"According to the floor housekeeper Alena checked with, the bed had been slept in by two people; extra towels had been used—lipstick and fragrant oils on several of them—and there was some very expensive lingerie lying on the bathroom floor. Amusing, considering the man makes himself out to be a choirboy.

"What's more interesting is the third fact—that Netski was speaking fluent Russian on the phone when Alena came in. You remember she's a Czech who grew up under the Soviet Union and was forced to learn Russian in school. Netski was talking to someone he kept calling 'Big Brother' and telling him everything was going according to their plan, despite minor difficulties which he'd taken care of. She reported that Netski wanted to be sure that whoever was on the other end of the phone had arranged transportation and installation for the Xmas present.

"Knowing that Netski had grown up in Prague, Alena started talking Czech. He looked blankly at her in complete incomprehension, so she switched to English in a heartbeat."

"Odd, very odd," Momo mused.

"Do you remember Carlos Morales, young, Mexican lad who started as a valet parker at the Kestrel in Santa Monica and now runs the pool of house Bentleys at the Audley in Beverly Hills?"

"Vaguely," Momo answered.

"The day before yesterday, Jimmy Lee arrived at the hotel, driven by Netski. They had a drink in the lobby and Netski went off in the direction of his home. Lee then met with two Caucasians for about an hour, Americans in their mid-thirties, one with a crewcut and built like a fireplug, the other tall and built like a basketball player. The two of them arrived together in a new 7-Series BMW. Jimmy Lee offered the 'basketball player' a lift in the Bentley, taking him back to the Santa Monica property. The driver told Carlos that Jimmy Lee had forgotten to put up the electric blackout screen between the front and the back seats, so he was able to hear the conversation."

"What did they talk about?" Momo asked.

"The American kept asking for more money for some job he'd recently done for Lee. He kept saying how the job had been riskier, more dangerous and expensive than Lee had told him, but that he had executed his instructions perfectly, and kept Lee's people completely clean. Lee kept saying that a deal was a deal and he couldn't go back to his masters for more. Then the man became strident. Lee told him that if he knew what was good for him he'd shut up and not play games. It was more of a threat than a suggestion."

"Then what?"

"After the American had been dropped off in Westwood, Lee dialed a number on the car's phone and started speaking angrily in Chinese for about ten minutes. When the Bentley finally returned to the Beverly Hills property, the driver told Carlos what had happened. Morales took down the number Lee had dialed and called it himself. It was the Chinese Consulate in L.A."

Rolfe put down the yellow sheets of paper and shook his head. "It always amazes me how people think hotel staff are blind, deaf and dumb. Guests seem to think they take invisible pills when they check into a hotel. If you heard the stories in the staff dining room or room service kitchen, you'd cringe. Hotel people don't miss anything. By the way, you should see what people do in the elevators. They don't realize that there are security cameras on all the time. Just for fun, I'll show you some tapes one day; quite pornographic.

"Anyway, I've given you just a few of the bits and pieces I've been told. There's more." He waived the papers in frustration. "Doormen, front desk managers, mini-bar attendants, housekeepers, and so on. I've no idea what it all means. What do you make of all of this?"

"Battini's a creep, Dieter Weiss isn't who he says he is, the Russian connection gets more obvious daily, Netski's not Czech, and Jimmy Lee is up to something with Chinese officials and . . . "

"And what?" Rolfe asked.

"And I have no idea."

"Me neither. That's why I couldn't sleep."

Momo Ritter looked at her husband. "It's time to get the oracle involved again."

Rolfe nodded and dialed a number. "Ron, we have a puzzle."

Chapter 40
San Diego

Matt and Pete Wilson stood under the *porte cochère,* watching the Resort's Bentley depart. "Those guys are in charge of diplomatic protocol?" Pete grumbled. "The mind boggles. They're just a pair of glorified flunkies."

"And we have to kiss their WASP asses: Whatever the State Department wishes . . . Jesus! It's galling." The men turned toward the lobby, automatically checking the cleanliness of the limestone floor, the symmetry and freshness of the monochromatic flower arrangements, each calla-lily its proscribed length, the precise location of the seating. "And now I'm to be graced with an audience with our security guru."

Pete picked up a tiny shard of paper and put it in his pocket. "That officious prick. He makes the most difficult guest a pleasure to deal with."

"How are you going to handle State's orders?"

"You mean the Russian foreign minister needing three extra suites, one for his wife the others for his mistresses?"

Matt laughed. "And that ain't all."

"Naturally we need to build a Shinto shrine for the Japanese PM. God forbid he should go off the grounds. How could we have missed that? And the German number three—a bed large enough to accommodate him and his two assistants, one male, one female. At least he's an equal-opportunity pervert."

"We mustn't forget the French," Matt said.

"Surely not the delightful French." Pete was laughing too. "Their president demands a suite larger than our president's. Their PM insists on a bed 2.25 meters square with 278 springs. What's he going to do at night? Use it as a fucking trampoline? Sealy doesn't have it in stock, no one makes anything like that. We'll have to the make the damned bed by hand. And Madame President? Her food's to be served on cream Limoges crockery and made only with herbs from her Parisian herbier. Thank heavens they gave up on insisting her chef take over part of the kitchen to make her meals. That would have caused mayhem and we would have had a war with all of our damned prima donna chefs. And, only French art on her walls, of course. *Mais oui*, not those bourgeois Frank Stellas."

They reached Matt's office. "Mr. Marshall's waiting," Olivia Wade said sternly.

Matt shook Pete's hand. "What kind of mood is he in?"

Olivia cocked an eyebrow. "As Queen Victoria said, 'We are not amused.'"

*

"If you won't tell me your source, why should I believe you?" Matt put his palms on the desk and glared at the senior vice president of corporate security.

"I don't have to tell you anything," Marshall sneered. "I report to Mr. Netski."

"This is my hotel!" Matt roared, knowing he'd been emasculated by his corporate superiors and it was no longer true.

Marshall seemed impervious to Matt's anger. "You don't get it, do you?"

"What do you mean?"

"Security means just that. When Mr. Netski wants you to know something, I'll tell you."

"Would he want me to know where you got the information about Ben Winnick?"

"No. All you need to know is that someone I trust told me he was a user. I searched his office. *Voila*! Hidden in a kids metal savings box in a locked drawer, three grams of cocaine."

Not Ben, Matt thought. This was a frameup. "How do you know it's his? What if someone planted it?" Someone from Blenheim Partners.

"It's a combination lock. Only he knows the code."

"All the same, I'm sure he's innocent. What do you want me to do?"

"That dope-head's clearly a security risk. Fire his fucking ass."

"What if I say no?"

Marshall sighed. "I've already discussed this with Mr. Weiss. He'll find a replacement. And remember, you were the one who insisted he stay on when you were specifically told he should be terminated."

Matt slumped in his chair. "I'll speak to Weiss myself."

"Go right ahead. But take my advice. Get Winnick out. Now. His isn't the only ass that can be put in a plane to Paraguay or Outer Mongolia."

*

"Backed the wrong horse, didn't you?" Dieter Weiss chortled.

"I've known the man for fifteen years. He's not on drugs."

"Are you calling Brad Marshall a liar?"

"Not really, simply misinformed. But . . ."

"But nothing. Your boy has been caught possessing cocaine. Not only was your judgment about him lousy, but you fucked up when you argued against Mr. Netski's decision to replace him months ago. Get him off the property now."

He would not give in, Matt knew. "*Jahrwohl, Mein Commandant.*"

"Is that supposed to be funny?"

Matt felt a tinge of pleasure. He ignored the question. "I strongly request that you authorize me to appoint Herve Tremont in Winnick's place. We're too far along for a newcomer to catch up, and Tremont knows the food and beverage arrangements for the Summit. His Executive Sous Chef Antoine Moreau can handle the kitchen side of things."

Weiss hesitated. "All right. Be it on your own head."

At least I can work with Herve, Matt thought. "Thank you, Dieter. I'll make it work."

"And you'll have help," Weiss said, his voice smooth as the Resort's famed crème brûlée. "I've asked Jimmy Lee to spend the next several months leading up to the Summit at the Resort. He's done a splendid job at the Kestrel Santa Monica. I know you'll be delighted to have him as part of your team."

Chapter 41
San Diego

"A Shulamit Lahav called for you," Olivia Wade told Dirksen when he returned from a meeting with the Summit Committee.

"Oh?" Matt tried to conceal his concern.

"She left a number."

"I'm sure it's not urgent. Probably thanking me for the donation I made to the charity she's set up in Gidon's name. Put it on my task list. I'll call back when I can."

He entered his office and closed the door. Olivia Wade placed a call to Los Angeles.

*

Later that evening, parked in the Starbucks lot near his home, he called Shulamit on his other cell phone.

Lahav's widow, still deeply emotional, planned to return to Israel with her children. Matt let her talk on until she got to her point.

"I found the phone bill for the month before Gidon died." Her voice was breathless. "There was one number in Israel I didn't recognize. Gidon called it half a dozen times. So I called it myself."

Matt's heartbeat accelerated. "And?"

"It was clear I was talking to a government security agent."

Mossad! "What did he say?"

"When he found out I was coming back to Jerusalem, not much. He told me to call as soon as I arrived and he would meet me. I did tell him Gidon was on his way to meet you in Hawaii."

"What then?"

"He got very excited. Wants you to call him." She gave Matt the number. "He said to make sure you call from a secure phone."

*

"Avi," Matt asked a few minutes later.

"Yes."

"Matt Dirksen. Shulamit Lahav told me to . . ."

"I know who you are. We not talk. Not on phone."

"How? You're in Israel, and I can't leave the Resort."

"There's Padres home game tomorrow. They play Dodgers. Go to 'Will Call' booth. There's ticket in your name. I find you."

"But if you're in Israel . . ."

"Does it matter? You see Avi."

*

For the first three innings, Matt concentrated less on the ballgame than on the empty seat beside him. In the bottom of the fourth, Halliday's home run descended into the left field stands and Matt stood with the rest of the Padres fans to watch its flight. He sat again.

"Giles has been in a slump," the man in the suddenly-occupied seat said. "Maybe this'll get him out of it." He was wearing tan shorts, a Hawaiian shirt, sneakers without socks and a two-day growth of beard.

Matt gawked. "Avi?"

"That's the name?"

"You the man I talked to yesterday?"

"Does it matter?"

"To me it does. Are you really Avi?"

"Does it matter?"

"Mossad?" Matt whispered.

"Does it matter?"

Clearly, this was not a voluble secret agent. "How do I know who I'm talking to?" Matt asked, irritated.

The man laughed and cracked open a peanut. "Look, Mr. Dirksen. I'm here because of Shulamit Lahav. You think Gidon's death was not a random carjacking, and I believe you're frightened for your own safety and that of Miss Taylor. Isn't that enough?"

It was more than enough. "Okay, tell me more."

"Gidon Lahav helped us out several times. We trusted him. He confided his suspicions about your company and his concerns both about Le Roi's death and about Leon Barken, his successor in Jerusalem. A plateful.

"We dug into it. There's certainly something odd going on, particularly at your company's Jerusalem hotel. Experience tells us it goes deeper than at one hotel. Anyway, we told him to back off. We needed time to investigate what Barken was up to and didn't want Gidon to alert anyone. If someone's up to no good in our capital city, we need to know about it immediately. Besides, we didn't want him at risk. He is—was—a friend." For the first time Avi's stoicism broke. His voice was hoarse.

"He wanted to see me," Matt said softly. "A matter of life or death."

"We didn't know anything about you until Shulamit called. I suppose he wanted to tell you to leave everything to us."

"Which I'm happy to do. But how can I help you now?"

"Watch the game. The Dodgers have tied it. And tell me everything you know."

*

As Matt talked, Avi prodded and probed, forcing Matt to remember details, circumstances, background he had forgotten or not realized he knew. When he came to Sammi's kidnapping, the Israeli was clearly taken aback.

"What do you think?" Matt asked when he had covered everything since Blenheim took over the company.

"*Zeh lo beseder.*"

"Meaning?"

"Something's not right. It smells as if it's much more than only a Jerusalem problem."

"Brilliant," Matt blurted, exasperated. "You didn't help Gidon, and now he's dead and that's all you can come up with. I thought you guys were supposed to be good."

"You told the Ritters and Beth Taylor." It was a statement, not a question. "Who else?"

"No one."

"Tell Ritter we've spoken. He knows who we are. Perhaps we'll want to speak with him, perhaps not."

"And me? What do I do."

"Stop investigating. Keep your head down and your mouth shut, especially if you're alone with Ms. Taylor."

Matt felt his cheeks burn. "You son-of-a-bitch! How did you know she and I . . ."

Avi was unfazed. "And be very careful. This is a serious matter, my good friend, Matt."

Good friend? Matt could have murdered him. A cheer rose from the crowd. Avi clutched his arm. "Kent popped out." Avi stood, leaned over to Matt and said, "That pipsqueak hasn't been able to hit in the clutch since he left the Giants."

Seconds later, Avi had disappeared into the crowd.

Chapter 42
San Diego Cliffs

"That was a nightmare," Matt said as he and Pete Wilson walked toward their offices. "Telling the Home Owners Association they had to leave or submit to full background security checks in order to stay in their own homes during the Summit was like dropping a raw lamb chop into a den of hungry lions."

"A bunch of dyspeptic billionaires baying for our blood," Wilson agreed. "Not a pretty sound."

"Your offer to lease out their homes to Summit participants? Where'd you come up with that one? Those guys need the rent like Eskimos need ice."

Pete chuckled. "You're right. I don't know what got into me. But most of them'll leave anyway. The thought of Fernando Ancira going through an FBI check is hysterical. Rumor is that he makes his money as an arms dealer. Pays all our invoices in cash. To say nothing of Cynthia Litt, our retired Madam. Background on her would explode their computers."

"We sell to those who can afford and don't ask questions; discretion is our middle name," Matt said, laughing. He indicated a group of workers outside the engineering complex. "Who're they?"

"German specialists from the factory in Germany here to install the new systems and electronic equipment. Not a one of them speaks English, but McGregor seems on top of it, and they've been cleared by the Almighty Marshall."

Matt sighed. "Give it a break, Pete. He's got a job to do."

"That obnoxious prick? You can't stand him either."

"True, but his life only gets harder from here. The *Times Union* reports there'll be at least a hundred thousand protesters camped out during the Summit. It's his job to keep them out of here. I'm starting to feel sorry for him."

"Tough shit," Wilson said. "I've got my own problems. All the extra staff we're training are falling over themselves while the security groups from the member nations start installing their own security equipment. It's a damned zoo and I feel like the zoo-keeper. And we've had to dramatically increase the numbers of new uniforms we've ordered. Now the manufacturer's saying he doubts he can get them here on time?"

"Yeah, sure." Matt grimaced. "He's sticking it to us for more dough."

"Like most of our friendly suppliers. They know a gold mine when they see it. The words longterm relationships seem to have escaped their greedy little minds. Fuck 'em! We'll get our payback when the Summit's over and we can put out all contracts for competitive bids."

They approached the workers. Matt went up to a large, ruddy-complexioned man, obviously the foreman. "*Bitte, mein Herr,*" he said. "*Ich bin Herr Dirksen, der Direcktor General von hotel. Kennen wir sprechen fur einen minuten*?"

The red-faced man, dressed in jeans and a denim jacket, looked at him blankly.

"*Vielicht sie sprechen etwas Englisch*?

Shrugged shoulders was the response. Behind him, Matt heard two of the workers making what was, judging from their barely repressed laughter, a joke at his expense.

"Come on, Pete, let's go." Dirksen's lips pursed tightly. He turned and strode toward the main building.

"You seem upset," Pete said, struggling to keep up with Dirksen.

"I am. My German's not so bad that it's unintelligible. But that guy didn't understand a word I said. And those two goons behind him? They weren't speaking any German I've ever heard."

They stopped outside Matt's office and shook hands gravely. "What language do you think it was?"

Matt's eyes blazed as he stared at him. "I'm not a hundred percent sure, but I'll bet it was Russian."

*

"You must have scared the daylights out of him," McGregor said uncomfortably, when Matt told him about the foreman. "You're the big cheese around here and he probably panicked."

Matt struggled to keep his voice steady. "That's bullshit and you know it."

The chief engineer's eyes darted around his office, focusing everywhere but on Matt. "Obviously, this particular team came from East Germany. One of the factories is just outside of Leipzig. The closer to the Russian border you get, the stronger the dialects are."

You may be a good engineer, Matt thought. But you're one lousy liar.

*

Matt marched past Olivia Wade's desk en route to his office. "Get me the security clearance files for those workers from the German factory," he demanded.

"Mr. Marshall's waiting in your office," Olivia said. "I'll ask him for the files when he leaves."

Marshall sat relaxed on Matt's couch. "McGregor called. He tells me you think something's strange with the Leipzig installation team. Can I help?"

"Yes, you damned well can. I want their files. Germans my ass."

Marshall raised a placating hand. Words as soothing as the specially blended Chanel moisturizer in the guest bathrooms oozed from the corporate security officer's mouth. "McGregor doesn't know who those guys are. Given that the factory's in Leipzig, he naturally assumed they were Germans. I handled the clearance process myself. That particular team is Russian who made their way to Germany after the breakup of the Soviet Union. Lots of skilled workers went west looking for work. Nothing unusual."

"That clarifies it. Still, you won't mind if I have a quick look at their files."

"I damned well do mind!" Marshall exploded. "Who the hell do you think you are, questioning me? I'm the officer in charge of security for the entire company, and you're just a . . ." He stopped short.

"Just a what? An insignificant hotel flunky with an IQ just above vegetable life who is kept around only to do exactly what he's told by his omnipotent masters?" Matt put his hands in his pockets to hide his trembling fury. The two men glared at each other. Dirksen took a deep breath. "Let me make this clear. I don't care what position your hold at Blenheim. For all I care, you could be tsar. But I'm responsible if anything goes wrong here, and if I want information on anything that goes on in this hotel, I'll damn well get it."

Marshall smiled, his demeanor suddenly changed. "You're right. If you want the files, you shall have them. I sent them to corporate for safekeeping. I'll have them sent down here ASAP and we can go through them together."

Matt wondered if 'ASAP' meant a year or a decade. "Good," he said. "Let me know when they arrive."

Chapter 43
Santa Monica

Jimmy Lee sauntered into Beth's office just as her phone rang. "Hold the call," she told her assistant. "Mr. Lee's here and I . . ."

"Take it," Lee said.

"It's all right," she told him. "I can call back."

"Take it!"

She picked up the phone, aware that her boss was watching her closely.

"Mommy?"

"Britney!" Beth's heart stopped cold. When it returned it beat irregularly, as though propelled by some fantastic, primordial drum. Sweat covered her hands, and she had to catch on to the corner of her desk to keep from falling. From the corner of her clouded eyes, she could see Jimmy Lee's mocking glance.

"Darling," Beth whispered. "Are you all right?"

"Are you really my mother?"

"I am. I promise you I am. Where are you?"

Britney's voice was cheerful; Beth couldn't tell if her tone hid fear—of if, in fact, it was Britney's voice at all. Deep down she knew for certain that she was talking to her own daughter "I'm not allowed to tell. They told me they'd bring me to you soon, but only if I kept where I'm staying a secret."

"Oh, Britney, I've thought about you every day since you were born. I've seen your picture and I know you're beautiful. I want to know about your childhood. If the Kisels took good care of you. What kind of girl you are."

"I want to know about you, too," Britney said. "I only found out yesterday that you were my birth mother. You run a luxury hotel, they said. They arranged for me to call you at this time precisely. I didn't believe them. But I have, and you're there. I don't think I've ever been so excited in my life. I have a thousand questions but above all I want to know why . . ."

Beth was barely aware of Lee's approach until he shut off the phone. Dazed, filled with a dozen inchoate emotions, she could only glare at him. "That's enough for now," he said calmly. "I'm sure you and your daughter both want to get acquainted, and I wanted you to know I can make that happen—or not." He spoke to her as if she were a little girl. "I've been assigned to the Audley San Diego Cliffs for a few weeks. Summit duties. I'll be in and out of here on an irregular schedule and I want to be sure you'll behave yourself while I'm gone. You will, won't you?"

Beth nodded dumbly, wondering who they were that Britney referred to. Where was her daughter speaking from? Beth's mind was a melee of emotions—excitement, guilt and fear being foremost. She nodded again, her face a window for her tumultuous feelings.

"Good. The Gary Cooper Suite needs work, I've noticed. It's sloppy and totally unacceptable. I'm surprised at you, allowing it to be sold to our guests. I want it—what do you Americans say?—spick-and-span when I return. Get your act together Taylor, or else."

*

The scene in her head was vivid in its details, no matter how hard she tried to banish her memories: the slovenliness of her threadbare, one-room apartment, Mr. and Mrs. Kisel standing hand-in-hand, beaming at the baby in her arms, the social services woman an unsmiling figure—a prison guard—behind them. This was highly unusual, Beth knew, the baby being given away with the mother present. But she had begged the Kisels, and these good-hearted souls agreed. A good sign.

Beth held Britney fiercely and whispered in her ear, though the infant was too young to understand. "This is your new mommy and daddy," she said. "They love you. They'll love you always just like me. And I'll come to visit. You'll be safe and protected and have a good life. Good food to eat. Toys, books." Only then was she aware of the tears spilling down her cheeks. "That's why I gave you life. So you'll be happy."

She held out the baby to Mrs. Kisel, wanting to die. There were papers to sign, and she did so, barely seeing them through a veil of misty eyes. I'll see her again, she told herself, though it was small consolation. She was barely conscious of the door opening behind her, only long enough to allow in a faint smell of spring, quickly gone.

*

After Lee left, her first impulse was to call Matt. They had their new phones; she could speak to him undetected. But she was afraid he'd do something rash, try to help her, try to find Britney on his own, and the risk to him was too great, let alone to the daughter she had just been reunited with after a lifetime of being apart. Alone in her bedroom that night, she was literally paralyzed by doubt. Questions attacked her like hungry vultures.

Should she try to reach her daughter by herself, and if so, how? Or should she wait until after the Summit, agree to everything Lee wanted, and hope he'd keep his promise? Was there anyone she could trust? Would she perish as Bertrand had, and Le Roi, Lahav? Would Matt? Would she be kidnapped like Chalabi, her life a hostage to God knows what? She couldn't run, not while there was a chance of being with Britney. But was it really Britney who had called? What if Lee were embarked on some monstrous plan involving her and Matt and Blenheim? My God! What if Matt were part of the plan, pretending to love her on Lee's orders? It was possible. Anything was possible.

Memories exacerbated her torment: Her father spanking her when, at age six, she was rude to their neighbor, Mrs. Carlson (strange how vivid such a minor incident remained—it was the look on her father's face that stayed with her); the harsh, rasping sound of her lover's voice when he told her to get an abortion; the life-ending hollowness when Britney was taken away. Matt's rage when she told him she'd betrayed him.

Beth lay on her bed, eyes open, staring at demons.

The demons stared back at their vulnerable victim.

*

"Mr. Ritter? It's Beth Taylor." Beth made the call at five-thirty in the morning, using her new cell phone.

"Hello, Beth. I had the feeling you might call. And it's Rolfe by the way. No need for formality now."

Rolfe. Mr. Ritter. What difference did that make? "I need your help!" she cried, her voice sounding shrill on the deserted beach. "You're my only hope. Can you talk?"

His voice was calm, reassuring. "Isn't that a question for you? I'm at Sloan Kettering with my wife; it's her day for chemo, and so far as I know nobody's listened in on me since I left Blenheim's clutches. But you . . ."

"I'm on Venice Beach. It's where I come to clear my head. We took your advice about the cell phones. There's nobody around for miles."

"Then tell me."

His gentleness breached her defenses, her fears, and she poured out her story, telling him about Britney without any of the guilt or humiliation she felt when she confided in Matt.

"You don't know where she's being kept? No idea?" Rolfe asked when she finished.

"No."

"And you're not sure it was Britney who called."

"I think it was. She called me Mommy."

Rolfe thought for a moment. "That could have been scripted."

"I know, I know. But in my innermost heart, I'm positive it was she."

"I believe it too," Rolfe said. "They're clever enough to have found her, and that makes the threat much more potent."

"I told Matt about Britney, but haven't told him about the call. I'm worried he'll do something rash."

"Your call. I hope he's smarter than that," Rolfe answered.

"There's one more thing. Something that has nothing to do with my daughter, Britney."

She could virtually hear his antenna go up. "My bellman's family came from China and he speaks fluent Cantonese. He told me he'd overheard Jimmy Lee on his call phone reassuring some-one that deliveries were going smoothly and everything would be ready for the Summit. He said, 'Our barbarian friends have done everything they've promised.'"

"So Lee's a bigot. Nothing strange about that."

"When he made the call, he announced himself as Tang Shen-ming, not Jimmy Lee."

"Lots of Chinese take anglicized names when they come to the States."

"I know. The bellman told me it's impossible to translate Tang Shen-ming into English. But that's only half the point. The other half is that Lee spoke with great deference and kept calling whoever was at the other end of the phone 'Sir.' Mr. Ritter, as far as I know, neither Mr. Netski nor Mr. Weiss speak Cantonese."

Rolfe paused so long Beth was afraid they'd been disconnected. Finally he said, "Is it still safe for you to call Matt?"

"I think so. We use the phones rarely, hardly talk. We're both terrified, but I don't think they're on to us yet."

"Good. Call him. Tell him I want to speak to him. In person."

Chapter 44
New York City

The walls of Fabrizio Battini's spacious forty-second-floor Madison Avenue office closed in on him under Dimitri Netski's withering barrage.

"You chose him. You bragged what a wonderful job he was doing. So tell me, how the fuck did this happen?"

Battini sank deeper into his chair. "I . . . I . . ."

Netski's eyes were on fire. "I . . . I . . . That sums you up. Everything's about 'I.' You prance around New York like the fucking pansy you are, spending our money like a drunk buying drinks for everyone in the bar. You buy tables at every charity event in town and big-time it 'cause you're the figurehead chairman of Kestrel Hotels and Resorts. You strut about in your extensive wardrobe of tuxedos like some playboy on fucking steroids getting your photo in the society pages. But can you do something simply, like putting a general manager in a job who'll do what he's told? Can you?"

"Er . . . Er . . ."

Netski jumped out of his chair and loomed over the Italian. "That's all you can say? 'Er'? You make me sick. I'm the one who gets calls from the Israeli fucking police. I'm the one some fucking security official from their L.A. counsel general's office comes to interview. Not you. Not Mr. fucking chairman!"

He turned and walked to the window, breathing heavily. Battini watched Netski's anger ebb. His shoulders sagged, his hands unballed themselves, and he slowly took his seat opposite the terrified Italian.

"I told that inscrutable Israeli that I was mortified to hear about Leon Barken's activities and that Kestrel would cooperate in every way. This young squirt proceeds to chronicle a dozen things they're convinced Barken's up to, blackmail on top of the list. They found videotapes in his apartment of diplomats from all over the world fucking their brains out with women, men, even kids. They found lock-picking equipment for every conceivable piece of luggage. There's even evidence he's on the Iranian government's payroll. And on Saudi Arabia's as well. Shias, Sunnis—seems he doesn't give a shit, so long as they pay him."

Battini blanched but said nothing.

"It gets better! They showed me his visa application. Turns out there is no Leon Barken. He's a fake! But you knew that, didn't you? You signed the reference letter and the original transfer request."

Battini, slackjawed, stayed silent.

"You fucking moron! Of all countries to send some goon who you dragged out of some nowhere gutter, you chose Israel, and even then you chose Jerusalem, the place with the tightest security in the world. For God's fucking sake, what possessed you?"

"You wanted someone quickly," Battini said with surprising force. "You told me to get rid of Ritter's people immediately. I did. Look, Dimitri, Barken was only doing what we asked him to do originally."

"What 'we'? You! I told you we had to have legitimate replacements. You put in this oaf. I told you he had to make changes slowly and subtly and take orders only from us. Barken seems to have ignored that part completely. We had a specific list of operations we needed to execute in Israel which would have destabilized the country even further, but your two-bit hood couldn't wait to set himself in business for his fucking own account, could he? Finally, as soon as we were given the Summit, I made it clear that all other activities anywhere in the world had to stop. Period. What part of that order didn't you understand?"

"I'm sorry," Battini said, his spine once more collapsed. "I thought Barken would cooperate and obey those instructions. I promise you, Dimitri, they were explicit and unambiguous."

"Well, you thought wrong, didn't you?"

"What are we going to do now?"

"'We're' not doing any fucking thing. As always, I have to clean up your mess. As soon as I heard from the Israeli police, I had Barken out of the hotel in minutes. Some of my men trussed him like a chicken, packed him in a crate and carried him out the back door along with the rest of the garbage. Cost us a small fortune to arrange that little enterprise."

"Where is he now?" Battini's tone was flat, expressionless.

"In a safehouse in East Jerusalem. He's telling us every fucking little thing he's done so we can close every goddamned hole. What's more, I've arranged for bank accounts to be set up under various aliases in the Caymans, Switzerland, London and Hong Kong. The aliases can all be traced back to Barken. I've arranged his employment application to be backdated, showing Barken lied to us when he asked you for employment. In short, I've made Barken a clever criminal who'd simply outfoxed us. We're creating a legend, Fabrizio, for the fucking Israelis to follow so they can find out he's got a track record of working on his own. I'm covering up for you and you'd better be fucking grateful."

"What will you do with him?"

Netski's eyes were wild again. "We're in this together, Battini. This is your fucking mess. I've gotten us out of it. Waste disposal is up to you."

Chapter 45
New York

The conference room that connected to Ron Falkman's office had six chairs around its oval table. File boxes were piled against one wall while a book shelf with Lucite deal trophies, awards given to the venerable lawyer and engraved gifts from foreign potentates, presidents, prime ministers and assorted dignitaries filled the opposite wall. Falkman's back was to the window that looked over Park Avenue towards the East River.

"What do you make of all of those random bits of information? "Rolfe asked, having recited his long list of snippets that he had written down on sheaves of lined, yellow paper.

"I didn't realize you had such an army of informers. I hope you don't go into the blackmailing business with them!" Falkman quipped. Seeing the self-satisfied smirk on his client's face, he added, "What was I thinking? I'd forgotten who I was talking to."

"On top of everything, we now know the hold that Blenheim has over Beth Taylor. Who the hell knows where they have hidden her daughter," Rolfe added.

"If, indeed, she was talking to her real daughter."

"After I talked to Beth, I had a chat with young Dirksen and gave him the pep talk about more communication between him and Beth. The guy doesn't fully trust Beth, not sure she's even got a daughter, and is seeing ghosts everywhere."

"If I recall correctly, you're the one who told him not to trust anybody. Besides, maybe he is seeing ghosts—Le Roi and Lahav's. I'd like to meet the man. Why don't you see if he'll come here? I'll wager we'll get more information from him in person. Perhaps both of us can talk some sense into him?"

Rolfe nodded as Falkman absent-mindedly stroked his chin. "My original supposition seems increasingly correct: The Russian connection is getter stronger and stronger. Obviously there is a

Chinese involvement somehow, but I have no idea what it could be, or why."

"What happened with your connections at the Justice Department?" Rolfe asked.

"Nothing yet, they are unusually slow in getting back to me. Maybe I'm nuts, but I think I'm getting the runaround. If so, someone's got some very powerful flushing water. God knows who? Anyway, I have one more trick up my sleeve. I have an old buddy at the CIA I'm going to pick his brains, if he'll let me. He's never lied to me and if he doesn't tell me something, it will speak volumes."

"What should I be doing?"

"Keep your antennas up, make sure you keep in touch with Beth and Matt and that they tell you everything that's going on in their world. I bet they don't have a clue about what they really know. Keep your intel army going, if nothing else, it's titillating gossip. See what else you can find out about Netski's lady. If she's a hooker, she's a very classy and expensive one. Mmm . . . maybe with your wealth we could pay her to turn on your successor. If not, then perhaps there's a lead we can follow."

Chapter 46
Jerusalem

No matter how many times Father Luca Maria walked the worn stones beneath the Crusader façade in the Constantine Church of the Holy Sepulchre, he felt the same elation. Here he was, the fourth son of a poor Tuscan farmer, for the past two years daily charged with opening up the Chapel of St. Mary Magdalene in one of the most holy sites in all of Christianity. God had truly blessed him.

Every morning, as the sky changed from dawn's slate grey to Jerusalem's vivid azure, he followed the same path to the Rock of Adam, from where he could gaze toward the bare rock beneath Golgotha and marvel at the glory of the Holy Spirit before continuing up the stairway for his first task, ensuring that the Chapel of the Nailing of the Cross was ready to receive the daily influx of tourists and pilgrims.

Usually, he would look with joy at the twelfth-century mosaic of Jesus on the Cross behind a Medici alter from Florence, Italy, the city of his birth. Today, however, he stared in horror at the scene before him, his bible falling unnoticed on the Chapel's floor. The silhouette of a male body, like a spectral scarecrow, swayed almost imperceptibly in the shadows.

Father Luca Maria's screams echoed throughout the ancient church. Guards came running from every direction.

Chapter 47
New York City

"How did you get here without anybody knowing?" Rolfe asked.

Matt grinned. "As soon as I got your e-mail, I told my assistant to book me a round trip to Dulles, explaining that I had to see meeting planners in D.C. I checked into the Audley Georgetown, left my clothes and toilet kit spread out in the room, met briefly with the planners, grabbed a cab to Reagan Airport, jumped on the shuttle, and *voila*, here I am. As far as anyone knows, I'm doing the rounds of D.C. I'll be back in Georgetown for dinner with the general manager, regaling him with terms of my success with those finicky meeting planners."

"You're learning," Rolfe laughed, leading his protégé into the living room. "Matt, this is Ron Falkman. You can trust him as you would me."

"In other words, count your fingers before you leave," Ron said with a twinkle, not rising from his seat on the couch next to the emaciated, beturbaned Momo.

Matt liked him immediately.

*

"First the FBI dropped our concerns like a hot potato and then the Justice Department essentially told me I was a paranoid old fool," Falkman reported.

"They blew you off?" Rolfe asked incredulously.

"Like Hurricane Katrina. It was odd, as if they'd been primed to ignore anyone and anything questioning security at the Summit. Shades of my rough treatment at the hands of the FBI. They said I'd read too many spy books, and if anything was going on they'd have uncovered it. In other words, go to Miami Beach and play pinochle with the other old New York Jews."

"What did you say?" Momo asked, her voice alive with curiosity.

"As soon as I realized I was wasting my time, I shut up and revealed nothing. Then I did what every good lawyer does. I thanked them for their wisdom and thought, 'Go fuck yourselves.'" He scowled at the memory. "Rolfe, do you remember I mentioned an old friend at the CIA? He's survived three decades of different bosses, is real smart, has abundant commonsense coupled with well-honed instincts, and is so close to retirement that he doesn't give a damn about internal politics. He agreed to meet and I've arranged to have a quiet word with him. Maybe he's got some suggestions. Your turn, Rolfe. What could your British intelligence man—I forget his name—have to add?"

"Kenneth Palmer. Unlike our government, he took the whole thing seriously. He said my instincts are good. His organization's had prior experience with my instincts—and he'd dig into the matter with the prime minister's security detail."

"That's it?" Momo asked, obviously disappointed.

"Not quite. Palmer called back to say his people were concerned enough to raise the matter with the Americans—Britspeak for 'It stinks to high heaven.' But when they brought the few facts we know to the attention of their colleagues in the U.S. government, they were told everything was under control and the British should mind our own business. MI6 were officially satisfied; Kenneth said they couldn't infringe on the American's turf. However, Palmer's own team within counter intelligence was anything but comforted by the response. 'Too glib by far' was Kenneth's understated comment. In other words, they want to stay involved."

"Meaning?" Matt asked.

"That's why I e-mailed you to get here as soon as possible. Palmer wants you to put a couple of their people on the Resort payroll."

"Doing what?"

"Anything you can think up for them. The more senior the position, the better."

Trouble, Matt thought. How could he put in new people when Blenheim had overloaded him with substitutes as it stood? "I suppose I can get one into Food and Beverage," he said at last.

"It's the only place I don't have Brad Marshall looking over my shoulder. Maybe I can get another into the front office. Make sure the guys have experience with hotels and can stand up to Marshall's inquisition."

"Will do." Rolfe Ritter smiled at the worried general manager. "I know that look, Ron; what's wrong?"

"Something's odd. It's one thing for Justice and the FBI to ignore me, but it's another to tell MI6 to go to hell. Strange . . ." The lawyer shook his head slowly from side to side. "By the way, I had a talk on the phone with your friend, Avi."

"Really!" The news was surprising to Matt. "The Israeli Avi or the Dodger fan Avi?"

"I've no idea," Falkman admitted. "Mossad's people are all very strange and secretive. However, I get the sense that the man I spoke with is a very experienced *Katsa*—that's what they call a case officer."

"Did he tell you anything?"

"Only that he and his colleagues are increasingly concerned. By the time they went to interview Leon Barken at the Kestrel Jerusalem, he'd disappeared. Dimitri Netski was cooperative, allowed them full access to Barken's home and office, and they found all sorts of incriminating evidence—but no Barken. Avi's people think someone tipped him off. Most likely someone within Kestrel. They assumed Barken had slipped out of the country."

"Assumed or assume?" Matt asked, catching the distinction.

"Assumed—and they were wrong. Barken was found yesterday hanging in front of the main alter in the Church of the Holy Sepulchre in Jerusalem."

"My God! Blenheim—assuming it was Blenheim—would even kill their own men." Matt felt enmeshed in an increasingly complex and multidimensional conspiracy, vicious and untamed. He thought of Beth. Was she too doomed? Was he?

"The Israeli police officially think he was murdered by a fringe group of Opus Dei. They found a copy of Josemaria Escriva's *My Way* in Barken's pocket, and some letters from a man named J.B. discussing some apocalyptic event in the Old City.

There's an endless stream of messianic lunatics, soothsayers and plots in Jerusalem and this looks like part of one."

"So it was some kind of religious killing?" Momo asked.

"The Mossad doesn't believe it for a second. They think he was murdered by whoever his paymasters were at the hotel."

"So Barken was killed to keep him quiet," Rolfe said.

"Exactly. The stuff in the church was meant to derail the police. They weren't fooled for a minute; however, they concluded there was more chance of whoever did it becoming complacent and making a mistake by pretending to buy the story."

Rolfe leaned forward. "Now what?"

"Now nothing. As I said, Barken's death is a police matter; the management of the Kestrel are cooperating; any corruption at the hotel has been rooted out. End of story."

"You've got to be joking!" Matt said, springing to his feet. "Another GM killed. Sammi Chalabi still missing. Beth's daughter a hostage. The FBI and the Secret Service don't want to hear about it, and the Brits want to put in an undercover waiter. Talk about Alice in Wonderland."

"It's not quite that bad," Falkman said quietly. "The Israelis aren't involved in the Summit, but they think something's wrong. They perpetually face a conundrum in situations like this. If something does go wrong at the Summit and word leaks that Israel either had some hand in it or could have stopped it, then there'll be one hell of an international scandal and, as usual, Israel will get blamed for everything, with all the punishment that inevitably brings. They want to know what went on at the Kestrel Jerusalem, why and how it fits together with everything else that's gone on involving Kestrel. They're going to help, but they can't seem to be involved. We've got to do their spying for them."

Rolfe, Momo and Ron looked at Matt expectantly. "Shit," he said. "That means me. Me and Beth."

"And Rolfe. They need his contacts and experience as well. In Mossad terms, they need all of you to be *mabilot*, non-Jewish helpers."

"This is for real isn't it?" Matt asked, as if hoping to be woken up from a bad dream.

Rolfe nodded. “Right. Your alternative is to take Beth and run like crazy.”

“We can’t. They’ve got Britney. And I’m not running till we get her back,” Matt said with far more conviction than he felt.

Rolfe stood and put his hand on Matt’s shoulder. “Very noble,” he said, “and very dangerous. Have you got the balls?”

Matt had trouble breathing. “Have I a choice? Have any of us?” He looked at his mentor and allowed himself a surreptitious thought: I wish this man was my father.

Chapter 48
Santa Monica

No alarm clock was ever needed to wake Beth Taylor up at her regular time of five a.m. As her eyes opened, she would jump out of bed, excited to exercise, get her adrenaline levels up and start her work day.

Until lately. Now, when she woke, she would lie in bed staring at the bedroom's ceiling, her stomach wrapped in a Gordian knot of dread, her legs heavy, her body sluggish, exercise turned from a joy to a chore. Her concentration levels dropped and her temper noticeably shortened as she fought to separate her multiple personalities: consummate, unflappable and suave professional hotelier, anguished and guilt-ridden mother, treacherous lover and deceitful spy.

There was never a moment in her day that Beth Taylor found a moment of solace and joy. Every act was tempered by the drug-laden ugly past she could never forget, the danger to her abandoned daughter, and the knowledge that both she and Matt were in death's path, and all that she had hoped for lay in shards around her.

Gradually the nexus of her angst became clear, manifested in the form of Jimmy Lee, her daughter's prison-keeper and her own tormentor. Hate for the man built up daily until the sight of him or mere mention of his name would cause her heartbeat to rapidly rise and her fists to clench until her long fingers dug deeply into her soft palms, drawing blood on more than one occasion.

Obsessed with the dapper Chinese man, she wanted to know what he was doing at every moment he was in her hotel. Enlisting her loyal assistant, Claire Antonika, as her co-conspirator, the two women would keep each other informed of Jimmy Lee's comings and goings, who he was seeing and what requests he was making of the hotel's associates.

Beth was on the phone, when the breathless Claire rushed into her boss's office.

"What is it?" Beth asked, having hurriedly terminated her call to the corporate accounting office.

"You remember the package of reports you asked me to give to Mr. Lee?"

Beth nodded impatiently.

"When I went into his office's ante room, I could hear raised voices behind his closed office door. I listened carefully and recognized not only J.L.'s voice, but also Dieter Weiss's. They were having a heck of an argument."

"Did you hear what it was about?"

"Some of it. It was about you. It was . . . horrible!"

"That doesn't matter. What did they say?"

"Mr. Weiss wanted to get rid of you, as you weren't doing what you were meant to do. Mr. Lee kept repeating that it was his decision and he was handling you in his own way. That nasty German said that he would take care of matters if Lee didn't have the balls for it. At that point in the conversation, J.L. started shouting that he'd had enough of Weiss's backstabbing and interference and that Weiss should remember who really called the shots. The office door slammed open and Dieter Weiss stormed out, brushing past me without a word."

"Then what happened?" Beth asked, trying hard to control her panic.

"Mr. Lee saw me and asked what I was doing there. I tried not to bluster and gave him the reports. He looked at me suspiciously, waved me to get out, went into his office and quickly shut the door. I saw the light on the phone in his line in the ante room go on, so I assumed he was talking to someone."

"You did well, Claire, very well. I'm grateful." Beth said, knowing she had to call Rolfe Ritter as soon as she could. Her fear level elevated to the breaking point. He was the only straw she could clutch at.

Chapter 49
Los Angeles

"Dieter? It's Brad Marshall."

"What do you want now?"

"Why don't you listen before you start busting my chops?"

"All right. I'm listening."

"I just got a call from one of our electronic surveillance people. Dirksen's personal credit card popped up on his computer."

"He went shopping, bought some gas. What the fuck do I care?"

"You care because Wonder Boy bought a Delta Shuttle ticket from D.C. to La Guardia and three hours later flew back. He wasn't in New York long enough to take in a show."

Weiss reflected. Marshall was right to be troubled. "Has he any business in New York?"

"None that Olivia Wade knows about. His business was ostensibly in Washington, drumming up business from the meeting planners, a courtesy visit to the State Department in order to update them on the hotel's Summit preparations. Besides, if he was on company business he'd have used his corporate credit card or told her to book the ticket."

"Did Olivia ask him about it?"

"Dieter, do you think I fell off a fucking turnip truck? Of course she asked how his meetings went. Dirksen told her he didn't have a spare second in Washington. Didn't mention New York."

"Shit. You were right to call. What about Beth Taylor? She say anything to Jimmy about this?"

"Not a word. According to surveillance, she hasn't spoken to Dirksen in days, let alone fucked him."

"I don't like this." He stopped for a moment, considering. "Ritter's in New York! What if Dirksen went to see him?"

"Possible," Marshall growled. "More than possible."

"Okay. Tell Taylor to see Dirksen regularly. Wait in front of his fucking house at night for all I care. She has a job, she'd better do it. Make sure she asks that interfering son of a bitch the right questions and reports everything he says to Jimmy Lee. I want to know how many times he comes and how much he spurts out. If the motherfucker farts, I want to know about it."

Chapter 50
La Jolla

Matt insisted they sit in the center of the row of tables, their backs to the wall of water that was the centerpiece of the Hyatt Regency La Jolla's packed and noisy Japango restaurant. They had greeted each other cautiously, each skittish after the intense emotions of the night at her apartment. Matt's heart was still uneasy. Her explanation had convinced him—nearly; but so much was unexplained. Was her admission that she was working for Blenheim nothing more than another twist to their devious plans? Had they said "get him to trust you," so that he'd reveal more?

"I chose the place and the table carefully," he explained when they were seated. "Rolfe told me to assume we were being followed, watched and listened to at all times. Your warned me as well, remember?"

Patiently, Matt recounted his conversation with the Ritters and Ron Falkman. Beth listened intently, asking few questions. "You're holding something back. What is it?" she asked when he'd finished.

Reluctantly, Matt described Leon Barken's gruesome murder in the Church of the Holy Sepulchre. Beth pushed her sashimi aside and gulped ice cold sake from her square wooden cup.

"Jesus! I was so excited when Jimmy ordered me to see you. Dieter Weiss wants to get rid of me, but for some reason Lee is keeping me around. I suppose to spy on you. At last I thought I'd have you to hold me, calm me, love me. But another murder. What does it mean for us? For Britney? Are they going to kill us all? Tell me everything's going to be okay."

He took her hand but avoided her eyes. Was her sweet talk poisoned? "We can't panic. It's imperative we find out what's going on. Look, we're not alone. Both British Counter Intelligence and Mossad believe there's something serious going on. They'll help. So will Rolfe."

Who is this man? Beth wondered. A virtual stranger despite their intimacy. All her life she'd been self-reliant, all her life she'd been scared. Was he working for Blenheim, as she was? For a second, she wished she was still on the streets; at least their terrors were familiar and she would always have the predictable oblivion from street drugs. She exploded, "Who in God's name are you kidding? A couple of low-level Brits in the food and beverage department or at the front desk? One Israeli baseball fan? A geriatric lawyer? A man whose wife has cancer? Grow up, for God's sake! We're at Blenheim's mercy." She began to cry.

"I know," he said. "I'm as scared and frustrated as you are. But what can I do? I barely have control over the Resort. Dieter Weiss treats me like dog shit on his shoes, Jimmy Lee's on my back when Brad Marshall's not stabbing it. It's as if I have a shadow everywhere I go, even when I take a crap. Those bastards keep me around only because the Summit's organizers want me. And you around so you can spy on me."

"I'm supposed to tell Jimmy everything you say," she said. "Even when we're making love."

"Then let's make love quietly. We'll think of something you can report to him, just enough to keep him satisfied, no more. He's with me at the Audley now. Maybe while he's gone, you can . . ."

"Steal his files? Search his home? Put poison in his toothpaste? Matt, I'm not going to do anything to jeopardize my daughter." She began to tremble.

But she'd have to help. Rolfe knew it, and so did he. He wondered for a second if Britney were real, or an imaginary child like the one in *Who's Afraid of Virginia Wolfe*? "I'm so frightened," she whispered, clutching his hand so hard he winced. "For Britney, for me, for you. Jimmy Lee's a monster. He's evil. I hate him so much I—I want to kill him."

"If he harms you or Britney, I'll do it myself!" Matt snarled. "Meanwhile let's go back to my place. We can make love and . . ."

She smiled at him through her tears. "And?"

"And I'll tell you something you can report back to Jimmy Lee."

They stood. "Which is?"

He pulled her toward the exit. "That I love you." Even as he said it, he wondered if the words were true.

*

They were so hungry for each other that when Matt pulled his BMW into his garage neither he nor Beth saw the gray Ford Taurus pull up on the opposite side of the street. Nor did they notice that even when its headlights switched off, the two passengers remained motionless inside the dark car.

Inside the townhouse Beth clasped him with an urgency driven as much by fear as desire. This is our time. This is my proof. Please, God, let me show him my love.

They stood in the unlit foyer saying nothing, Matt stroking her hair and face until she could feel her body relax, feel the warmth of her blood.

"Come," he said, leading her up the stairs to his bedroom. There he cupped her face in his hands, kissed her closed eyelids, the warm tears on her cheeks and, finally, her lips. Her mouth opened and she returned his kisses fiercely, with an urgency that surprised her.

He caressed her breasts, and bent to kiss her nipples through the white silk of her dress. Wordlessly, she kicked off her shoes and started to unbutton his shirt, her fingers as sure as a fine lacemaker's. His hands found the zipper at the back of her dress and the dress slipped off her body. He lifted her thick hair and kissed the smooth nape of her neck. She sighed ecstatically. His tongue gently explored Beth's ear. Her body writhed in pent-up passion.

"Get your clothes off now," she said hoarsely. Her brain free of thought, all she knew was sensation.

Matt obeyed. In seconds he was naked and fell backwards onto the bed, pulling Beth with him. She helped him remove her bra and thong. Hurling them to a corner of the room as though throwing away inhibition, she then placed her hand on his chest and pushed herself up to see if he was ready. He was. She settled herself on him with an uninhibited cry of frenzy and his answering moan told her of his gratitude. Their rhythms coincided. Nothing mattered at that moment except pleasure, and they looked into each other's eyes with joyful passion that transcended rationality until at last she shouted "Now," and he, her willing slave, obeyed.

It was only when they had finished that his doubts returned, while hers—the doubts of a decade—were wiped away.

*

"Weiss will enjoy listening to that episode," the older of the two men in the Ford Taurus chuckled as he pulled off his headphones.

His companion snickered, "I need a goddamned cold shower!"

*

Beth Taylor didn't let Matt sleep that night. Whispered endearments exchanged between increasingly tender lovemaking, their glistening bodies hot on the sheet, dancing shadows from melting candles illuminating the room, the couple explored each other with an intensity that surprised them both. At dawn, they lay immobile, spent and satiated. Beth's head nestled on Matt's shoulder, her flowing red hair vivid against the cream-white pillow. Tension gone, words spoken and unspoken, meanings understood, their fingers caressed increasingly familiar bodies, this time with love, not unrequited passion. Her words didn't convince him of her love. Her body almost did.

Finally, sleep won its battle.

*

"Come on, sleepyhead, my infamous coffee awaits."

Beth squinted at Matt standing above her, and accepted the robe he held open for her. She stood drowsily and followed him to the balcony where he had placed two cups of steaming cappuccino on a small table beside a chaise. Bending, he gently kissed her eyelids, then silently returned to the bedroom. Soon the sound of soft jazz surrounded her, and he was by her side.

"Why music so early?" she asked.

"Remember, we have to assume we're being listened to or watched. That's why coffee is served outdoors. The music is on to cover our conversation."

Beth blushed. "Does that mean they could have heard us last night?"

"If they had, they'd know you were doing your job. Splendidly, I might add."

"The torment I have to endure in Blenheim's cause," she sighed with a knowing smile. "I've been thinking about our conversation in Japango. You're right. We can't be passive. It's an invitation for those shits to do whatever they want."

He glanced at her, struck by the excitement in her voice. "I can tell you have an idea. What is it?"

"I'm not quite sure," she said, leaning over to kiss him. "Let me think about it."

*

The Ford Taurus remained in its spot. "Can you hear what they're saying?" one of the passengers asked.

"The music's drowning them out."

"Listening to them, all I got last night was an erection."

"She didn't do much to make him talk," his companion agreed. "Mr. Lee will be disappointed."

"I'm not so sure. Maybe we're here to check on her as well as him. She seemed to be enjoying herself entirely too much."

Chapter 51
Santa Monica

The shrill of smoke detectors shattered the night. Four fire engines, speeding down Ocean Boulevard in response, roused only the homeless sleeping under the park benches overlooking the Pacific.

Guests of the Kestrel Hotel and Resort, Santa Monica, eyes heavy with sleep, looked over the atrium's balcony to see their grumbling compatriots milling in the lobby, clad in everything from pajamas to undershorts to jeans and tee-shirts, to—in the case of two Japanese men—suits and ties.

"This is not a drill," a loudspeaker blared. "Please evacuate your rooms and come to the lobby."

The smell of smoke was in the air, but from the atrium and the lobby, no one could see flames.

*

Beth Taylor, wearing slacks and a silk shirt, greeted the chief fire officer under the *porte cochère*. "You got here fast," she said. "All we know is that the smoke detectors and sprinklers went off on the South Wing on the fourth floor. Smoke's coming from that area. One of the security team reported a fire in the back of the house elevator."

"Have you closed down the elevators?"

"Of course. Our protocol mandates that we return service and guest elevators to the lower level and shut them down. We have staff on all levels escorting guests down the emergency staircases. All guests on the West Wing have been accounted for. Security personnel are on guard to prevent theft."

"Excellent!" the chief said. "My men are already on their way to the fourth floor."

*

An hour later, Beth and the fire chief watched the firemen roll up their hoses and stack their equipment back on the truck. "The fire started in the laundry chute on the fourth floor where the maids' storage rooms and service elevators are located and, fortunately, was contained in that area," the chief explained. "I'm afraid we had to smash through the back wall to get to that area."

It could have been worse, Beth thought. "Any chance the bedrooms on that wing will be habitable?"

"Not a chance. The smoke was bad. My guess is you'll need to do dry-out, and then shampoo the carpets and sort out the mattresses and boxsprings. The sprinklers messed them up good."

Outside the hotel, police had cordoned off the *porte cochère.* TV crews milled around, looking for people to interview and reporters buttonholed the firemen as they left.

Beth sighed. "I've got to get this place organized and the guests back to their rooms. We'll have to find rooms somehow for the fourth-floor guests." She waved expansively at the people in the lobby. "Tomorrow this whole group will want their money back and then there'll be the oddball lawsuits to drive us mad. I have to notify our insurance company and they'll want a copy of your report. Can do?"

He smiled sympathetically. "You'll have it this afternoon."

"Thanks." She felt guilty, as though the fire were her fault. "Want my job, chief?"

"No way. Mine's hard enough. Sorry for the mess."

Beth and her team began to organize the guests, arranged cleanup squads and sent them into action. It was four a.m. The next day promised to be hell on earth.

*

"I've got to see you immediately."

Matt looked at the number on his secure cell phone. Beth had called from hers. "I heard the news," he said. "Poor darling. You okay?"

"Can you drive up here now?"

"No," was the answer. Matt was feeling overwhelmed. "Sure. What's up?"

"Not over the phone. Call when you're close and we'll meet at Germaine's on Third Street."

*

"Kiss me. Hold my hand. Make it look like you're consoling me after last night's shock. I've been telling everybody the fire threw me for a loop."

Matt grinned. "My pleasure. But why?"

"They may be watching. Besides, I want to be kissed."

He complied enthusiastically. She told him the events of the previous night. "I forgot to tell the chief who set the fire in the laundry chute."

Matt's eyes widened. "You know?"

"Yes. It was me. I lit a bunch of oily rags and tossed them in. We had a test a few days earlier, so I knew the safety systems worked, but I hadn't counted on that much damage."

"Why in heaven's name did you do it?"

"Jimmy Lee's office is three rooms away from the chute. I knew it would be cordoned off. I was allowed in the area, of course, so when I had a chance I went into the office and rummaged through the files. I took anything that looked remotely interesting, a lot of it in Chinese. I photocopied it all, then replaced it as best I could. Also, I opened his computer—we had his general passwords on file in case of emergency—and downloaded everything onto a disc. I couldn't get into his secure files, but even so his contact list was on general access. Interesting names. When I'd finished, I sent him an e-mail reporting the fire, saying his office wasn't badly harmed, but I had to send a crew to clean up and I'd made sure the head of security stayed in his office while the crew worked. Pretty clever, eh?"

He gazed at her admiringly. "You're a genius. Where's all this information?"

"In a briefcase under the table."

"What!"

"What did you expect me to do with it? I called Rolfe just before I met you. He says go to the Kinko and FedEx it to him in New York. He'll get it to the right people."

A snake of suspicion wound through his gut. What if she was bringing misinformation? "But they'll be watching me," Matt said. "His plan won't work."

She smiled. "Leave it to Rolfe to anticipate the question. You should go to Rizzoli's, buy your father a large coffee table book on San Diego or anything remotely relevant, and FedEx it to him at the same time you send the stuff to Rolfe. You may be the only GM that wouldn't ship it from the property, but at least they'll think you're honest—stupid, but honest. Like your father is, now." He had told her of the Blenheim blackmail.

The mention of his father reminded Matt guiltily that he hadn't thought of that threat for days or spoken to his dad since he had left Chesterton for New York, so intense was his worry about Beth. As usual, someone else was being proactive while he let himself be swayed by events. His father's style. He took her hand. "You must have been terrified."

"I've never been so scared in my life. For my next job I'll take up something safer, sky diving without a parachute."

They kissed goodbye. "Let's hope Rolfe comes up with something," Matt said.

"Let's hope Jimmy Lee doesn't find out what I've done."

Chapter 52
San Diego

Exasperation replaced Pete Wilson's normally calm demeanor. "You're not leaving those crates here."

"I'll leave them any damn place I want," Keith McGregor snapped.

"Move them. What the hell do you think this place is? A warehouse? I assume they contain all the new electronics and systems that Mr. Weiss shipped from Germany, but I don't give a flying fuck. I'm in charge of operations around here, and those unsightly things can't be left in view of the guests. Besides, we agreed they'd be staged in the staff parking lot."

"You decided. It's ridiculous to store them a quarter of a mile from where they're to be installed." The Scot pointed to the equipment rooms not thirty yards away, their cream, stucco facades, windows, doors and roofs matching the guest suites. "And another thing, I don't report to you and you damn well know it."

The house manager's face turned purple. He called his boss from his cell phone. "Matt, we've got a problem by the equipment rooms that needs your attention. Now."

Minutes later, Dirksen arrived, clearly irritated. "What is it?"

Wilson, fists clenched, explained the issue.

"Those crates are enormous. What the hell's inside them?" Matt asked.

"Everything Mr. Weiss ordered from Germany—operating systems, electronics, boilers," McGregor answered impatiently.

Matt's loathing of his German boss blinded him. "Well, they're not staying here. Move 'em. Now!"

"Take it up with Mr. Weiss. I'm just in charge of installation." The Scot answered patronizingly.

"I don't care whether the fucking crown jewels of England are in those crates. Get them out of here and into the goddamned staff parking lot," Wilson shouted, his jutted jaw close to McGregor's face.

"Calm down, both of you," Matt said, recovering his composure. "I know all our nerves are frayed, mine included, but we've still got a lot of work to do before the Summit. Getting into a contest to see whose balls are bigger isn't going to help. Understand?"

"I'm sorry," Wilson said.

Before the Scot could answer, a familiar voice boomed, "Those crates stay here!"

Matt turned. Brad Marshall stood behind him, hands on hips, like an overseer of a chain gang. Matt wondered how long his nemesis had been near them. "Why is this any of your business?" Matt asked. "It's an operational issue. There are no security matters involved."

"Excuse me." Marshall glared at Matt. "You don't decide what's a security matter and what isn't. That's my job. These crates stay right where they are."

Dirksen could see Wilson staring at him and McGregor wearing an insolent smirk. "I'm not interfering on security issues. Dieter Weiss made it clear you have control. Please help me understand what the location of the crates has to do with security." Matt fought to keep his voice pleasant, difficult given his smoldering rage.

Marshall sighed. "This equipment is going to be critical for the Summit. You know its installation was a condition of us getting the event. Sabotage would be disastrous. The closer the crates stay to the main buildings, the more secure they are. We're expecting more than 100,000 protesters. God knows what they'd do if they could get to the equipment."

Nonsense, Matt thought, shaking his head wearily. But he knew the matter was closed. "Pete, the crates stay here. Organize the yellow and black striped fabric coverings we had manufactured when we were redoing the façade on the main building, the ones in the company's colors. McGregor, you'll build a frame and pin the fabric to it to shield the crates. When you've done that, get the florist to make up five-dozen or six-dozen pots with midsized trees and place them in front of the shield. Okay, Pete? Okay, Keith?"

Both nodded, Matt strode away, followed by Wilson.

"That fucking cocksucker wouldn't survive one night on Glasgow's streets," McGregor sneered.

Marshall shrugged. "Forget it. The Summit's in four months. After that, Dirksen will be out of our lives forever."

Chapter 53
New York

Penn Station teemed as rush-hour approached and an increasing crowd of tired commuters stared at the departure boards for notice of their departure platforms.

The two men, engrossed in conversation sitting on one of the many solid wooden benches, went unnoticed by the self-absorbed throng.

“The Summit’s a hot topic, but we’ve been told to keep our noses out of it,” the veteran CIA man commented.

“Isn’t that unusual?” Falkman asked.

“There’s so much internecine politics these days, it’s difficult to know. I can tell you one thing, the orders to keep out of this come from on high. The Summit’s definitely radioactive inside the company.”

“Rick, I’ve known you for over two decades, you’re not telling me something. What is it?”

Rick Caverly hesitated, looked around and said, “I’ll deny knowing you, let alone saying this, but something’s decidedly odd about all of this. I wouldn’t have taken it seriously if not for you telling me both British Counter Intelligence and Mossad think something is up. They’re not dummies. Tell me everything you know.”

Falkman talked for twenty minutes.

“Shit! There’s enough here to raise red flags everywhere. I don’t get it,” Caverly said.

“What can you do about it?” the lawyer asked.

“I’m damned if I know. Someone has to connect the dots, but getting involved in this could be a career-ender for me.”

“So that’s a no?”

“After twenty-something years of our relationship, you still have to ask that stupid question? I’m nearly at retirement age, what’s the worst they can do, force me into early retirement? If they can't take a joke, fuck 'em! I'll dig around some, who knows what shit will float to the surface. For God's sake, Ron, never mention my name or involvement to anyone, not even in your dreams."

Chapter 54
Los Angeles

The hot Santa Ana wind shook the windowpanes in Dimitri Netski's Bel Air mansion. His normally clear views of Los Angeles from the library's wall of windows were obscured in a sandy haze.

Netski paced the room, clad in navy-blue Zegna slacks and a light-blue Dunhill silk shirt, a half-drunk glass of pepper vodka in his hand.

Fabrizio Battini watched him with growing anxiety. "Are you positive the Israeli police think Barken's death was a local incident?" Netski asked, his voice suspiciously pleasant.

"Absolutely. As far as they're concerned, Barken was involved in a right-wing Catholic group, then tried to back out. Exit Barken."

Netski's grunt expressed his skepticism.

"Look, Dimitri. Jerusalem's always had dozens of fanatic sects. Every year or so some lunatic proclaims himself the Messiah and attracts a bunch of crazies ready to blow up the Wailing Wall or the Al Aqsa Mosque. We left enough clues to make Barken look like just another religious nut."

"Why did you try to link him to Opus Dei?" Dieter Weiss sniped from a chair in the corner. "Who do you think you are? Author of the next *Da Vinci Code*?"

"I did the best I could on short notice. Anyway, the Jerusalem police told me there's no need to involve Blenheim in any further investigation."

"Stop bickering," Netski commanded. "It bores me. "Dieter, what's the status at the Resort?"

"Most of the team's in place, per our schedule, including all the key players. The balance arrive during the next three weeks."

Battini wiped his brow with a handkerchief. Despite the air-conditioning, the room felt hot to him. “What about the systems and equipment? Get there on time?”

“Safe and sound. Our engineers are starting to install it now. McGregor and the team Dimitri sent from Russia are overseeing it.”

“How’s Brad Marshall doing?” Netski asked.

“Seems on top of everything. He’s made friends with the advance teams from every country and has a good relationship with the American secret service detail in charge of the Summit preparations. Dirksen abominates him, which I take to be a good sign. If you ask me, it’s safe to get rid of both Dirksen and the Taylor woman. With the Summit getting closer, there’s no chance for a change of venue now.”

Netski loomed over the seated German. “No one’s asked you. How stupid can you be? Our friend Mr. Dirksen is the organizers darling. I even received a letter from Tim Matheson at the State Department complimenting me on what a fine job Dirksen and his team are doing with the Summit preparations. Why set off alarms by getting rid of him? He stays until the damn thing is over. ” He turned to Jimmy Lee. “How’s he behaving?”

The Chinese jerked to attention. “Doing his job and that’s about it. Works twenty-hour days. Trying to pull off the Summit is like herding cats. He only loses his calm around Brad Marshall.”

“He’s banging our Santa Monica GM every chance he gets,” Weiss leered. “Most imaginative, those two. Quite the acrobats. But our surveillance team has no trace of his going to New York. He either left his cell phone in D.C.—unlikely—or simply stayed where he said he’d stay. The other day Olivia Wade asked him casually if he was going to submit expenses for his New York trip. He looked at her as if she was crazy. ‘What New York trip’?”

“Is the Taylor woman cooperating?” Netski asked Lee.

“She’s been a pussycat since I let her talk to her daughter. Tells me everything about her meetings with Dirksen. Humiliation is a powerful weapon. I ask her what kind of underwear he wears, how many times he comes, whether he likes his balls scratched. That way she remembers who she works for and what’s at stake.

She tells me Dirksen's focused entirely on the Summit, making a name for himself, and then getting out of Blenheim as quickly as he can."

"And you believe her?"

"She knows what will happen to her daughter if she lies."

"Good." Netski smiled mirthlessly. "Anything else?"

"There's one thing." Lee's voice grew quiet. "There was a fire at the Santa Monica property last week."

"I heard about it. Our insurance will cover it."

"That's not the point."

"Go on."

"Beth handled everything according to the company's policies, so there's no problem there. Only I checked my computer access dates. Someone had used it the day of the fire. When I checked with the guard overseeing the cleanup, he told me no one had turned it on."

"Good God!" Weiss exploded. "That means Taylor . . . Did you ask her about it?"

"Of course. She said she'd checked it to make sure it hadn't been damaged. A reasonable explanation, but . . ."

Netski stared at him through half-closed eyes. "But what?"

"She was nervous. Avoided eye contact. Usually she's straight with me, but this time . . . I don't like it."

The four men were silent. Finally Netski said, "It may be nothing. Perhaps our Ms. Taylor was only trying to find out about her daughter."

"What do you want me to do about it?" Lee asked.

"Not you. Blenheim. It's time to send Taylor and Dirksen a reminder of what they have to lose."

Chapter 55
New York

Discarded sections of the Sunday *New York Times* lay neatly piled by the side of the leather wing-backed chair in Ron Falkman's library. Casually dressed for the octogenarian lawyer and Talmudic scholar meant Gucci loafers, gray mohair slacks and a monogrammed dress shirt unbuttoned at the collar. The ever-present grey suede yarmulke was perched on his mop of receded grey hair. A glass of lemon tea in one hand, he was about to start on "The Week in Review" when the phone intruded.

He lifted the receiver. "Mr. Falkman?" An unknown voice.

"Speaking."

"*Shalom.* It's Avi."

"I'm afraid I can't place the name."

"Avi the baseball fan. Mr. Dirksen probably mentioned our conversation."

The penny dropped. "Of course, *boker tov*, Avi. What can I do for you?"

"You can buy me lox and new green pickles. What else for a Jewish friend?"

Falkman loved the cat-and-mouse of it. "I see. Where?"

"Where else? Zabars."

"I see you have good taste. It's perhaps the best delicatessen in the world. You'll meet me there?"

"In half an hour."

"How will I know you?"

The voice chuckled. "Mr. Falkman, you've danced to this music before and so you know the answer. I'll know you."

*

The mellow sun beamed onto the Ritters' terrace where Rolfe, Momo—color in her high-boned cheeks, her condition momentarily stable—and Falkman were drinking their morning coffee.

"The Jimmy Lee files must have contained interesting information, judging by the reactions we had from Palmer," Rolfe said. To Falkman's disdain, his feet were bare and a rumpled tee-shirt hung loosely over frayed jeans.

"And from Mossad," the lawyer said. "Yesterday I met with Dirksen's baseball buddy, Avi, though he sure didn't match Matt's description. He must have been ten years older."

"So it wasn't the same man?" Momo asked from her chaise, a blanket pulled up to her chin.

"I asked him. He said, what difference, if all I wanted was to know what his organization thought of the Chinese's files."

"And?" Rolfe asked.

"The Lee papers left them with more questions than answers."

Rolfe took a savage bite of the rugula Ron had supplied from Zabar's. "Jesus! Just what Palmer said. What was Avi's conclusion?"

"His boss wants to have a meeting with you, me and your friend Palmer."

"Then it must be important," Rolfe said. "Palmer admitted—and I quote—that the situation was a trifle worrying."

"Bloody English," Momo muttered, her face animated. "If a nuclear bomb went off in Parliament, all they'd say is, 'there's been a spot of bother.' So where and when's this spook's summit?"

Rolfe shook his head, grinning. "Palmer wants it in London."

"And Avi in Tel Aviv," Ron said.

"Then the matter's settled," the turbaned Momo said. "Wild horses wouldn't stop me from attending. I'm not allowed to travel. So New York it is."

Chapter 56
La Jolla

The ringing of his telephone woke Matt at 3:26 a.m. He sat up groggily. “Hello.”

A disembodied voice said, “Tune in to CNN.”

“Who is this?”

The dial tone resonated in Matt’s ear. He switched on the news channel just as the half-hour lead stories started to play.

He recognized the Kestrel logo, then the ivy and bougainvillea-covered *porte cochère* of Blenheim’s Lima hotel. An earnest young reporter stood in the cobblestoned driveway.

“Less than an hour ago, a black Mercedes sped to the front of Lima’s finest hotel. And, just where I’m standing now, its passenger door opened and a package the size of a soccer ball was thrown at the feet of the doorman. Only it wasn’t a soccer ball. It was a human head.

“The police have identified the head as that of Sammi Chalabi, the hotel’s missing general manager, believed to have been kidnapped by the terrorist organization, Shining Path . . .”

Matt switched off the channel and dropped the remote. Blood pounded in his head like hammer on anvil. Chalabi’s murder was his fault! He should have reached his friend, should have somehow warned him, should have stayed away, should have stayed closer, should have—shit! He was his impotent father’s impotent child.

The phone rang again. He grabbed it eagerly. “Beth! Did you see the news?”

The same eerie voice. “This isn’t your whore. We wanted you to see what happens to nosey and uncooperative general managers. The next head could be hers, or perhaps her daughter’s.”

Fear made him sweat. “What do you want?”

“We want you to do exactly as you’re told, but you and Taylor, like Chalabi, have been nosey and haven’t been cooperating. You’re being watched and overheard; we know everything you do and you'd better not forget it. Don't even dream of digging into our plans, let alone interfering. Both of you do your jobs and keep your mouths tightly shut, and you and those around you might keep your heads." The line went dead.

Rage blew in him like a sandstorm. His impotence left him weak. Hand trembling, he lifted the receiver.

*

They sat opposite each other in "their" diner outside Santa Monica. "Not ten minutes after you called, so did Jimmy Lee," Beth said, trying to ignore his bloodshot eyes and her own curdled feeling of impending doom.

Matt was unable to mask his tone of despair. "What did he want?"

"To tell me about Sammi Chalabi. But it was a crock of shit. The real message was for me to behave and to make sure you follow instructions, even if you were told to wear a bowler hat and a hula skirt and walk on your hands and knees on Ocean Boulevard whistling "America the Beautiful." For good measure, the bastard added that Britney was still safe, at least for the moment."

"Still," Matt muttered the operative word. "How can I act as if nothing's happened?"

Tears filled her eyes at his suffering. "You have to for my daughter's sake."

"Of course. It's just so difficult." He cupped her hand with his, wishing with all his heart that there'd been no daughter. He wondered if he'd ever be sure about her, realizing how noxious his suspicions were. Blenheim was responsible for this, too. "When this is over, let's never get out of bed."

She managed a smile. "Come back with me now. We can practice."

"I can't. The State Department people are coming at eleven. After Sammi, it'll be tough to be hail-fellow-well-met."

"Then you'd better get going. The traffic's murder." They stood and hugged. "Please promise you'll be careful."

"I'll take it slow, don't worry."

"I wasn't talking about the drive."

*

Beth made two calls after Matt left.

"It went well," she reported to Jimmy Lee. "He'll behave, just as I will. He told me that he was so shaken up by Sammi's murder that he was going to call Mr. Netski today and quit. I begged him not to, again, for my daughter's sake. As he was leaving, I asked him, 'Why call Mr. Netski, not Dieter Weiss?' He made some strange comment, inferring that Weiss was not loyal to Blenheim and may have his own agenda."

"What did he mean by that?"

"No idea. I asked. He said for me to forget he'd said anything, he was just angry. I made him promise to keep his head down, mouth shut and do his job, for my sake and for Britney's. He lightened up when he was kissing me goodbye and asked me if a blowjob was out of the question. He's going to behave. I'm sure of it."

"Excellent. You're a good girl, Beth, just as I knew you'd be."

His self-satisfaction made her gasp. "Your wish is my command."

She used her other cell phone for the second call. It was answered immediately. "Rolfe Ritter speaking . . ."

Chapter 57
Manhattan

From his chair opposite his lawyer's desk, Rolfe Ritter inspected a new photo of Ron Falkman standing next to King Abdullah of Saudi Arabia, their arms around each other's shoulders, while Ron explained his difficulty in setting up the meeting.

"It's the location. The Israelis want it at their consul general's office, 2nd Avenue between 42nd and 43rd. The Brits say their consul general's office, right around the corner from me on Third, between 51st and 52nd. Both claim security reasons, but the truth is neither wants to be seen going into the other's place."

"So which is it?"

Ron cackled. "Neither. I told them you didn't want to be seen going into either."

"You're kidding!"

"Actually, yes. But, nevertheless, we agreed on your apartment."

Rolfe jumped up. "Are you nuts? Our place won't be secure enough for Palmer, let alone the Israelis with their paranoia. Besides, I'm not sure Momo's up to it."

"She is. I asked her before I suggested it."

"Why her and not me?" Rolfe shook his head. "I know, I know. She's the boss." He smiled. "But what about security?"

"Here's how it'll work," Falkman said. "The Israelis will send some people over in the morning dressed as TV repair men who'll sweep the place for listening devices. In the afternoon the Brits will come in through the garage elevators and the Israelis through the back entrance and use the service elevators. The doormen will be trying to break up an altercation in front of the building."

"How convenient."

"I thought so."

"I suppose Momo will have given our staff the day off and provided food?"

"We'll sit at the dining-room table. I like round, don't you? It's what they used in Oslo."

"Why am I always the last to know?" Rolfe grumbled. "When's Momo's Spook Summit?"

"Tomorrow." Ron bowed from his waist. "Will that be soon enough, m'lord?"

Chapter 58
San Diego

Matt's mind filled with dark visions on the drive back. He saw Sammi's head severed by a scimitar, his own blown to pieces by a pistol shot, Beth strangled in her bedroom. He kept reciting the growing list of dead hotel GMs. Would he indeed be next? Would Beth? Would her daughter? What about his own father?

At last he came to a stop at the Resort's gate house. A cursory wave at the guards and he was inside what were once comfortable surroundings that today seemed alien and forbidden.

Inside his office, Olivia Wade handed him his list of appointments and messages. "You look like someone dragged you through a hedge backwards," she said. "Those pompous popinjays from State are already here and waiting for you with Pete Wilson. But you'd better clean up a bit before you see them."

He washed, shaved and put on a fresh shirt and tie before heading toward the boardroom, wishing that Tim Matheson was here rather than the second-raters for the State Department whom Tim had charged with logistics. "By the way, Pete needs to speak to you when the meeting's over," Olivia called after him.

He turned. "What happened?"

"He wouldn't say—just that you'd be pissed."

"Great! Something else to look forward to."

*

Pete Wilson had provided a sumptuous feast for his four guests—all under forty, all dressed in gray suits and red ties, all with skin the color of three-day-old Dover sole. On the sideboard sat Danish pastries, sliced tropical fruits, toast wrapped in pale, yellow napkins, croissants, mini-bagels, butters, jams, cut cheese, sliced meats, thin strips of Scottish smoked salmon, coffees and teas in silver urns, bottled water and soft drinks, the Resort's signature scrambled eggs with porcini mushrooms and truffles, bacon, pork, turkey, and chicken herb-spiced sausages. Also grilled Canadian bacon, grilled basic and truffle-oiled tomatoes, mushrooms with lime juice and oregano, and Matt's own creation, thinly sliced red new potatoes, fried over lightly with glazed button onions and finely sliced red, green and yellow peppers, flavored with cilantro.

Matt nearly retched at the sight of it. Boardrooms were not five-star restaurants. Most of the food would be tossed into the garbage when the meeting was over. He wondered how much it had all cost. How many man-hours went into its preparation? How many more hours would go into the cleanup and equipment storage? Pete would never have been so lavish on his own; he was acting on orders from Dieter Weiss.

Pete made the introductions, focusing on Theodor Goforth, a small, lean, mousey-haired, thin-lipped, bespectacled man with the weakest handshake Matt could remember. The man from State acknowledged Matt's apologies for tardiness without graciousness. Obviously too self-important for mere mortals like me, he thought, his mood dark.

"Under Secretary of State Goforth is here to do a site inspection and to tell us of certain changes," Pete announced.

"What changes?" Matt asked abruptly, instantly sorry for his rudeness. It's all too much, he thought. I'm losing my touch. Just hold on.

"Some delegate changes," Goforth stated, barely moving his thin, bloodless lips.

"No sweat. We expected some shuffling back and forth." Matt's attempt at politeness came out as a croak.

"I'm relieved to hear that." The Under Secretary forced a smile. "Mr. Wilson thought it might be a problem."

Matt looked at Pete, whose face was deep red, choleric. "What problem?

"It isn't shuffling. State wants to add four delegations. Twenty-eight new people."

"I see. And house them where?" Matt's incredulity was obvious.

"In the Resort, of course," one of Goforth's lackeys said.

"I see. Again, no sweat, provided you can expand the Resort to accommodate them."

"I don't think you understand, Mr. Dirksen," Goforth said, puffing up like a pompous frog. "We discussed this with your corporate office. They approved the addition of the Uzbekistan, Kazakhstan, Bulgarian, and Serbian delegations. 'Honored guests of the United States' and all that. The subject being raised at this meeting is not for your consent, but for logistical purposes."

"Did corporate suggest where we might house them?"

"They had every confidence you could find room." Goforth leaned back smugly.

Matt balled his fists. How he longed to smash this narcissist's smile off his face. Instead he smiled. In fact, he thought, their confidence was well founded. This at least was something he did well. "Then I'd best get to it. We can save any other matters for this afternoon. Come with me, Pete. This won't be as simple as Mr. Goforth seems to expect."

Wilson followed him to the door. Matt turned back.

"Enjoy the food, gentlemen." He paused to look at the plates in front of them. "Oh, I see that you already have."

*

"We'll have to convert the staff housing on the edge of the property to guest accommodation." Dirksen and Wilson, weary soldiers in an ongoing war, were seated in Matt's office. "Get with McGregor and fast-track the conversion. Make do with whatever you can find. Shit! As far as I'm concerned, go to the Furniture Mart and buy stuff off the floor. Fuck it, Pete, it may not be perfect but it'll have to do."

Wilson shook his head. "Christ alive! Have you any idea what this will cost? It's last-minute requisitions. Every supplier and subcontractor will screw us blind."

"Why should we give a shit? Weiss doesn't."

"Where are we going to house the replaced stuff?"

"Fucking burn it! Set up tents somewhere. Your problem." Matt began to pace. "What a Mickey Mouse way to run a global company. You'd better get hold of the chef and let him know he'll have to feed four more sets of divas, each more important than God. Call the convention services department. Each of the delegations will want their own meeting room, so that's got to be sorted out. And you'll have to talk to those arrogant pricks from State, tell them to figure out who doesn't like who and whether World War Three will erupt if the Bulgarians are next to the Japanese or if the Serbs can smell the French in the conference room."

Pete grinned despite himself. "I'll get hold of Brad Marshall immediately. He knows from smells."

"You're the best," Matt said fervently. "Without you, I'm yesterday's dog poop. Olivia said there was something you wanted to talk to me about."

"Given your mood, I'm not sure this is the right time."

Matt sighed. "What difference does it make? Adds to the shitty day."

"There's been an incident with one of the Russians installing the new electronic equipment."

"Tell McGregor. Those guys are his problem."

"Not this time. It involves Mrs. Dickenson."

Matt groaned, "Go on." Martha Dickenson, age forty-three, widowed two years previously, had inherited her husband's wealth from his Ohio bolt-making business. She now spent four months a year at the Resort, her bill, as Pete once put it, greater than the national debt of Lithuania.

"This particular Russian got friendly with our lovely heiress. Seems she's learning Russian and used him to practice with. Whatever the signals, he took it as an invitation for a nocturnal visit and knocked on her door around midnight. She'd ordered some ice, thought room service had arrived, and opened the door. He pushed his way into the room and started to fondle her. He must weigh 220 pounds; Mrs. Dickensen can't be more than 110. An unfair fight. As Mrs. Dickenson reported, he 'had his way with her.'"

"Dear God!" Guests had been through unpleasant encounters, even here at the Resort, but this was the worst.

"It gets uglier. She claims he took money from her purse and her Bulgari watch."

"I assume you called Brad Marshall?"

"Immediately. But here's the funny part. The Russian claimed she'd invited him in on many occasions and he, knowing the rules, refused. And Marshall backed him! As far as he's concerned, Mrs. Dickerson made up the story to cover the fact she's lost her watch."

Matt felt his brain explode. Everything seemed part of a gigantic puzzle and he had no way of figuring it out. He could trust Beth—or could he? Pete seemed loyal—but how could he be sure? Nausea ate at him.

"The closed TV-security system we just installed has pictures of the Russian crossing the property and getting close to her suite about a quarter-to-twelve," Pete said.

"What did Marshall say to that?"

"'Case closed.' We needed every skilled worker if we're to finish the work on time and he wasn't going to let 'some hysterical bitch' in heat screw up the schedule. The only thing he promised was to keep the Russian away from Mrs. Dickerson from now on."

"I'll go see her," Matt said. "Let her know that at least one person believes her."

Pete glanced at him. "Make that two."

Chapter 59
Manhattan

"Sorry I'm late," Ron Falkman said. "New York traffic."

Seated around the Ritters' dining-room table were Rolfe, Momo, and two strangers, one a lanky, lean, gray-haired man, dressed as though he'd stepped out of a Saville Row ad, who rose when Ron entered.

"Kenneth, this is the infamous Ronald Falkman," Rolfe said. "Ron, this is the equally infamous Kenneth Palmer." The two men shook hands. "I've heard a lot about you over the years," the Englishman said.

"And probably read a lot more. The British government's Secret Intelligence Service, otherwise known as MI6, would never rely on the word of a reprobate like Ritter."

"*Touché*," Palmer said, laughing.

"*Shalom, Mah* Falkman." The booming voice belonged to the other stranger, who remained seated, though he too extended his hand in greeting. Luminous blue eyes stared from a square head atop an equally square body.

"*Shalom, Adoni.*"

"My name is Amnon," the square man said.

"Then you're not another Avi? That's refreshing. You're also a baseball fan?"

"Basketball. An ardent supporter of Maccabi Tel Aviv. As to who I am, I suspect Mr. Palmer knows." His English was perfect.

"I never had the pleasure of meeting this gentleman before today," Palmer said. "But this is Amnon Sapir, Mossad's number two and in line for the top spot—first amongst equals, I believe the Israelis call it—before too long, when Meir Dagan, the long-serving Director General, decides to retire. His being here speaks to the importance of this meeting."

"If you say so," the Israeli said, taking the cup of coffee Momo handed him. "Why don't we start?"

Falkman kissed a disturbingly wan Momo on the cheek and accepted an espresso as well. He sat down next to her. "Good idea."

"Quite a treasure-trove Beth Taylor provided us," Palmer said. "Don't you agree, Amnon?"

Amnon nodded. "The more we investigated, the more we became seriously concerned that something very dangerous may be happening with Kestrel Hotels, including the property in Jerusalem. Too many incidents in too many places. But we're still left with more questions than answers. Though the deaths worldwide of Blenheim GMs can't possibly be coincidental, what's the purpose behind them? If the pressures on Mr. Dirksen and Ms. Taylor are connected to the Summit, why attack GMs whose countries, such as ours, aren't represented? If we're only looking at a Blenheim power grab, replacing Mr. Ritter's people with their own, why the violence?"

"Here's what we do know," Palmer said. "Jimmy Lee and Tang Shen-ming certainly seem to be one and the same. That in itself isn't unusual. But what is of concern is that the letters and memos are from Te-Wu, our counterparts within the Chinese government, which almost certainly means he's one of their operating agents. Indeed, on three separate occasions in the past couple of weeks, Mr. Lee met with the Chinese government's assistant consul general in Los Angeles, a longtime, senior Te-Wu man."

"What do the documents say?" Momo asked, leaning forward.

Palmer and Sapir exchanged glances, as if to agree that the information could be shared with the Ritters and Falkman. "The documents Lee passed on originated from an organization calling itself 'Dark Winter' with headquarters in Moscow. They concern events that coincidentally date back to Blenheim's acquisition of Kestrel, events that coincide with dates when there was an unpleasant incident at or near a Kestrel Property."

Rolfe whistled. "Starting with St. Paul de Vence and Bali. Those bastards! No question, it's part of a plan."

"But what plan?" Falkman asked. "Could we be looking for the link that ties these random and disconnected events together or are we seeing hobgoblins in the dark?"

"You mean, could it be a coincidence?" the Israeli snorted. "We don't believe in them and suspect Mr. Palmer's organization doesn't either."

The Englishman nodded in agreement. "Of paramount concern to the counter intelligence unit for which I am responsible is the increasing spate of recent communications asking for progress reports pertaining to something called 'Snow Festival,' and whether the 'Xmas Present' has been received."

"Meaning what?"

"We think 'Snow Festival' most likely refers to the Summit, but we've no idea what 'Xmas Present' stands for. A present you wouldn't want to receive, I'd wager."

Amnon's expression was grave. "'Dark Winter' is apparently a Russian organization," he said, "but we don't know if it's government-sponsored or some sort of rogue group. We've had an influx of Russian immigrants into Israel over the past decade, many of them Mafia big shots with international ambitions. That's part of our concern."

"Whereas ours is the Summit." Palmer couldn't hide the anger he was feeling. "If there's something ugly in store, we need to know about it. In addition to my country's prime minister, seems like half of our government's planning to attend."

Silence. "You haven't mentioned the disc containing the download from Lee's computer," Falkman said at last.

Palmer shrugged. "Not much there. Mostly company matters. Lee's address book has a list of names unconnected to Blenheim, and we're looking into them, but without much hope of great revelations. Nonetheless, information is key and knowledge is power."

Rolfe sat back, electrified. Palmer used the same mantra his predecessor, Rolfe's "Uncle Mike," had drilled into him from an early age. There was something strangely comforting about hearing it now.

"Still, there's one thing slightly odd about the correspondence," Palmer continued, oblivious to Rolfe's reaction. "It's as if Lee was giving instructions to Blenheim, not taking instructions from them. Then there was the strange row between Lee and Weiss that Ms. Taylor reported."

Sapir stood, walked to the window, then turned to face Palmer. "Slightly odd? You British with your understatement. The whole thing stinks to high heaven. I tell you this is a conspiracy, and it's deadly serious. If there's a catastrophe at the Summit, it'll be our responsibility. And if there's a hint of an Israeli link, the whole world will blame us."

"Isn't that a bit jingoistic, Amnon?" Palmer asked. The two men glowered at each other.

"Gentlemen," Falkman said. "Let's think about this rationally." He glanced at notes he had taken since the start of the meeting, which he knew he would destroy before leaving the Ritters' apartment. "We know the Chinese government's involved, and quite possibly the Russian. We think the Summit's involved and that the Kestrel disasters are somehow connected. We have murders of Kestrel GMs, Dirksen's beating, the threat against his father and the kidnapping of Ms. Taylor's daughter. What else do we know?"

"A lot." Rolfe extracted some papers from a plastic file in front of him. "I promised Dirksen I'd dig into Dieter Weiss, so I contacted the best, Longstreet Investigations. I asked them to find out about Netski, too."

"What's their story?" Sapir asked before Palmer could.

"Dieter Weiss doesn't exist. His credit cards are registered to Blenheim. He has no driver's license, social security number, work permit, green card, citizenship papers. Longstreet checked his German records. Nothing. The man's a ghost. Except for the name on the passport the San Francisco housekeeper saw."

"We're following up on that lead," Palmer commented.

"And Netski?" Sapir queried.

"Exists. Grew up in Prague, parents both dead in a car crash when he was a teenager. No siblings. No other family of any kind in Prague or anywhere else. Impeccable high school record, honors graduate in economics at Charles University in Prague, great references for a variety of companies he worked for after graduation. No credit problems. Squeaky clean."

"Nothing amiss there," Falkman concluded.

"Longstreet thinks it's too clean. There's no record of a parking ticket anywhere in the world. He's never owned any property.

He must be in perfect health since there are no medical or dental records. Shit, the man's forty-five and he's never dated anyone, let alone been married. There's never even been a photo of him published before he came to the U.S."

"Immigration status?" Sapir asked.

"The man has a green card—shortest writeup Longstreet's ever seen. The FBI checked the box as okay. Processed in less than a month with the help of a senior congressman from New York. No interview. A cakewalk. Frankly, I suspect someone got paid off. Added to this is the fact that the man speaks Russian but didn't understand a word of Czech. He also had a well-clad lady in his New York suite, so we know he's straight. If we could find out who she is, then perhaps . . ."

"So it's a cover," Palmer sighed. "Netski's another person whose real identity we don't know."

"As I said, it stinks. So let's be adults and acknowledge it," Sapir's voice rose. It sounds like those guys have heavy-duty influence, access, plenty of money for bribes. Add blackmail and violence and you have the Russian Mafia's modus operandi. I'll have our people look into Netski. Thanks to the influx from the ex-Soviet Union we now have wonderful assets in that part of the world. Rolfe, can you see if your friends in the hotels can find out any more about Netski's lady."

Falkman smiled knowingly as Rolfe responded. "I already have." He tossed a disc onto the table. "This is a copy of the security tapes from the night that Netski was in the Audley down the street." He threw a second disc to join the first. "This one's from the London property a few weeks earlier. Other than Netski, you'll see one common face in the elevators, in the corridors and at the entrance to Netski's suite. In both cases the tall, good-looking, slim, very expensively dressed blonde has the key to the suite and looks like she's visited before. This lady is no call girl."

Sapir grabbed the discs and grunted at Palmer, "I'll have copies made for you. In the meantime, I'll see what we can find out about the mysterious blonde." He finished his coffee, stood up and stretched. "I'm hungry. Let's have lunch."

*

"If the two of you are so concerned, why haven't you brought up the matter formally with the American authorities?" Momo asked. She had insisted on clearing the lunch dishes herself and now sat, flushed and slightly winded, at the head of the table.

"Actually, we did," Palmer said. We contacted the FBI and the Secret Service."

"Who brushed you off," Rolfe guessed.

"Right. The FBI told us we were inventing plots—said that ever since Kim Philby we've been paranoid. The Secret Service simply treated us like village idiots. Insulting, really, but it's what we've come to expect from our special partnership."

Sapir laughed. "That's nothing. They told us to mind our own business as we had 'no skin in the game,' given we weren't involved in the Summit. The head of the CIA's station in Tel Aviv told me personally that when we could control Hamas and Hezbollah perhaps they'd have more time for us interfering in their own back yard."

"Ron, didn't you reach out to someone in the CIA?" Momo asked.

The lawyer nodded warily. "I can't tell you his name; however, when I explained the whole situation, he agreed there could be a pattern and he would look into it."

"And?" Momo pressed.

"And he told me officially the CIA views the various incidents as local and under the jurisdiction of the various authorities in the countries involved. Anything to do with the Summit is within the purview of the FBI and the Secret Service, and the CIA can have nothing to do with it."

"So that's that!" Momo's voice strained.

"Not quite," Falkman answered warily. "My friend told me off-the-record that there's serious and heavyweight pressure on the CIA to keep their noses out of the matter. He thinks there's something fishy going on and is going to keep digging."

"In other words, we're precisely nowhere," Rolfe said. "Matt's in over his head. Beth will do anything to save her daughter. In the meantime, those motherfuckers are walking all over them."

Momo gave him a weak smile. "Don't give up. You have the resources of both MI6's counter intelligence unit and the Mossad. You have Beth, who they think is spying for them, and Matt, who's only pretending to buckle under to their threats. As long as they have each other, they'll fight."

"Even at the risk of their lives?" Rolfe asked.

"They think their lives are forfeit anyway. What have they got to lose?" Momo snapped. "Anyway, we have a secret weapon."

Falkman gazed at her admiringly. "Which is what?"

"You, Rolfe and I. We have money, connections, reputation and many line-employees loyal to Rolfe who are still in place. They'll know everything that's going on at the hotels. Besides, you and Rolfe have seen every dirty trick in the book."

"And done most of them," Palmer said.

Rolfe shot the Englishman a withering glance, blithely ignored.

"You know, Kenneth, she's right," Sapir said solemnly. "It's time to go on the offense."

Chapter 60
San Jose Del Cabo, Mexico

The 143-foot navy-blue and cream Benetti Vision cruised serenely north on the Sea of Cortez, one-and-a-half miles out, parallel to the coastline, Cabot San Lucas long-since passed. Powerful stabilizers ensured the ship's stability, so the choppy waters went unnoticed by the four passengers seated on deck.

Dressed in white linen pants and a pale-blue linen shirt, sleeves neatly rolled halfway up his forearms, he was very much the quintessential rich man showing off his new boat to his similarly dressed friends. Anyone looking—and there were several like boats on the water—would assume the talk was of women, fast cars and business success, and that a stream of fine food and alcohol would be served by an obsequious crew.

But the crystal glasses in front of the men were filled with Pellegrino water, no food had been served, and no crew was within earshot. Theirs was a private conversation.

"You're convinced Dirksen and Taylor will present no problems until after the Summit's over?" Netski asked Jimmy Lee.

"Absolutely. Taylor's reporting every word Dirksen says. She really seems fond of the guy—they plan to live together after the Summit."

"Long life to them!" Battini said ironically. "Where have you put the daughter?"

"It's not important for you to know." Lee's disdain for the Italian seeped out of him.

"I'm curious, too," Netski glared at Lee. "Where is she?"

"In China. Her school ran an essay contest, the winner to get a lengthy study trip to the Great Wall and places well off the normal tourist track. Amazingly, Britney Kisel won. She's under constant supervision in a remote part of China. No one can communicate with her unless we say so."

Dieter Weiss scowled. "What a waste of time. Why not just snatch the kid, lock her in a basement, threaten her mother that she'll receive bits of her in the mail if they alert the police, maybe send an ear as a warning, and be done with it?"

"Dieter, Dieter," Netski sighed. "Learn some subtlety. Why run risks if you don't have to?"

"What was so subtle about cutting off Chalabi's head and dumping it in front of the Lima Kestrel?" Weiss countered.

"That wasn't supposed to be subtle. We wanted to send a crystal clear and very harsh message to Dirksen that he'd better behave—or else. Jimmy says he got the message."

"What about Ritter?" Battini asked.

"Olivia hasn't reported any phone contacts between him and Dirksen. Our technology people say there've been no received e-mails or calls on Dirksen's Blackberry. Luckily Ritter's wife is worse. He's spending most of his time at Sloan Kettering Cancer Clinic. I doubt if he's got anything else on his mind."

Netski refilled his water glass. "But two things worry me. I have a report that a private investigator named Longstreet's been checking up on me. Of course there was nothing for him to find, but still . . . More, our contacts inside the FBI and the Secret Service tell me that there've been security concerns voiced about Blenheim."

"By whom?" Lee asked.

"The British and the Israelis."

"I thought the Jerusalem incident was long over," Battini said quickly.

Weiss sneered. "You're the one who announced it was a closed case."

"I have assurances from the Israeli police. The property's not performing well, but there's nothing going on the authorities have any interest in."

"But someone's interested enough to make enquiries," Weiss pointed out.

"Stop acting like adolescents," Netski said sharply. "Fortunately, all of our security systems have been quadruple-checked and our money's bought us high-level people in both the FBI and the

Secret Service who are paid to ensure that any enquiries meet quick dead-ends."

Lee smiled. "In other words, mind your own business."

"Precisely. What's the status of our Summit preparations?"

Weiss stretched contentedly. "Everything's going smoothly at the Resort. Our people are in place and the equipment installation is proceeding on schedule without a hitch. Dirksen and his people have the day-to-day side under control."

"How's Brad Marshall performing?"

"I see him daily," Jimmy Lee answered. "He's earned the confidence of the security people and he's still the Secret Service's pet poodle. So he knows everything they're thinking and doing."

"He and Dirksen don't get along," Weiss growled. "Dirksen complained to me, and I told him that whatever Marshall says, goes."

"How did he take that?"

"It was a few days after poor Mr. Chalabi got his head mown off. He took it like a lamb."

The meeting was over. Netski stood. "A poodle and a lamb," he mused, "waiting for a circus."

Chapter 61
San Diego

Brad Marshall and Jimmy Lee reported that as an added security measure all the line staff would have different uniforms each day.

"You're nuts," Matt howled when they told him. "Think of the complications. First, we'd have to get them designed and ordered in time; second, we'd have to tailor, launder and store them; third, every day we'd have to move the previous uniforms offsite and replace them with the new ones. With hundreds of temporary staff coming in, it'll be logistical chaos."

"Probably," Marshall acknowledged. "But that's your problem; you're the operational grand poobah. The Secret Service thought it was a good idea and so did corporate."

"What's wrong with our system, bar-coded security passes for all employees with their information and allowed access points stored on them? We planned to change their color, shape and information size daily, so no one will know what they look like and thus won't be able to copy them."

"You're right of course." Jimmy Lee was, as always, imperturbable. "We'll have both systems. Better to be safe than sorry."

*

They lay on the sand, Beth's head resting on Matt's stomach while he unthinkingly played with her hair. Her half empty glass of chardonnay was balanced precariously on her own stomach; the base of his empty glass was buried in the sand.

"Thinking about how much you love me?" she asked.

"I always think about that, but sometimes it's a subtext. I wake up every morning with a hollow feeling in my gut and go to sleep at night feeling even worse. You remember Rolfe asked me to put yet more people on the staff? The last two showed up the day before yesterday."

"What positions?"

"This time the spooks sent us one night cleaner, two in housekeeping, one steward and one at the front desk. Their paperwork sailed through Brad Marshall almost too easily. Pete says the young woman at the desk's a star. Go figure!"

She laughed. "Between Weiss's people and Rolfe's, you're not a hotelier any more, you're a zookeeper."

"The San Diego Zoo has nothing on us," he acknowledged. "Between the installation of the equipment near the Conference Center; the Secret Service putting in God knows what—miles of fiber-optic cable constantly being installed; chefs showing up from all over the world to practice and develop even more complicated menus, which need specialist equipment we haven't got but must buy; renting two mobile army kitchens to handle the extra events being added; building yet more storage for the food and booze; the State Department's endless whining, nagging and requests; and, beyond that, having the devil's own job of making sure our regular guests are happy, I'm wearing down like a tractor tire. Besides, Marshall treats me like an old dishcloth and Jimmy Lee commandeered my conference room for an office without . . ."

She pushed herself to kiss his chin. "I'm scared for you."

He hugged her. "And I for you. Terrified. Great, isn't it? Protected by the Israelis, the British and Rolfe Ritter, and we're no safer than a plywood house in a hurricane."

They were quiet for a moment, holding each other tightly.

"Rolfe asked me to take pictures of Jimmy Lee," Beth said. "I've done it. Any idea of what that's about?"

"Not a clue. I've taken some, too, and of Brad Marshall plus his key goons . . . I mean lieutenants. I've instructions to take that scumbag Weiss's photo, but he hasn't showed up yet. I assume Rolfe has a purpose, but damned if I know what it is. What did Momo say about Britney?"

"Only that they're looking for her, pulled out all the stops, found nothing yet. Hardly reassuring if two of the world's most sophisticated intelligence agencies can't find one teenager. I asked Jimmy if I could talk to her. He gave me the Chinese equivalent of 'Go fuck yourself.'"

Her vulnerability made his heart contract. He could barely imagine the extent of her suffering—if in fact she was suffering at all. A swarm of summer butterflies of doubt danced inside his brain "Each day my hate for those shits grows; I want to kill them."

"No," she said. "Love me."

He eased her body upwards and found her mouth with his. Her body relaxed, and he could feel her urgency. "Is the beach deserted?" she asked.

"Yes. Why?"

"It's time for me to do my job."

But their passion, when spent, brought them little solace.

Chapter 62
London

Kenneth Palmer was looking forward to the end of the work day, when he could perform his evening ritual of feeding the ducks from his favorite bench along the Birdcage Walk of the side of the lake in St. James Park.

The phone rang. He answered. "Yes, Rolfe."

"Off to feed the ducks? You're my Uncle Mike's successor. He'd insist."

"Actually," Palmer said, "I've come to enjoy it. The beastly birds are a grateful bunch, and I can see the houses of Parliament, the Cabinet War Rooms, and Buckingham Palace. Even that bloody Ferris wheel they erected for the Millennium celebrations, London Eye they call it; I call it London's Black Eye."

Rolfe chuckled. "I'll bet you sit on the same damn bench."

"Spot on the impression made by the Great Man's Arse. What can I do for you?"

"Just checking in for an update. Any news on Beth's daughter?"

"Nothing you should tell Beth. We had someone interview her nonbirth mother, Mrs. Kisel, who says Britney's on a trip to China. Won some sort of essay contest to get there. Gets regular post-cards."

"China? A contest? Sure. Jesus, they have her where we can't touch her. The relationship between the Russians and the Chinese seems increasingly evident."

"That appears to be the case. But we have some connections close to the top in Beijing, and we may be able to find out something, although so far there's a cone of silence."

"Keep trying," Rolfe urged. "The mother's desperate!"

"Of course. You're a strange man, Rolfe. Sometimes, you're the embodiment of Machiavelli and sometimes you're so linear, I could scream. Surely you understand that if Britney was in our hands, then there's no reason for Taylor and Dirksen to hang around. I bet they'd both be so far away from Southern California that we'd never find them. From our selfish perspective, if they were gone, we'd lose our eyes and ears inside Blenheim. Those two are the best chance we've got."

"You're a cold bastard, aren't you? Not like my Godfather," Rolfe gasped.

"Don't be so naïve. Mike just sugar-coated things better. That man had nothing but ice in his veins. It comes with the territory." Palmer kept his voice calm. "By the way, Sapir and I are sending some accounting types to you and Mr. Falkman. We need your hotel expertise."

"They'll get it. But why?"

"We want to throw Blenheim off balance a little. Stir the pot, so to speak, and see what floats to the surface."

"I have an idea along the same lines," Rolfe said, thinking that Uncle Mike chose the right man in Palmer. "Want to hear it?"

"Why naturally, dear boy. Pray tell."

The ducks would have to wait.

Chapter 63
Los Angeles

Kestrel Hotels and Resorts's diminutive general counsel, the white-haired, skinny-lipped Victor Hawken, cowered in the far corner of Dimitri Netski's office, ducking invectives in Russian and English as if they were missiles. The papers he had put in front of Netski had been hurled at his face and now lay strewn at his feet.

"You fucking idiot. You stupid fucking idiot!" Netski's finger pointed ominously at a spot between the lawyer's eyes. "I pay you a fortune to take care of problems, and you bring me this bullshit?" The fingers moved down to the papers. "Fuck off and fix it. Otherwise . . ."

Hawken knew the 'otherwise' did not mean a simple letter of resignation and a severance package. "Er, er . . . " he stammered.

"Out with it, you moron."

The lawyer took a deep breath. "Last week I received a letter from lawyers representing the owner of the Kestrel Cleveland, claiming Blenheim was not only negligent in the way we managed the hotel for his client, but that we had plotted to defraud him of his profits and were systematically stealing from the operation. They sent us a formal notice of default and then filed a complaint with the Ohio court."

Netski stared at him wordlessly.

"They demanded a deposition from you, Fabrizio Battini and Dieter Weiss, and will issue subpoenas to ensure compliance," Hawken hurried on, hoping to ward off physical violence. "On Monday, Ernst and Young will be undertaking a forensic audit of the hotel accounts, contracts and agreements, as well all of the corporate charges we paid ourselves from the hotel's bank accounts. Ernst and Young is amongst the most powerful auditing firms in America. If we attempt to delay or interfere with the audit, the hotel's owners will file with the court for access under their contract."

"What the fuck's a forensic audit?" Netski's voice grew surprisingly calm.

Hawken preened. For this brief moment he was on solid ground. "The owner brings in specialist auditors trained to look for every inconsistency, every detail that could lead them to a trail of who did what to whom and when. If they find even a penny not spent or allocated correctly, they'll use it to fuel a law suit like this one."

"In other words, they're accountant proctologists."

"And they dig deep, without an anesthetic. They're expensive and thorough. They can tie Blenheim's accounting and legal team into knots for years."

"Will they find anything?" Netski's anger had cooled. Hawken could virtually see his brain work.

"It's hard to tell. Who knows what mistakes some accounting clerk might have made. My guess is the real risk is in the way we charge the hotels for head office costs such as corporate marketing, reservations, insurance, internal audit, accounting, even the share of this office's rent and overhead which we allocate back to the departments—anything we do centrally or regionally that's charged back to the hotels. I'm sure we have set formulas, but anyone can argue with formulas."

Netski thought for a long moment. "Okay. Give me the name and address of the owner, and I'll deal with him."

It was the moment Hawken dreaded. "It's not that easy. The owner's Franklin National Insurance Company. Through Ritter, EUF sold the Cleveland Kestrel to them in '05. They're a giant corporation that operates by consensus. There's no person with whom to make a deal or threaten, blackmail and bribe," the general counsel thought. "And . . ." he hesitated, "there are others."

"Others?"

"Different letters, same import, from Detroit, Seattle, Dallas, Jacksonville, St. Louis, Montreal, Edinburgh, Lyons, Seville, Hamburg, Pusan, Perth, and, just yesterday, Foz Do Iguacu."

Netski leaned his elbows on his desk and covered his face with his hands. "Foz Do . . . ?"

"Iguacu. In Southern Brazil. Great waterfalls."

"I hope you drown in them." Netski began to pace. A dormant volcano, Hawken thought. "My God! I'll be tied up in depositions forever."

"And you'll be tied up in courtrooms all over the world, with all the publicity to match. Lord only knows how Battini and Weiss will hold up," the lawyer replied, unable to hide a hint of satisfaction for this bully's discomfort.

"Buy them off. One at a time."

"I wish we could. I spoke to the Cleveland, Dallas and St. Louis people. They're so pissed they want to take this to court." Hawken was beginning to enjoy himself. "It gets worse. Today we received a class action suit filed in federal court from the same pitbull litigators who won giant settlements from the tobacco companies. As mean and tough a bunch as you're likely to find. They represent the owners of some of the properties we manage for others, and claim they have evidence of fraud and systematic pillaging of their rightful funds. These guys never give up if they smell blood. It's clear they think they have us by the balls. They've also filed a RICO claim."

"What the hell's that?"

"The Racketeer Influenced and Corrupt Organizations Act"

"And that gobbledygook means?"

"Racketeering charges."

Netski gripped the side of his desk for support. "Racketeering? If anything like that was going on inside this company, I'd know about it, and whoever was involved would be dealt with. There's not a crook within fifty miles of us. Who the fuck are these bastards kidding? We're about to host the Summit. It's the most important thing that's going on in this company. If the press gets hold of this . . ."

"They already have," Hawken whispered. "*The New York Times, Los Angeles Times, Washington Post, Wall Street Journal* and *Financial Times* have already called, wanting our reaction to the law suits and the press conference held this afternoon in the lawyers' office."

"Press conference? What did those bloodsucking lawyers say?"

"That we were blatant criminals engaged in a global conspiracy to rape, loot, plunder and pillage the owners, many of whom are pensions funds-entrusted with the many billions of assets hard-earned by construction workers, teachers, garbage men, nurses, truckers—the entire working class—all of whom depended on these investments for their retirement. They said it was a disgrace that the government not only let Blenheim go unchecked but, worse, condoned it by selecting the Audley San Diego Cliffs as the host hotel for the Summit. They called on our State Department to change the venue at once."

"What was State's response?" Netski's voice was so low Hawken had to strain to hear it.

"That they'd review the whole situation and give us a chance to defend ourselves. You know perfectly well they couldn't possibly change venues now without incredible problems and embarrassment. There's too little time."

Again, Netski was silent for a long time. "Is that all?" he said at last.

"Isn't that enough?"

Netski glared. "Yes."

The Blenheim CEO slumped back into his chair looking, Hawken thought, like a senator caught in bed with a page. "Thank you, Mr. Hawken," he said, in a frigid voice the lawyer had never heard before. "You're excused."

*

Fifteen minutes later, his course of action planned, Dimitri Netski picked up his phone and dialed a fourteen-digit number. It was answered at once.

Netski spoke. "Yuri?"

Chapter 64
Washington, D.C.

The sun had long set over The State Department's offices at 2201 C Street in the nation's capital, when the phone was wearily answered by the lone remaining employee on the east wing of the third floor.

"Matheson speaking."

"It's Matt Dirksen, Tim. What the hell's going on?"

"Christ, your company doesn't make my life easy, do they?"

"All hell's broken loose on the property since the press release crossed the wire. Rumors are flying around with the speed of summer lightning, and the foreign staff we've imported for the Summit are already packing their bags to go home."

"Well it ain't all peaches and cream for me either," Matheson grumbled. "That lawsuit created one hell of a shit storm, and all of a sudden I'm a pariah. One day, everyone else is taking credit for the decision to use your property for the Summit; the next, I'm the Lone Ranger bullying the choice through for my own advantage, whatever that is."

"Tim, for God's sake, be straight with me. Have we lost the Summit or not?"

"I wish I knew, I really do. I'm stuck here writing two reports for my masters. The first one is why we recommended your Resort in the first place. That's easy, I have the original telephone book-sized approval memorandum and due diligence report to draw on. The second is the problem; our options for moving the fucking thing to another venue."

Dirksen's disappointment was obvious "Shit, Tim, you and I both know that would be a disaster for everyone."

"I know, I know," Matheson answered, trying unsuccessfully to stop the Resort's general manager in full flow.

"This place has been wired and rewired for security and communications reasons so often it looks like an Italian spaghetti banquet. Everything is on track, all the requests, event locations, menus, rooming lists . . . Christ, even the new equipment is being tested. If you moved the Summit to another venue, you'd have a half-cocked, Mickey Mouse event that would make the United States look like buffoons. I can't even imagine the cost implications. My guess is the new place would have you over a barrel and financially screw the shit out of you. On top of everything, you have a binding contract with Kestrel and I can't imagine they'd just slink off into the fucking night!"

"Calm down, Matt. No one's made any decisions yet. All I said is I'm writing a report on what our options are. I'll conclude that moving the Summit to another venue is an undesirable conclusion."

"Which means?"

"It's a political decision, not a practical one. Logically, it's a no-brainer. Whatever happens, stick with your Resort. But this is D.C. If things were logical, men would be riding the bikes without the crossbars!"

Chapter 65
New York

LUXURY HOTEL COMPANY SETTLES CLASS ACTION SUIT

"In a dramatic midday announcement at the offices of Wilbourne, Clark, Fenster and Abernathy, attorney Harold Abernathy announced that multiple owners of the hotels managed and branded by Kestrel Hotels and Resorts have agreed to settle the class action and other law suits against Blenheim Ltd., Kestrel's parent company, filed over the past two weeks in various states and countries in their relevant courts of law.

"The class action suit itself was only filed in federal court this past Thursday. When asked about the speed of the settlement and its contents, Mr. Abernathy commented, "Kestrel Hotels and Resorts provided our clients with adequate explanations to our queries. The balance of this matter remains confidential.

"Informed sources report that the financial consideration for the settlement was in excess of $1.5 billion and the amount was paid in full at the time of signature of the settlement agreement. If true, the amount represents the largest settlement of any of the owner/operator litigations that have plagued the lodging industry since 2003 . . ."

Rolfe Ritter, propped up next to Momo on their king-sized bed, passed her the business section of *The Times*.

"I'd have liked to see it played out in court," she said when she'd finished reading. "Watched those bastards publicly squirm."

"No you wouldn't," Rolfe said. "I'd have been sucked into it. It's not as if I was a vestal virgin when I owned the company. Forgotten so soon?"

"Forgotten? I still remember you pushing me away when you were so frightened and didn't want me hurt. You're right. I don't want to relive it." She brought his hand to her lips and kissed it. "What it shows is that the Kestrel and Audley owners wish you were still running the company. They'd never have sued if you were in charge."

"I'd never have screwed them the way Blenheim has," he acknowledged. "Or at least I'd have done it more subtly. And now they're my allies."

Her laughter was interrupted by the ringing or their phone. Rolfe answered. "Hello, Ron. Wait a second while I put this on speaker. Momo's right next to me."

"I have Amnon and Kenneth on the line," the lawyer said.

"When I told you to go ahead with your plan, I didn't realize you had this in mind," Palmer growled.

"I take responsibility," Falkman interrupted. "I told Rolfe if he was going to pull a stunt like this, he'd better make it for big stakes, or Blenheim would brush it off like a fly."

Palmer continued, "Well, they didn't brush it off, but they surely settled quickly. It proves they've got something serious to hide. The financial ramifications of losing the Summit are peanuts compared to this giant settlement. No self-respecting business would have acted so precipitously to shut off a law suit. They're terrified of things coming out—but what things? Why? We checked with Lloyd's of London. They're not covered for this, so the money came straight from Blenheim's pocket. We'll see what happens when we start phase two."

Amnon's gruff voice boomed through the speaker, "Before you get too self-congratulatory, you have, I presume, considered the ramifications."

"What do you mean?" Falkman asked.

"Rolfe has just cost Blenheim $1.5 billion to settle a problem he personally made for them. Do you really think they won't find out he was behind it and won't want revenge?"

"Those owners are my friends," Rolfe said quickly. "They promised confidentiality and I trust them."

"Don't be a putz. Bribes, threats, blackmail, murder. These guys will use anything, do anything, to find out who fucked them. And they will, sooner or later."

Palmer cleared his throat. "Amnon has a point. Perhaps you did overreach a wee bit."

"You'll need protection; best get you and Momo out of town," Amnon said. "Either Kenneth or I can get you to a safehouse."

Rolfe quickly glanced at Momo, saw her grimace and shrugged. "Not possible."

"Essential."

"I'm still having chemo at Sloane Kettering," Momo said quietly. "We can't leave the city."

Neither intelligence officer was stupid enough to suggest Rolfe go alone.

"That means we'll have to give you twenty-four-hour protection," Palmer said matter-of-factly, as though guarding Rolfe were routine. "In the meantime you two had better be very careful."

Momo could see her husband shudder. She knew he was re-living haunted memories. Once again, their lives were in danger.

Chapter 66
Santa Monica

The guests attending Pfizer's latest product launch had checked out, and the weekend crowd was checking into immaculately made-up rooms, each garnished with the Kestrel Santa Monica's specially bred Cambria-Nojo orchid.

Dressed in an Armani shoulderless black dress to attend the hotel's Friday Night Welcome cocktail party, Beth knocked on Jimmy Lee's office door.

"Come in."

The windows on two walls were open and a gentle breeze swayed the tiny leaves of Lee's Bonsai plant. The office, as always, looked unoccupied, even though its inhabitant was seated behind his desk.

"Yes?" Lee spat the word out in his 'why are you wasting my time' voice.

Beth sat without being asked. "Welcome back from San Diego," she said, then hurried on. "I've stumbled on something unusual. I thought you should know and tell me what to do."

He snapped upright. "About the Summit?"

"No."

He relaxed. "Go on."

"When I was checking our quarterly profit and loss accounts and balance sheet, I came across some strange entries and dug into the backup."

Lee made an obvious effort to concentrate. "And?"

"The numbers on the checks were out of sequence. In fact, they had no relationship to the rest of that month's checks whatsoever."

"Checks get out of order. What's the point?"

"When I asked the accountants, they told me they hadn't written the checks—indeed, hadn't even received blank checks with those numbers." She took a deep breath. "The checks were made out to suppliers not on our authorized list and we have no record of receipt of the goods ordered."

She had Lee's full attention. Perfect! "We tried to call the suppliers. Even sent people to the addresses on the invoices. There was nothing there. No offices, warehouses, nothing. They simply don't exist. Even their tax IDs are fake."

"Fraud," Lee whispered. "Someone's stealing. Good work, Taylor. How long was it going on before you caught it?"

"We've traced it back five months. It might have been longer."

"How much have we lost?"

"Four-hundred thousand per month."

"That's at least two million!" Lee's black eyes seemed to penetrate Beth's soul. "How come you didn't catch it before?"

"The invoices were charged, capitalized, to the new building projects. If they'd been in the P and L accounts, I'd have seen them immediately. But corporate's taken preparation of the balance sheets away from the individual hotels. That's how come I only see the quarterlies."

Lee bore in on her. "Do your job. There must be corporate procedures for fraud. Follow them. This is a criminal offense. The police must be notified."

"I'm not so sure you want the police," Beth said cautiously. "Jimmy, the thing is we did follow procedure. We worked with corporate accounting and found, buried in a wrong file, a corporate officer's authorization for those suppliers."

Lee gasped. "Who signed? Which officer?"

"I don't want to tell you. You should know that we recovered the checks used to pay the fake suppliers. Although the name is different from the authorization form, our investigators brought in a handwriting expert—the same person signed both, the same corporate officer. Also, there were similar authorizations with identical signatures for similar supplies for five of our other California properties."

His skin was waxen as an artificial peach and his breathing was labored. "I want to know now! Who is it?"

"I need you to protect me from retribution. Corporate's powerful. I'm scared."

"Damn it!" Lee shouted. "You stupid woman, I have all the sway needed to protect you from corporate. You won't be hurt. Who?"

Beth looked at him with innocent eyes. "Dieter Weiss."

Chapter 67
San Diego

By mid-afternoon, Matt was exhausted and the most unpleasant part of his day lay ahead: A *New York Times* interview under the working heading "The Best Hotel Manager in North America," something Rolfe had set up on the grounds that the more Matt seemed indispensable in the public's eyes, the safer he would be from Blenheim. With a twinge of satisfaction, he slumped into his tan Christian Liaigre leather sofa, put his feet on the coffee table and closed his eyes, hoping for at least a half hour's peace.

Peace was unavailable. He saw his father's ashen face, heard the desolation in his voice, wondered if the old man would give up and die. Guilt gnawed at him like a rat. I'll go to him right after the Summit, he thought. Blenheim will have no hold on him after that. But he knew in his gut that Blenheim would never let him go free. At the least, they'd keep him from talking by retaining their hold on his father. At worst . . .

Visions of Beth filled his mind. Frantic Beth, loving Beth, funny Beth, Beth in the throes of ecstasy, Beth at the brink of despair. He guessed she had as much chance of getting her daughter back as he did protecting his father. And Britney (the mythical Britney, perhaps?) made it impossible for them to act, to be together, to escape. But, like him, she was powerless against Blenheim. The one thing that kept him going was Rolfe's optimism. He and Beth had allies, but the Ritters brought him small comfort. He didn't know what Blenheim was planning, only that it involved the Summit—every indication pointed that way. Something catastrophic was about to happen, he was sure. And when it erupted, what would be the consequences?

*

Leona Grann, *The Times* reporter, had a voice like a cheese grater and an attitude to match. "Best in North America?" she seemed to say. Prove it. She wanted to know who stayed at the Resort, how often, how much did they pay, who was getting what suites for the Summit, wasn't he too young for such an important job? Then, suddenly, "What's it like working for Blenheim instead of Rolfe Ritter?"

"Very different," Matt blurted, knowing instantly that this quote was the one she'd print, taken out of context. For an instant he thought of elaborating: how Jimmy Lee had been badgering him all day about trivial matters when important ones had yet to be settled; how corporate accounting had asked him questions about invoices for items he knew nothing of; how Brad Marshall had insisted he fire two excellent chefs just because "It's a security matter and I say so;" how Gianni Mantagazzi, one of the Resort's most valued regulars, threatened to never come back because of construction noise and poor service from newcomers . . . "Eastern Europeans," he spat out derisorily to the staff.

Matt recalled how Mantagazzi elaborated, "New showerhead don't work. Normally someone come, five, six minute. Today one hour, then this . . . person arrive. Uniform filthy, wearing old sneaker, tattoo on arm and neck. Fix shower, then hold out hand for tip. I no give him one. He threaten me. 'I won't forget you,' he say."

"What was his name?" Matt asked, appalled. It would have been embroidered into his uniform above his right shirt pocket."

"I look. No tag, no name." To Mantagazzi this seemed the most heinous crime of all.

Matt had promised reform and sent the Italian away with a precious bottle of 1947 port to sample. He called in Keith McGregor to complain.

"What did you expect?" the chief engineer said. "You're the man who kept the Resort open while we prepared for the Summit. Every time we test a new system or installation, something switches off and leads to chaos. Don't bitch at me. It's a damn miracle that anyone got to that puffed-up Italian and fixed his shower at all." His nerves are as shot as mine, Matt remembered thinking.

"Do you have anything to add?" Leona Grann asked, snapping him out of his reverie.

"Only that you're right: I'm too young to have fully earned a title as 'Best' anything. But the Resort is the best in North America, and I've done my damndest to keep it that way, whether working for Mr. Ritter or Blenheim. Would you like to stay for dinner, Ms. Grann? It's early, but I'm sure the chef can whip up something, or perhaps you might like to taste one or two of our unique specialties and, of course, the incredible matching wines we're offering at the Summit are simply too good not to sample. Good color for your story, perhaps?"

*

At nine that night, someone rapped on his door. A cleaning man whose name, Murray, adorned his uniform, stood respectfully outside. "You weren't expecting me?" he asked.

"I was expecting someone," Matt answered, taken somewhat off guard. "Who sent you?"

"Avi."

"Avi who?"

"Avi the baseball fan."

The recognition password sequence was complete. "Let's go."

They moved quickly to the door of Brad Marshall's office. Matt gently knocked. When he got no response, he used a plastic, master keycard to let them in.

The meek night cleaner was galvanized. A pencil beam emitted from a tiny torch as he swept the office. He put on rubber gloves. "Don't move. Don't touch a thing."

The man held the torch in his mouth while he dug into his overalls pocket and brought out a black piece of equipment with a small screen and overlaid it on the alarm panel next to the door. It lit up. Numbers filled-in nine discrete boxes. The machine beeped.

"All clear," the agent announced, delving into his pocket again, extracting a piece of equipment no bigger than a cell phone, which he waved over the phones, cabinets, TV, computer and desk. "Good. No security devices. Careless, I must say."

He fixed electronic devices no bigger than toothpicks to the underside of the desk chair, the back of the TV, the bottom of the credenza, and the tiny gap between carpet and wall.

"What about the phone?" Matt whispered.

"Too obvious."

Again the agent activated the device with the screen. It lit up, numbers filling the boxes. Once more the machine beeped.

"All set." He opened the office door and peered out. "All clear."

Matt, stumbling in the darkness, followed him into the corridor, but by the time he got there, the night cleaner had disappeared.

Chapter 68
New York

"I became a Beatles fan as a teenager, never stopped since, and always get nostalgic coming to this place," Rick Caverly said, as he waved his arms expansively over Strawberry Fields in Central Park.

"Never cared for them myself. I'm a generation too old, I suppose," Falkman answered, straining to see Rolfe Ritter's penthouse apartment across the park from the east, facing adjacent to the mosaic monument with the word "Imagine" at its center. The two men sat at the bench where they'd arranged to meet, ostensibly old friends casually sharing the warmth of the mid-afternoon sun.

"Anything new for me?" Caverly asked.

Falkman brought him up-to-date and handed him copies of the discs that Rolfe had given to Amnon Sapir. "What have you learned?"

"Brad Marshall had quite a reputation within the Company. Not all good, but certainly an experienced Russian hand. I came across him once or twice. Hard nut, very much a loner. No ideology whatsoever. I always had the feeling he was out for himself. I've used whatever connections I still have with the old guard in Russia to quietly and unofficially dig around. There's a code amongst us Cold War old-timers, we look out for each other. If there's anything being planned by the Russian government, or even a rogue group within the FSB, there's not a whisper around. My guess is this is a Mafia organization who have a scam going. My Russian buddies are going to keep their ears open for any chatter."

"That's it?" Falkman queried.

"Something else. Odd perhaps. You remember you told me about the mysterious four Pakistanis from the Bali Resort incident?'

"Sure, the late Sammi Chalabi briefed Dirksen on them," the lawyer responded.

"The section head in Islamabad is a pal of mine. We grew up in the organization together. Apparently there's been an increasing amount of chatter in Pakistan lately that has been picked up on our voice- and word-activated tracking satellites. The current feeling is that Al Qaeda are planning an attack at the Summit. It's no more than a guess, but . . ."

"My God, are all these things connected?"

"Seems unlikely to me. Russian hoods, Chinese officials, Al Qaeda? Can't see it personally other than in a Hollywood movie. However, you never know, stranger things happen and this Summit has a giant bull's-eye splashed across it as a terrorist target. Probably too inviting to ignore. You'd think the whole world would figure out that security would be tighter than a tick's ass and no one would try anything; but many of these fanatics are such lunatics that I wouldn't put anything past them."

"So what now? Sit back and wait?" Falkman muttered, his frustration evident.

"Not my style, you know that all too well from our past activities," Caverly laughed, remembering their adventures together in Libya, Sudan and Columbia, when the canny lawyer had assisted the CIA through his business connections and his political access. "No, I'm convinced something bad is brewing. Lord knows what, but I'm going to keep digging around until my masters fire my weary old ass. Something may come up. I sure hope so before it is too late."

Chapter 69
San Diego / Los Angeles

Dieter Weiss spent a glorious evening. Victor Fusilli, GM of the Kestrel Hotel in San Diego (the large, dominant meetings hotel set on a prominent perch in downtown San Diego), treated him like the Blenheim royalty he was, arranging for a snack of knockwurst, bratwurst, black bread, rough mustard and white beer to be delivered to his suite upon arrival, followed by one long-limbed, Latina lady and an equally long-limbed, light-skinned mulatto lady. Both ladies gave a new meaning to the term "room service."

They pleasured each other as Weiss watched, making sure that no orifice was neglected, then turned their attention to him, massaging his genitals and nipples with scented oils and spanking him with increasing ferocity, thus bringing him to the edge of climax but not beyond for nearly an hour until at last he could stand it no more and they allowed him release.

The Kestrel, of course, would be picking up the tab, but his companions were so adept that he tipped them each $100 of his own money, generosity he regretted only after they had left the room. He slept well, awoke refreshed, breakfasted on a smoked salmon and caviar omelet and strawberries with crème fraiche, and set out for the Audley San Diego Cliffs. Matt Dirksen had been acting too independently for some days now and needed a little discipline.

*

"You're a difficult man to find," Dimitri Netski said when he reached Weiss's cell phone. His voice was pleasant, soothing. "Took the night off, did you?"

"Not at all. I wanted check on our properties in San Diego. The Kestrel last night, the Audley later this morning."

"How gratifying. Always on the job. But something's come up. Forget the Audley. Return to L.A. Come to my office as soon as you get here. Drive carefully, though. The traffic can be brutal."

Unease soured the crème fraiche in Weiss's stomach. His boss could be even more ominously pleasant than when he was grim. "Can you tell me what the 'something' is?"

There was no reply. Netski had hung up.

*

Weiss drove his Mercedes into his designated parking space and started for the elevator. Two huge men, heads shaved and dressed in black pants and tee-shirts, appeared in front of him. Weiss recognized them as Netski's body guards.

"The boss wants to see you," the younger man with the small ears growled.

"I know. I'm on my way up now."

"Not in his office. Come with us." He was led into a small storage room located off the garage. "Sit."

A single, rust-colored, metal chair was placed in the midst of file boxes stacked from floor to ceiling. An electric light bulb shone above it. Weiss felt sweat drip down his face and arms. He fought the urge to urinate.

The door eventually opened. Netski entered carrying a thick file. Weiss tried to stand. Unseen hands on his shoulders rendered him immobile. Netski slapped his face with on open hand—once, twice, a third time. His nose and mouth began to bleed. The German looked at his tormentor. "What have I done? Tell me."

Fury flashed from Netski's eyes. His face contorted. "Do I have to tell you? Do I look that stupid?" He drew back his fist but did not strike. "Why did you steal from me?"

"Steal what? What are you talking about."

Netski's fist drove deep into the German's stomach. His bodyguards prevented the chair from toppling.

"Two million from Santa Monica alone! What's the matter? I don't pay you enough? You don't even pay for your whores, what do you need the money for? Don't you trust me?"

Weiss vomited. Netski looked at his subordinate with disgust. "Tell me who your accomplices are."

"Accomplices? I don't understand."

The slap of Netski's hand across the German's face reverberated throughout the dank room.

Tears mingled with the sweat on Weiss's cheeks. "As God is my judge, I've never stolen a penny from you."

"God's not your judge. I am. Liar!" Netski struck Weiss again. This time the chair toppled. Weiss lay in a fetal position on the concrete floor, gasping. Netski threw the files at him.

"There's your proof. Your handwriting condemns you."

Netski nodded to the taller of the bodyguards. The man produced a Glock 10mm pistol from this belt and slowly, with pleasure, screwed in a dark-grey silencer.

Weiss scrambled for the papers surrounding him, scanning one and then another. "It's not my handwriting! For God's sake, look here. Look here!"

Another nod. The bodyguard aimed the Glock at Weiss's forehead with one hand, and steadied it with the other.

The silencer was effective. To anyone who might have heard the shot, it would have sounded at most like a distant backfire.

Netski stepped over the German's body, careful not to soil his shoes with blood or brains.

Chapter 70
New York

"How do you like your new phone?" Kenneth Palmer asked from London.

Rolfe chuckled, "It's fine."

"Don't let him fool you," Momo interjected. "It's his favorite new toy. A secure line with a scrambler and a device that tells you if anyone's listening in? He's as happy as a pig in mud. You know how much he wanted to be like his father. At last he believes he's playing with the big boys."

Rolfe's late father, Wim Den Ritter, known as The Kestrel, was still a legend at MI6 and the Dutch Counter Terrorism Agency.

"I wonder if any of the guests or the staff at the Kestrels knows where the name originated," Palmer mused.

"None, I hope. If they do, your security stinks." Amnon Sapir's impatience resonated through the speakerphone in the Ritters' apartment. "Have we finished with the pleasantries? Can we get down to business."

"Hello, Amnon. Falkman speaking." Ron paced the living room. "It's good to hear you're your usual jovial and pleasant self this morning—or should I say this afternoon? I assume you're in Tel Aviv."

"Assumptions are bad in this business. Kenneth, do you want to start?"

Palmer's tone was sober, dark. "I talked to a friend of mine in the *Sûreté*. He took a look at Bertrand Le Roi's file. The file had been sealed tight after Le Roi's death on the orders of a 'very powerful person' in the French Ministry of Defense. My friend wouldn't give me his name, said it was too dangerous for him. But he told me the person was 'far less than a thousand kilometers' from the president's office."

"Would he let you look at the file?"

"Not a chance in hell. He didn't look at it himself."

"So that gets us nowhere," Rolfe said. "What else?

"I had our people in Indonesia investigate those fires in the Bali resorts. The Indonesian police blamed them on local terrorists, and since there've been no more incidents for months, they've dropped the investigation."

"Yeah. There were only some thirty deaths at Nusa Dua Cliffs and fifty or so at the Regent," Sapir scoffed. "Someone got to them the same way they got to the damned French. I assume the mysterious Pakistanis never surfaced, if they were ever looked for in the first place?"

"Did you do any better in Peru?" Palmer asked, offended by Amnon's tone.

"About Chalabi? Another Shining Path attack. 'A most regrettable incident.' Case closed."

Rolfe's temper flared. "'Case closed, case goddamned closed.' In every other instance, too, I'll bet you. Jesus, the cover-ups are worldwide, and your renowned services are hamstrung."

Silence from both agents, acknowledged his accusation.

"I've got something," Falkman said. "About Blenheim. They bought National Security Associates last year, a company based in Bethesda, Maryland. Provides guards for corporate executives, VIPs, second-tier energy producers, industrial plants and, yes, hotels. Guess who one of the owners was."

More silence.

"Ta-da! Brad Marshall. And guess where he was before he started National. The CIA! And not as an analyst, but a field operative. Venue? Eastern Europe. My friend in the CIA told me that Marshall didn't resign but was pushed out because of a tendency to be in business for himself. "

"Another road pointing east," Amnon said. "Very promising."

"Amnon, are you hearing anything in your neck of the woods about Al Qaeda plans for the Summit?" Falkman enquired.

"Why do you ask?"

"Just a feeling," Falkman responded enigmatically.

"My musical ear just told me that Mr. Falkman's CIA man has heard something," Palmer said.

The Israeli snorted, "I haven't heard anything, but I'll find out what chatter we're hearing. If something's going on, we'll soon know. By the way, a few days ago Matt Dirksen—well, actually, one of our *neviot*, surveillance specialists, with Dirksen's help—planted bugs in Marshall's office. We've had a tasty tidbit already. Netski called Marshall and told him that from now on he'd no longer be reporting to Weiss, but to him. Rolfe, see if Dirksen knows what's behind it. Probably has to do with Beth Taylor's disinformation scheme. We'll see if Weiss surfaces. If not . . ."

"I talk to Matt frequently," Rolfe said. "We use his private phone, the one he changes numbers for every other week. He's got so many different Sim cards, he can start his own store. He's becoming quite the little spy."

Momo laughed. "Reminds me of someone else when he was younger."

Rolfe swiped at her playfully, "If you were feeling better I'd . . . " He bit his tongue. "I've had quite a few calls from the Kestrel owners in the class action suit. Blenheim's putting all sorts of pressure on to find out who instigated it. No one's said anything about me."

"It's the ones who don't call you have to worry about," Palmer said. "Someone will break, believe me. And when they discover it's you . . ."

"We want you out of New York the moment Momo's treatments are over," Amnon broke in. "Meanwhile, our guards are in place."

"No promises," Rolfe said. "All I'll say is, we'll think about it."

Palmer sighed. "Okay. Back to work. I think it's time we had a little fun with the elegant Mr. Lee and the foppish Signor Battini."

Chapter 71
New York

Fabrizio Battini sat behind his Louis XV walnut and ormolu desk and drummed his varnished fingernails on its antique leather top, his handmade Loeb shoes tapping on the silk Persian rug in time with his fingers. He had just returned from dinner and still wore his Saville Row bespoke suit, Pucci foulard tie, cream shirt, and personally designed gold and onyx cufflinks. But sweat stained his underarms and his heart rate was abnormally high.

The Italian was nervous.

At last the phone rang. He grabbed it like a man possessed.

"Battini here."

"What's the urgency?"

"Dimitri! Thank you for calling back so promptly."

"Get on with it."

The Italian mopped his forehead with a blue, silk handkerchief. "When I got home from dinner at Harry Cipriani's . . ."

"I don't give a shit where you ate dinner."

"I think someone broke into my apartment."

"Think? Don't you know?"

"I'm sure. Nothing's been taken, but there are signs."

"What signs?"

"Books not how I left them. Files rearranged on my desk. My, er, things in my bathroom not how I left them."

"You mean the toys you fuck your boyfriends with? Your pills and potions that get your dick hard?"

He knows everything about me, Battini marveled, grateful to be on the other side of the country, so Netski couldn't see the shame on his face.

"What about your safe?"

"I opened it. Everything seems to be in order."

"Seems? You make me sick."

"Yes, but only seems . . ." Battini's hands began to shake. "Again, things rearranged, nothing taken."

The secure transcontinental line was silent.

"Dimitri? There's something more."

"I'm listening."

Battini could barely get out the words. "The reason I am so sure there was a break-in is there was an envelope waiting for me on my desk. Contained 8 x 10 glossies plus a DVD."

"Shit! How bad were the pictures?"

"Very bad. They showed me having sex with someone in my bedroom. We were using the toys."

"Save the photos and the DVD. I'd like to see them on my next visit." Netski laughed humorlessly. "So would Mr. Weiss and Mr. Lee. They're with me now. Sorry. I should have told you this was a conference call. Say hello, Jimmy."

"Hello, Fabrizio. I'm sorry about . . ."

"Enough!" Netski interrupted. "Your colleagues want to see the pictures too."

His humiliation complete, Fabrizio Battini began to cry. "My partner's birth certificate was included with the pictures. He was only fifteen years old."

"You fucking moron!" Netski screamed. "If those pictures are released they'd not only ruin you but more negative publicity would be devastating for Blenheim and Kestrel." It took him a minute to calm down. "Was there a note with them? Any demands?"

"Just the pictures and the birth certificate."

Netski's breath was loud in Battini's ear. "It's obvious what happened. Your apartment was bugged, and they managed to put in a video feed. I'll send a cleaning crew in tomorrow morning, but it's too late. You've already had your starring role. Whoever did this has what they want, and they'll use it, though God knows how or when. It won't be good for us, I promise. Just the threat of this stuff hanging over us is problem enough." He paused, thinking. "I'm not pleased. Not pleased at all. The only reason I'm letting you live is because the Summit's only a few weeks away. It would create more problems if you disappeared as well than if we left you around. Another fucking scandal is the last thing I want. But I could change my mind, believe me. Meanwhile, your cock stays where it belongs, firmly sipped up inside your pants."

*

The call ended. Battini's pulse pounded as if he'd sprinted up a flight of stairs. Gradually his mind cleared and a hollow feeling grew. If I disappeared as well? he thought. So someone else had disappeared who had earned Netski's wrath. Who? Realization dawned. It had been a conference call. Netski had ranted, Lee had spoken. But from Dieter Weiss, his ever-present tormentor, not a word.

Chapter 72
San Diego

Matt cut himself while shaving. Irritated, he patted off the blood with a tissue and looked into the bathroom mirror, not liking what he saw: his cheeks were pale, his eyes sallow, his mouth set like the mask of tragedy. The Summit should be the apex of his career, yet it loomed ominously, a dark cloud not a golden one. Dread ratcheted through his stomach; these days, he sucked on Pepcid tablets as though they were M&Ms.

Why, he asked himself, if Blenheim's and his goal was identical—a smooth Summit bringing honor to all—were he and Beth kept forcibly in Netski's thrall? Why kidnap Britney, blackmail his father, surround him with a bodyguard of spies? Why turn him, an ally, into an enemy? What in God's name was being plotted?

The search for answers exhausted him, depressed him, frustrated him. He felt sour, an alien. The inner man was as unrecognizable as the one in the mirror. The only course, he knew, was to keep working, the dutiful employee with a smile on his face. If he lost himself in the Audley and its problems, perhaps he could keep himself hidden, even to himself.

*

Matt had installed digital clocks counting down the number of days to the Summit, throughout the back of the house areas. Locker rooms, staff dining rooms, kitchens, laundry rooms, engineering rooms, even the loading and receiving docks—all had the ubiquitous clock. No one could miss it.

Translators worked overtime converting menus, maps, in-room information packets. signs, and daily activity sheets into the dozen or so languages of the various attendees. Different teams of translators worked on instructions for the staff imported from Kestrel and Audley properties around the world. The concierge team was inundated by requests from the Summit's participants, each confidential, each more important than any of the others, some more bizarre than most others, verging on the illegal. Purchasing and Procurement worked twenty hours a day to take care of requests from the various delegations. Human capital ironed out housing problems, baggage, visas, logistics, transportation, medical emergencies, family traumas "back home," and a plethora of personal issues.

Installation of the extensive equipment that Dieter Weiss had ordered went smoothly, though the Eastern European technical team sporadically disrupted power throughout the Resort, as they experimented with the new systems. The Resort's landscapers tried to keep up with the building and rebuilding that disrupted the normally serene grounds, while Japanese topiarists shaped thick ficus hedges into the shapes of the nation's national flags. Lighting subcontractors were nearly trampled as they tried to illuminate the topiarists' masterpieces.

Disputes erupted among the Resort's staff—permanent against temporary, Japanese against Korean, Hindu against Muslims, Croat against Serb, Jew against Arab, tent builder against landscaper, front desk against housekeeping, food and beverage against laundry. None could be satisfactorily settled, yet somehow the work went on.

Extra security cameras were installed, despite the staff's complaints of invasion of privacy, in the cold rooms, maintenance workshops, food and beverage storage rooms, maids' storage areas, the electric golf cart recharging area outside the Clubhouse.

Outside the Resort, protests erupted around the property's perimeter. Small and spontaneous at first, they became nastier as opening day grew closer, and it became obvious that they were part of organized patterns. Meetings among Matt, Brad Marshall, the San Diego police chief, the state's superintendant of police and the head of the Secret Service detail led to a series of ever widening road blocks and the acceleration of a plan to establish three widely separated cordoned off areas for the protesters, each of which would be surrounded by mounted police officers from around the state, water cannons, fire trucks and SWAT teams.

Pete Wilson was supplied with pictures of known terrorists, leaders of protest groups with a history of violence, and people who had made threats against the government in the past, and told to post them throughout the back of the house areas. Fire drills were held at irregular intervals. Trained sniffer dogs and bomb-detection squads started their regular patrols, adding to the general confusion.

Matt lived through it all on automatic pilot. He worked tirelessly, adjudicating disputes, giving interviews to a rapidly increasing press corps, attending daily security meetings, overseeing staff, placating those few regular guests who chose to stay on amid the turmoil. Each second of each minute of each hour of each day was occupied. His father, Beth, Blenheim, Rolfe, Palmer and Sapir—each receded from his immediate consciousness as though a distant star rushing further and further from his universe. When a press release from Netski arrived announcing Dieter Weiss's resignation from the company, he e-mailed it to Rolfe Ritter and merely registered it without calling Beth to gloat. Jimmy Lee was ever-present. Matt ignored him.

*

Brad Marshall was awoken at four a.m. by the ringing of the cell phone by his bed.

"What is it?"

"Sweep your office. You have many people listening to your conversations."

He recognized neither the voice nor the accent. Asian? Hispanic? "Who is this?"

"Someone who cares."

He rushed to his office, withdrew an electronic listening-device detector from his safe, and swept the room. The devices had infested his office like termites, top of the line models, he knew, used only by the most sophisticated clandestine organizations.

Who had placed them? his frantic mind asked. The Secret Service? The FBI? Both had vetted him thoroughly. One of the G8 countries? Illogical. Matt Dirksen? Matt hated him and had the master key. But it was laughable. Matt would never have access to these devices, let alone get through the security system he'd had installed. Anyway, for what purpose?

Two names came to mind, both of which filled him with apprehension: Jimmy Lee, who had Te-Wu colleagues, or Dimitri Netski, with his multi-tentacled connections. It had to be one or the other. But why? He was as loyal to them as any captain to a general. Did they not trust him? Didn't they know he shared their goals? He went back to his apartment, not ten minutes from the Resort, and lay down, knowing that sleep was impossible.

The phone rang again, loud as a scream. He picked it up with trembling hands.

"Look under the mat outside your front door."

The phone went dead. He staggered to the front door. There was a large manila envelope under the mat. He placed it unopened on his dining-room table and examined it. No writing, no labels, no postage, nothing to hint at the identity of the sender. He opened the envelope and shook out its contents, an 8 x 10 black and white photo. He stared at it. Answers to his questions, like pieces of a jigsaw puzzle, fell into place.

Chapter 73
Washington, D.C.

As the elderly lawyer exited the Acela express in Washington, D.C., Rick Caverly signaled Falkman to follow him. Minutes later, they were ensconced in the weary CIA agent's battered Jeep Cherokee parked outside of Union Station.

"What's so urgent that you had to schlep me from Manhattan on such short notice?" the lawyer asked, reaching over to turn up the noisy air-conditioning.

"Doors shut on me everywhere I turn, but one thing I can tell you is that Dimitri Netski's girlfriend is a Russian named Olga Petrova. This looker dresses like a top fashion model; she's the only child of Alexei Petrova, now a major shareholder in, and chief executive of, Az-Ram, one of Russia's largest steel companies. Under the Yeltsin regime, Petrova, an ex-KGBer, became a buddy of the late Boris Yeltsin and magically got a large chunk of the company when Yeltsin privatized a number of industries. He's a critic of Vladimir Putin and wisely spends much of his time outside of Russia, constantly protected by a phalanx of well-armed bodyguards. My friends tell me he is rumored to have close connections to one of the crime syndicates. If my pals know which one, they sure aren't telling. This Petrova is one powerful guy.

"The very delectable Olga's now in her thirties, and despite having earned a reputation as a spoiled bitch hellraiser is the apple of her father's eye. She runs the family's non-steel industry businesses. Reputed to be as ruthless as her old man and just as ambitious. Word is that she is, or was, seeing some big time Mafia guy, but no one can or will tell me who the guy is. That conflicts with Dimitri Netski merely being a Czech corporate professional, doesn't it?"

"What do you want from me?" Falkman was clearly intrigued.

"Simple. Get your Mossad and MI6 buddies to get all over this and put her under close surveillance. They have the resources I can't get access to. Once we know who Netski really is and where he fits in the Russian pecking order, we'll have more to go on and maybe can finally connect some of the dots."

Chapter 74
Los Angeles

By the time Dimitri Netski arrived at Century City that morning, Brad Marshall had been waiting over an hour.

"Mr. Marshall doesn't have an appointment," Netski's assistant said, "but he insists on seeing you."

Marshall stood. "It's important."

Netski sighed, "You'd best come in." He ushered Marshall into his office and closed the door. "This had better not be a waste of time."

Marshall produced a small plastic bag containing the listening devices and recounted the story of his early morning calls.

"Hmmm. Ominous." Netski separated the devices through the plastic as though they were worry beads.

Marshall proffered the envelope. "As soon as I opened this, I knew you had to see it."

The bugs dropped onto Netski's desk. His eyes widened as he examined the picture. "You know who these people are?"

"Yes, sir. Obviously the man on the right is Jimmy Lee. The man he's talking to is Sergei Fedorov. He's the number three under Nicolai Petrushev who runs the FSB, Russian Federal Security Service, the successor to the KGB."

"Precisely. There's a date on this photo. Do you know where Lee was that day?"

"I checked with his assistant while I was waiting for you. His calendar shows he was in Vancouver for the weekend. But the picture says otherwise."

The general stared at his captain. "Go on."

"Behind them is the Flame of Liberty statue on the *Pont D'Alma* in Paris. They must have been at one of those cafes at the bottom of Avenue Wilson."

"Lee went a long way from Vancouver for a cup of coffee." He spoke as though Marshall were no longer in the room.

"Mr. Netski, why would Lee bug my office, lie about where he was going, and have a meeting with an agent of the FSB?"

Netski stood. "An equally important question is who took the picture and sent it to you?" He walked to the door, then turned back to Marshall. "I want you to watch Lee closely. Don't let him get suspicious. Report anything unusual, anything at all, to me. I think it's time we did some switching. Have Lee followed twenty-four hours a day, and let's bug that fucking shithead's offices both at the Resort and in Santa Monica."

Chapter 75
New York

"Why meet here?" Ron Falkman asked, sitting with Rolfe in the red-lacquered bar of the Carlyle Hotel on Madison Avenue.

"Because I have to get out of the damned apartment or I'll go mad. Momo sleeps most of the day, the security guards don't play canasta, "The Days of Our Lives" is too complicated to follow, and if I see another blonde bimbo telling me what's going on in North Korea, Iran or D.C. I'm going to break the bloody set. I can't concentrate enough to read anything more than magazines and I'm beginning to obsess about the Summit day and night. Besides, the Carlyle's close enough to the apartment that I can get home in five minutes if Momo's in trouble."

Falkman sipped Pellegrino water. "Have you heard from Matt or Beth?"

Rolfe swigged a Bombay martini. "Both. Dirksen's overwhelmed, Beth is in the dumps. They've only seen each other once in the past week. Apparently it wasn't much of a reunion, since he fell asleep before she got under the covers."

"Who'd you get that from?" Falkman laughed.

"Each of them told me. They thought it was funny. But they're worried, Ron, worried sick about what'll happen to them and to Britney after the Summit. Matt told me he's even wondered whether Beth's telling him the truth or even whether Britney really exists."

"Poor guy. He's getting paranoid. Do they have any ideas of what Blenheim's up to?"

"None. It's a goddamned mystery." He raised his hand for another martini. "Anything new from Frick and Frack?"

"You mean Spooks Incorporated?"

Rolfe chuckled as he sipped his drink.

"Palmer's scheme of telling Brad Marshall about Sapir's bugs drove Marshall nuts. The photo MI6 doctored to show Lee and an

FSB officer canoodling in Paris rocketed him to Netski's office; hopefully it's driven a wedge between Netski and Lee. With Weiss gone God knows where, Netski's got no one to turn to except Battini, whom he loathes and I'm sure treats like the disgraced lackey he is. We've got him sweating all right, but it doesn't get us closer to his plans."

"Was the information from your CIA ghost about the Russian woman useful?"

"Sapir has had his people all over it. He believes he's established a connection between the Petrova family and one of the more dangerous crime syndicates."

"Does it lead Amnon to more on Netski's identity?"

"That's the bad news. Mossad thinks—and I stress 'thinks'—that Alexei Petrova is somehow tied up with Yuri Borotin, who's reputed to control one of the most powerful Mafia organizations in Russia. If so, it's ugly. Yuri Borotin is someone even Putin doesn't mess with."

"If Olga and Yuri are an item, then does that mean Dimitri Netski is Yuri Borotin?" Rolfe asked, shaking his head in confusion.

"I asked the same question. The answer is no. If there is a tie-up between Petrova and Borotin—and I stress, that's a big if—then Amnon's people have a feeling that your successor at Kestrel, Dimitri Netski, could be Vasily Borotin, Yuri's younger brother. They're trying to get fingerprints and even a DNA sample. Mossad has someone on the Kestrel corporate office cleaning squad and is trying to get into Netski's domain. However the security team in the office watches the cleaners like hawks, so who knows what they'll be able to accomplish."

"Christ! If it's the Borotin brothers, what the hell's their game and what has Te-Wu and the Chinese government got to do with it?"

"Amnon has no idea. Palmer speculates that the Chinese may have subcontracted an operation to the Borotins, perhaps involving the Summit."

"But Blenheim bought Kestrel before the Summit deal was made. Why?"

Falkman shrugged. "Sapir says that when an opportunity arises, a good operative will adjust to take advantage of it. Simple as that."

Rolfe looked dubious. "Did Palmer tell the U.S. Secret Service his suspicions concerning the Borotins?"

"Of course. Basically, he was told that his precious PM would be safe and he should take his paranoia home with him. With contingency plans on contingency plans and more agents guarding the Resort than all the delegates combined, he and his British colleagues could sleep soundly in their beds."

"So they'll do nothing more?"

"You've got it."

"By the way," the lawyer continued, toying with the lemon wedge in his glass, "I told my friend at the CIA about the possibility the Borotins are involved. He would only say that it put an interesting complexion on things. When I pressed him he was, to say the very least, enigmatic, merely allowing that his organization had been interested in Yuri Borotin for a while, and the Russian would not be on the White House Christmas Card list."

"That's it? Anything else?"

"That's all he said. When these guys don't want you to know something, it's easier getting blood out of a stone."

"What should I tell Matt and Beth?"

"Tell Beth to suggest to Jimmy Lee that she'd be more use to him if she was at the San Diego Cliffs. If he's on the outs with Netski, he might figure Beth could help him spy on the Russian, if that's what he is. And tell Matt to watch Marshall. The closer to the Summit, the more pressure he will feel. If anyone's going to break, this one will. He's got to be just the dispensable hired-hand and knows it."

Rolfe swirled the cocktail stick around in his half-full glass with its four olives, no longer thirsty. "I'll have to see Matt personally. I'm the only one he'll listen to, and by now any phone's too dangerous."

"Ridiculous!" Ron pounded his hand on the table. "Matt can't possibly leave the resort and you can't leave Momo. Besides, you'd probably be gunned down the minute you got off the plane."

The two men glared at each other. Reluctantly Rolfe said, “You’re right. But it’s crucial that Matt and I meet. Tell Palmer and Sapir to work it out.”

Chapter 76
Moscow

The sole passenger aboard the 126-foot-long Boeing Business Jet slept in the bedroom much of the way from Los Angeles to Moscow's Domodedevo Airport, although he took a solitary walk during the brief refueling stop in Paris's Le Bourget Airport. As dusk fell, the plane taxied directly into a hanger on the airfield's north side, the hanger's doors slid closed and stairs were rolled up to the opened door. At the bottom of the stairs the passenger was met by one of the most powerful mobsters in the world, who embraced his younger brother with a hug that would render a lesser man than Vasily unable to speak.

Vasily left out no detail.

"I'm not pleased," Yuri said. He picked up the photograph of Jimmy Lee that Vasily had included in his file and tossed it on the laminate coffee table of the hanger's stark office. "Sergei Fedorov is totally loyal to Putin. He's the worst kind of FSB man—can't be bought or blackmailed. He'd love to see you and me dead."

"And vice versa." Vasily glanced at the pockmarked face and bushy eyebrows of his brother with emotion. How much they had shared together! "I asked Brad Marshall why he was sent the photo. He guessed someone in the CIA had sent it, wanting to look out for their ex-comrade."

"Makes sense, but better not to trust this Brad Marshall. Have him watched." Yuri poured both of them a vodka. "The bigger question is why did Federov and Lee meet?"

"Exactly, I've been thinking of nothing else. That's why I decided to talk to you in person."

The older brother set his vodka down without tasting it. "There's only one explanation, not a pretty one. The Chinese must have decided to eliminate us after the Summit. Lee's warning the FSB that something will happen, though of course he doesn't know what. Of course, the FSB will have to warn their good friend Putin that when the Summit fails we're behind it. The fucking Chinese save billions, look blameless and win—game, set and match."

"Son-of-a-bitch!" Vasily exploded. "I'll have that fucking snake Lee cut into ribbons."

"You'll do no such thing, Little Brother," Yuri said sternly, gulping his vodka and pouring them both refills. "They don't know we have the photo. The worst thing you could do is alert Lee. He'll run like a scalded cat. Hands off for now. At the right time, you'll clean up without leaving anything that could point to us. As to our friends Marshall, Taylor, Dirksen, and Battini—well, there's no need to deviate from our original plan."

Vasily Borotin nodded. "Will you take care of the misinformation?"

"Absolutely. Dirksen, Taylor and that pest of her daughter—kaput!" He drew the stretched fingers of his right hand across the front of his neck with a nonchalant leer. "We'll show that Battini was on the Chinese payroll for years and that Marshall was his accomplice. They'll have a long trail of clandestine meetings with Beijing that the CIA will find out about. Sadly, by the time the Americans find Battini and Marshall they will be singing with the heavenly choir. Too bad Le Roi, Chalabi and Lahav discovered the scheme and had to be killed by the Chinese to cover their tracks."

"What about me? Wouldn't I have had to be involved?"

"At the very center. But there'll be an accident a day or so before the Summit opens. Maybe your plane will catch fire on the ground. Whatever, a body will be found, identified as you. Dimitri Netski, dead. Vasily Borotin, alive and well in Moscow. Voila."

"Brilliant!"

"I thought so. There'll be a trail difficult to follow, but not for highly trained agents, leading to Beijing, as Battini's and Marshall's killers. Maybe I'll let the Americans find it. Another reason to hate the Chinese."

The brothers laughed and tossed back their vodka. Yuri's mood darkened. "There's one piece of unfinished business, Vasily. I don't like spending a billion-and-a-half dollars to settle a bogus class action suit."

Vasily's eyes widened. "Bogus?"

"Well master-minded. I've found out who put the Kestrel owners up to it."

Vasily leaned forward. "Who is it? He's a dead man."

The older man patted his brother's shoulder tolerantly. "The man you said was finished, not worth wasting our time and effort on."

"Who the fuck is it?"

"Rolfe Ritter."

Chapter 77
New York / La Jolla

At 1:49 a.m. a white Chevrolet Express, with MANHATTAN PLUMBING SERVICE announced on its sides, pulled up to the apartment building where the Ritters lived.

Two Hispanic men, one short, the other tall, both wearing MPS baseball hats pulled over the eyes, disembarked and, tools in hand, rang the night porter's bell. "Manhattan Plumbing," the taller one announced. "Mr. Ritter called."

The porter rang Rolfe's apartment. "The plumbers are here, Mr. Ritter."

"Thanks, Joe. Send them up. Why do kitchen sinks only overflow in the middle of the night?"

The porter laughed. "Murphy's Law. Let me know when they're finished and I'll let them out."

"Will do."

Fifty minutes later, Rolfe called down. "All through," he told Joe. "Three hundred bucks for one clogged pipe. It's a disgrace. I'd have waited till morning, only Mrs. Ritter's preparing dinner for eight guests tonight, and she insists on getting started early. Women!"

Joe duly let the workmen out, and a minute later, the van disappeared into the Manhattan night.

*

As the van turned onto the West Side Highway, the man in the passenger seat took off his cap, shrugged off his overalls, and reached for the double-breasted blazer hanging behind him.

"All set, Mr. Ritter?" the driver asked, turning onto the exit for the George Washington Bridge.

"I feel like James Bond," Rolfe said, thoroughly enjoying himself. "But now I bet Mrs. Ritter's giving your pal Shlomo the best coffee he's ever drunk."

"There's some benefit in being tall," the driver muttered. Both he and Shlomo were members of Sapir's team guarding the Ritters.

"May he watch over her safely," Rolfe murmured.

Within fifteen minutes, the van pulled up alongside a Falcon 900 EX in a dimly lit part of New Jersey's Teterboro Airport. Rolfe was inside the plane in seconds, and minutes later it was turning west in its climb to 45,000 feet.

*

A starlit sky greeted Rolfe as he stepped into a Lexus ES with tinted windows. The olive-skinned driver didn't say a word. Rolfe adjusted his watch to local time: 4:53 a.m., a few minutes ahead of schedule.

The Lexus pulled up one street away from Matt Dirksen's house. Rolfe hugged the shadows and approached, alert to any movement or noise. Nothing.

As arranged, a burglar-alarm shrieked from a house on the block behind him. Taking advantage of the distraction, Rolfe opened the back gate to Matt's neat postage-stamp garden and, moments later, was shaking his protégé's hand in the quiet of the kitchen.

Matt flipped a switch on the entertainment system. "You are without question the best lover in Southern California," Beth Taylor's recorded voice said. "Let's have some music." Norah Jones's dulcet tones crooned "Come Away With Me."

The two men silently made their way to an upstairs bedroom. "Beth's in the other one," Matt said. "Asleep, I hope. This room's clean," Matt said. "We can talk safely here."

Rolfe talked. Just over ninety minutes later he watched as Beth's car drove away from the house, followed by Matt's, and then, a few seconds later, a gray Ford Taurus. More of Blenheim's men, Rolfe knew. He thanked the heavens for Mossad's meticulous reconnoitering and information. What would he have done without them?

*

"Hard day, Mr. Ritter?" Shlomo asked when Rolfe entered the Ritters' apartment. "You'd better get some sleep."

"Sleep?" Momo asked, kissing her husband. "He's a chef and has to prepare dinner for eight people. I'm in no way up to it."

Chapter 78
San Diego

Each time Brad Marshall set his eyes on Jimmy Lee, he seethed. Furious that he had not been informed about Beth Taylor's interim transfer to the Resort, he had challenged Lee.

"Who do you think you are, Marshall? If I remember correctly, you're merely a functionary," Lee had responded dis-misssively.

Now, all too often for Brad Marshall's liking, he saw Lee and Taylor locked in whispered conversations, avoiding Marshall's eyes whenever they saw him watching. To add to the security chief's angst was Matt Dirksen, who until now had avoided Jimmy Lee, but was spending increasing an amount of time behind closed doors in meetings with the young Chinese.

"Anything I should know about as a result of your meetings with Mr. Lee?" Marshall casually asked Matt Dirksen after one of the twice-daily Summit briefings.

"If our conversations had anything to do with security, of course you would be the first to know about them," Dirksen responded innocently.

The surveillance team Marshall placed on Jimmy Lee was achieving little. Following him to and from the Chinese Consulate in L.A., learning nothing from the listening devices they placed in his apartment and his car, they were unable to penetrate the codes on his laptop; and, on the rare occasions they were able to place bugs on his cell phone, they heard nothing but static, despite seeing Lee walking around with the phone glued to his ear.

The call at three-forty-five that morning added to Brad Marshall's black mood. He had answered his cell phone to that same Asian or Hispanic voice: "Remember you aren't in the inner circle and are expendable. Ask yourself, if you know too much. If you rightly answer yes then, of course, you know the consequences."

"I don't know what you're talking about," he answered, his mouth suddenly as dry as a desert sand storm.

"Watch your back and be very careful. Trust no one, especially not your so-called friends."

"Who are you? What do you want?"

"We care about you. Maybe we're the only ones. We want you to live."

Chapter 79
La Jolla

"What's a girl got to do around here to get laid?" Beth asked, emerging from the shower wrapped in a bath towel. She lit a candle on Matt's bureau.

"All the work," Matt replied honestly, eyes gritty, body aching with fatigue. He had been at the Resort for eighteen hours, and only now, at midnight, in his own bed, could he try to forget the Summit.

"Whatever you say, my lord." Beth let the towel fall. Her breasts were silhouetted in candlelight; he saw that her nipples were already hard.

"It's a start," he acknowledged, reaching for her.

"Be obedient." She knelt beside him on the bed and caressed his nipples with her tongue. "Don't move a muscle." His penis hardened. "Okay. One muscle." Her tongue moved down Matt's chest while the tips of her fingers gently massaged the tip of his penis and his scrotum.

Matt's body writhed with pleasure. He tried to enfold her, but she pushed his arms back to his sides. Her mouth took him in.

He moaned. "Beth . . ."

"Not yet. Tonight, I'm on top. You will do as I command." She raised herself so she could see the lust in his eyes, then guided him inside her with a wide-eyed gasp of pleasure. Together they fought to postpone orgasm.

After fifteen minutes, their efforts failed.

*

The lovers lay entwined, sated.

"Oh, dear God, if we could just be this way together. Only us, left alone without being scared." Beth stifled a sob. "Will it happen, Matt?"

"No matter what, we have to believe it." He wished he could believe it himself, fully believe in her, just once. Matt rose and walked to the stereo. Instantly the mellifluous sounds of Antonio Carlos Jobim's "*Desafinado*" filled the room. "If we talk softly, the music will cover what we say." He slid into bed. "What's your news?"

"When I asked Jimmy Lee to assign me to the San Diego Hills so I could know exactly what you were doing and saying, I didn't realize how much time I had to spend with him."

"Rolfe wanted that to happen, puts more pressure on Marshall and lets you keep an eye on that Chinese shit."

"But it's awful. He's awful! He keeps telling me that if I let you put one foot out of line, I'd see Britney soon, but not in this world."

He felt a spasm of anger. If there was no Britney, his own task would be made immeasurably simpler. Something was about to happen at the Summit, he was sure of it. Something set up by Blenheim, controlled by them. Without Beth—without her daughter, if there really was one—he'd be free to investigate, free to act, free to run. For a moment, as he looked at Beth's anguished face, he resented her.

He swallowed his feelings as though they were harsh medicines. "I know it's torture for you, but it is our chance. You'll get her back, somehow. Only a few more days, and the Summit's over. Meanwhile, I'm trying to find places for the three more people Rolfe asked me to add."

"Sounds like there's a 'but.'"

"Brad Marshall's increasingly suspicious of everything I do. He won't process any more security clearances, so I'll have to think of a way around him. Or Rolfe will." He tried to control his voice; his own fear, he was sure, was leaking out of him. "Brad's got problems, so maybe that'll give us an opening. Yesterday a few protesters got through one of the Resort's side fences and started waving banners near the loading dock. Brad's men pounced on them and beat them with nightsticks. When Marshall showed up, brandishing a gun, the beating stopped, and he ordered the protesters to be taken by a Resort's vans to be dumped at the edge of one of the camps springing up around the edges of the security cordon. Who knows what really happened to them."

"Won't there be legal repercussions?"

"There might be. Pete Wilson asked Brad to notify the police about it. Pete says Marshall only sneered, 'The police? We've handled them.'"

"Can you do anything?"

"What? They've made me into a damned eunuch. Besides, aren't you here to make sure I stay one?"

She looked at him sharply. You sound like you're blaming me, as if I'm part of Blenheim's team."

He shrugged. "Well, aren't you? It's the same effect."

She jumped from the bed, threw on a robe and glared at him. "My daughter's life is in danger!"

"So is yours, so is mine."

"So fuck Britney. Every man for himself. Is that what you're saying?"

His head hurt. He rubbed his temples. "Of course not."

"I don't believe you."

"Believe what you like. You do anyway."

She began to dress. "Goodbye, Matt."

"Where are you going?"

"Out of your life. I've got my child to attend to. You've got your precious Resort; that's more important to you than Britney, than me."

He reached for her hand, but she pivoted away. "I didn't mean . . ."

"I know exactly what you mean. And I thought . . ." She forced herself to hold her anguished words back. "I'll tell Jimmy you threw me out as you suspect I've been spying on you, and that I can give him no more information. Britney and I are at his mercy. Maybe he'll tell me to return to Santa Monica. If so, what choice will I have? I'll have to wait to see what he does."

"Try to understand," he said, his anguish lodged like a cancer in his chest. "They're planning something for the Summit. I don't know what and I don't know how, but something big, something earth-shattering. And I'm the only one who may be able to stop it. If only I knew what in God's name it was."

Her expression was ice cold; already she had frozen him out. "I see. It's a matter of priorities. You, this fucking Summit, me, my daughter. Oh, I get it—you're Matt Dirksen, savior of the Free World!"

"I'll help," he said. "You can't go on alone." But even as he said this, even as he meant it, a heretical thought ate into his brain like a ravenous termite: Good.

Chapter 80
New York

“Momo, wake up” Rolfe Ritter gently shook his wife as she dozed on a chaise longue in front of their bedroom’s TV.

“What . . . ? What is it?” she replied, repressing a yawn.

“I’ve just got off the phone with Beth Taylor. She and Matt have split up. She says he’s more concerned about the Summit than about her daughter.”

“Oh, God! Poor woman. How’s she handling it?”

“On the outside, stoically. Inside she’s in terrible pain. She told me she can’t go on.”

“What choice does she have?” Momo asked. “While they have Britney, they have Beth’s body and soul.”

“I’m damned if I know what to do. My talking to Matt will only stress him out more, but I’m not sure I have a choice. Any ideas?”

Momo stretched and reached out for her husband to help her stand. “I’ll talk to Beth, tell her men are weak idiots. Explain that she can never go wrong by underestimating their understanding of women, and at least give her an ally.”

“You don’t really believe that, do you?” Rolfe asked seriously.

Momo giggled, “If you don’t understand that I want you to strip me, gently lay me on the bed, and slowly make love to me now, then you’ll prove my point.”

No one had ever accused Rolfe Ritter of being a slow learner.

Chapter 81
San Diego

The countdown continued relentlessly. Eighteen-hour days took their toll. Tensions mounted. Tempers frayed. Mediating arguments became an increasingly time-consuming component of Matt's days.

State Department officials poured into the Resort, each countermanding the orders of their fussy predecessors. Ever calm, Tim Matheson interceded time and again, his well-practiced diplomatic skills calming troubled waters. Chiefs of protocol from the member states haggled over who would sit next to whom at the dinners, which prime minister would precede which president into the daily meetings, who would get to be photographed with the President of the United States, and in which order.

The Secret Service daily searched the suites where the nations' leaders and their key ministers would be staying. Carpets were shampooed once more, light bulbs changed, air-conditioning filters renewed, wall vinyl replaced, paint touched up, real or imagined scuff marks eradicated. Teams of landscapers manicured already trim lawns, replaced flowers in bloom, ensured that cables were disguised as if non-existent, and that every hedge, tree, branch and leaf were exactly in place.

Sniffer dogs prowled the grounds day and night, towing their bored handlers in their wakes. Metal detectors, body scanners, X-ray machines were installed at the entrances to the Conference Center and banqueting rooms.

Miles of secure cables snaked their way to the newly created Security Control Room, the nerve center for the Secret Service, off limits to any foreigner and all Americans without Zone Four clearance. Shifts of two unsmiling Secret Service agents vigilantly guarded the entrance around the clock. Multi-screen monitors for dozens of closed-circuit televisions newly installed throughout the Resort blazed twenty-four hours a day. Landlines, secure satellite, protected wireless, plus access to all Homeland Security computer systems had homes at each of the thirty-two cubicles inside the Control Room. The marquee housing the media center was completed on the parking lot and satellite linkups for each of the over four hundred accredited media personnel and their technical retinues were tested and ready, while hundreds more of their envious colleagues vied for property tours and snippets of information.

Keith McGregor gleefully reported that the new boilers, electrical and electronic systems were functioning better than ever. Indeed, most of the installation team had left, leaving only a handful behind for emergencies.

Only perfection would satisfy the demanding GM overseeing the work, Matt couldn't imagine how an ant, let alone a saboteur, could enter the place without being noticed.

*

Jimmy Lee denied Beth's request that she go back to Santa Monica. "You don't have to keep fucking Dirksen, if what you say in true," he snarled. "But I still need you here. Maybe you'll pick up stuff on Dirksen from Pete Wilson. I want to know about your activities, what you see, what you hear. I want you where I can see you so you don't get up to any mischief."

So she shared Wilson's office, acting as liaison with the State Department on the ever-changing arrival and departure scheduling. And every day at noon and six p.m. she reported to Jimmy Lee on Matt's activities, even though there was nothing new to tell him. She did not tell him of her brief, occasional daily calls with Momo Ritter, her only link to an increasingly elusive hope of salvation.

What she did not know, and thus could not tell the Te-Wu agent, was that Matt, in turn, called Rolfe Ritter at least once every day. He used a different phone for each call. In turn, Ritter briefed Momo and the relentlessly logical Ron Falkman, who updated both the increasingly agitated Sapir and worried Palmer on every development.

*

The cell phone's shrill ring startled Beth. Only Matt and the Ritters knew the number, and it had been silent since that cathartic last night she and Matt had spent together in his La Jolla townhouse. Her heart leapt in relief. Without looking at the screen she pressed the answer button, throwing reticence to the winds. "Matt, Matt, I've missed you. Are you okay?"

"I know this will disappoint you; it's Momo Ritter."

Beth's face flushed bright red with embarrassment as she stammered, "I . . . I apologize. I thought it was . . ."

"I know who you thought it was, and I'm the one that's sorry."

"Sorry? What for?"

"Sorry that I'm not Matt. Actually, that's the reason I'm calling."

"I don't understand, has something happened to him?"

"Not that I know of. Nothing except the two of you are apart."

"Oh . . ."

"I know it's none of my business and I shouldn't interfere, however I thought that you might need someone to talk to."

"Mrs. Ritter, that's kind of you but I'm fine. It didn't work out. Probably wasn't meant to be in the first place," Beth said stoically, biting her bottom lip to restrain herself from breaking down.

"I bet you're not as fine as you're saying," Momo chided. "I've been around a long time, am married to one of the most complex men in the universe, and I could tell you stories about my husband that would make your hair curl. I understand men, their egos, weakness and sometimes self-destructing pride."

"Mrs. Ritter, I appreciate your kindness but . . ."

"Let me finish. Just listen for a couple more minutes."

Beth's silence was the acknowledgment Momo needed. "Rolfe and I had a wonderful relationship going until my naiveté got in the way and we split up. You see, I wanted Rolfe to change, to be the way I needed him to be, not the man he really was and had to be. I demanded I be the sun to his moon and for everything to revolve around me. I'd concluded that if he wouldn't change to suit me, then he didn't love me. It wasn't 'til long after I'd left him that I realized my life was empty without the only man I'd ever really loved. The more I thought about it, the more I realized that I loved him for what he was, and that if he changed it would be unnatural, as futile as asking a lion to behave like a horse; and anyway, he wouldn't be the same man I loved for all of his strengths and weaknesses.

"I think it may be the same with you and Matt. You're frantic with worry about your daughter. Matt says he loves you, therefore you came to the immediate conclusion that you and your daughter should be the only focus in his life, and all else—his father, the Resort, the Summit, his worries about whether you're on Blenheim's side, his fears about making a lifetime commitment to you—should be instantly swept aside in this overwhelming love. Well, I have news for you; life's not like that. Maybe it is in movies, maybe it is in the teens or early twenties, but you and Matt both know that fairy tales don't exist.

"Even, if Matt did exactly what you wanted, it wouldn't take long for him to resent you and that would inevitably lead to bitterness and . . ."

"And it would be over anyway. Is that what you're saying?" Beth challenged.

"Whether you want to hear it or not, it's exactly what I'm saying."

"This is different! My daughter's life is at stake!"

"Believe me, I understand. All I'm asking you to do is think about Matt's perception of what's real and his own stresses as well as yours. It took me a long and unhappy time of being apart from Rolfe to realize all of this. All I'm asking is for you to think about what I've said, and remember my mistakes. Maybe there are some parallels for you."

Momo Ritter's words stung Beth like angry bees, as she struggled to ignore them, to refute their implications. "Thank you Mrs. Ritter, I appreciate you telling me about your situation and I'm equally sure you appreciate that these circumstances are very different from yours. Nonetheless, I'm grateful for your call."

Momo ignored the coldness in Beth's tone, "You're right, every circumstance is different. Know only that Rolfe and I are worried about you and care deeply for you both, together or apart.

We want you to know you're not alone, that we're here for you. We're doing everything we can to find Britney, to stop whatever may be planned for the Summit, to help, and are here for you. As a woman with a crazy, difficult and wonderful hotelier husband, I empathize and want you to feel free to call me, talk to me, lean on me at any time of the day or night. I care, I really do."

"Thank you, Mrs. Ritter. I'm grateful. Please give my best to Mr. Ritter," Beth whispered and disconnected the call.

*

Tears coursed down Beth Taylor's cheeks as she stared vacantly into the windowless office, her mind a melee of emotions. She struggled to balance resentment at Momo Ritter's interference with the logic of her words. Beth's heart wanted to accept them, to run back to Matt and be safe in his arms; but as her doubt grew like fungus after a storm, she wondered if Momo's call was contrived, only an act. After all, having her and Matt working in concert gave the Ritters and their cohorts a better team in place to find out what Blenheim was planning.

Screw them! She thought. To hell with them all! I'm on my own. I'll find Britney by myself.

Chapter 82
Bel Air

"What's the mystery?" Dmitri Netski asked.

"I wanted to make sure we wouldn't be overheard," Brad Marshall answered. "That's why I wanted to see you in person." They were meeting in Netski's Bel Air residence. Now, seeing the glower on his boss's face, Marshall wondered whether he should have used a phone after all.

"Get on with it." Netski tapped his foot on the limestone floor of his library. He was drinking coffee but had offered none to his visitor.

Marshall glanced around the library as if seeking help from an unseen power. The room was sterile as a laboratory. Books lined the shelves as if they'd been brought in by an overzealous decorator. An antique globe on its wood and metal stand appeared only to serve the purpose of filling an unused space. He could see no pictures, no mementos, no objects anywhere. The place is as soul-less as its owner, he thought.

"I reviewed the tapes of the calls we could translate from Jimmy Lee," he blurted.

For the first time, Netski showed interest. "What did that treacherous bastard say?"

"That you'd excluded him from the Summit planning. He thinks you're suspicious of him."

Netski chuckled, "With good reason. How did his Te-Wu controller respond?"

"He told Lee to carry on as usual, but to come to you to review the planning. If Lee senses anything unusual, he's to make sure you understand the ramifications of a double cross."

Netski exploded. "Who's double crossing who?" he shouted. "Do they think we're fucking stupid? That I don't know what they're up to?"

Marshall waited for the storm to pass. "What can I do?"

"You and I are going to tell Lee of all our plans."

Marshall, who had not been invited to sit, took a step back. "But I thought . . ."

"We'll make sure you have Lee's fingerprints on any documents we show him."

"What documents?"

"The ones you'll get made up. Among others, those with incriminating evidence on our slippery Chinese friend."

Marshall grinned. "I get it."

"Some of it. Don't forget, you don't know all the plans and neither will Lee. If he makes any problems, I'll call him immediately and tell him we won't use them unless he and his friends cooperate with our plans. Our methods." Netski finished his coffee and stood. "Thank you for your cooperation, Mr. Marshall. You'll receive your just reward in the future."

The phrase terrified Marshall. "There's something else," he stammered.

"Oh?"

"Olivia Wade's seen Dirksen talking on his cell phone on the grounds of the property."

Netski glanced contemptuously at his underling. "So fucking what?"

"She checked the electronic monitoring device we put on his cell phone. There was no record of any calls. Then she saw him use the phone again. Same result." He had his boss's attention now. "I asked Lee for the tape of Dirksen's last tryst with Beth Taylor. Music, sex—and whispers."

"Whispers?"

"A virtually inaudible conversation."

"I presume you gave the tape to the electronic boys."

Marshall produced a laptop from his briefcase and powered it up. "Of course. Here's the result."

Netski sat. He could make out a male voice and a female reply, but the words were undecipherable. "Useless."

"Not entirely. This is what I wanted you to hear."

He typed in an instruction. Matt's scratchy voice said, ". . . your news."

And Beth's—almost, but not completely unintelligible—said, "As Rolfe instructed when he was here."

Netski slammed his left fist into the palm of his left hand. "Ritter again! First our money, and now this. I should have dealt with him in the beginning." His jaw tightened and his nostrils flared—a bull preparing to charge. "Get back to the Resort. You're the security chief and the place is as secure as a chat room. I want Dirksen monitored as if he has a wire up his ass."

"What about Ritter?" Marshall could barely conceal the tremor in his voice.

"He's my problem. Taylor and Dirksen are yours. Now get out. Meet with Lee. Tell him we need to get together. Taylor and Dirksen can't see each other again." He leaned forward. "Then do exactly as I instructed. I want that motherfucker, Jimmy Lee, framed!"

Marshall turned to go. His legs seized up so badly he almost buckled.

Chapter 83
New York

The sandy-haired, overweight CIA agent nursed the large Starbucks cup perched on his protruding belly, as talked to Ron Falkman on an adjacent bench to the one they had previously occupied at Penn Station.

"Yuri Borotin has virtually dropped out of sight. Security around him has been tighter than a tick's ass and all of our sources have dried up. Have your Mossad buddies had any better luck?" Rick Caverly asked.

"They seem increasingly convinced that Netski is Vasily Borotin, but have no idea what that means."

"It means something bad. That's for damned sure. Vasily is one hell of an operational planner and plays to an audience of one person only—his big brother. He'll do anything, absolutely anything to impress Yuri. The man is reputed to have no soul."

"Why has the agency got an interest in Yuri Borotin?" Falkman whispered.

"As much as I trust you, there are some things I can't tell you. Suffice it to say, the man doesn't care what he sells or to whom. His only god is money and he only prays at the Temple of Mammon."

"Hmm," Falkman murmured. "According to the Israelis, Olga Petrova returned to Moscow last week. The flight manifest on her Gulfstream G450 listed Los Angeles as the point of departure."

"No prizes for guessing what, or who, she was doing in California," Caverly snorted.

"Apparently she spent a couple of days doing the rounds of shops and restaurants in Moscow, plus a few pictures in the society pages, and now she's dropped out of sight as well. Her plane's sitting in its hanger. Her apartment is unoccupied except for the staff. She hasn't been near her office. There's not a trace of the woman anywhere."

"Shit! I hope like hell she turns up soon. Maybe we can figure something out by her movements." Rick Caverly shook his head slowly. "Tell your boys that my sources in China have shut up like a clam. The Chinese don't even acknowledge they know about the Summit. My instinct tells me they're too damned quiet."

"My Israeli friend wants you to know that they picked up some chatter in Yemen, which may fit into the puzzle. They picked up two Pakistani names for your people to look into: Yusaf Khel Hajari and Chaudry Abdul Hamid. He also said to tell you the chatter level is rising, whatever that means."

"Add everything together, it means all the signs are ominous. Something bad is going to happen and we still don't have a goddamned clue!"

Chapter 84
Moscow

Among the elite's *kottedzhi*, surrounded by high walls and CCTV along *Rublyovo-Uspenskoye Shosse*, the guarded road that leads to Vladimir Putin's dacha at *Novoyo Ogaryovo*, Yuri Borotin's mansion stood out. Replete with balustrades, towers and flying buttresses, the property was more of a fortress than a home, a concept usually fortified by around-the-clock shifts of ten security guards and the latest electronics. Yuri's neighbors marveled at how ugly the forbidding building was. His increasing number of enemies realized it was impregnable, even more so over the past weeks, as supplemental security patrols appeared around the property's perimeter, the only visible manifestation of recently increased security measures.

Sun streamed through the windows of the Victorian conservatory that Yuri had imported from Britain—a taste of the Cotswalds he boasted about to his erudite friends. Dressed in Armani jeans and a black silk tee-shirt covered by a tan Zegna thin-suede unbuttoned outer shirt, the barefoot Russian lounged in a black Corbusier leather armchair with his feet on the custom-designed Lalique coffee table and talked into his scrambled portable phone.

"Vasily, Vasily," he said patiently. "I will tell you again: don't overreact."

"I'm not overreacting. You're not on the front line. I am," Vasily Borotin replied.

"Sometimes it's easier to see clearly from afar, Little Brother. There are always difficulties in complex operations. We simply have to deal with the unforeseen."

"What if Ritter knows what we're planning?"

"He doesn't. If he did, the Secret Service would also know and either we'd know or there'd be no Summit. You'd be on the run, and they'd be hanging Marshall and Battini from their testicles to squeeze information out of them."

The younger Borotin's venom crackled over the secure line. His Bel Air study seemed hot despite its air-conditioning. "I'm still worried about Ritter. I should never have allowed him to live in the first place. That was a mistake I won't make again. Allow me to finish him off."

"I have no objections, so long as you're not discovered, but it won't be easy."

"Why?"

"He has twenty-four-hour protection."

"So what? A couple of agency security guards? Light work."

"Hardly agency guards. Ritter has round-the-clock Mossad protection."

Vasily Borotin's silence testified to his surprise. Then he blurted out, "Mossad! How the fuck did they get involved?"

"Maybe the botched Jerusalem job alerted them." Yuri's voice was uninflected.

"But why would they have an interest in the Summit? Israel's not involved."

"I've no idea. It doesn't matter. But you can see how eliminating Ritter might be difficult. Probably best to leave things alone. He can't hurt us from New York."

"Not true. He's in contact with Dirksen. Killing that interfering son-of-a-bitch would leave our precious resort manager without an ally."

"Except the Taylor woman."

Vasily coughed up phlegm. "Don't worry about her. I have an interesting use for that lady."

The Moscow sun disappeared behind the clouds, darkening the conservatory. Yuri switched on the lights using the remote control on the coffee table. "The sooner the Summit's over, the better," he told his brother. "If you say Taylor's under control, I'll deal with Ritter, once and for all."

Chapter 85
New York

"Let's get out and walk," Rolfe said. "It'll be faster."

His suggestion left his two Israeli companions unmoved. Stocky, shaven Yoram kept driving down Lexington Avenue. Lanky Yossi's eyes searched the crowd for potential trouble.

"For once be patient and do as you're told," Momo said. Rolfe had tried to persuade her not to join him for this last minute meeting at the British Consul General's office, but she had scoffed at his suggestion. "I'm not a cripple," she'd snarled. "I'm merely fighting cancer." Even if she were dying, she'd added, Rolfe couldn't keep her from watching Sapir and Palmer compete with each other like a pair of hormonal teenagers showing off in front of a good-looking girl. Dressed in cream linen pants, a coral linen long-sleeved top, and a cream linen turban, she looked, Rolfe thought, like an exotic fashion model. He hadn't seen her so energetic in weeks.

Finally the Israeli stopped the car between 51st and 52nd Streets in front of the building that housed the British Consulate.

"Don't get out," Yossi said sharply.

Rolfe's hand was on the door handle. "Why not?"

"Because we've had company for the past few blocks." Yoram opened the driver's door and got out. Yossi exited the passenger side.

It was not until they were sure it was safe that they let Rolfe and Momo dash into the Consulate's lobby.

*

"Your receptionist told me that Sir Kenneth was expecting us. What's with this 'Sir' shit?"

Palmer motioned Rolfe and Momo to chairs. "It's nothing. Happened a couple of years ago."

"Bloody hell, they give out knighthoods like balloons," Rolfe laughed. "Congratulations. Why didn't you say anything?"

"It's not that important. I just use the title to impress Americans, anyway."

"And Jews like me from the desert." Amnon Sapir, who'd been sitting on a couch against the wall, rose to greet the newcomers.

"Kenneth knows the real truth. The Brits figured out it's cheaper to give out titles than raises to their civil servants."

Ron Falkman, who'd been sitting next to Sapir and remained on the couch, fidgeted and impatiently adjusted his yarmulke. "Let's get serious, shall we? Rolfe, what have you heard from Matt Dirksen?"

"Precious little. The property's ready for the Summit. Daily dramas, of course, but nothing ominous. The bad news is that he can't get your people jobs. Brad Marshall slammed the door in his face."

Palmer frowned. "Any particular reason?"

"Just showing Matt who's boss, he thinks. And Jimmy Lee's out of the loop. He hasn't been present at any of the Summit team meetings. Until a couple of weeks ago, Lee was ubiquitous. Now he's roadkill."

"But still on the property?" Ron asked.

"Yeah. According to Matt, spends all day at his computer except when he gets Beth Taylor's reports."

"Which say?" Sapir asked.

"Nothing much. She and Matt barely talk and, when they do, it's purely business."

"So what does she tell Lee?" Sapir bored in.

"That Matt's an obedient puppy. Lies down just where he's told. Marshall seems to be wilting under the stress, some of which we added for good measure—temper like an exposed hot wire. Same thing with McGregor, though the installations are complete and working well. Matt mentioned there were some anomalies between the plans that were submitted to the authorities and the systems that were actually built. He talked to San Diego's Mayor, who agreed to have the matter deferred until after the Summit."

"So Dirksen still doesn't know what Blenheim's planning," Palmer said dolefully.

"Not a clue."

"What about you, Amnon? Any news from your side?" Falkman asked.

"We managed to get one of our men into Kestrel's Century City office. He got hold of a Netski itinerary. Seems Blenheim's CEO made a turn-around trip to Moscow."

"So?"

"Guess who met Netski at the airport."

"Yuri Borotin," Palmer said quietly.

"Bingo! They met in Borotin's private hanger, surrounded by two-dozen bodyguards."

"Christ!" Rolfe gasped. "The man has a private army."

"A formidable opponent," Palmer agreed.

Sapir snorted, "My man at the airport bribed one of the hanger workers who confirmed that the man with Yuri Borotin was Vasily Borotin—'Little Brother.' Hard son-of-a-bitch; engineered the takeover of the major Kazakhstan oil fields and then used a particularly vicious combination of intimidation, murder and blackmail to force the government into buying them back from his big brother for an eye-watering sum of money. The DNA reports finally came back and Dimitri and Vasily are one and the same. I'd say two formidable opponents, wouldn't you?"

"Any sightings of the girlfriend, Olga Petrova?" Falkman asked.

The Israeli shook his head. "Nothing. Maybe she's holed up in her father's dacha or even in Borotin's estate."

Silence permeated the room. Finally Momo spoke, her voice a whisper. "What does it all mean?"

"I've been thinking about this since Amnon told me about the Borotins," Palmer said, choosing his words carefully. "The only logical conclusion to our granted limited information is that the Chinese government, through Te-Wu, has enlisted the Borotins to do some kind of mischief at the Summit. Major mischief, given what Blenheim's already spent. But we've no idea what it is. With all those world leaders present, any incident could be a bloody catastrophe. I'd hoped Dirksen would provide us with something, anything, enough to give us a clue. He hasn't been able to, and now he's virtually impotent."

"Surely we've enough to cancel the Summit," Falkman blurted.

"Cancel?" Sapir laughed derisively "Are you crazy? That would be political suicide for the administration. It would make the U.S. look like it was swayed by terrorism and couldn't look after an event in its own country."

"What if the United Kingdom cancelled? Wouldn't that be enough to at least postpone the event?"

Palmer sighed. "I talked to my PM and the Foreign Secretary. They think I'm barking mad, ready for immediate retirement. The Summit will go on, they said, with Her Majesty's government standing with the Americans." He shook his head. "All I can say is, God have pity on us."

"There's more," Sapir said.

Falkman laughed mirthlessly. "I suspected there would be."

"My government believes that the Borotin brothers have set up an organization in Israel made up of some of the more than one million immigrants from what was the Soviet Union that we've had to absorb. How many? Some believe upwards of a thousand. A few have already gained access to our leadership, and we believe they already have three members of the Knesset on their payroll, but have yet to prove it. Judging by the leaks, there could even be a cabinet minister in their thrall. It appears they've contracted with Hezbollah, and are selling them sophisticated Russian weaponry and sensitive information."

"Good God!" Palmer said. "Information about what?"

Sapir shook his head. "You know better than that. Good try, Kenneth. Just not good enough."

Both spies laughed.

"There's one more thing," Sapir continued. "Over the past few days there's been increased surveillance on Momo and Rolfe. Today, for example, they were followed to this meeting. We don't know what the Borotins know, but we have to assume the worst."

"What's the worst?" Momo's voice was surprisingly calm.

"They may have found out about Rolfe's trip to La Jolla. His meeting with Taylor and Dirksen might have been monitored."

"Unlikely," Rolfe said.

"But possible." Despite his withering glare aimed at Rolfe, Falkman's tone, too, was calm. "If so, what's your conclusion, Amnon?"

"The Borotins intend to kill Rolfe."

"Rolfe, I insist you and Momo move to a safehouse immediately." Palmer's no-nonsense tone surprised everyone.

Rolfe sighed, "I suppose we have no choice."

Momo leapt from her seat. "What do you mean 'no choice?' No fucking Russian's driving me out of my home!"

"If we were to move, where would you put us?" Rolfe asked. Momo looked at him, realizing by his question how serious the situation was.

"We've a safehouse in New Jersey," Palmer said. "Just outside Fort Lee. Momo, you could go back and forth to Sloane Kettering for treatments. You could vary your appointments, use an alias. No one would know."

"Too risky," Sapir said. "Better find another cancer center. There's a fine one in Philadelphia. I have a better idea, move Momo to Israel. We have the finest cancer centers in the world, and there I can guarantee her safety."

"Let's compromise," Momo said, clearly exhausted by her emotional outburst. "I agree to the safehouse if you get me to and from Sloan-Kettering. I'm not leaving Dr. Sheinkop. Not at this juncture."

"I still don't like it."

"Live with it." Rolfe smiled fondly. "It's bad strategy to mess too much with an Asian tiger."

"What do we do about the Summit?" Falkman asked.

"We pray," Palmer answered. "That's all we can do. Pray that Dirksen or Taylor stumble onto something."

*

"They've disappeared."

Yuri Borotin slammed his fist on his coffee table. "Disappeared?" he shouted at Boris Gremalkin, his top agent in New York. "Impossible."

"I'm standing in the street, looking up at their apartment. Nothing's moved in two days. No one's there. No deliveries, not even the newspaper. We've had directional mikes trained at their windows. Nothing. I don't think they ever came back from that trip to the British Consulate."

There was a long pause. When Borotin spoke again, his voice was dry ice. "You will find them. You will find them quickly. As if your own life depended on it."

Chapter 86
San Diego

"Five days to go and the place is a madhouse," Pete Wilson complained. He and Matt were making the first of their twice-daily inspections of the Resort."

"It's worse outside," Matt said. "Three times the number of protesters the police expected, camps overflowing, not nearly enough Port-O-Potties, and yesterdays rain makes the grounds look like Woodstock."

"Do the police expect violence?"

"Not only the police, but the Secret Service as well. There are people out there already on their watch-list. The Summit's delegates won't be in any danger. I spoke to Jeff Hartman, who heads the Secret Service group on our property; he says there's no way anyone will get on the grounds. But Jesus, I wish I hadn't pitched the damn business in the first place."

"I don't know what more we can do to get ready. As it is the place is a like an Olympic Village, all of the staff ready to explode into action. If the Summit was delayed we'd have a powder keg ready to explode," Wilson blithely continued, oblivious to the wide-eyed expression on his boss's face. "The advance parties from the eight nations arrive tomorrow and start plenary sessions the next morning. Then come the dramas, the litany of complaints, the inevitable changes, the endless requests for 'just one more thing.' It's 24-7 duty for both of us."

Matt felt a rush of warmth for his long-time colleague. "I'll have cots brought to my office and yours. Look, Pete, we're in the homestretch and you've done a fantastic job. The property looks great, nobody's murdered anyone, we're set." Tears, surprisingly, came to his eyes. "I've never been so proud of this place."

"Couldn't have done it without Beth Taylor," Pete said.

"Oh?" Matt's voice was guarded. "I haven't seen her in a few days."

"She's worked her butt off since the moment she arrived. A natural take-charge leader who accomplishes every task diplomatically, no matter how important or menial, that's handed out. Keeps Jimmy Lee off everyone's backs, is even pleasant to that son-of-a-bitch Brad Marshall. I don't know how she does it—the woman is both immaculate and cheerful twenty-four hours a day, she has a smile for everyone. That one's going places, you'll see. She's in Santa Monica today—her regular Executive Committee meeting at the Kestrel. Should be back by evening. If you do see her, tell her how grateful to her we all are."

"Mmmm . . . ," Matt mumbled noncommittally, unable to shuck off his feelings of guilt-ridden loss and knowing he'd avoid her if it were possible.

Chapter 87
Santa Monica

The Executive Meeting at the Santa Monica Kestrel ended at noon. Beth walked toward the garage for her car, wondering why Jimmy Lee had stopped asking for her reports. He hadn't even commented or asked how long she would be away, when she'd told him she was returning to the Kestrel for a staff meeting. Did he accept that she was no longer with her lover? Or was he, like everybody else, too caught up in the Summit to worry about anything else? After all, what could Matt do now? When she looked into the uncertain future for them both, she could see only darkness.

She took the elevator to the underground garage and pressed the electronic button on her car key. The taillights on her car flashed.

A voice behind her said, "Miss Taylor. One moment please."

She turned to the sound of the accented voice. Two men faced her, dressed in faded jeans, tee-shirts and open cracked-leather bomber jackets. One was Hispanic, medium height, stomach overflowing a garish belt, drooping, ill kempt mustache, and lank, black hair dropping over his forehead, hiding his eyes. The other was Slavic, tall, wiry, bald, with small protruding ears and small, expressionless eyes. He held an aerosol can at arm's length.

"Miss Taylor," he said again, inflectionless.

Fear rose like bile in Beth's throat. "Yes."

Aerosol spray hit her full in the face. The smell was the last thing she remembered. She dropped her briefcase and her knees crumpled.

The short man caught her before she fell, grabbed her left breast and licked his lips. "Lady, I could do things to you," he said with a Mexican accent.

"Stop! No time for that!," the Slav instructed, angrily. "Let's get her into the van."

The Mexican dragged Beth toward a light-blue battered van. The heel of her right shoe broke off, unheeded. The Slav picked up her briefcase and opened the van's back doors. Together, the men threw Beth into the van as if she were a sack of grain. The Mexican leapt in beside her, rolled her inert body over, secured her wrists with a plastic tie, tightly bound her ankles with a second tie, and stuck a strip of silver duct tape over Beth Taylor's mouth. The Slav tossed the briefcase in behind her, then ran to the driver's seat and started the engine. Seconds later, the Mexican was seated beside him. They sped up the ramp.

The cashier took the offered ticket from the bald man and scanned it through the electronic reader. "Twenty-two dollars," he said. "Did you enjoy your stay at the Santa Monica Kestrel?"

Not answering, the Slav handed him the exact amount.

"Receipt?"

But the van was already moving through the opened gate and onto Ocean Avenue.

Chapter 88
Manhattan

The outside temperature rose to ninety-eight degrees as the black Mercedes E63 AMG sedan, with its matching black-tinted windows, glided onto the Triborough Bridge, leaving Queens's melting sidewalks behind.

The driver adjusted the air conditioner down to sixty-six degrees as he drew up to the toll booth, but his two companions did not seem to notice. Each was engrossed in images of what was to come.

Not a word was exchanged, the only sound the incessant finger tapping on the tan raincoat next to the open-shirted passenger occupying the back seat. Neither of the men up front had asked why their comrade needed a raincoat on a cloudless day. They knew.

The Mercedes pulled onto the 71st Street exit of the FDR Drive, turned left on York Avenue and stopped at the corner of 70th Street, the car facing south. Engine idling, the passenger in the front seat pressed an automatic dial button on the mobile phone he'd been cradling in his sweating palm.

"In place, on schedule," he said, disconnecting without waiting for an answer. He turned to the man behind him. "Be ready. Now we wait."

The man in the back seat lifted the raincoat and picked up the Sig Sauer Sig556 semi-automatic rifle it had covered. Weighing less than eight pounds, the gas piston, rotating bolt system had never let him down. He stroked the sixteen-inch forged barrel as if it were his wife's breast and checked the thirty-round magazine. Satisfied, he inserted the flip-up combat sight and, with one eye, aligned it with the barrel. He wouldn't need it, but knew it was better to be prepared, for his masters were unforgiving. He grunted. "Ready."

He had never failed before. He wouldn't now.

*

Dr. Mitchell Sheinkop was the best the Sloan-Kettering Cancer Center had to offer. Although he counted statesmen, princes, billionaires and first-tier celebrities among his patients, he also treated many who could not under normal circumstances afford his services. Healing, not money, motivated him, and he selected only those patients he liked, or those he felt he could rescue from almost certain death.

The patient facing him in his small office had been introduced to him by his childhood friend, Ron Falkman. The lawyer had been a mentor to him since the would-be doctor was a teenager, and had helped pay off Mitch's medical school debts when times were bleak for his family after his father died.

Anyone Falkman sent him would be accommodated. In this case, it had been Sheinkop's pleasure, since he'd been taken in by the woman's beauty and charm. He'd one day warned her that if he'd been any younger, her husband would have a dangerous rival for her affections.

Today, dressed as usual in an immaculate white coat, his trademark pink shirt and an Hermes tie, he was feeling particularly avuncular toward Momo Ritter. For the first time since he had first met his patient, Dr. Mitch Sheinkop had positive news.

"Your treatments are going well," he told her. You're not out of the woods by any means, but the cancerous cells have stopped growing. We'll have to see if they diminish, but I'm optimistic. The tests we took today will tell. In the meantime, we'll continue the treatments. Better not to take any chances."

Rolfe, sitting beside his wife, squeezed her hand. She sat stoically—other seemingly good news had been met by setbacks—but his own blood was warm with hope and tears filled his eyes.

"Changing appointments?" Sheinkop said.

The words broke his reverie. "I'm sorry?"

"What's this cloak and dagger stuff? Changing appointments, false names? You guys going Hollywood on me?"

"It's better you don't know," Momo said. "Rolfe has some enemies and you never know when they'll try something stupid. We decided to be careful."

"That would account for your Israeli friend outside. He's one of the better behaved bodyguards we see around here."

Rolfe chuckled, "Nothing escapes you, does it?"

"The only thing that escapes me is why this beautiful woman was attracted to a reprobate like you."

"It wasn't his money," Momo answered with a grin. "'Cause he didn't have any."

"I see. You married him out of sympathy."

"Right," Rolfe said. "She swept me off my knees."

Their laughter continued as Sheinkop ushered them to his door. Momo kissed his cheek. "Thanks, Mitch. For everything."

The doctor rubbed the spot. "Be still, my beating heart."

Yoram stood and punched in numbers on his cell phone. "Yossi, bring the car 'round now. To the 69th Street entrance."

The Israeli failed to mark the short, pasty-faced, razor-thin orderly with lank brown hair watching the entourage from the corridor's shadows.

*

The man in the passenger seat of the Mercedes answered his cell phone as soon as it rang. "Two minutes," he announced to his companions.

The driver revved the motor in anticipation. The passenger in the back checked the weapon's magazine one last time, closed his eyes, and breathed deeply to slow his heart rate.

The cell phone rang twice and cut off. Their signal. The car edged forward, stopping for a light at 69th Street. The light changed. The driver pressed a button and the back seat, curbside, tinted window lowered. The shooter readied his weapon. The Mercedes crept toward the hospital's driveway.

*

Yossi carefully maneuvered the stage-four armored Cadillac Escalade to the front of the hospital entrance. Yoram, looking left and right, hurried Rolfe and Momo out through the hospital doors. Yossi jumped out and opened the passenger side's rear door, positioning himself to create a buffer between it and the Ritters.

Rolfe heard the roar of an engine at his left side. A car, black and ominous, was bearing down on them. Yoram's mouth flew open and he shouted something incomprehensible; he jerked like a puppet toward the Ritters. Yossi started toward Rolfe, then raced toward the driver's seat. Rolfe could see the black car clearly now—a Mercedes, he registered—then shoved Momo face first onto the back seat of the Escalade.

The black car came closer. Rolfe made out an emotionless face at the back window, and the sinister barrel of a rifle aimed unwaveringly straight towards him. In an instant, all was clear. Death stared at him the same way it had stared at his father in that horrific summer of 1955, when he was run down by a black Mercedes outside of his Amsterdam office.

"No!" he screamed reflexively. Something struck him; his body registered the impact. He catapulted toward the ground, arms flailing as his father's had over fifty years ago.

He smelled his own blood. The last sound he heard was Momo's disembodied wail, as if echoing from the depths of a bottomless underground cave, "Rolfe! Rolfe . . . !"

*

The Mercedes accelerated along the driveway and into a melee of traffic on York Avenue. The back window slid closed. The man in the back seat calmly dismantled the combat sight and covered the rifle with his raincoat.

The front seat passenger dialed his phone. "It's done," he said.

This time he was answered. "Are you sure?"

"He went down like a fallen deer. Blood everywhere."

"Our man on the scene corroborates," the voice said. "Good work."

The phone disconnected. The front seat passenger turned to shake the smiling killer's hand.

Chapter 89
Los Angeles

The battered blue van wound its way out of Los Angeles, doubling back and forth through side streets to confuse any would-be followers, its driver checking the rearview mirror every ten or twenty seconds. If the comatose woman in the rear got jostled, so be it.

He heard her moan. With a curse, the Latino passenger in the front seat turned, inspected the bound woman as if she were a sack of coal, sprayed her face again, and watched her body relax as the drug took hold for the second time. They came to Long Beach.

"Turn here," the passenger said. The van followed a winding road through a 1950s industrial park, its sidewalks long disintegrated, garbage littering the way, spectral relics of abandoned warehouses haunting every turn.

They arrived at a building that, according to the faded brown letters on its side, had once housed the Lee Ho Fuk Provisioning Company. "Here?" the driver asked.

"Here."

The driver followed its potholed driveway to the rear of the building. Surrounded by a sea of empty oil drums, rotting wooden pallets, overturned garbage cans, and a surprisingly intact twelve-foot-high metal fence, the ramped loading dock led to a rusted, metal rolldown shutter, only a fleck of color indicating that it had once been painted brown.

The passenger got out and inspected the desolate yard. Satisfied, he pressed an electronic device produced from his pocket; the shutter rose fluidly on well-oiled tracks. The Slav drove the van inside the warehouse, and another press on the device closed the shutter. With obvious familiarity, the Latino man pressed a switch on the side wall. A dangling sixty-watt bulb cast shadows on the narrow passage between the shutter and a solid brick wall, where the passenger punched nine numbers into a newly installed digital pad. A single iron door, set to one side, slid open with a sigh.

Together, the two men picked up Beth Taylor's inert body and, carrying her through the door as unemotionally as if they were delivering groceries, threw her on the concrete floor.

"It stinks in here," the Slav complained.

"Did you expect a flushing toilet? You wanna Marriott?" The Mexican manacled Beth's left ankle to a pole set in the concrete and anchored into a steel beam in the ceiling. "Let's go." Neither looked back as the door shut and they reversed the van into the yard.

Inside the warehouse, a second manacled prisoner looked with horror at the new arrival.

Chapter 90
San Diego

Matt Dirksen was frantic. Yes, he and Beth had agreed not to see each other; however, he was the one that had forced her away—what choice had he given her but to leave? The realization stunned him, her invisibility a growing tumor, mercilessly throbbing in his brain. After his conversation with Pete Wilson about her, he realized how much of a fool he had been. Rolfe Ritter had been right when he sharply questioned Matt's judgment concerning Beth. Matt had mentally dismissed his mentor's criticism as self-interested. After all, having Matt and Beth working together was better for Rolfe and his friends than having them working on their own. Now he felt ashamed. What had he been thinking? How could he have deserted her? What difference were Blenheim's plans? What mattered were her and Britney, and he had failed them. Sick at his own hubris and selfish stupidity, Matt felt as he did when his mother died: guilty and helpless.

Well, not this time! He wouldn't just accept things. He wouldn't run away from Beth like he had with every other woman. He wasn't his father, he was his own man! It wasn't too late. The need to hear from her, see her, were paramount, all consuming, overwhelming. He didn't care if Blenheim knew he was contacting her. He only wanted to know if she was all right; what was wrong with that? Maybe Jimmy Lee would even be pleased. He dialed her cell phone number.

"Hi. This is Beth Taylor. I can't take your call right now, but leave your name and number . . ." He disconnected and waited. Five minutes later he called again. Same answer. He dialed once more. Same answer.

He called her office and reached her assistant. Beth had left three hours ago. Everyone assumed she was immediately driving back to the Audley, but it wasn't clear if she was stopping off anywhere on the way; nor did Beth's assistant know when her boss was planning to return to the Santa Monica property. He dialed her apartment. Leaving a hurried message on her voicemail, he rushed out of his office and, in every violation of the speed limit, drove north to his house. Beth's car was not in his driveway. He called and called, always getting the same robotic response. He went back to his house and sat in his armchair, trying to fight the ugly images in his brain. Had there been a traffic accident? Had she cracked under the strain of Blenheim's threats—her kidnapped daughter—and simply run and kept on running? Had she, her assignment with him finished, simply gone to Blenheim to be welcomed as a heroine? He battled the thought, realizing that was the old Matt; the man who rationalized pushing away every woman who came too close, forcing them to be the ones who made the decision to leave, to make him the wronged one, the victim. No more. He needed Beth, had to find her, had to make things right.

As the night grew darker, so did his thoughts. Had Netski found out that she'd been lying to Jimmy Lee for months? Had they hurt her? Killed her? Unthinkable! Tasting bile, he fought back vomit.

Dawn filtered through the windows. He realized he hadn't moved all night. He dialed the Kestrel hotel in Santa Monica and asked for security. "Come on, come on. Answer!"

"Mr. Dirksen, how can I help you?" The security officer was well aware of Matt's name.

He kept his voice calm with superhuman effort. "Miss Taylor is due at the Resort in an hour or so. I'm not sure if she took a limo or drove herself. Security's so tight here I have to preclear the vehicle, otherwise she won't be allowed in. Do you know if she drove?"

"Not a clue, I'm afraid."

"Could you check with the garage's manager? Have him call me?"

"Sure thing, Mr. Dirksen. Scott Fusilli's on duty now. I'll get hold of him immediately."

*

It was close to twenty tormenting minutes before Fusilli called. "It's real early, Mr. Dirksen, so I might not have the full story, but here's what I know." His Boston accent grated. "Miss Taylor's car is still in the garage. It hasn't been moved since it came in at since 6:07 yesterday morning."

The words hit Matt like body blows. "Thanks, Scott. I guess she took a limo."

"There's more, Mr. Dirksen. Stuff that's odd."

The pain in his gut mushroomed. "What stuff?"

"Miss T's garment bag is hanging in the back of the car. Makes me think she was planning to put on a change of clothes. And there's the heel . . ."

"The heel? What in heaven's name are you talking about?"

"I found the heel of a woman's shoe near the car. A Jimmy Choo shoe, like the kind she usually wears."

She loves those shoes. Matt could hardly breathe. "What do you think?"

"I think something's fishy, Mr. Dirksen. Real strange. If she doesn't show up at the Resort, call me and I'll call the police. There may be a reasonable explanation, but as an ex-cop, I'd say this stinks."

*

Matt showered, shaved, put on fresh clothes and drove to the Resort in a daze. He pulled his bag from the trunk and shuffled like an old man to his office.

Olivia Wade was already at her desk, but it barely registered that it was only seven a.m. and she usually came in at eight-thirty. He slammed his office door behind him, threw the duffle on a couch, and slumped into his desk chair, unable to censor visions of Beth's broken, bloody body lying . . . where?

An idea! He reached for his cell phone and started to call Rolfe's secret number, then abruptly stopped. On his desk, opened to the News Summary, lay *The New York Times*. The efficient Olivia had circled an item in red:

> "Hotel Titan Murdered on Manhattan Street: Just after 12 noon yesterday, hotel magnate Rolfe Ritter, founder of Kestrel Hotels and Resorts, was gunned down at the front entrance of the Sloan-Kettering Cancer Clinic where his wife was undergoing treatment for breast cancer. Witnesses described the shots as coming from a black Mercedes that sped away from the scene. The police have no leads at this time for what appears to be an organized crime reminiscent of Mafia slayings in the past."

Matt's eyes clouded. He could no longer read the type. In total desolation, he knew only one thing: Beth, if she was alive, was in mortal danger and had to be saved, but he, like her, was utterly and totally alone and had no idea what to do next.

Chapter 91
Philadelphia

"Thanks for splitting the difference and meeting me in Philly," Falkman said as he sat down in Bucks County Coffee Co. at Philadelphia's 30th Street Station.

"This is real urgent, otherwise I wouldn't have made such a fuss," Caverly said, brushing thin, grey hair from his wrinkled forehead, as his southern drawl betrayed his Memphian roots. "I need you to get hold of your Mossad guy immediately, maybe even your Brit friend."

"Why?"

"I ran the two Pakistani names he gave me through our computers and found out these are real players. They have a few aliases so we tracked those down, and they were in Bali on three occasions—and the dates magically coincide with the bombings at the hotels."

"I don't understand the urgency?" Falkman's confusion was clear.

"Their aliases cropped up again. Three days ago, they entered the United States by way of the Mexican border at Tijuana. My bet is they're holed up in a safehouse somewhere near the Resort."

"Good God, man, why do you need the Israelis? Talk to your own people, the FBI, Secret Service, Department of Homeland Security. Surely someone'll listen?"

"Don't you think I tried? Talk about rebuffed at every turn. On top of everything, the feds complained about me and my own superiors have reprimanded me for interfering when I was warned off. Right now I am so radioactive within the agency that even the cafeteria staff doesn't want to acknowledge I exist. In all my years, I've never known anything like this. I just don't get it."

"What do you want my friends to do?" Falkman was shocked at his longtime unflappable friend's worried pallor.

Caverly passed the lawyer a sealed, brown envelope. "Inside is a list of the Pakistanis' aliases, photos, visa applications, passport details—everything we've got on the two of them. If my bosses ever find out I have given this information to you, being fired will be the least of my problems. Your guys should do everything they can to find them. For sure, no one else is looking."

Chapter 92
Long Beach

Beth's eyes flickered open, then shut again. Her breathing quickened. Her leg was cramped and she tried to stretch it; cold metal held it back.

She gagged as the stench of feces and stale urine overpowered her. She tried to move her arms, but they were bound behind her. She tried to scream; the duct tape still covered her mouth. Her throat was parched and her lips felt like blubber; the inside of her mouth and throat had an acrid, antiseptic taste. She remembered being sprayed in the garage and vaguely recalled the two men who had captured her. They had taken her here—where?—and left her. Would they return? What would they do to her if they did? Beth Taylor was beyond terror.

The concrete floor beneath her was cold, and she tried vainly to raise her body. The manacle's sharp edge bit into her ankle and she moaned in pain. Don't panic. Think!

To her right, a shadow moved. Her body tensed.

"Thank God you're alive. I was afraid they'd killed you."

A stranger's voice. A woman's. Beth's heart rate rose. With immense effort, she rotated her body toward the sound. The woman was sitting with her back against the pole, around which the manacle was secured. She could see the outline of a head silhouetted in the semi-light, surrounded by a halo of wild hair.

Its owner shimmied toward Beth, accompanied by the echoing clank of a chain. Beth felt the woman's hands touch her face. "This might hurt. I'm sorry." The woman—rancid-smelling but young—tore the duct tape from Beth's mouth.

"Yeeooow!"

"The next part's harder. I have to break open the binder they used to tie your hands. I'll use this metal rod I found near the pole; must have been too dark for them to notice it. It might be painful and take some time. I guess time's all we've got." The young woman pushed the rod under the plastic tie and began to stretch and turn it, first clockwise, then counter-clockwise. Beth thought she'd pass out from the pain.

"When the two guys dumped you, I played dead," the woman said. "They didn't care about me; they were in a hurry to finish with you and get out. I hoped they'd brought food. Nothing. All I've had is dirty water and a few slices of stale bread."

"How long have you been here?" Beth asked.

"I'm not sure. There's no daylight, and my watch broke when they threw me into their stinking van at the airport."

"They?"

"Two men. Not the same who brought you."

"Why did they kidnap you?"

"I've no idea." The woman began to cry. "I've been so lonely. So scared."

"Do you have any idea where we are?"

"Not a clue. Just that we drove for hours from the airport."

"Did they spray you like they sprayed me?"

"You mean drugged? No. They told me they were sent by the tour organizer to take me home. When we reached the parking garage at LAX, they shoved me into the back of a van, slapped my face three times, put tape over my mouth, and tied my wrists and ankles with more of the tape. By the time we reached here, I'd loosened it enough to free my hands. I didn't want them to know that so I kept the tape on my mouth. Then they chained me to the pole and scrammed."

The woman talked so articulately, so pleasantly, all the while working on the binders, that Beth let herself relax a little. She imagined how it must have been for the woman with no one to talk to, then said, "I can barely feel my hands."

"Shouldn't be much longer."

Maybe talk will distract me from the pain, Beth thought. "Where did you fly from?"

"Beijing. I won an essay contest on why I wanted to go to China. The prize was a trip to China. I was bowled over when I won and off I went."

"Good trip?"

"Until the end." The young woman finished twisting the plastic. "There, that should do it. Try pulling your hands out, one at a time. Gently, now."

Despite her aching elbow, Beth released her hands, oblivious to the tug of the binders, then shook both wrists, trying to get the blood circulating. What felt like a thousand needles jabbed inside her skin. "Yikes!"

She reached down to her manacled ankle and rubbed it cautiously. "Get me out of this and you win the gold medal," she told the woman.

"No can do. Unless you can think of a way to unlock them, we're both stuck for as long as they want to keep us."

She started to cry again. Beth sat up painfully and turned to face her. "Crying won't help. We'll think of some . . ."

Recognition stirred. The hair was different, the face obscured by filth, but she'd seen the young woman before. Yes! In a photo. In the picture Jimmy Lee had shown her.

"What's your name?" Beth whispered, aware her heart had stopped.

"Britney. Britney Kisel. What's yours?"

All the longing and terror, the love and hate, the hope and despair she'd fought to control these past months exploded out of her in a wail that echoed through the room. "Oh my God!"

"What is it?" Britney asked.

"My name is . . . my name's Beth Taylor."

The name brought no response from the young woman.

"Beth Taylor, I'm your mother."

*

Beth waited for a reaction. Any reaction. Britney's awful silence was like a death sentence. "I'm so sorry," Beth said, "So very sorry." She peered at her daughter's face, recoiling at the shocked sadness she saw written there.

Minutes passed. Britney spoke at last. "Cherri Kisel's my mother. Jim Kisel's my father." Her voice was flat, expressionless.

"True," Beth said quickly. "Your adoptive parents. I let them have you to save your life."

"Mine or yours?"

Beth had tortured herself with the question ever since she gave her daughter up.

"I don't have a good answer. I've struggled for sixteen years trying to find a good reason for what I did. Selfishness? Probably. I was very young and couldn't have taken care of you. So I gave you away to people who would—and lived with the shame for all these years."

"You've had to live with shame?" the young woman exploded. "That's all you can say? How do you think I've felt all of my life? I'm the one that was abandoned. I'm the one who's had to live with being rejected. Every single day of my life I've had to wonder why. Your life's been great. You're the fancy hotel manager, no responsibilities, no child to take care of. You've never loved me, just yourself."

The unjustness of her accusation cut into Beth Taylor's brain like acid. "That's not true! I came to see you regularly. I was your Aunt Beth."

Britney moved closer and stared into her mother's face. "I barely remember," she admitted reluctantly.

"It was me, darling! After a while the Kisels felt I was getting too attached to you and asked me to stop visiting. It broke my heart, but I did what they wanted. For weeks I'd watch their house to catch a glimpse of you, but Jim saw me one day and they both asked me to back off, for your sake as well as theirs."

She forced herself to look into Britney's eyes. She would tell her daughter everything. "He was right, of course, though Lord how I resented it. Anyway, I did what any nineteen-year-old, miserable girl would do: I drank, did everything bad you could think of, drugged myself silly every day and every night until one night I was picked up by the cops in the park for possession of drugs—plus, for good measure, loud and lewd behavior—and dragged down to the police station. It changed my life."

The young woman's curiosity overcame her agitation. "How?"

"My companions were petty criminals and prostitutes. 'Mini-me's. One of them, a hooker named Amy—she was nineteen too—befriended me. This was her second arrest for solicitation in three months, and she faced prison time. But instead of worrying about herself, she worried about me. This was a girl who became pregnant at fifteen and was thrown out of her house by her father's girlfriend. She went to live with an aunt but when the baby, a boy, was born with undersized lungs, the aunt told her to move on. The state tried to take the baby away, so she ran—ran straight into the arms of a pimp who beat her and forced her to sell herself to earn enough for the baby's drugs. After two years she escaped from him and shared an apartment with two other girls, but the boy still needed his medication, and hooking was the only way she knew of to make money."

"Interesting," Britney said coldly, her disbelief evident. "Most moving. But I don't see how that changed your life."

"Amy told me I had two choices: to end up like her or to make something of myself. I told her about you, and she said I'd made the right decision. But it couldn't be right unless I did something with it. She kept pressing me: What did I want to do with my life?"

Beth paused. Her mouth was parched, but she did not ask her daughter for water; nor was it offered. "Well, what did you tell her? What did you want to do?" Britney asked.

"The answer came to me at dawn in that prison cell. I wanted to work at a hotel. A nice hotel. My parents, your grandparents, stayed in them all the time, mostly fleapits and dumps, but I'd never stayed in a really good one," she said with a laugh, "but they sure seemed a damn sight more attractive than a cell. 'Go for it,' Amy yelled and gave me the warmest, nicest hug I've ever had, before or since. Eventually the police let me go with a warning. I went to the courthouse and provided bail money for Amy; it was the least I could do."

"What happened to Amy?"

"I don't know what happened to her or the boy. She didn't repay the bail money—not that I expected her to. Maybe she's living a normal life, maybe she died. Anyway, I enrolled in Sacramento Community College's course in hotel management, and a decade-and-a-half later I run one of the swankest hotels in L.A. Today, drugs come from the pharmacy and any loud and lewd behavior comes from the guests, not the general manager."

In the ensuing silence, Beth scrutinized her daughter. Beautiful, she thought—an oval face with an aquiline nose and full lips. A high, rounded forehead accentuated the almond shape of her eyes, although Beth couldn't discern their color in the gloom. A long neck atop what looked to be a full body, though it was difficult to tell. Limbs longer than her mother's. Britney was filthy and her tee-shirt was ripped at the sleeve, but to Beth Taylor she was perfection incarnate.

"Tell me about my father," Britney said, anger gone from her tone.

Beth answered carefully. "Alan Campbell. I first saw him at a summer camp where I was a counselor. He had an eight-year-old daughter in the day program. He was thirty-three, an architect, as handsome as you are beautiful. He seemed to me the quintessence of sophistication; I couldn't take my eyes off him. He saw me staring and stared back. We started an affair. I was madly in love with him and he told me he felt the same about me. The problem was he was married."

"Nice," Britney said bitterly.

Beth went on before she could say more. "He told me he'd leave his wife as soon as I'd graduated. It made me reckless in my passion. I was pregnant when I graduated. Surprise, surprise! He stayed with his wife. When I told him I wanted to have his baby, he took it as a form of blackmail, said he wanted nothing to do with it, and told me to grow up. It was as if he'd knifed me. I'd never felt such pain."

"Did you see him again?" There was little compassion in Beth's daughter's voice.

"Never. I never heard a word from him."

Britney turned her face away and began to weep. Beth reached out to touch her, but she withdrew her hand. All she could do was listen to her daughter's breathing.

*

Beth's heart, newly lifted by the euphoria of finding Britney, plummeted, not only at the hopelessness of their situation, but with the certain knowledge that she had been the cause of her daughter's unhappiness and now her imprisonment. She cursed Jimmy Lee and Dieter Weiss, and maybe Matt most of all, but she also cursed herself.

"The stink comes from that," Britney said, pointing to an aluminum bucket a chain's length from the pole. She dragged her chain in the opposite direction and picked up a second bucket. "This is all the water we've got. It's better than nothing. They left bread next to it, but I'm afraid I've eaten it all." She smiled wryly. "I didn't know you were coming or I'd have saved you some."

Beth drank as little as possible, determined to make it last, though she longed to finish it all.

Britney watched her mother carefully. "I can only assume I'm here because of you. Tell me why."

Beth and Britney talked for hours.

Chapter 93
Bel Air

"Isn't this an odd time for a meeting?" Jimmy Lee asked.

Dmitri Netski, opposite Lee and Brad Marshall at Netski's dining-room table, offered them double espressos. "Two a.m. is as good a time as any. This'll keep you alert. During the day you're both needed at the Resort."

"You're right. I've a meeting in four hours with a Jeff Hartman, he's coordinating the Secret Service's activities at the Resort," Marshall said. "Why the high drama?"

"And why did you risk the operation by taking out Ritter?" Lee asked. "My masters want to know."

"It was necessary." Netski said no more.

The Te-Wu agent slumped in his chair. He knew enough not to prod Netski further.

"What's the status of the Taylor woman and her bastard daughter?" Netski eventually asked.

"They're sharing a room as Te-Wu's guests in a Long Beach warehouse. Not quite the Kestrel Santa Monica, but we'll make sure they stay alive, at least for the time being."

"Are they secure?" Marshall asked.

Lee flared. "Do you think I'm an idiot? Of course they're secure."

"We may need them once more," Netski said, "so be careful. Nothing happens until the Summit's over. Understood?"

The Chinese slowly nodded in acquiescence.

Netski turned to Marshall. "Status?"

"Everything under control. The Secret Service swears by me, and Hartman treats me as his confidant. I know everything they and their foreign counterparts are doing. I assure you, the Summit will work according to plan."

"Dirksen?"

"That motherfucker knows his business, I'll grant him that. The Resort's running like a Rolex."

"That's not what I mean."

"You want to know if he's snooping around. Not bloody likely, what with Ritter dead and his whore chained up in some forgotten warehouse in the middle of nowhere. Right now he's sleeping on his office couch—if he's sleeping. Somehow he seems depressed. Obedient and depressed."

"I couldn't give a flying fuck what his mood is. Just make sure he behaves."

Lee grinned, a lion about to devour his prey. "I'll reinforce that message when I get back. I have a little surprise for him."

"And I have a surprise for you. We're changing the schedule. Here's the new one. We're moving up ours to the opening ceremonies." Netski passed Jimmy Lee a sheet of paper, watched him absorb the information, then carefully took it from his hands and placed it in a blue plastic folder.

"But you can't change anything," Lee gasped, dumbfounded. "The plans for the closing event have been in place for months."

Netski leaned forward, jabbing his finger at the Chinese agent's face. "The word 'can't' isn't in your vocabulary when you're talking to me. Only, 'Yes, Mr. Netski. We can, Mr. Netski.' Understand?"

Lee nodded.

"Here are some other instructions concerning the aftermath," Netski said, passing over a two-page document and, once Lee had absorbed the new information, placing it in the blue folder.

"Good. Brad, can you handle the changes?"

"Yes, Mr. Netski. But it's going to be hard. We've only got four days till the Summit begins."

"Do I look like I give a shit how fucking hard it is. Getting it done is the only option."

Only the slightest tremor in his cheek muscles betrayed Marshall's terror. "Don't worry, Mr. Netski. I'll get it done."

*

Netski threw open the door to his kitchen. “Oleg, did you get everything?”

A curly-haired man in his mid-thirties, wearing jeans and a black tee-shirt, looked up from his recording equipment. “Sure did.”

“Good. Now listen carefully. I want you to edit the recording, delete every word I said. The entire conversation took place between Lee and Marshall. I wasn’t even present. I don’t exist. Understand?”

“Piece of cake.” Oleg chewed his ever present gum.

“This has to be your very best work. Be sure even the most experienced experts can’t detect the tape’s been doctored. My brother told me you’re the best in the business. Prove it.”

“Your brother’s right,” Oleg said, unperturbed by Netski’s threatening urgency.

“As soon as you’ve finished, copy the edited recording onto three discs. Leave one in a sealed envelope in the safe behind the tie rack in my dressing room. If you swivel the rack from its horizontal position, you’ll see the safe. There’s a slot for depositing documents. Swivel the tie rack back when the tape’s secure. Leave without touching anything else. If I find out you have . . .”

Oleg’s bravado disappeared when he saw the gun. “Whatever you say, Mr. Netski.”

He followed Netski into the living room where his employer pulled a double CD case from a large selection in a cabinet. “You will put the remaining two discs into this Bruce Springsteen box and place them in this briefcase.” He selected eight more from his collection, dropped them in, and handed the young man the briefcase.

“Tonight, you will take the eight p.m. Lufthansa flight to Frankfurt and connect with the Lufthansa flight to Moscow. You will dress neatly, shave before you leave, and keep the documents with Jimmy Lee’s fingerprints on them and some other files I’ll give you, as a cover inside the briefcase. Do not lock the briefcase. It must appear that there’s nothing valuable inside it, just a bunch of business papers and your favorite CDs. You will buy a carton of American cigarettes and a liter of Johnny Walker Blue Label at the airport Duty Free. You're a businessman returning from a quick trip to the U.S. You will be respectful to everyone and not draw attention to yourself. Any questions so far?"

"It's all perfectly clear, Mr. Netski."

"When you clear customs in Moscow, there will be a grey Mercedes 320 at Arrivals with a driver sitting in the car waiting in front of baggage claim. A man in tan slacks and a brown tweed jacket will be standing at the passenger door. He will introduce himself as Yvgeny. You will give him the briefcase and he will open the passenger door for you. He will get in the back seat. While the driver is taking you to your apartment, you will open the glove compartment and remove a package bound with tape. Inside the package will be your payment, $50,000 in $100 bills. It's more than we agreed. Look at it as thanks for a job well done."

Oleg beamed. He thought of his darling Natasha's joy now that he could afford to propose to her. "The job will go smoothly. You can rely on me."

"I'm sure I can," Netski said, knowing that Oleg would not live long enough to reach his apartment, let alone spend the money that the young technician's killer, sitting in the back seat of the car, would keep as payment for his services.

*

Dmitri Netski sipped cognac in his soundproofed library and dialed his elder brother's cell phone. "The recording is being edited as we speak."

"Perfect," Yuri Borotin replied. "What's more, we'll have Marshall and Lee's fingerprints plastered over the documents in the briefcase. It's enough to prove Lee engineered everything and Marshall was his willing accomplice."

As always, Yuri's cackle made Vasily smile. "Everything else is in order," he affirmed. "Lee has Beth Taylor and her daughter ready for post-Summit disposal. At that time our effete friend Battini will commit suicide, his shame over the catastrophe too much for him to bear."

"And Dirksen?"

"We didn't train Olivia Wade to fail. She'll find Dirksen in the chaos and inject him with the poison we've provided. Then she'll flee to Tijuana where, alas, she'll be struck by a runaway truck. Happens all the time in that part of Mexico. Just to be sure, we'll have a car bomb set in Dirksen's car. One flip of the ignition and body parts will rain on what's left of the Resort. We'll use the same device for Marshall's car. As a backup there will be a bomb under Marshall's bed at his home, naturally replete with not too hard to find clues linking it to the Te-Wu. The Chinese obviously couldn't afford to let him live."

"You've left out something." Yuri was obviously enjoying himself.

"You mean the mastermind behind the Summit disaster? Dmitri Netski? Kestrel's Boeing Business Jet will explode on route from New York to San Diego the day before the Summit. It's a flight for Netski alone, summoned by Miss Wade on behalf of Mr. Dirksen from a business meeting with his investment bankers in Manhattan, to make sure everything goes smoothly at the Resort. The pilots and stewardess, alas, will be what the Americans so quaintly call 'collateral damage.' In the wreckage of the plane, of course, will be evidence also linking the explosion to Te-Wu." He sighed. "I'll be glad to be home in Moscow."

"And I'll be glad to have you home. So will Olga, I suspect. Goodbye, Mr. Netski. This will be our final farewell."

Chapter 94
Tel Aviv

Tova Shiboleth, sixty-one, diminutive, slate-grey-haired grandmother to three high-spirited girls all under ten, held the highest security clearance in Israel. As Amnon Sapir's personal assistant, "Tovalah" (as Sapir called her to her constant irritation) was party to too many secrets and stayed awake at night too scared to sleep, knowing what threats her fragile Mediterranean nation faced.

In the office, she knew what calls were important for her boss to take and which ones could be diverted elsewhere.

Ron Falkman's calls were always taken. As a longtime *sayan*—a Jewish volunteer helping Mossad—the elderly lawyer was well respected inside the organization. Sapir's frustration at the lack of information about the Borotins' plans had poisoned the office like nerve gas, the frustration shared by the New York lawyer. Tova had listened to her boss's conversations with him and with Sir Kenneth Palmer, sick at their lack of progress. Disappointed by their dismal dearth of knowledge and infuriated by the incident at the Sloan-Kettering Cancer Center, Sapir and Palmer wanted answers but also revenge.

"So, what's new?" Sapir asked, his joviality unable to mask his worry.

"*Shalom*, Amnon. I'm afraid I'm not going to make you feel any better," the lawyer answered sadly.

"Given that it's the middle of the night where you are, I didn't think this was a social call."

"Momo Ritter called a few minutes ago on the verge of hysteria. Matt Dirksen reached her on Ritter's secure cell phone. Beth Taylor's disappeared. He can't find her anywhere. He's convinced she's been kidnapped. Between that and reading about Rolfe's murder, the poor guy's desperate."

"Shit, shit, shit! I should have put protection detail on her."

"It's too late for self-recrimination. We've got to go forward."

"Does Kenneth know?"

"Not yet. Will you tell him?"

"Of course. Where's Dirksen now?"

"At the Resort. He's not sure how much longer he can go on. Momo said he sounded like he's at the breaking point. She's going to call him back, update him with the latest, give him a pep talk as best she can. That's why I'm calling you."

"I've been checking with my operatives. All seems normal for a hectic Summit. They say security's so tight even a mosquito couldn't get clearance. Palmer's people say the same thing."

"Then there's nothing the two of you can do?"

"Beyond what we're doing, no." Sapir's professional veneer almost cracked. "My guess is that the Borotins are holding Taylor hostage so that Dirksen behaves during the Summit."

"And after?"

"I wouldn't hold out much chance for her—or her daughter."

"Can I help?" Falkman's voice was a whisper.

"Tell Momo to stay calm and, more importantly, persuade Dirksen to stay where he is and do his job. Whatever happens, he must act normally. If he doesn't, my guess is Taylor's dead body will turn up nearby. It may anyway. When or where we'll find her daughter remains to be seen. More importantly . . ." The Israeli paused.

"More importantly, what?" Falkman snapped.

"He's all we have between us and whatever the Russians have planned."

Chapter 95
San Diego

The countdown clocks throughout the Resort all showed the number 3. Three days to go.

The area around the Audley had been transformed into a netherworld of protesters behind barbed-wire barriers, and hour-long traffic jams due to street closings, diversions, road blocks and security checkpoints. The influx of cars from Summit participants, lobbyists, gawkers, and reporters further flooded the already inadequate roads.

Most of the protest marches started peacefully and ended with scraps between the marchers—inflamed by violent agent provocateurs—and the riot police. The acrid smell of tear gas hung in the air long after the rioters dispersed and reformed to march again.

Local hospital emergency rooms staffed up to tend to the bruised, battered, gassed, clubbed and rubber-bullet victims among the protesters. They lay side by side with police officers injured in the running sorties.

Police isolated and identified ringleaders with a history of violence, but hundreds more protesters flowed in, attracted by the publicity, the excitement, their own heartfelt political beliefs.

Hovering helicopters became part of the background, vying for airspace to the extent that the Secret Service banned all non-security aircraft from the vicinity. Scalpers traded hotel rooms on the black market. Rooms auctioned on E-bay went for record prices. Reporters, swarming the area like bees seeking honey, dubbed the accommodation scandal "Hotel-Gate," and entry passes to the official press conferences became the hottest ticket for journalists since the Michael Jackson trial.

Talking heads filled the networks and cable stations, their hyperbole increasing with every report. Initially, much was made of the recent Manhattan murder of Rolfe Ritter—the creative genius behind the Audley San Diego Cliffs—but Matt Dirksen was the main story in the final pre-Summit days. *People* magazine ran a piece on him entitled "The Hotel Industry's Most Eligible Bachelor—If He Didn't Exist, Would Hollywood Invent Him?"

The real Matt Dirksen was leading a double life. To the arrivals, he was the impeccable, calm, unflappable sophisticated hotelier, acting as if each guest filled his very existence. The executive office's conference room—the War Room, as it became known—became command central where disputes were settled, staffers mollified, dignitaries soothed, meetings arranged, every manner of crisis averted. Unkindly dubbed "Boy Cheerleader" by Brad Marshall, he adopted the name as a rallying cry and used the initials B.C.L. to sign his e-mails. Marshall was not amused.

However, in the privacy of his office, the other Matt emerged, overwhelmed with guilt about his treatment of Beth, frantic with worry about her disappearance, consumed with terror about his own fate after the Summit ended, desperate—despite the security—that a catastrophe had been planned by his bosses at Blenheim and that he would be powerless to prevent it. Alone, he brooded in a depression that only his public performance could alleviate—something he found increasingly difficult to pull off.

*

Scott Fusilli, the security officer at the Kestrel Santa Monica, located the tape from the garage showing the arrival and departure of the blue van.

"What about the license number?" Matt asked when Fusilli reported in.

"Bad news, Mr. Dirksen. The guys were pros. The licenses were covered in mud—or paint. Still, with the help of my old boss at LAPD, the pictures of the vehicle are clear and they've been circulated to every police department in California. The van's distinctive. Sooner or later it'll show up."

Small comfort. Matt translated the word "later," as "too late" and spent a sleepless night drowned in self-pity, as visions of Rolfe's mutilated body was superimposed over Beth's in his mind. When he tried to imagine Britney, all he could see were grade-school children snatched by masked marauders from the playground.

His calls to Momo, more and more risky each time he used the secret phone, did nothing to alleviate his agony. She reported that Palmer and Sapir had no idea where Beth was. Worse, they had no leads on what Blenheim was up to at the Resort.

"Look out for anything strange," she warned him, which threw him into fury. Strange? Everything was strange! But he knew Mo- [illegible] was grieving, and he said nothing.

[illegible] The countdown to the Summit inexorably continued.

*

[illegible]att was awakened from a dream-plagued sleep by the sound [illegible]nging at his office. Dazed, he looked at his watch. Damn! [illegible]lept forty minutes when he'd intended only ten.

[illegible]oming!" he called, lifted himself from his metal cot and [illegible]ed to the door. When he undid the lock, it flew open. Jimmy [illegible]ed at him.

[illegible] down, Dirksen," the Te-Wu agent said. "We have to talk."

Chapter 96
Long Beach

Mother and daughter talked until both were hoarse. Britney told of her years with the Kisels—the generous, warmhearted Kisels who brought her up in a small home on the border between Goleta and Santa Barbara, but who could never replace her real mother in her bitter thoughts. She told of her youth, her school, her volleyball prowess, her first boyfriends and their clumsy attempts at petting. In turn, Beth described her own parents and their erratic actors' life, her itinerant childhood and the resultant lack of real friends, her education, the problems confronting a female hotelier in a man's world. Like her daughter, she tried to keep her stories light, but she couldn't help describing her inner torment when she let Britney go and the joy she felt—no matter her daughter's own feelings—at this reunion. She told her only a little about Matt: how they had come together and parted because of Blenheim; how they now had to go on separately, both with a different priority. Her heart was wrenched in pain as she tried to unemotionally gloss over the reasons for their parting. Unmentioned was her resentment. She knew Britney remained in his way, but she could not accept his dismissal of her child—and her. He would, she imagined, be crazed by her disappearance, no matter his present feelings. She hoped so.

Britney reached out to touch her mother's hand, then snuggled against her. The gesture, more moving than words, brought sobs to Beth's throat.

The girl pulled slightly away. "How did you and I get here? You mentioned a company called Blenheim. Jimmy Lee works for them, doesn't he?"

Beth told her, omitting nothing.

"Then we're in danger. Terrible danger." Britney's voice betrayed her fear.

"I don't know. They may let us go when the Summit's over and Matt's behaved as they want him to."

Britney looked at her closely. "Do you believe that?"

"I'd like to."

"Thanks for your honesty. I'd like to as well." She managed a wry smile. "It sounds like you really love this Matt."

"I used to," Beth cried. "But I betrayed him from the start, and he never really believed me when I told him the betrayal had changed to love. Oh, it's awful! He won't trust me, can't trust me, yet I love him with all my heart."

"So much that you'd agreed to sacrifice yourself—and me?"

Me yes, you never! Beth wanted to say as her face flushed with her guilt-ridden feelings, only the answer was more complicated than that, and she paused so she could get it right.

Britney covered her mother's mouth with her hand. "Shhh. Someone's coming."

*

A whirr preceded the clanking of the warehouse's rollup shutter, its ghoulish sounds echoing through the dark, cavernous warehouse.

Both women stared toward the direction of the rumbling noise, which stopped, then started again. The shutter had been raised—someone had entered the warehouse—then it closed again, Beth reasoned. She clutched her daughter's hands; like Britney's, her own palm was damp from fear.

With a soft hiss, the door in the wall of the cavernous room slid open, allowing a shaft of incandescent yellow light to throw eerie shadows. Both women blinked, rubbed their eyes. The silhouette of a medium-height, heavyset figure appeared in the doorway, then disappeared as the door closed. They could hear the intruder's footsteps approach and vaguely make out a spectral shadow. A man! He loomed over them like a monster.

"*Señora*, *señorita*, I have brought you food and water." His voice was pleasant underneath his heavy accent.

Beth could make out that he held a bucket in one hand, a small plastic shopping bag in the other. She reached to take them.

Their captor stepped away. "Not so fast. You must earn it."

"Please. We need food, water. What must we do?" Beth croaked through dry, cracked lips.

"Follow instructions." Now the man's voice had a bite to it. "If you behave, you will get fresh water and some bread. If you don't . . ." he waved the bag ". . . *Que lastima*."

"Who are you?" Britney asked. "How do we know the water's not poisoned?"

"My name doesn't matter. You'll have to take my word that the water is pure."

"Let us go," Beth said. "Please. How can one human being be so cruel?"

"The world is cruel, *señora*. Besides, I was not given the key, only instructions." He put the bucket down and reached in his pocket. The object he handed her was a cell phone. "All you have to do is make a phone call and say exactly what I tell you. *Enteindes*?"

Chapter 97
San Diego

"Sit down."

A command. Matt obeyed. The Te-Wu agent raised the blackout curtains; shards of sun streamed through the window. Silhouetted in the sharp light, he approached Matt's desk like the Angel of Death.

"You stupid man!" Jimmy Lee spat. "You stupid, interfering man. Why wouldn't you simply do as you were told?" His normally emotionless face was infused with rage.

Matt felt no fear. Lee was not there to kill him, not with the Summit ahead of them, and besides, this man was no more than an errand boy. "I don't know what you're talking about."

"Oh, but you do. I know everything: the betrayal by Beth Taylor, the calls to Rolfe Ritter. The conspiracy against us. Do you think we're stupid?"

Matt Dirksen stared at him defiantly. "That remains to be seen," he said quietly.

The words further inflamed Lee. "Now that Ritter's dead and your precious Beth's vanished, who will you talk to? Who can save you?" In a fury, he paced back and forth between door and window. "How many more deaths do you want on your conscience?" He tossed a manila envelope on the desk. "This one?"

Fear exploded in Matt's stomach.

"Open it!"

Photographs. Not Beth. Please, God, not Beth!

He pulled out the photos. They showed his father, stooped and obviously failing, getting into his rusting car, opening the door to his house, eating in his kitchen, sleeping in his bed.

Matt looked up. "For God's sake. Leave him alone!"

Lee's face was expressionless. "That's up to you. Up to now, we haven't touched him. Your father's life is in your hands. Don't bother warning him that we've been watching him—and don't call the police. There's nowhere he can go. One call from me, and he'll be dead within the half hour. I realize you're not as close to him as Ms. Taylor is to her daughter, but you wouldn't want to be responsible for his death, now would you? Your sister would know why he died and would never forgive you, even if you forgave yourself."

With a roar of rage, Matt leapt at his enemy. "You murdering son-of-a-bitch! I'll kill you!"

"With what?" Lee asked, stepping easily out of range. "Run me down with a maid's cart? Beat me to death with a room service menu? Get real and sit down, Mr. Dirksen, then listen very carefully."

Matt had no choice. He obeyed.

"From now until the end of the Summit, you will do nothing but your job. No phone calls except on Resort business, no more 'secret' conversations with any of Ritter's friends." He held out his hand. "You'll start by giving me your cell phones. Not the company one, the ones you've been using to call your precious friends."

"I don't know what you're talking about."

Lee took out his own cell phone. "Don't you even want to say goodbye to your father? I can tell my men to hold off until you do."

Matt reached into his briefcase and produced a phone, tossing it onto the desk.

"Now the other one."

"What other one?"

The Chinese pursed his thin lips. "I've been patient so far. That's over. Now give me the other phone. Now!" Lee's clenched fist pounded the desk.

Matt shuddered, sighed, pulled out the second phone and gently pushed it towards the other man. Lee put both cell phones in his pocket, his eyes never leaving Matt's face. "See how easy that was? Now let me have your Blackberry and your laptop."

"That's ridiculous. How will I be able to communicate within the Resort?"

"From this minute forward all e-mails addressed to you will go through Olivia Wade. She'll read them and pass along anything she deems worthy of your attention. You're to send none yourself. Olivia will say you're too busy. You and your team have the internal radio system for the important decisions—how to arrange the flowers, for instance."

Humiliated, Matt handed over the Blackberry and laptop.

"One more thing." Lee looked at his watch. "A surprise. You'll have to wait two minutes and twelve seconds to find out what it is."

The two men stared at each other. The seconds passed, very slowly.

Matt's desk phone rang. He moved toward it, but Lee stilled his hand and picked it up himself. He listened. "Good." He handed the receiver to Matt. "It's for you."

"Dirksen speaking," he said automatically.

"Matt, help us! Please, please help us."

His hands shook so violently he almost dropped the receiver. "Beth. You're alive!"

"You have to do what they tell you," she said quickly, her voice tightly controlled.

"Who's they? Who's us? Beth, I . . ."

"There's a man here. He doesn't speak much English, and he won't let me talk long, I'm sure. Britney's with me. We're in a warehouse, chained to a post, only I don't know where. You mustn't try to find us. If you don't do what Mr. Lee tells you, they'll kill us."

"Are you hurt? Is Britney?"

"No. Just frightened. So, so frightened!"

"Don't hang up!" Matt shouted. He heard the sound of a slap. Beth cried out. The phone went dead.

Jimmy Lee watched him triumphantly. "Convinced?"

Not entirely. The smallest part of him wondered if this was the last part of the cruel hoax.

Chapter 98
Tel Aviv

"Tovelah, where the hell is Kenneth Palmer?" Amnon Sapir shouted through his open office door.

"I'm trying to find him. His assistant told me he's traveling and will call you back as soon as she gets hold of him."

"It's a hell of a time to disappear," Sapir grumbled, fingers drumming on the red plastic file Tova Mandel had placed on his desk, its contents prompting the call to his British associate. He'd just returned from briefing his worried prime minister on the lack of progress of their Summit investigation. It was not a pleasant conversation, certainly not one that augured well for his long awaited promotion.

"Sir Kenneth on the line," Tova announced.

Sapir closed the door and picked up the scrambled phone. "Finally! Where the fuck are you?"

"And good afternoon to you, Amnon. I'm in the States of course, at the British Consul General's residence in Los Angeles, to be precise. Do you realize it's five a.m. in California? I haven't had my morning tea, so do try to be pleasant."

"Don't give me that British shit. I've no intention of being pleasant and you're just as worried as I am."

"More than worried. Frustrated and frantic. Everybody at Downing Street thinks I'm crying wolf; I can't get anyone's attention. The reason I'm here and not at the Resort with less than two days to go shows how little my presence would be welcomed by my prime minister's personal security detail, let alone my own colleagues in MI6. Now, why did you call? Did you come up with something on Falkman's mysterious Pakistanis?"

"Only that they're for real. Other than that, nothing. Lots of chatter from the satellites, lots of talk about the Summit, plenty of it from Pakistan, but no substance. You?"

"Not a peep, nothing to go on. Come on, what's the drama?"

"We both have people working at the Resort, remember?"

"Of course."

Well, Dirksen created a job for one of my men as a night cleaner. Together they got access to Brad Marshall's office and bugged it."

"That's old news. Go on," Sir Kenneth said impatiently.

"He's the only agent Dirksen knows personally."

"I don't follow."

"My man was on duty last night, part of the crew cleaning the lobby. Dirksen 'accidentally' bumped into him, palmed him a note, apologized for being clumsy and left. My man went to the men's room, photo'd the note with his cell phone and e-mailed it to me."

Palmer was impatient no longer. Sapir could hear his steady, controlled breathing. "What does it say?"

"I'll read it.

"Please pass this to your boss. Explain that I have no other means of communication since Jimmy Lee has confiscated my cell phones, laptop and Blackberry. Too, I'm watched 24/7 by Brad Marshall's security force. They sleep in the same room as me and even follow me to the bathroom.

Yesterday, Lee threatened to have my father killed if I didn't behave. He let me speak to Beth Taylor, held captive with her daughter in a warehouse, chained to a post, I have no idea where, hostages to my good behavior.

Marshall's cut off my contacts with the Secret Service and the FBI so I have no idea what's being done to protect our guests. I'm not sure what 'behave' means, but I'd guess if I see something strange, I'm not to say anything about it and that whatever Blenheim says, goes.

I realize that Blenheim has no reason to keep me alive, so when the Summit ends, I'll try to slip out without being seen and start running but I can't leave California without trying to find Beth and her daughter.

That's where you come in. The LAPD has information on Beth's kidnappers. There are pictures of a blue van. Please let them know how serious this is—they must do everything they can to find the van. It's the only lead to Beth. I know you are going to depend on me for information during the Summit. I'll help you if I can.

Can you figure out a way to get me out of here without Blenheim knowing?

I am filled with dread. Getting Beth back is the only thing that prevents me from going mad."

"That's some note," Palmer said. "Poor fellow."

"It took guts to pass it on," Sapir agreed.

Sir Kenneth paused, reflecting. "My people can communicate with Dirksen, but I don't have any influence with the LAPD. Do you?"

"Perhaps some. There are lots of Jews in L.A., many very wealthy and more very political. I'll get them involved, someone will have enough stroke that the police will have to pay attention. Let's face the fact that Taylor and her daughter will probably be in the van when they find it—with their throats cut." Sapir's tone was unemotional.

"I'll work on a plan to get Dirksen out of the Resort—maybe pass him off as a member of our delegation."

"Say we save him. We still have no idea what Blenheim's planning."

"That's not quite accurate, Amnon. The fact that Lee and Marshall are so overtly threatening means that something will happen. There's a real plot. But who is it aimed at? When? How? I've no idea. All we can hope is that Matt somehow stumbles on their plans."

"Yeah." Amnon's gravelly voice was pitched low. "And he's a dead man walking."

Chapter 99
White Plains, NY

Dimitri Netski contently sipped coffee. His brother's Gulfstream G550 was waiting at Westchester County's airport. He boarded, looked at his watch—5:48 a.m.—and dialed a number on his cell phone.

"Marshall speaking." The security chief's voice was sleepy.

"Brad, it's Dimitri Netski. Sorry to call you so early."

"No problem, Mr. Netski. I was just dozing. It's been a long few days."

"Days that are nearly over. I've decided to leave New York early and come to the Resort to make sure everything goes according to plan. I'm on my plane. My assistant will track it and let you know when you should pick me up. We need to talk before I get to the property."

"I'll be waiting for you, sir."

Obsequious idiot. "One last thing, Brad. If I have to change schedule or something comes up, I want you to execute the plan exactly as discussed. Exactly. Meticulously. Precisely according to schedule. Is that clear?"

"You can count on me."

"I do. And you can count on another $5 million in your Swiss bank account. However, if you fail . . ."

Vasily Borotin turned off the phone, leaving the threat unspecified. Nodding to the pilot, the plane in which he was the lone passenger revved up its engines and took off on its long journey east, to Saint Petersburg, Russia. Minutes later a Boeing Business Jet, bearing the Kestrel Hotels and Resorts logo, took off from the same runway and headed west.

Chapter 100
San Diego

Everyone could read the clocks. One day left to the G8 Summit.

*

"Why are those goons following you everywhere?" Pete Wilson asked, indicating the two security officers trailing them.

"Brad Marshall's idea," Matt said. "He says its Secret Service orders, but I'll be damned if he isn't having me watched. Apparently I have no choice."

The two men walked on in silence, noticing everything in their path. Wilson picked up two dead leaves that had somehow gone unnoticed by the grounds crew on their half-hourly sweeps, while Matt straightened the name tag on a bellman hurrying to deliver a package to one of the suites.

"The place is a zoo," Wilson complained.

"It's about to get worse. Netski's uber-assistant called this morning to say the Great Man's flying from New York for a personal inspection. Just what we need. More interference." The news was sinister. Netski's presence could only mean that Blenheim's plan was about to be ignited.

Matt kept his thoughts to himself. "You say it's a zoo. Why?"

Wilson sighed. "How's this for openers? Last night, the snipers set up on the roofs of the main building, Conference Center and laundry complex. We had a power outage when Fox News tried some new equipment that sucked the juice out of the system. The emergency generator kicked in, but only satisfied the basics. Took me over an hour to get it fixed, pissing off every temperamental journalist in the place. Then the CBS head honcho busted my ass because we didn't have the right brands of booze in the mini bar. As for those nervous pricks from State . . ."

Matt chuckled, delighted to have some light relief. "You think you got troubles? Just after midnight, one of your State Department flunkies showed up in my office telling me they'd decided to add a half-day session called 'Outreach Africa.' Shouldn't be too hard to organize, he said. They've invited the presidents of Nigeria, Egypt, South Africa, Algeria, Ghana and Senegal. I told him I'd get you right on it."

Wilson exploded, "You've got to be fucking joking! There's no place to put them unless we set up tents on the lawn."

"No need." Matt patted Wilson on the shoulder; he didn't want his only friend ruffled. "I took care of it myself. The presidents will stay at the Ritz-Carlton, Laguna Niguel, where they'll be treated like kings wish they could be treated. They'll show up here for lunch, attend the session, have their pictures taken with our president, and get back to living it up in Laguna at our government's expense."

"Have you told F. and B.?" Wilson asked, mollified.

"Yup. They whined about seating plans, dietary requirements and staff shortages. When they finished complaining, I told them I didn't give a flying fuck about their problems—just get it done without ever talking to me about it again."

"What did our chef say?"

"That I deserved to die. I think I am in danger of being decapitated with a butcher's knife, but . . ."

"Mr. Dirksen! Mr. Wilson!"

The two men turned. Melanie Berman, Wilson's normally calm and disciplined administrative assistant, raced toward then.

"What's the matter?" Wilson asked.

Melanie fought to catch her breath. "It's Mr. Netski!"

"Fuck!" Matt didn't usually swear in front of employees, but this news was too much. The man wasn't supposed to arrive for hours. Now he'd have to spend the day babysitting his boss. "Is he here already?"

"No, no! That's not it at all." The woman's distress level had peaked. "Mr. Netski's assistant tried to reach Olivia, but she's not at her desk, so I took the call."

"What call?" Wilson asked.

"Oh, it's horrible. Horrible!"

Had it started? Matt wondered. His body trembled. “What’s horrible, Melanie?”

“Half hour ago, Mr. Netski’s plane exploded over the Rockies. There were no survivors.”

Chapter 101
Los Angeles

"All clear, Sir Kenneth."

"Thank you, gentlemen." Palmer watched the two MI6 operatives who had swept his office in the British government's Los Angeles consulate leave, marveling as always at the technical skills of men who barely speak English. He picked up the secure phone and dialed. "Did I wake you?" he asked the voice that answered.

"If I were in Tel Aviv you might have," Sapir answered. "Not that I'm able to sleep under this pressure."

"Where in the world are you, dear boy?"

"Does it matter?" Amnon was clearly in a foul mood.

Palmer chuckled. "You'd lie anyway. It's in our genes."

"Any news?"

"Vasily Borotin's plane exploded over Colorado with him in it."

"You don't think I know that?"

"I presumed you did. What do you make of it?"

"It reaffirms that something big's about to happen. That's why I can't sleep. As far as the younger Borotin's concerned, there are two possible scenarios. First, the bad guys have fallen out with each other and the Chinese decided to get rid of our friend Vasily. That would piss his brother off, leading to God knows what."

"And the other?"

"It's a fake. Borotin's alive and well. The U.S. will find the plane and a body will be identified as Netski's. But it won't be his. Just some stooge unfortunate enough to look like him."

"Yes, I'd thought of both scenarios myself. What's your bet?"

"Same as yours. Borotin faked his own death. By now that son-of-a-bitch is on his way to Russia."

"You know what it means, of course."

"Borotin's putting distance between himself and his alter ego, Netski. Everything will be Netski's fault—Netski who's already dead."

Palmer's collar became uncomfortably tight. He unbuttoned it. "Here's something you probably didn't know. My team reported that Jimmy Lee, a.k.a. Tang Shen-ming, drove out of the Resort less than a quarter-hour after learning the Netski news. The man hasn't returned, nor has he shown up at the Santa Monica property.

Sapir's tone was grim. "That's nearly ten hours. I'll have someone stake out the Chinese Consulate, but we wouldn't be able to touch him if that's where he is. Fucking diplomatic immunity."

"Tell you the truth, Amnon, I've never been so frustrated in my life," Palmer admitted. "We've got nothing new. Despite the chatter, nothing more on the Pakistanis. The fact that the Russian and Chinese birds have flown scares the hell out of me. We both know something horrific's going to happen, we both have people in the Resort who've found out nothing. My own prime minister thinks I'm crazy, the U.S. Secret Service doesn't want to listen, the FBI's shut us out, and our only hope is a general manager whose estranged girlfriend's being held as a hostage to his good behavior."

"My own prime minister's equally frustrated. He thinks I've lost my touch. We can only hope we've got enough agents in place to fend off any attack."

"You don't believe that, do you?"

"I wish I did. This is not a full-front assault, nor a one-shot suicide bomber. I haven't a clue what in God's name the attack will look like. I am convinced it will come. Talking of God, perhaps hoping for divine intervention is what it comes down to." The Israeli was silent for a moment. "Remember I said I'd use the Jewish influence with the LAPD to be more aggressive in their investigation of the Beth Taylor kidnapping?"

"Frankly, I haven't given it much thought. Seems like a hopeless quest."

"Probably is. But they've found the van used to kidnap her." A sliver of hope, like a crescent moon in a dark sky, lit Palmer's heart. "Really! Where?"

“A town called Vernon in L.A. County. Plenty of small manufacturing setups, so the vehicle didn’t stand out.”

“How did the police know it’s the right van?”

Sapir’s laughter made Palmer smile. “The perps didn’t do a good job cleaning up. They found prints on the doors and the steering wheel, and fingerprints, hair and blood in the back of the van. Taylor’s fingerprints. And Taylor’s briefcase, for Christ’s sake, that had slipped behind the passenger seat and was jammed on the floor underneath it.”

“Okay, it was the van. But what good that does that do us? It doesn’t tell us where she was taken.”

“No, but the fingerprints in the front tell us who the driver was.”

“Jesus! Who?”

“Mexican national, name of Pablo Fuentes. And one guess who *señor* Fuentes works for.”

“Don’t play games. I’ve no bloody idea.”

“Fuentes is a driver for the Chinese Consulate in Los Angeles.”

Palmer felt his blood pressure rise, “I presume the police contacted the Consulate. What did they say?”

“That Fuentes was a contract driver, that he hasn’t been used in over a month, and would the police stop harassing them.”

“That means the police’ll have to find him.”

“There’s an all-points-bulletin out. We’ve used what little influence we have to get the FBI to issue an alert across the country. If Fuentes hasn’t fled to Mexico, sooner or later he’ll be picked up.”

Sooner or later. The moonlight dimmed. “By which time it’ll be too late for Beth Taylor and her daughter.”

“Right. And too late to stop whatever’s going down at the Summit.”

Chapter 102
San Diego

Bertrand Le Roi. Gidon Lahav. Sammi Chalabi. Leon Barken. Rolfe Ritter. Names and faces scrolled through Matt's mind like ghosts. He slumped at his desk, shoes off, tie askew, so exhausted he could not lift his head or erase the images. It was near midnight, minutes before the first day of the Summit.

And precious Beth. He remembered her smile when they met at the Hotel Del Coronado, her uninhibited ways of making love, his glow in their passion's aftermath; he heard her fear when she called from her invisible dungeon—fear for Britney, for herself, for him. Gone was his feeling that her call was part of Blenheim's plan for setting him up. No actress alive could have feigned such distress, such terror. How wrong he had been about her! Yes, she was working for Blenheim at the start, but her protestations of love, her ardor, her gentleness, her courage—those had not been faked. And her protestations of love were real and true and all-important. He reviled himself for his suspicions. Why the fuck had he decided to work alone? Why had he pushed her away like every other woman he had loved? Her safety was more important than anything that might happen at the Summit, and out of stupidity and anger he had given up the chance of helping her, no matter how remote that was. Despair suffocated him. His tormentors at Blenheim would never let Beth, Britney and him live beyond the Summit.

An hour ago, his messenger, the stealthy night cleaner, had contrived to bump into him. "We'll take care of you if the time comes. Look for a sign. It will be obvious." The man in the fawn overalls had talked so quickly and quietly that Matt wondered if he had imagined the exchange.

If Beth died, what matter if he lived?

The roar of a heavy vehicle sounded outside. With the effort of a man of ninety, he roused himself and went to the window. The

American president's personal ambulance pulled into Matt's own parking space behind the executive offices. Was the president himself inside? Did Matt's warnings have enough impact to warrant this simple subterfuge? He hoped so.

Time for one last inspection. The food and beverage team would continue preparing hundreds of today's meals: rack upon rack of flash-grilled beef, veal, lamb and poultry would be stored for last minute finishing for the gala banquet and legions of bakers would work through the night. The ice sculptors would be in newly created freezers chiseling out their intricate designs for the opening gala dinner; the countless flower arrangements would be stored in temporary coolers. He knew he should look too at the Conference Center with its elaborate set and multi-dimensional audio and video equipment, programmed to showcase the United States as host of this—the most expensive and elaborate G8 Summit in the history of such events.

Yet, as he put on his shoes, he recalled his words to a group who had come whining to his office, needing his arbitration. "Enough!" he'd shouted. "Get out! You're confusing me with someone who gives a shit!"

The door to his office opened. "Can't you knock?" he shouted.

"I don't have to," Brad Marshall said. The man was impeccably groomed, like the official greeter at a society fund-raiser.

"What do you mean?" Matt said.

"I'm here to remind you to behave."

"I don't need the reminder. And never barge in on me again!"

"For fuck's sake, we have your girlfriend and her bastard daughter. Your father's a phone call away from meeting his maker. And you're giving me orders? From this point on, I am your boss. If I tell you to fart, you answer how loud. If I tell you to do something, any fucking thing, you hop! Is that clear?"

Matt said nothing. Marshall rested his hand on the general manager's desk and leaned over close enough for Matt to see his faint stubble. "Is that clear?"

"Yes," Matt whispered, beaten.

Chapter 103
San Diego

Four a.m. The countdown clocks read zero. Matt trudged from his office to the meeting room set aside for the final pre-Summit conference. Sniffer dogs, ears twitching like antennas, somehow realizing that the rehearsals were over, roamed the grounds intently, taking their handlers where their trained noses led them. An army of Secret Service and FBI agents, wearing Kevlar vests, checked every nook and corner with metal detectors; others were carefully turning over and examining each gold-brocaded chair in the Conference Center and meeting rooms. Their companions would be crawling under the stage, through the audio-visual and lighting control rooms, the staging and setup areas, the narrow crawl space between the ceiling and the Conference Center's reinforced concrete roof, the air-conditioning ducts, the kitchens, cold rooms and service areas. Nothing could go undetected—at least so Matt prayed.

His heart full of dread, he walked into the packed meeting room. A wave of caffeine-fueled nervous chatter hit his ears and he took his place at the end of the table, silencing the crowd. His staff was weary, he knew, yet the men were clean-shaven, the women freshly made up. Their adrenaline rush would get them through opening day.

"No motivational speeches from me," he said, thinking that this should have been the proudest moment of his life. "You all know what your jobs are and what needs to be done. So let's get down to business."

One by one, the staffers gave their reports. Occasionally, he'd ask a question, offer advice, suggest a change. No one could have suspected that there was anything on his mind other than running the G8 Summit.

Keith McGregor, the chief engineer, looked apprehensive, shifting in his chair, his face abnormally pale.

"Keith?"

"Everything's as it should be. Just as it's been for weeks."

"You look troubled. No issues with the boilers, air-conditioning, electronics?"

"I said everything's fine. There won't be any glitches." He bit his lower lip and looked away.

"Any risks of power overloads or shortages when everything's cranked up to full?" Pete Wilson asked.

"Damn it!" McGregor shouted. "Think I don't know what I'm doing? You want my job as well?"

"Hold on, both of you," Matt interceded. "Everyone's on edge. Let's move on."

The group dispersed. Wilson and Dirksen left together. "Why wasn't Marshall here?" Wilson asked.

"He's got his hands full. You know that." He caught up to McGregor. "Keith, a word." He rested his hand on the Scot's forearm.

McGregor wrenched his arm away.

"Anything I can do?" Matt asked gently. "Stress getting to you?"

The engineer pursed his lips as if restraining himself. Then, without answering, he marched away, leaving Matt staring at his back.

*

Two days ago McGregor was on top of things, Matt reflected back in his office. Now he's a nervous wreck. Why? As he struggled to find the answer—was it in McGregor's domain where the attack would come and had he somehow found out about it? Was the Scot being blackmailed and threatened like Matt?—Brad Marshall loomed at his door.

"Dirksen, you're wanted in the Control Center. Now."

"Why?" Matt asked automatically.

"Because I say so. The Secret Service wants to review your instructions for today."

Stifling his fury, Matt walked toward the Control Center, Marshall following close behind. Inside, Matt gasped. The room's long wall was filled from floor to ceiling with numbered flatscreen monitors. In front of them were three rows of banquet tables, the first standing on the floor, the second on a raised platform, the third on an even higher plinth, so the team manning the desks had an unobstructed view of each monitor. The desks were covered with telephones, cell phones, laptops, strewn pens, partially used pads of lined yellow paper, coffee cups and plates of congealed, half-eaten food. Behind the third row were five individual tables, each a desk for the senior Secret Service agents. No one, it seemed, had slept; men and women looked similarly disheveled. Matt caught snippets of a Babel of conversations: "Switch to three." "Take a look at the face in twenty-two." "ETD for POTUS from Andrews in one-forty."

The multiple monitors showed images of the Resort from every conceivable angle. From the front gates to the loading dock, the main lawn, the suites set aside for the presidents and prime ministers, the laundry rooms and meetings rooms—closed circuit TV cameras left no corner unseen.

The cameras covered the outside as well. Monitor after monitor showed the protestors' camps. On one screen, the camera zeroed in on two men talking under a tree by the dumpsters San Diego County had provided in a valiant but vain attempt to control the ever-growing mounds of garbage.

"Give me sound," a male voice from the second row shouted.

"That's as loud as it'll go," a woman answered.

"Then get me a goddamned lip reader!"

"They don't come on duty until six a.m."

"Shit!"

Smiling, Matt looked at the monitors showing San Diego Airport, now closed for all but Secret Service-cleared traffic, as was the surrounding airspace. Other monitors showed all the roads in the no-go area surrounding the Resort, looking eerily abandoned save for police and other security vehicles.

"Interesting, isn't it?" a voice behind Matt said.

"Fascinating." He turned to acknowledge Jeff Hartman, the forty-three-year-old secret service agent responsible for the Resort. He and Matt had worked together for the past months, and Matt had grown to not only like him, but to consider him an ally. The ultra-fit ex-Notre Dame running back had been cooperative, unobtrusive and unfailingly friendly—characteristics not shared by anyone at Blenheim.

"Dress up for me?" Matt joked, noting Hartman's dark suit, white shirt and red tie.

The agent rubbed his face. "I seem to be shaving every two hours. I'm the one each of the 'High-and-Mighties' calls if there's a hint of a problem, and I'm the liaison with the security details of the foreign poobahs. God pity me if I don't look like a recruiting poster for the Secret Service."

"Brad Marshall said you wanted to see me."

"With his customary tact and charm?"

Matt grinned. "Some day he'll make an ambassador to some far off, very remote and sparsely populated place—only not soon enough."

"I thought you and I should review the day ahead. If we wait any longer, it'll be mayhem."

"This isn't mayhem?" Matt gestured toward the desks.

"You ain't seen nothing yet. Wait till POTUS and FLOTUS arrive."

"I thought they'd come last night in an ambulance."

"That was just to throw off the would-be bad guys. Here's what's going to happen. The president and first lady will take off from Andrews in less than two hours. An air corridor will be cleared for Air Force One across the country until it lands in San Diego. Marine One, the president's helicopter, will bring them here, with the rest of the entourage coming by SUV in a police-protected convoy. There will be two other identical helicopters, so any bad guys won't know which one carries the president.

"All the other leaders will be here by the time POTUS and FLOTUS arrive. You'll have greeted each one personally and escorted them to their suites, posing with each of them for the usual photos I know you're dying to hang from your office wall."

What office? Matt thought, a jolt of adrenaline hurling him back into his situation.

Hartman pressed on, oblivious to the change in Dirksen's demeanor. "By the time the president and the first lady arrive, we will be in Closed Protection Protocol mode. Every area the president goes through will be inspected and protected in advance. We've already instituted complete Perimeter Protection protocols—doesn't that sound nice?—so this place now is as secure as any on earth.

"As soon as it's light, we'll go into full helicopter patrol mode. We'll have every damned road in San Diego County in human and video sight at all times. The National Guard's tripled the assistance they're providing the local police. If a protester so much as scratches his balls, we'll nab him."

"You sound very casual about it all," Matt said.

"You should see my stomach. Knotted worse than the Unicorn Tapestry." He feigned a burp. "When POTUS and FLOTUS arrive on the main lawn, you'll be the first to greet them. You have ten seconds for your welcoming speech. You'll have your picture taken with them. POTUS will hold an eight-minute press conference using the helicopter as backdrop. Then you'll drive the president in a gold golf cart to the front door of his suite and escort him inside. Pete Wilson will chauffeur the first lady."

"Then what?" Matt asked, already fatigued.

"Then, my friend, you'll do what you're paid to do. Produce a Summit the president and the people of America can be proud of."

"Okay. One final time: Are you satisfied everything's one hundred percent secure?"

"I've asked myself that a thousand times. The answer's yes. We're as safe as anyone could hope for. Oh, and you must thank Brad Marshall. For all his rough ways, he's taken much of the burden, made my job a lot easier."

Matt was anything but reassured.

Chapter 104
New York

Since the nightmarish events at the entrance to the Sloan-Kettering Cancer Center, Momo had paid little attention to her sickness, inhabiting a strange and lonely netherworld, living for the moment, making no plans longer than hours ahead. The only objective person she could talk to was Ron Falkman. He, Rolfe's best friend, had kept Rolfe from too many mistakes to count, and now the aging lawyer provided her with much needed balance.

She spent too much time watching television, having neither the energy nor interest to read. An image, a story, shocked her into picking up the phone.

"Ron, it's Momo. Turn on CNN."

Falkman used the remote on his desk to activate the TV in time to see the President of the United States shaking hands with Matt Dirksen on the great lawn of the Audley Resort.

"It hurts," Momo said. "Suddenly I realized this was for real. All the conversations, the hypothetical plots we've talked about for months, the Sloan-Kettering . . ."

"I know, my dear. We'll only know what they've planned when it happens. It's sad to acknowledge that the great Mossad, the fabled MI6. and our own brains haven't figured out anything."

"What if nothing happens?" she asked listlessly. "What if we've got it wrong and the Borotins are only up to some financial scam?"

"You know better than that. The deaths, the kidnappings, the Russians and the Chinese. Something's going down that's more than a financial rip-off."

The screen showed Matt and the president drive away out of the camera's view. "The place looks great," Momo said. "How proud Rolfe would have been to be in the midst of the event and to have seen his jewel so resplendent."

"Young Dirksen seems to be holding up despite his burdens."

"You can't tell from a picture. God, how he must be suffering!" She took a deep breath. "Any more news on Beth and her daughter?"

Ron tried to sound optimistic. "The reward you offered for information leading to Fuentes resulted in some leads. The LAPD's pretty sure he's still in the city, in which case they'll find him."

"And if they do, and if he leads them to Beth and Britney, what then?"

Falkman let the question hang.

Chapter 105
San Diego

Matt Dirksen felt like a deflated balloon. In the past few hours, he had escorted every head of state, each prime minister, the Secretary General of the United Nations, the President of the European Commission, the Director of the International Monetary Fund and the head of the World Bank to their suites; had the obligatory photos taken with each; arranged for whatever services they required; dealt with the complaints of their sycophantic and self-important attendants; listened to Pete Wilson's tales of woe when it came to his charges, the second tier dignitaries; made the latest series of changes to the agenda demanded by self-important State Department staffers; dealt with a minor fire in the exhaust hood of one of the kitchens; reworked and reinforced the cordons for the internal No-Go areas, enduring the vituperation of the media; and then suffered through individual interviews with the major networks, CNN, Sky News and the BBC.

He and Wilson together watched the coverage of the escalating violence between protesters and police as the unexpectedly large crowds surged through the first perimeter lines manned by the National Guard.

At last alone in the bathroom attached to his office, he showered and shaved for the third time that day, toweled off, sat for a moment and experienced the feeling of impending disaster he had been repressing all day.

Beth was doomed. He was doomed. There was no hope for either of them. When he looked in the mirror to comb his hair, the thought that welled up in him—this may be my last day on earth—buckled his knees, and he slowly slid down the wall, ending up on the cold marble floor, his back against the cold ceramic tiles, hands holding his face while unstoppable tears of despair dripped unnoticed onto his bare torso.

The sound of his sobbing brought his two Marshall-appointed minders to the bathroom door. Stony faced, they made no move to comfort him.

*

The business of the Summit began in earnest. Meetings between the various heads of state went as choreographed; press conferences occurred with pre-scripted answers to obviously planted questions; hastily arranged meetings of junior ministers caused turmoil among the Resort's staff as they reshuffled meeting room assignments to make space available and arranged for catering, as if it had all been planned months in advance.

Russia's Under Secretary for Foreign Affairs collapsed during an argument with his French counterpart in one of the meeting rooms. Following the Resort's standard protocol, the director of catering called 911 while one of the Resort's doctors rushed to the room with a defibrillator. The Russian's colleagues refused to allow the doctor to touch their comrade, however, and located their own doctor at last, wrapped in scented, purified hot mud in the spa's steam room.

Furious at having his sojourn interrupted, the Russian doctor examined his patient, pronounced a heart attack, and piled into an ambulance with the Secretary and a Russian security officer. It was doubtful if anyone would see the Under Secretary again.

No one in the meeting room could have guessed that only fifteen minutes earlier, the Resort's general manager had climbed out of his deep vat of self-pity, dressed in a new shirt, tie and suit, and forced himself downstairs to attend to whatever additional crises would inevitably occur.

*

On the other side of the Resort, Brad Marshall watched the simultaneous translation team receive their final briefing and climb the flight of stairs to their positions in the tinted, mirrored glass booths overlooking the stage of the Conference Center's auditorium, where the opening ceremonies would take place in less than two hours. Florists put final touches to the trees, planters and floral arrangements that lined the auditorium and surrounded the stage. The Resort's staff set up each nation's flag in the order decided upon after days of negotiation, the "Stars and Stripes" central among them. Marshall noted with satisfaction that his own security staff had taken up their assigned positions and mingled easily with the anxious retinue from the Secret Service.

He beckoned to Keith McGregor, who had just completed his final inspection of the Center's internal systems. "Everything in order? Backup systems functioning?"

The chief engineer saluted. "Aye. Like clockwork."

"Good," Marshall said. "We wouldn't want any surprises, would we?"

Chapter 106
Los Angeles

"Amnon! What a surprise! What brings you to Los Angeles?"

The Israeli grinned. "First, it isn't a surprise—you knew I was here all along. Second, you know exactly what brings me here."

Palmer remained unflappable. "Let me amend. What brings you to my temporary office this early morning?"

"News, good and bad." The Israeli sat across from Palmer's desk at the British Consulate and leaned forward. "The police have Carlos Fuentes in custody."

"Where? How?" The head of British Counter Intelligence could not control a tremor of excitement.

"Momo's offer of a reward helped. Fuentes was holed up in one of those anonymous apartment complexes near the airport, staying with a friend. His friend thought it his compelling civic duty to let the police know. He's a hundred thousand richer and Fuentes is in a holding cell."

"With friends like that . . . What's the bad?"

"Fuentes got himself a big-time lawyer who won't let him say a word. God knows where he got the money, but I'd venture it's Borotin's dough. I've been trying to get in to see him. Ten minutes with me, and he'll be singing like Bruce Springsteen."

"The niceties of American justice do have a tendency to get in the way," Palmer acknowledged.

"I thought maybe you could get me a one-on-one interview. Israeli influence only goes so far."

"If I can't persuade my prime minister there's something going on, what makes you think I'd have better luck with the LAPD?"

Sapir looked at the portrait of Elizabeth II occupying the center of an otherwise empty wall. "Maybe you should call her," he joked.

Palmer followed his gaze. "Mmmm."

"What that supposed to mean?

"It means I have an idea . . . "

Chapter 107

Long Beach

Beth and Britney—after each attempt to break out of their manacles failed, every quixotic escape plan was squashed, faint hope long disappeared, their food long ago devoured, and only a couple of swallows of water remained—were too exhausted, too hungry, too dehydrated to talk.

Mother and daughter simply lay side by side on the cold floor of the dark, dank warehouse, hugging each other for meager comfort, and waited for the inevitable . . . reunited in life and now in their impending death.

Chapter 108
San Diego

The food and beverage team, which had prepared and set up the opening night's gala dinner, gathered around Matt in the otherwise unoccupied glittering ballroom.

"My hat's off to all of you," he said. The room's never looked better, the food's perfection. I'm proud of you all. Here's the process: First, the regular delegates will enter, followed by the leaders of the G8 countries, who'll be seated on the stage. We're allowing three television cameras and a dozen pooled still-photographers on the sidelines. The president will make his remarks after the main course, but before the dessert. Your job—our job—will be to make every delegate feel special, as if we were catering a dinner party for two in their own homes."

Matt paused to look around the ballroom. The walls and ceilings were washed in muted lights. Gold and silver chair coverings and table cloths shimmered; crystal stemware created by Steuben especially for this event would, Dirksen knew, sparkle with the reflections of the dozen candles adorning each table. Should conversation lag, the delegates could turn their attention to the apparently seamless ten-foot-high screens wrapped around the entire ballroom, showing videos of previous Summits and—an innovation—not only pictures of every delegate taken minutes before at the lavish pre-dinner cocktail party, but also videos of attendees while they lavishly wined and dined, taken from twenty ceiling track-mounted, remote-controlled roving cameras.

He felt oddly moved. The Resort was resplendent. No other general manager, no other resort or hotel, could have outshone his own work or the Audley's opulence. He had set the bar as high as it could go, and as he thought grimly of the almost certain reward, his heart was heavy.

"I can't begin to tell you how impressed I am by all you've achieved, how grateful I am for your incredible effort and how proud I am to be part of your team," he said. "This is your night. Relish every minute. Remember it forever. It's an historic event and you are an integral part of it. You've done exactly what I asked you to do when we undertook this journey together. You've proven you are the very best professionals and have earned the respect of everyone in our business. Now let's go back to work and show the world what we can do. Let's set a standard that others who follow will have to struggle to even get within striking distance of our incredible achievement." Matt left the room to sustained applause, knowing from his own experience that it was more for themselves than for his words.

"Mister Dirksen?"

Li Yong-zheng, executive chef from the Shanghai Kestrel, hurried after him.

"Yes?"

"Have you seen Mr. Lee?"

The little man was plainly agitated. "Not in the last day or so. Why?"

"Since I have been here, I became friendly with him. His family came from downtown Shanghai, off Nanjing Xi Lu, where I live, so we spent time talking about home. I'm a little—what's the word? Homesick?—and it made me feel better talking Chinese with . . ."

"Yong-zheng, you must forgive, but I'm very busy," Matt interrupted kindly. "Please come to the point."

"Of course, of course. Mr. Lee was interested in the Chinese fusion dishes I'm preparing for tomorrow's Festival of Nations dinner. I promised I would do a special tasting for him this afternoon—he is an important man, and it would be an honor for me. Yesterday, I saw him getting into his car and I asked him at what time he would like to come to my kitchen tomorrow to taste the banquet's dishes. He looked at me as if I were crazy and said something very strange."

Matt felt his heart rate quicken. "What did he tell you?"

"He said, 'It doesn't matter. No one will eat it.' Then he drove off. Do you know where he is so I can apologize for whatever it is I've done to offend Mr. Lee?"

"I'll try to find him and let you know." Matt could barely get out the words.

A flash of light entered his brain with palpable force, causing him to lean against the wall to steady himself. "'It doesn't matter. No one will eat it.' No one will need food tomorrow?" he said out loud. "That means today!"

*

Only Amnon, Kenneth and Ron Falkman would believe him, he knew, and without facts he couldn't go to the police or Secret Service. Besides, Marshall's men would know in an instant if he tried to make a call. He was as tightly chained as Beth and Britney.

What had Blenheim planned? What form would the attack take, and where would be its epicenter? He had missed something vital that would click the odd events into place, but what was it? He knew it existed. He knew it was obvious. The elusive answer fluttered in front of his eyes like a feather in the wind. Think, you dimwit! Think or you'll die, they'll die, all of us will die.

He was interrupted by a knocking at his door. "Matt?"

His thoughts evaporated like soap bubbles. He recognized the voice. "Come in, Tim."

Matt's relationship with Tim Matheson had grown into friendship during the months of planning, dramas and challenges they had endured together. Without Tim's wisdom, support, morale boosts and constant mediation, Matt knew the Summit would not have come together as efficiently as it had, and the extraordinarily high standard that was once a dream could never have been a reality. Matt Dirksen also knew Tim would lose his job if anything went wrong, and had long ago vowed to make him proud of his selection.

Matt forced himself to concentrate, roughly shoving aside the thought that he probably wouldn't see tomorrow's dawn. Would Tim Matheson?

"I just want to thank you and your amazing team for making me look good," Tim said. "I expected to see you at the Conference Center, but Pete Wilson said you'd fled to escape the hubbub."

"I should be the one thanking you. You gave us an amazing opportunity, trusted us, and allowed us to showcase the Resort in front of the world."

"So far so good. All the delegates are inside, the media are frenzied as ever. There are 700 people crammed into the Conference Center—it's the Tower of Babel all over again."

Yes, Matt thought. And look what happened there.

"The protesters are under control, if you can describe that barely contained mayhem in any way as 'controlled'," Matheson went on, "although the sight of a TV camera sends them into the usual frenzy." He looked at his watch. "We'd best get going. In less than three minutes the G8 leaders will enter the Center. Our president will come in last, take his seat in the middle—and hey, presto, magic, the performance begins."

"I've checked with the ballroom people and can assure you tonight's event will leave everyone wowed."

"I never doubted it." Both men stood. Matheson put a fatherly hand on Matt's shoulder. "You know, Matt, I had faith in you the first time we met and you haven't disappointed me for a second. You and I have made one hell of a good team. But I have to say I am astonished by what a job you've done. Amazing! You accomplished things we'd never have dreamed of asking for: the repainting, the landscaping, the topiaries, new furniture, upgrading the air-conditioning, and even entirely new boilers on top of the electrical and electronic systems for the Conference Center. You went way over the top on that one. That's initiative, man. I owe you big time. You made me look like a hero. If it hadn't been for you . . ." He stopped, stared. "What's the matter?"

Matt turned pale. "What did you just say?"

"I said you made me look like a hero."

"No. Before that. What did you say about the boilers."

Matheson continued to stare. "What I meant was, they seemed fine to us when we did our pre-selection inspection. Changing the boilers for bigger ones was an unnecessary bonus."

"You mean you didn't ask for new ones?" Matt's voice trembled. He vividly remembered McGregor mentioning them earlier, during the incident in the parking lot. At the time the word 'boilers' hadn't penetrated.

"Of course not, why would we?"

Everything fell into place in the general manager's brain like the jackpot line in a Las Vegas casino's slot machine.

The boilers! It has to be the goddamned boilers!

Cursing himself for his stupidity, Matt grabbed Tim's arm and pulled him out of the office. "Jesus Christ! Run! For God's sake, run!"

They sped past Matt's shocked minders along the executive offices corridor.

"What's going on? Have you lost your mind?" Tim shouted, struggling for breath.

"Listen," Matt said. The two were sprinting now. "We're out of time. Get hold of Jeff Hartman and tell him I think there's a bomb in the boilers beneath the Conference Center. I'm going to the Control Room next to the chief engineer's office. If anyone sees McGregor or Marshall, whatever happens hold them and don't let them go. And get the president out of the Center. Now. For the love of Christ, move Tim, move! It may already be too late."

Chapter 109
San Diego

"Code Black!" Matt yelled, racing through the main lobby, Matheson at his heels. "Implement now!"

Reacting automatically, the front office manager pressed the red buttons recessed under the check-in pod's onyx counter top. Instantly, the electro-magnetic seals holding back both sets of recessed doors to the lobby released, and the thick walnut doors began to close. Stainless steel shutters ground their way down, closing off the windows.

"Stop those two men," Matt screamed, pointing at the minders who ran after him. "Don't let them out of here until the Secret Service arrives. Be careful, they're armed!"

Matt and Matheson jumped through the few inches left before the lobby doors closed in their locked position. The Resort's own security guards, he was sure, would face down his pursuers until the Secret Service men could make their way up from the basement.

*

Matheson and Matt split up as soon as they left the building. Adrenaline sped Matt across the main lawn and onto the path leading to the Control Room next to Keith McGregor's office. There had to be some way to deactivate the bomb—and the more Matt thought about it the more he was sure it was a bomb—planted somewhere in the boiler system, that could be activated by the newly installed electronic systems.

His brain worked at warp speed. Everything fit: The State Department hadn't asked for new boilers, Netski had lied about that; Dieter Weiss controlling the purchase and installation of the boilers; the installation team was Russian, not German; the row with Brad Marshall when the crates arrived; the installation not being the same as the plans approved by the city; getting our

Director of Engineering, Dick Jamieson, out of the company—he would have seen this in a flash; McGregor's nervousness. It all fit together. The equipment was the "Xmas Present" referred to in the papers Beth had stolen from Jimmy Lee's office. It hadn't come from Germany, it had to be from Russia or China. Probably China. The bastards had built fully functioning equipment around a bomb, almost surely surrounded by lead or some material which would deflect any x-ray when they brought it into this country. It had to be a bomb, massive enough to destroy the entire Conference Center, perhaps filled with anthrax or Ebola? Maybe even a nuclear device? What difference? It would be exploded at the "Snow Festival"—the Summit; devastate the Resort, wipe out the leadership of much of the world, kill hundreds, maybe thousands of people. The installation team wasn't using a German dialect, as Weiss had claimed. The Russians and the Chinese had collaborated—the Russians were the "Dark Winter" in Lee's documents. And Lee himself had disappeared because he knew the bomb would be detonated today. Now. In minutes. Maybe less.

Brad Marshall! He controlled all the vetting of the clearances for all security personnel. He was Blenheim's tool, the lynchpin of their operation at the Resort, the man who brought in all of Blenheim's people. Jesus! That son-of-a-bitch was the one who coordinated with the Secret Service and FBI, made himself their best friend. He would know everything they were doing and be able to adjust Blenheim's plans accordingly. Weiss was the front man for the Russians and the Chinese. And McGregor, the dour Scot who seemed the consummate professional? Had he been corrupted by money or blackmail or both? Matt wondered. McGregor was essential. The Scot had to supervise the installations and make sure no one asked questions.

The logical place to hide the detonating equipment was in the Control Room, McGregor's fiercely guarded domain. Matt tried to visualize the room from which McGregor had tried to bar him . . . the master control panel, set before the monitors that scanned the insides of the Resort. It had to be the nerve center! Not only did it operate the lights, the master electronic systems, the air-conditioning and the boilers, it would operate the bomb. With a jolt of horror, Matt realized that only McGregor and Marshall knew how to work it. What if they had a remote detonating device, gone into hiding and were ready to set it off? What if it had already been primed? What if it was already ticking down to cataclysm?

His mind reeled at the possibilities. In less than a minute, the leaders of the G8 nations would be assembled together on one podium for the first time this Summit. The only other time would be at the end of the conference, and who knew what might happen in between. That was why Dark Winter had to detonate their device now. Lee's own words had confirmed it.

Matt accelerated. He had run a marathon over the 200 yards from lobby to the chief engineer's building.

The doors were locked! Wasting precious seconds, he found his plastic, master electronic keycard in his wallet and, with fumbling hands, scanned the card over the black electronic pad. More precious seconds passed. Had they changed the lock? No! The green light blinked. He pushed open the doors.

Half falling down the short flight of stairs, Matt righted himself and raced down the starkly lit, dark-green and white painted corridor, turning the corner near McGregor's office. Its lights were off. He moved to the Control Room itself and put his ear to the door. A voice: Marshall's. Talking over what seemed to be a hand-held radio. Matt could barely hear the words, his heart was pounding so loud.

"Current status?" Marshall barked.

"Delegates seated, leaders walking onto the stage," a disembodied voice crackled through a walkie-talkie.

"Tell me when they're seated." Matt thought he could hear the tension behind Marshall's outwardly calm tone.

A pause. "Seated."

"Tell our people to stay where they are. Wait in position until you get my order." It was, Matt knew, a death sentence for the thirty-four men and women on Marshall's staff.

"Roger that." The crackle went silent.

Matt waited.

"Are you ready?" Marshall asked.

Silence.

"Are you ready?"Marshall's voice grew louder, more insistent.
"Ready," came McGregor's unsteady response.
"On my count of three."
"Okay."
"One."
Matt's muscles cramped, released.
"Two."

*

Now! Matt pushed the door with his shoulder and plunged into the Control Room, momentarily blinded by the unexpectedly bright neon light. An image of Beth's face in the throes of passion flashed through his mind and just as quickly disappeared.

The macabre tableau in front of him froze as his mind processed it. Keith McGregor, at the far end of the room, stopped the downward motion of his hand, his face contorted in shock, the Scot's stubby finger poised inches above a dark-red button set in a sleek, black, wall-mounted box, a green light blinking at its top. Neatly coiled red, blue and yellow wires linked the box to the control panel set six inches away on the same wall.

Brad Marshall had turned toward the sound. Eyes blazing in hate, lips tightly pursed, he leveled a black and grey pistol at Matt's chest.

Conscious thought evaporated. Matt flung himself at Marshall; Marshall fired. One shot. Another.

Neither the violence of the impact in Matt's shoulder and side nor the excruciating pain that followed were enough to stop his forward momentum. Marshall raised his gun. The men's bodies collided and collapsed to the floor.

"Motherfucker!" Marshall yelled.

A third explosion, this one muffled between the two bodies.

Silence.

Chapter 110
San Diego

Keith McGregor recoiled in horror; his ears deafened by the sound of the explosions, and clenched his fists tightly to control his shaking hands. He stared at the two inert bodies lying in an ever-expanding pool of blood, then raised his eyes to the black box, its green light blinking hypnotically. Decision made, he inhaled deeply and moved his index finger toward the red button.

*

McGregor's body launched against the wall, his chest an ever-expanding pattern of red wounds. Nine-millimeter parabellum bullets continued to strike him from the micro Uzi semi-automatic weapons held by Jeff Hartman and the two Secret Service agents in his detail. Over two hundred rounds struck the Scot; his dead, twitching, shredded body slid slowly into a crumpled heap on the Control Room's bare concrete floor, leaving in its wake a ghoulish patchwork of dripping blood and shattered plaster.

The agents, puffing hard from their sprint across the Resort's grounds, kept their guns trained on Matt and Marshall, while Hartman examined their inert bodies lying entwined in a blood-drenched love-knot just feet away the control panel.

"Jesus Christ! What a fucking mess!" He spoke into his wrist radio, his voice emotionless. "Control Room secure; explosive device still live. Remove POTUS and FLOTUS immediately, then evacuate the Conference Center right away, Repeat, evacuate the delegates now. We've got casualties. Get ambulances here quick. This Summit's over."

Chapter 111
New York

Quinton Thomas, a Harlem-raised kid who'd managed to escape the projects, led a squad of four FBI agents to the door of Fabrizio Battini's midtown apartment.

Like the others, the barrel-chested, thirty-eight-year-old was dressed in a blue nylon vest, FBI initials emblazoned in white on the back; like the others, he had drawn his automatic pistol. He glanced at the nervous building superintendent. "Unlock the door."

The superintendent complied. Thomas pushed the door open. The agents rushed in, footsteps loud on the marble floor, and began their search of the apartment.

The woman among them, Agent Rebecca Morales, found Battini's body in the bedroom. "In here," she called, placing two fingers against the Italian's carotid artery. "There's a pulse," she told Thomas. "A faint one."

"Call an ambulance," Thomas instructed the agent by his side. "Get it here quick!"

He spotted a snifter and a half-empty bottle of Hine cognac on the bedside table next to an open porcelain box, half-full with white powder. Thomas dipped his finger into the powder and tasted it. "Coke," he said, wrinkling his nose.

He ripped off the burgundy silk sheet covering Battini's body. As he expected, there was a two-thirds empty medicine vial next to Battini's left hand.

Thomas read the pharmacist's label. "Valium, ten milligrams, fifty capsules. God knows how many he's taken. It was yesterday's date, can't have taken too many before now. Ugly combination with booze and cocaine. Come on, Morales, help me sit him up."

*

Agent Justin Waring shouted from Battini's study, "I think I've found something."

Thomas watched the ambulance crew cart Battini off on a gurney, then went to the agent's side. Waring, hunched over a Sony Vaio SZ series laptop, had already opened the last e-mail Battini had sent.

> TO: dnetski@kestrelhotels.com
> FROM: fbattini@blenheimpartners.com
>
> I can't live any longer with my shame.
> Jimmy Lee blackmailed me into doing it.
> If I'd been strong, I'd never have gone along with his terrible plan.
> I should have told you from the beginning. I was too frightened.
> What a mess I've caused.
> I'm sorry.
> Please forgive me.
> May God also forgive me.

Thomas turned to Agent Morales. "If we're lucky, they'll revive him. If he's lucky, the son-of-a-bitch will die on the way to the hospital."

Chapter 112
Ensenada, Mexico

When her white Mercedes 320 was waived through Mexican Customs, Olivia Wade felt her shoulder muscles relax, and opened the driver's window to suck in huge gulps of humid air—the air, she thought, of escape.

Brad Marshall had changed the plans for her to dispose of Dirksen and had told her exactly when to flee. She'd gratefully packed her suitcases the night before and stowed them in the car's trunk. Forcing herself through a busy day, she'd left the Resort's executive offices, told the receptionist she was on her way to the dinner at the convention center, announced to the security guard she was going home to change, and drove off the Resort. Nobody seemed to care.

With the border forty miles behind her, she allowed herself to think of her two-bedroom, white, stucco house nestled in the arid hills above Cabot St. Lucas. Another few hours of driving, and she would start her new life. She tuned her radio to an all-news channel out of San Diego, smiling in anticipation. The smile vanished as she listened to the newsreader's dramatic interpretation of events as they unfolded in the aftermath of the failed bombing attempt.

She stopped the car on a dusty roadside as she struggled to catch her breath. This can't be? Maybe the news was just part of an elaborate Borotin disinformation scheme? She switched station after station, hoping to find a different message.

Her final remnants of optimism evaporated as the minutes passed. Fear overwhelmed her. Grasping the steering wheel tightly, she gasped in pain. Gradually her breathing slowed and she could think clearly. She was out of the country, no one knew where. She'd carry out her plans, disappear. She patted her handbag as if to reassure herself that her new passport, birth certificate and credit cards were in place; not the set that had been given to her courtesy of Brad Marshall—they were in a safe deposit box in a bank in Carlsbad—but the set she'd had made up by her own contacts in Zurich. Finally she allowed herself to smile, slipped the car into drive and, dust churning in the car's wake, sped off to her new life. Goodbye, Olivia Wade, she thought. Julia Clements, welcome to Mexico.

*

Olivia Wade failed to notice the Ford Taurus in her rearview mirror. Had she not been so self-engrossed, she might have realized that the grey vehicle had never been more than 200 yards behind her ever since she left the Resort.

The Ford's unsmiling driver looked into his own rearview mirror—nothing in sight—and then ahead at the empty road, as it wound its way through the cuts in the bare, sun-baked, rocky hills. "It's time," he said emotionlessly to his passenger.

"Okay."

The passenger pressed the button on a remote-control device. The Taurus slowed. Both occupants watched the rear axle of the Mercedes explode and the car careen off the road into the craggy hillside. The passenger pushed a second button. A second bomb, this one planted directly below Olivia Wade's seat, went off, sending sheets of orange flame twenty feet into the air.

"Good job," the driver said, turning off Highway 1 at the Ensenada exit to wait on an overpass. Certain they had not been followed, he steered the car back onto the highway and headed north to Tijuana and the good ole U.S. of A.

Chapter 113
San Diego

"What a fucking mess!" Pete Wilson thought, watching the parade of limousines backed up from the main gates to the *porte cochère* and on to the parking garage and remote lots. The president and first lady had been evacuated aboard Marine One. The presidents and prime ministers of the member nations had also been airlifted to safety. Now the ministers, secretaries, translators, aides-de-camp, and the pell-mell of additional sundry officials were scrambling to get out of the Resort as quickly as possible—meaning there was virtually no movement at all.

Word of a hidden bomb had spread through the Conference Center like a California wildfire, causing chaos. Reporters went into frenzy as rumors swept the Media Center and fragmented information was eked out in frustratingly small portions. Denied access to the overwhelmed Secret Service and FBI details, breathless journalists broadcast half fact, half fiction, while social media stories flooded the Internet and flourished like mosquitoes after a tropical rainstorm.

The protesters and crowds surrounding the Resort panicked over tales of nuclear bombs about to explode. Barriers were overrun, police and National Guard troops pushed aside. Traffic on every road in the county gridlocked.

Not everyone tried to get away. Gangs of looters appeared smashing down doors of shops and stores wherever they could find them. The Resort's grim-faced security guards held them off the Resort grounds with tightly clutched rifles, safety switches off.

Pete Wilson, desperately trying to reach Dirksen on his walkie-talkie, tried to herd waves of human traffic from the Conference Center. Long minutes later, he was told that the general manager had been in the midst of a shooting incident in the Control Room.

"Shot? What do you mean? For God's sake, where is he?"

Delegates forgotten, he fought his way through the crowds until he reached his office, in time to see Matt's two handcuffed minders being handed over to the FBI by the front desk staff.

"Get the executive committee here immediately," he shouted to his assistant, vaguely registering that she had stayed by her post amidst the turmoil. He looked out his office window to see yet another helicopter landing from the fleet that swarmed the cerulean blue sky, like frantic bees around honey.

No one came to the meeting. All Wilson could find out was that two bodies on gurneys, one surrounded by medics with hand-held intravenous drips and the other in a dull-green body bag, had been evacuated on one of the helicopters.

*

"What a fucking mess!" Pete Wilson repeated aloud, three hours after the Secret Service had ordered evacuation of the Conference Center.

"For both of us," Tim Matheson, sitting across from him, agreed.

"Why you? You helped stop a calamity."

"No one will see it that way," a despondent Matheson sighed. "Everyone will be looking for a scapegoat. I was the man who picked this place, so I guess it'll be me."

"Ridiculous! No one could have foreseen anything like this. Christ, the damned Secret Service has been all over the Resort from the beginning, and they didn't pick up so much as a clue."

"You understand facts, but not the D.C. shuffle. By the time this thing sorts itself out, everyone within the Beltway will claim they were against using the Resort, but I bullied it through for my own benefit." He managed a smile. "Got a job for me in the hotel business?"

Wilson felt as if pounds of lead were sitting in his stomach. "I can't find out where Matt is, let alone if he's alive. I've got to get the FBI to release the staff they still have on the property, use them to help me clear the Resort so the bomb squads can start dismantling every piece of equipment to see what's hidden inside. The place will be a wreck. Not that it matters; who's going to want to come here after this? It'll be the most publicized hotel in the world and not one fucking person'll want to stay here. Job for you? What about me? After this disaster, who'll want me?"

Chapter 114
Los Angeles

The phalanx of telephones on Sir Kenneth Palmer's desk had been ringing nonstop since the incident at the Audley Resort. This time, however, the call came to his secure cell phone.

"Palmer speaking."

"Had a good time so far?" Amnon Sapir's laughter boomed into the Englishman's ear.

"As much fun as my father's funeral."

"But surely you've been vindicated by today's near miss?" Sapir's voice was full of genuine concern.

"One would have thought so. Rather, I've been excoriated by the prime minister both for not spotting the plot sooner and for approving the Resort as acceptable. As if I had anything to do with the selection. The press have been all over me. I tell you, my job's in danger. Ignominious, forced early retirement was not exactly my plan."

"Whereas you should be given another knighthood."

"One's all most people get. Anyway, they're as valuable as a tube ticket." Bitterness rose in his throat.

"Anything I can do to help?"

"Tell me if you got anything from Fuentes."

"Only if you tell me how you got my men unsupervised access to his jail cell."

"Couldn't have been easier. Last year, our consul general here, Andrew Layton, gave a dinner party at the residence which included the L.A. Commissioner of Police. The man was an ardent Churchill fan, so Andrew arranged a private tour of the Cabinet War Rooms and the Churchill Museum when the Commissioner was in London; even sat in Churchill's red-leather swivel chair. The man was thrilled. Turns out his grandmother was English and London's in his blood. Layton had casually mentioned this little snippet of information to me and when you pointed to Her

Majesty's portrait, I had an idea and met with our anglophile Police Commissioner. After I told him a little of what was happening, I suggested Her Majesty's government would be grateful if a little quiet time could be arranged for *Señor* Fuentes together with some of my friends. I even hinted that an OBE might be bestowed as a sign of our gratitude. The man positively preened. See? Easy."

"Brilliant. What's an OBE?"

"Officer of the Most Excellent Order of the British Empire, jocularly known as "Other Buggers Efforts." Unlikely an American policeman would receive one, granted. But you never know."

"Maybe you can arrange one for me." Sapir chuckled. "Is it like your knighthood?"

"A notch or two below. You wouldn't want it, trust me. But come on, man, did Fuentes talk?"

"Not as eloquently as Churchill but certainly as volubly, though it took some time. Fuentes is one tough customer. He worked full time for the Chinese Consulate, reporting directly to Jimmy Lee, whose idea it was to grab Beth Taylor and her daughter. Here's the shocker: Taylor and her daughter are chained to a post in an abandoned Long Beach warehouse. You'll have to get your police commissioner friend to send a SWAT team to get them out."

"How much time do I have?"

"God knows. Fuentes told my boys he thought they'd be dead by now."

"Jesus! Did he tell you who's guarding them, how many, and if they're armed?"

"Sadly no. *Señor* Fuentes was unconscious by the time they got to those questions. I regret to say he may have a long hospital stay, if indeed he ever regains consciousness."

Chapter 115
Moscow

In dusk's gloom, less than twenty-four hours after the collapse of the Summit, a force of seven armed members of the FSB, the State Security Agency of the Russian Federation, descended on Yuri Borotin's *kottedzhi* on *Rublyovo-Uspenskaye Strosse* and, in a brief but bloody firefight, overwhelmed Borotin's two ten-men security teams, dismantled the extensive booby traps and entered the building.

A similar force entered Borotin's newly built granite, steel and glass office building on *Tverskaya* Street after meeting token resistance from his guards. And fifty-five miles to the south, five FSB men gained access to Borotin's hanger at Domodevo Airport.

The results were identical. Yuri Borotin, to say nothing of his two identical Gulfstream G550 planes, had vanished.

On board his new Iluyishin 11-9-300PU, returning from San Diego to Moscow, the President of the Russian Federation was furious. "Track that motherfucker down," he screamed at his intelligence chief. "Bring him back to Moscow. I want him now!"

Chapter 116
Long Beach

Headlights off in the moonless night, a convoy of four armored vehicles, five police cars and an ambulance moved through garbage-littered, deserted side-streets to the Lee Ho Fuk Provision Company's ostensibly long-abandoned warehouse.

Five helmeted, Kevlar-clad members of the Long Beach Police Department's SWAT team exited the lead vehicle and briskly trotted in crepe-soled boots to the warehouse to search its perimeter.

"No vehicles, no signs of booby traps, single entry point through metal roller shutter," the lead officer, Rufus Seward, reported into the microphone mounted in his helmet. The additional vehicles took up their positions in front of the shutter; their occupants, each carrying 5.56-caliber, gas-operated, MI6 Assault Rifles, fanned out around the building. Seward checked for a control mechanism to the shutter. Finding none, he and the nearest officer tried to raise the shutter by hand. No movement. Four other men joined them. The shutter would not budge.

"Any access from the roof?" Seward asked into his microphone.

"None. Welded steel panels. No way to insert a camera or mike."

Seward considered. "Bring a drum of C-4 and six wireless detonators. We're going in!"

Within a minute the explosives officer attached six balls of C-4 to the shutter in a rectangular pattern and inserted his detonators. He looked at Seward.

"Squad three to secure the perimeter. Squad four, provide safety cover. Squads one and two, follow me into the building. Night lights on. Prepare for firefight. On my go."

Seward nodded to the explosives officer, who immediately pressed the button on his detonator. The door exploded. "Go, go, go!" Seward yelled. Squads one and two ran into the acrid smoke and through the gaping hole. "Shit! A fucking wall," Seward said.

"Captain, I've found a door; slider with a combination lock."

"Don't shoot through it. They're probably inside," Seward said as calmly as his pumping heart allowed. "Explosives. Now. Single-charge detonator. Move your ass!"

"On my way."

The explosives officer fixed a small mound of C-4 to the combination lock. Seward nodded again. A muffled bang. Smoke. Members of squad two slid the door open.

"Go! Go! Night lights on. Shoot anyone with a weapon," Seward shouted. The two squads raced through the doorway.

"Talk to me," Seward commanded.

"Nothing here," said a member of squad two.

"Clear so far."

"Empty."

"Captain! Over here! Center left. Now!"

Seward rushed forward. A SWAT officer, rifle on the ground, squatted at the side of two bodies, curled into one as if lovers for eternity.

"Medics!" Seward screamed.

*

"Are they alive?"

The medic looked up. "Barely." He fitted as oxygen mask over Beth Taylor's pale face.

"Can you save them?"

"We're doing everything we can. The younger one's got a better chance. For Christ's sake, have your men hurry. We can't get them out of here until you get rid of those chains."

Chapter 117
Washington, D.C.

The CIA operative grabbed the receiver as soon as his desk phone began to ring. "Caverly speaking." He listened as the FBI agent introduced himself. "Okay Hank, what did you find?"

"Based on information you communicated to the head of the local office, I led an assault squad on the San Diego address you'd provided."

Caverly couldn't contain his impatience. "I don't want your official report Hank, just tell me what the hell you found when you broke in."

"Two men, two women dead. Heads blown in from the back, short-range, execution style. Smelt like sour apples inside the place. My guess is whoever did it pumped in some form of knock-out gas, and when they were unconscious, just waltzed in and murdered them. Very professional."

"Did the men's bodies match the photos I e-mailed your office?" Caverly asked.

"Sure did. One of the women's passports was in the name of Fatima Hameed, the other in the name of Frahana Khakwari. Both well-traveled."

"Any Indonesian stamps?" Caverly queried.

"Three entry and exit stamps."

"What a surprise!" The CIA agent's sarcasm was evident. "What else did you find?"

"When we pulled the place apart and lifted the floorboards, we found a pile of papers, a whole bunch in what I'm told is Urdu or Pashbu. They're with the translators now. We did find a series of plans for the Audley Resort and . . ."

"And what?"

"And detailed layouts of the new boilers. All signs point to a failed Al Qaeda operation and someone came to clean up. Did a sloppy job."

"Maybe," Rick Caverly said.

"Can I ask you a question?" Hank Abernathy queried. "How in heaven's name did you know where to find these guys?"

Rick Caverly smiled inwardly as he remembered the phone call he'd received from Ron Falkman. After he'd apologized for talking on an open line, the lawyer had said, "My British friend has an address for you in San Diego. It seems some of the people you're looking for have relatives in the North of England who eventually suggested your people pay a visit." It hadn't taken Caverly but a second or two to make the translation: MI6 had applied some heavy muscle to a few Pakistanis in the U.K. with known terrorist connections. Caverly had called the information through to the local FBI office. He had been politely thanked and the information ignored. Minutes after the failed attack at the Resort, he'd received a call from the head of the Bureau's San Diego office reporting that they were going to act on the information immediately.

Putting his feet up on his wooden desk and crossing his ankles, Rick Caverly grinned. "Just a lucky break I guess."

Chapter 118
Los Angeles

The newly opened one million square feet Ronald Reagan Medical Center, on the Westwood edge of UCLA's campus, was besieged. Throughout the night, helicopters bearing the injured, an assortment of protesters, soldiers and police, landed on the hospital roof. Secret Service and FBI agents patrolled the corridors, and an entire floor was cordoned off to accommodate the influx.

One of the first to arrive, comatose and bleeding badly from bullet holes in his abdomen and shattered shoulder, was Matthew Dirksen. Within minutes, he was wheeled into the operating room, whose entrance was guarded by two stony-faced, flack-jacketed, FBI agents.

*

"His eyes flickered," the nurse at Matt's bedside reported to the FBI agent stationed in the room.

"Any idea of how long before he regains consciousness?"

The nurse just looked at him.

Two other visitors sat calmly on chairs nearby. Both were engrossed in their copies of *The Los Angeles Times*. Headlines screamed at them.

*

Matt's eyes opened, closed, opened again. He had been dreaming about his father, posing as a Russian agent, with electrical wires streaming from his eyes.

"Good morning," the nurse said. "You're in a hospital. UCLA." The nurse pressed the buzzer to alert the doctor on duty.

"Beth?" Matt whispered.

One of the visitors stood up. "Beth and Britney are . . ."

The voice seemed familiar to Matt before he slipped back into the void.

*

At 2:49 a.m. Matt opened his eyes to a darkened room. Curtains opened to a starless night; the only outside illumination shone from the nearby buildings on the campus.

"Thirsty," he murmured through bruised, dry lips.

The nurse brought a glass of crushed ice and a straw. "Drink slowly." She put the straw in his mouth, removed it when he swallowed.

"More."

"Take it easy. You've been unconscious for two days since the surgery."

"Surgery?"

"The usual procedure for bullets in the shoulder and stomach," the nurse said dryly. "You were lucky it missed your lung."

"How long . . .?"

"You'll be here at least a week before you start rehab."

Memory, like a noxious gas, filled his brain. "Beth?" He spasmed, dreading the answer.

Sir Kenneth Palmer, awakened by the noise, unfolded himself from the recliner and approached the bed. "Beth and Britney survived. They're your next door neighbors."

"Don't understand . . ."

"They're on this floor, recovering well. They'll be fine."

Matt, mind dulled by morphine, could not process the information. "Who are you?" he rasped.

"Hush," Palmer said, father to a feverish child. "There'll be time for answers. Try to go back to sleep."

"The Resort?" The patient whispered as sleep overtook him.

*

A gentle hand touched Matt's good shoulder. He opened his eyes and beheld a miracle.

"Beth!"

"Damn it," she said in that resolute voice he adored. "Here I made myself as pretty as possible, and my tears ruined my mascara. I told myself I wouldn't cry, but when I saw you . . ." Her tears flowed again and she buried her head against his neck.

The voice he'd dreamed he heard last night, a voice he didn't recognize, came back to him. Not a dream at all. "Beth. You're safe." The reality of her presence unlocked his heart, and he bawled his exaltation in sobs that shook his body so severely that his day nurse had to hold him still. "I'm sorry," he murmured.

"A fine pair we are," Beth said. "Haven't seen each other in weeks and we've yet to kiss."

She bent to gently caress his cracked lips with hers. He tasted life. "Britney?" he asked.

"Just down the hall. She thought I should see you first before you meet her. Matt, I got to know her so well during that . . ." She straightened. "I know you'll love her."

He managed a painful grin. "Any daughter of yours . . ." Exhaustion overtook him and, despite himself, he slept.

*

"You'll never know how much I hated you."

Twenty-four hours had passed, and they were alone in his room, Beth still weak and pale in her hospital gown, her bloodshot eyes rimmed with black circles; Matt, stronger now with more sleep and, at last, some liquid nourishment.

He stared at her. She was thin, gaunt, worn down—beautiful. "I don't blame you. I drew you into this. Without me, you wouldn't have gone through hell. And then I abandoned you."

"In order to be a hero," she said softly.

"That's not it. I never planned to be a hero; I just wanted to do what was right."

"First and foremost, you wanted to save the Resort, not Beth, not me. How could I deal with that?" Sadness poured from Beth's eyes as he looked down at her raw hands.

He squirmed uncomfortably. "I didn't trust you, didn't know what to think. I was torn, confused, stressed, whatever . . . I made the wrong choice, I'll never forgive myself."

She couldn't meet his gaze. "When I woke up in that terrible place, that awful stinking prison, and found Britney there, the two of us chained to a pole like a pair of rabid dogs, I hated you so much I was sick from it."

"Beth, I . . ."

Now she was able to look into his eyes. "But I loved you too, don't you see? You taught me passion, and your passion wasn't just for me . . . ," she grinned ". . . though it sure felt good in bed. It was for everything you did. Your integrity and your belief in right and wrong were fundamental parts of you, the essence of you, and you couldn't have acted differently. Without you, I would never have known Britney, and as I talked to her about you, I discovered that I loved you for everything you are, not for what I wanted you to be—and that if you changed, it would diminish you, diminish me, and ultimately diminish our love."

He reached for her; she stepped away. "Let me finish. I've had plenty of time to prepare this speech I thought I'd never give. As we faced what we knew would be our certain death, Britney and I realized that our lives would have been incomplete if we hadn't known each other. I fell in love with her as a daughter as I did with you as a man. By the end, before we were too weak to talk more, we concluded two things. One, if by any chance we survived our nightmare, we'd figure out an arrangement with her adoptive parents that would allow us to see each other without changing the relationship—the love—she had with them."

The wonder of her filled his soul. "And two?"

"I decided that if I ever saw you again, I'd tell you that I loved you to the depths of my soul, and that if you'd have me, I'd spend the rest of my life with you."

*

The door swung open. "I'm sorry, Mr. Dirksen," the head nurse said. "They insisted on seeing you, no matter what. I told them you had a visitor, but . . ."

She was pushed aside by twin bulldozers. "Nothing could stop us," a familiar voice said.

Beth shrieked. Matt blinked and blinked again, trying to clear his sight of a fantasy that would mean Beth, too, existed only in his imagination. "You're dead," he gasped.

"It would seem not," Rolfe Ritter said.

"I can attest to it," Momo added. "Why, only last night . . ."

"You were gunned down in Manhattan," Matt insisted.

Momo's laughter rang through the room. "That'll teach you not to believe everything you read in the papers."

"Hello, Beth Taylor," Rolfe said, crossing to hug the pale woman. "To say it's a pleasure to see you again is an understatement of titanic proportions."

She pulled back and curtsied. "Mr. Ritter." Her hands went to her face. "Oh, I look awful. If I'd known . . ."

"You look like a Renoir," Rolfe said, "only a little thinner. You're still the most beautiful hotelier I know."

Momo embraced her; the two woman hugged tightly as Beth whispered, "Thank you, thank you a million times. Without your advice I . . . I wouldn't have . . ."

"Shhh . . . ," Momo quietly interrupted, "All I did was tell you what you already knew. You just needed to hear it from someone else."

Matt, a bystander, closed his eyes. He felt disembodied, as though he was watching from afar a magician pull wonders from a hat. His body began to tremble. So much joy swept through his heart he couldn't contain it.

Rolfe noticed. "Our friend's seeing ghosts," he said to the others. "Let's give him an hour to let the fact that we're real sink in."

*

Rolfe Ritter came back alone that afternoon. He was, Matt knew, very real, very alive; but there was still such a disconnect from his certain knowledge Rolfe had been killed that he could barely take in his presence. Beth was down the hall, her daughter with her. Now his patron, his friend, his mentor, his second father, was standing beside his bed. He was dizzy with the thought of it.

"You're a hero," Rolfe said. "A regular Jack Bauer. You stopped the bombs from being detonated, saved the Resort, and very possibly prevented God knows what. At the very least we'd have had an extended period of global chaos and mischief. Not a bad day's work for a kid from Chesterton, Indiana. The papers are calling you the 'Hotel Hero' and there are a couple of great caricatures of your head on Superman's body. Who knows, you may even get your own comic strip." He proffered a bunch of them. "Want to read them? I thought you'd prefer them to flowers."

"I'll read them later. First, tell me . . ." Matt stopped. Too many questions crowded his brain.

"About the Resort? It's a disaster area. The FBI's technicians are dismantling every piece of equipment in the place to see if there are any more surprises lurking around. I hear the laundry room looks like a giant Lego project. No one will ever put those particular bits back together again, that's for damned sure. Every reservation on the books has been cancelled, most by the customers; but for the few guests who must have been in a cave in the Himalayas when all this was happening, Pete Wilson's staff had to tell them the place was closed. Talking of Pete, he's a trooper and is returning deposits as best he can, or was—the hotels' bank accounts are all depleted. Kestrel's corporate offices are as empty as the Kalahari Desert with all Blenheim's stooges having either disappeared or in custody. There's no one left with signature authority to pay the bills, yet the money is still rolling into the company's bank accounts from the rest of the hotels around the world. I've never seen a situation like this, and I've created some gigantic messes myself!" Rolfe shook his head in bewilderment.

"What about the team on property? The staff?" Matt asked, trying to hold back tears.

"Pete Wilson has managed to persuade a few of the old hands to stick around and help. He's promised to pay them from his own money if no one else coughs up. The property-level Blenheim guys that didn't disappear are all in custody and are singing soprano to the authorities. The rest of the staff are being snapped up by the competition, who are having a field day at the Resort's expense. You can imagine the negative publicity. There's even a blog out on the Internet calling the place 'The Armageddon Resort'; even used the same typeface as the Audley logo. Pisses me off, I can tell you.

So to answer your next question, I don't know if or when it will ever reopen."

Dirksen's fallen face was testament to his emotions. Rolfe Ritter changed the subject.

"When you barged into the Control Room, the bullets you took weren't enough to stop your momentum and, evidently, you cannoned into Brad Marshall just as he was about to fire a third time. Your body pushed his arm and hand into his chest at the same moment he pulled the trigger, and ka-boom. Bullet went straight through his chin into his warped brain. Killed the son-of-a-bitch instantly."

"He's really dead?" Matt asked incredulously.

"Definitely dead; shuffled off his mortal coil; pushing up the daisies as we speak."

"What happened to McGregor?" Matt managed. "Were there really bombs in the boilers?"

"Two bombs. Bloody big ones. The Secret Service got to McGregor literally an instant before he could detonate it. His hand was on the detonator switch. It was that bloody close."

"My God!" Matt whispered, replaying the vivid tableau from the Control Room in his tormented mind.

"McGregor didn't survive a hail of bullets. Tore the bastard to bits. The few pieces that were left of him would fit into a match-box."

"What happened to Jimmy Lee?"

"Skipped."

"Netski? I assume his plane blowing up in mid-air wasn't an accident. Who murdered him and why?"

"You mean Vasily Borotin? If you believe Kenneth Palmer's theory, the body in that plane was just some dope misfortunate enough to resemble him. Anyway, that vicious son-of-a-bitch has disappeared, along with his snake of a big brother. The Russian government promises a world-wide search for them. Why do I think they'll never be found?"

"Then they can plan again. Try something new."

"I doubt it, hope not, but who the hell knows? The Summit adventure was a one-time-only event. It must have been sheer opportunism, and the Borotins will be running so fast they won't have time to sit down, let alone try another scheme. Besides, their pay masters would hardly use them again after they fucked up so grandly."

"Their pay masters? Who?"

Rolfe shrugged. "That's the big question, the key to this whole mess. We'll have to wait for Palmer or Sapir to provide us that answer, if they know it."

Enough about the conspiracy, Matt thought. At least for today. Rolfe had called him a hero. He thought of himself as a jackass. If he'd suspected the bomb earlier, if he hadn't been so self-centered and hadn't wallowed in his vat of self-pity, he'd have seen the obvious earlier. If he'd been able to find out more, if he'd been able to help Palmer and Sapir—talk about fuck-ups. Hero? Hell no! More like the village idiot! Pain pushed through his medications and he gasped aloud.

"I'd better be going," Rolfe said. "Momo's napping at the hotel and there's a Miss Taylor down the hall who seems to want your undivided attention."

"Not yet." Matt weakly held out a hand to restrain his visitor. "Tell me about you."

Rolfe smiled. "Still think I'm a ghost, do you? I might have been if it wasn't for our friend Amnon. Or rather his men."

"What do you mean?"

"Have you heard the phrase 'taking a bullet'? Well, one of our Mossad bodyguards, fellow named Yossi Bar El, took one for me. I'd brought Momo to Sloan-Kettering for a check-up. Yossi was with us and followed us out when the examination was finished. Yoram Livnati, our other guard, brought the SUV to the entrance and got out to open the door for us. At the same time, a black Mercedes roared up the street. I saw someone with a rifle at the back window aiming straight at me." He shuddered. "Brought back awful memories.

"Without thinking, I pushed Momo onto the floor of the SUV Yossi crashed into me just as the rifle fired. The bullet blew his head open, instead of mine. It missed me by millimeters."

Again Matt felt disconnected. Rolfe's tone was level, calm; the events he was describing seemed to Matt to have happened long ago, as in a fairy tale. Now, though, Ritter's voice grew husky.

"He saved my life at the expense of his. It'd be fatuous to say I wish I'd been in his place, but I wish it didn't have to happen. His family will be looked after for as long as they live. Amnon said the Mossad are soldiers. There's a regular boot camp in Israel called Glilot. Apparently inside the confines of the place are a mass of sandstone walls, assembled in the shape of a human brain. The names of the men and women in Israel's intelligence community that have been killed in the line of duty are inscribed on those walls. Yossi will be remembered with pride on that wall forever. That helps a little, but it still hurts. Another recurring nightmare to add to my growing collection."

"Oh, Rolfe, I have to be selfish about it; I thank God it was him, not you. You're my ally, my friend. What I owe you . . ."

Rolfe's wave cut him off. "Yoram decided to let the killers think they had killed me, not Yossi, so they wouldn't chase after us and try again. He pushed me on top of Momo, covered Yossi with his jacket so no one could see what remained of his head. The Mercedes had sped away, but still Yoram made us lie still—God knows, terrified as we were, we obliged—while he called Amnon. It was Amnon who decided to let the world think I was dead, and master-minded the publicity. That way there'd be no more attempts. Momo and I were already in a safehouse but Amnon moved me into another one that only he and his assistant knew about. I couldn't see or speak to anyone, not even Momo. Only Sapir, Yoram, Momo, Palmer and Ron Falkman knew I was alive. Yoram baby-sat me day and night while Momo played the grieving widow in public and Falkman the executor of my will. So there you have it—the illusion was complete." He chuckled. "It's fun reading your own obituary in *The Times*. Now that I've resurfaced, Momo and I haven't figured out how to handle the condolence letters; some of them were even sincere. Momo doesn't think it's very funny. She's still badly shaken up."

Ritter waited for the information to set in to his protégé's mind. "One more thing. The bad news is that you're a hero without a job and a paycheck. The good news is that you're the most famous hotelier around, so you will get your pick of the job litter."

"Stop!" Matt said. "Right now, all I want is to see if I can walk. The doctors promised I could give it a try after you leave."

Rolfe grinned. "It's only a few steps to her room. I know when to take a hint."

*

"So you're Britney. You're as beautiful as your mother." Matt, hooked up to a mobile I.V. machine, stood beaming by Britney's bed while her mother looked nervously on.

"I don't feel very beautiful," Britney said, self-consciously stroking her long red hair.

"Well, you are." He turned to Beth. "Isn't she?"

"In my biased opinion, yes. But it's good to have a man's confirmation."

"I feel I know you so well." Britney gazed at him with happy eyes. "After all, all my mother did was rave about you for days on end."

Beth Taylor blushed. "It was hardly raving. Anyway, we had to talk about something, didn't we?"

Chapter 119
Los Angeles

"Tylenol with Codeine," Dr. Gillespie said. "That's all he's to have."

"I need something stronger. How about morphine or a double dose of Vicodin?" Matt wailed. "I'm in agony every time I turn over on my side."

Gillespie was unmoved. "Physical therapy starts tomorrow." He gestured toward the bed. "If you think this is agony . . ." He swept out of the room, his entourage in his wake.

"A martini?" Matt called after him, to no avail.

Succor came in the form of Beth Taylor, who entered on the arm of a nurse Matt hadn't seen before. Her eyes twinkled.

"Look at me. One more day and I'm out of here. And Britney's leaving today. Back to the Kisels. I'll miss her."

"You'll be seeing plenty of her," Matt said, reaching for his lover's hand and guiding her to the side of his bed.

"As much as I can."

"And even more of me."

She grinned. "Don't be so sure. I might get sick of you."

"Tough. I plan to be with you every second of every day. You get in too much trouble when I'm not around."

She leaned to kiss him. "If you insist."

He remembered the feel of her, the joy of her, and despite the pain tried to pull her next to him.

"You'll have to wait," Beth said. "You've got visitors. A crowd."

*

"I'm Kenneth Palmer. We spoke when you were semi comatose." The dapper, bespectacled Englishman, resplendent in a pinstriped suit, light-blue shirt, and regimental tie, extended his hand.

Matt shook it and acknowledged Momo and Rolfe Ritter with a huge smile.

"You remember Ron Falkman, don't you?" Rolfe asked.

"I certainly do. Hello, Mr. Falkman."

"Despite my rapidly advancing decrepitude, I'd rather you called me Ron. All my friends do." He shook Matt's hand but kept his eyes on Beth. "And this is?"

"Beth Taylor. My fiancée."

Beth stared at him—the engagement was news to her—and blushed. "Charmed," she said, poking Matt in his sore ribcage.

"Congratulations," said a bulky man in an open-necked golf shirt and windbreaker who brought up the rear of the party.

"This is Amnon Sapir," Ron explained. "He's not here. At least not officially. But without him, you might not be around for the marriage."

"I owe my life to one of his agents," Rolfe said. "And we all owe him and Kenneth an immense debt of gratitude."

"*Shalom*," Sapir said with a shallow bow. "I understand you've been having fun and games. Nothing like saving the Free World to add spice to the days before Christmas."

"I wouldn't call it fun," Matt said. "And as for saving the world . . ."

"Maybe it's an exaggeration; however, fortunately we'll never know how much of one it really is." Kenneth Palmer's voice was so somber it seemed to darken the room.

"Maybe you can clear things up for me?" Matt asked. "I've been watching CNN and reading the newspapers and I'm beginning to feel like I've just stepped through Alice's looking glass. According to the media, a group of American ultra-nationalists was behind the attempted bombing, the only purpose of which was to kill the president because of his recent signing of the immigration bill. Officially, the Secret Service had known of the plot for months and was working to find out whom else, if anybody, was involved. The president was never in real danger. I was the unwitting hotel manager who stumbled into the middle of it, by chance, outed some of the bad guys and was caught in the crossfire. Instant hero status for getting shot!" He scratched his head. "Tell me, please, how all that squares with Netski, Lee and their cronies."

"The press reported what the Secret Service fed them," Palmer said. "They conferred with us, and Amnon and I agreed to let the story stand. I'm always amazed how gullible the media are, to say nothing of their listeners and readers. But imagine the uproar if they knew how close we were to real catastrophe."

Sapir approached the bed. "Let me tell you something, young man. With your bent for heroics, you should join our country's Golani Brigade—they're all as crazy as you. I'm glad you lived to talk about it. A few days ago, neither Kenneth nor I would have taken a bet on your survival. Or especially not yours, Miss Taylor."

Palmer chuckled paternally. "Seeing you alive, and being British, I am reminded that you epitomize an inevitable Churchill quote: '. . . live dangerously; take things as they come; dread naught; and all will be well.'"

Rolfe leaned against the window ledge. "I wanted everyone here so you both could get the full story at the same time Momo and I did."

"By the way," Momo added, "there's a gaggle of reporters camped outside the hospital waiting to speak to you. We told them you were in critical condition, but they won't leave. I suggest you delay it as long as you can, read a prepared statement—Kenneth can write it for you—answer a few planted questions, and claim you're not strong enough to talk any more. That'll at least give you time before you decide how much you ultimately want to say."

"Meanwhile," Palmer said, "talk to us. Before we start with our story, I want to know how you figured out that there were explosives inside the boilers and how in heaven's name you knew that'd be set to go off on opening day."

*

Matt explained. When he finished, Amnon looked at his British counterpart. "We were very lucky, fate plays strange games," he said. "Without Matt . . ."

"Thank heaven you were there," Palmer said. "It proves that despite our vaunted intelligence gathering machines, luck and instinct trump science and technology time and again."

"*Nu*," Falkman said. "Enough foreplay. What really happened?"

Sir Kenneth began. "It's a long and complicated story, so bear with us."

Matt grinned. "I'm not going anywhere."

Beth glared at him. "Nor am I. If he stays I stay."

"Good. Immediately after Matt's incredible display of courage and all broke loose at the Resort, the head of the Secret Service detail responsible for the Summit—he'd shut me out until that moment—contacted me at the British Consulate in L.A. He wanted to know what I knew; I have a feeling it was less curiosity than to cover his behind. I helicoptered down to the Resort and went through everything I knew about Blenheim and the Borotins with him and his team.

"Minutes later, the FBI rounded up Blenheim's engineering, maintenance and security people who hadn't slipped off the property. They're being questioned even as we speak. From what we've gleaned so far, there's no question that Jack Turner, the previous chief of security at the Resort, had his car brakes deliberately sabotaged. We assume it was a murder attempt—that's why he drove off the road. Luck was on Turner's side that day."

"Motherfuckers!" Matt's face was pale.

"His replacement, Brad Marshall, was the lynchpin in the recruitment and placement effort at the Resort, while Dieter Weiss headed up Blenheim's internal maneuvers."

"Including putting Jimmy Lee in over me," Beth interrupted. "I second Matt's remark."

"Thanks to Rolfe's people in the San Francisco hotel, we knew Weiss's real name was Manfred Wangen. When we dug into the mysterious Herr Wangen, we found out he was a controller who'd worked for a German chain until internal auditors discovered he'd colluded with the purchasing manager of the Frankfurter Hof to skim 20 percent off the top of everything the hotel bought. Two years in prison followed. When he got out, it didn't take long for the Borotins to recruit him and erase his previous history. Exit Wanger, enter Weiss."

Beth shivered. "He was the second most loathsome man I've ever known."

"The FBI haven't found even a trace of him yet. My guess is when you told Jimmy Lee that Weiss was stealing from the company and handed him the doctored accounts, Netski probably decided he'd been betrayed by his loyal lieutenant and had the German killed. If I'm correct, his body will never be found."

"A lingering death, I hope." Beth's eyes lit up at the idea.

"Who knows? Those folks don't believe in warnings; murder is just another part of their regular business day."

"But they warned me a dozen times," Matt protested. "How come I'm still alive?"

"Timing, my dear boy. Without you, the Resort wouldn't have been host to the Summit. According to your friend Tim Matheson, Dieter Weiss tried, on several occasions, to persuade the State Department that you weren't essential to the Summit. Tim put his foot down and would have none of it. In other words, if you weren't at the Resort, no Summit. When you got involved with other GMs from the Ritter Era, Blenheim had two choices: kill you and risk the Summit, or control you by all means possible. They planned to kill you once the bomb went off if, by any miracle, you weren't killed in the blast. The FBI found a bomb under the front seat of your car that would've exploded the moment you turned on the ignition, and I suspect there were two or three other plans for your untimely demise as well."

"My God, Matt!" Beth whispered. "So that's why they kept me around! I had to be your watchdog. It wasn't just about finding out what you were doing, it was in order for them to keep control."

Palmer's blue eyes connected with the young woman's. "Precisely. They didn't know about your previous personal history with Matt or count on you both falling in love with each other and you telling him what was happening. If you'd have been no use to them, they'd have fired you—or gotten rid of you in a more permanent way. Surely you and your daughter stood no chance if their plan had succeeded."

"Beth wasn't the only woman watching Matt," Sapir said. "Olivia Wade, real name Harriet Berner, was a longtime employee of the Borotins, based in Zug, Switzerland. According to the Resort's CCTV cameras, she left the grounds about an hour before the anticipated bombing. The Mexican police discovered the wreckage of her make of car just north of Ensenada. The few parts of her body they found were unrecognizable. DNA and dental records proved it was her. My guess is that the Borotins were simply clearing house. Standard operating procedure for them, I would guess."

"After they'd 'cleared' Bertrand, Gidon and Sammi," Matt muttered. "Why? Because they were asking too many questions?"

"Certainly Le Roi and Lahav were," Palmer answered. "We think Chalabi was kidnapped and saved for a time when his murder would be the clearest warning to you. But even that didn't stop you."

Punishment not only for Rolfe, but for him. The realization branded his brain like an iron. "Oh God, what have I done?" He began to sob.

Beth cradled the patient and smothered his face with gentle kisses. "My darling, it's history. You can't change the past. If Bertrand hadn't contacted you . . ."

"I know, but it's awful."

"Stop the self-pity," Rolfe said sternly. "Those men were doomed whether or not you had any contact with them. Once they started digging around they were finished. Their deaths are my responsibility, not yours. They were being loyal to the company I'd created; loyal to me. You couldn't have done anything for them. You did at least save hundreds, more likely thousands, of lives."

His mentor's words were no solace. His mind reeled as much as his heart ached. Matt tried to compose himself. "What about Leon Barken?"

"I can answer that," Amnon said. "He disobeyed Blenheim's instructions and set up shop for himself. Petty espionage, blackmail; stupid stuff. But when Lahav's tips started us investigating, the Blenheim group panicked and Battini came up with the stunt at the Church of the Holy Sepulchre. I told our police to let everyone think the investigation was over, but just to give us time to dig into the mess. Right now, there are more important matters."

"Like Fabrizio Battini," Kenneth Palmer said with a touch of pride. "We finally got the Secret Service to listen to us. The FBI sent a team to Battini's Manhattan apartment and found him near death—an overdose of valium compounded by a cocktail of cocaine and cognac. Apparently a suicide attempt. But the note he left on his laptop was patently a fake and his would-be killers fortunately were clumsy, rushed and botched things, and he's now snug in a New York State federal facility. The Feds have taken over Battini's offices and between what they found there and what they were able to reconstruct from his laptop, they report a treasure trove of goodies."

He stretched and preened. "The real treasure trove, of course, is Battini himself. At first, he wouldn't talk—seemed more terrified of Borotin's retribution than the U.S. system of justice. So he was given some options: a few days with Amnon's Mossad friends; an extended stay in Guantanamo; a cell with the meanest bunch of homophobes in nearby jails; location at a prison where Borotin's murderers could get to him. And, if he told us everything, a guarantee of full federal protection. That did the trick. Now the chairman of Blenheim Partners can't stop talking. It's more exciting than a le Carré thriller."

Beth interrupted excitedly. "Did Battini tell the FBI where they were holding Britney and me? Is that how we were rescued?"

Palmer shrugged. "Tell her, Amnon."

The Israeli looked at Momo. "The answer is no. Battini had no idea whatsoever. He was just a front man and kept well out of the loop. Mrs. Ritter had the idea of putting up a reward leading to the arrest of one of your kidnappers; man named Carlos Fuentes. You'd recognize him, I'm sure, by the smell of his breath."

Beth paled. "How much was the reward?"

"One hundred thousand dollars."

"My God!" She walked over to Rolfe's wife and bowed her head in supplication. "How can we ever repay you?"

"You've already done so," Momo said, visibly moved. "You're here."

"Fuentes's lawyer was a high-priced criminal defense attorney," Sapir continued quickly, lest the level of emotion grow too high. "I say 'was,' because as soon as he found out he would personally be investigated for his ties to this mess, the loyal counsel dropped the case like a red-hot potato, leaving Fuentes without an advocate. Somehow Sir Kenneth persuaded the LAPD to let my men spend some intimate time with *Señor* Fuentes. Miraculously, Fuentes provided the information of your whereabouts, proving that after all, he had a benign heart."

Beth shuddered. "I don't think I could bear to face him at his trial."

"You won't have to, my dear," Palmer said softly. "Fuentes apparently also had a weak heart and died in the prison hospital from injuries sustained during his capture."

"How convenient," Ron Falkman muttered.

Not a muscle moved on the faces of the two counter intelligence men.

"Time for a break," Rolfe announced after an uncomfortable silence. "Anyone for Starbucks?"

Only Beth stayed behind.

*

"Snake," she hissed. "Worm. Cockroach. Lowlife. Your fiancée?"

Matt glanced at her, all innocence. "Well, aren't you?"

"I don't know. Usually, an engagement depends on a proposal and the acceptance of that proposal by the other party."

"I could hardly get down on my knees. Besides, you looked so alluring standing there that the word just came out."

"Then propose, damn you. And I'll give you an answer."

"Will you marry me?"

"Of course, idiot."

She avoided the obstacles of an IV and a phalanx of bandages, and they kissed with the pent-up passion of hungry lovers too long abstinent.

Though the rest would have to wait.

*

"Battini's information enabled us to put together most of the puzzle," Palmer said, munching contentedly on a chocolate and banana muffin. They had brought back their coffees, including cups for Matt and Beth.

"Someone in the top echelons of the Chinese government reasoned that if the G8 nations—indeed, all the industrial countries with whom the Chinese did business—could be destabilized, those countries would have no choice but to turn to China, not only for economic reasons but for global leadership and, as a result, would fall into China's so-called 'sphere of influence.'

"The group the Chinese government assembled for this assignment determined that the catalyst would be industrial and political espionage, blackmail, assassinations, bombings and other assorted crimes, all aimed at their economic and trading national partners, blows that would weaken those nations politically and economically, and, inevitably, catapult China to world leadership.

"The problem was, how to pull this off in multiple countries at the same time?

"The answer: concentrate on hotels. Tourism is the global industry. Western hotels were proliferating everywhere, including China. Why not buy a major global hotel chain to use as a front for their activities. Best would be a U.S.-owned chain, so that if anyone linked the crimes to the chain, the world would assume the Americans were behind them, and the Chinese would be further benefited."

"Incredible!" Rolfe gasped.

"Brilliant!" Falkman added.

"Israel should have thought of this idea first," Sapir muttered.

Palmer put up his hand. "Let me continue. Brilliant it certainly was. But the planning group saw a major flaw. They didn't want the risk of being directly linked to the hotel chain, nor did they have the cultural or operational resources to run such a chain, let alone the people. All they had was unlimited money. They needed a partner without morals, ruthless enough to commit the crimes and to keep their mouths shut about the Chinese connection."

"Ta-da! Enter the Borotins," Momo announced. "The Russian Mafia."

"Precisely," Sapir said. "Big brother Yuri made the deal through the Te-Wu and delegated the planning and execution of the whole operation to his baby brother Vasily. Of course having Borotin and his pals involved was an added bonus for the Chinese. They would be able to make sure that there were enough clues implicating Russia and, by natural extension, its government in the whole affair, further making China look holier than thou and looking like the only alternative for world order. Gradual but inevitable Chinese domination. I've never seen anything as audacious."

Palmer again took center stage. "Vasily found the front man he needed, Fabrizio Battini, a completely amoral, small-time broker with expensive tastes and unsavory habits, who was all too happy to go to 'the dark side,' as Fabrizio himself put it.

"Under Vasily's tutelage Battini found a hungry, relatively new banking firm, Strands, to approach every multi-national hotel company chairman to find a chain willing to sell. Rebuffed time and again, they finally found one."

"My dear friend, Sir Martin bloody Treadway," Rolfe whispered.

"Exactly. He didn't do due diligence on Blenheim. Greed overwhelmed him. There was too much money for him in the deal."

Sapir grunted in disgust. "The Chinese government wrote a giant check for Kestrel Hotels and Resorts. And they paid three billion dollars up front to the Borotin brothers, with a further seven to come on the achievement of certain milestones on the road to achieving their objectives."

Rolfe swallowed; his throat was dry. "No wonder Blenheim didn't give a damn about profits. The Chinese didn't care and the Russians only wanted their pay-off."

"Amazing." Ron Falkman's face had lost its color. "The Chinese government simply sub-contracted their plan for global terrorism to the Borotins."

Beth's excitement was manifest in her shrill voice. "And sent Jimmy Lee to L.A. to report on what was going on."

"Yes to both. By the way, Jimmy Lee was in charge of certain clean-up matters and subcontracted work to locals in various parts of the world where the Borotins may not have had such influence," Sapir answered.

"A critical part of the plan mandated that Blenheim put its people in key positions in the target locations," Palmer commented.

"So getting rid of my people wasn't spite, only business," Rolfe said.

"Simple as that," Palmer responded. "The bombings and killings started at Kestrels and Audleys around the world. The Chinese were delighted. The Borotins weren't even particularly disturbed when Le Roi started digging. They just killed him, spread their money around the French police and selected government officials, and—*voila*!—the investigation evaporated."

He looked at Matt. "The big prize wasn't planned, it simply fell into their laps. You, Matt, told Dieter Weiss that the Resort had made it onto the State Department's short list for the Summit and bragged that you'd struck up a good relationship with the staff involved. Weiss told Battini. Battini told the Borotins, who then passed it on to Jimmy Lee. Imagine how their little evil hearts pounded. The G8. What an opportunity! The Chinese saw this as a way to shortcut matters and decided they wanted instant global domination."

Sapir sighed, "The Audley Resort was on top of State's short list but that wasn't good enough for the Borotins. Just to be sure, they blackmailed or greased State Department staffers and some well-placed politicians. Word is that the Resort would have got it without help."

Matt groaned.

"You look dismayed," Palmer went on. "But you were just doing your job—doing it better than any other GM in America."

Amnon drained his coffee. "Vasily came up with the idea of planting bombs in the equipment and figured out that the Chinese would be all too happy to oblige with the manufacturing. With one explosion he'd wipe out the most powerful leaders in the world, including his brother's own arch enemy, the President of Russia."

"And the leaderless world would immediately look to China for stability and salvation," Ron said.

"Simple," Sapir shrugged. "What's more, Vasily arranged for a trail of clues that would eventually lead through Pakistan to Al Qaeda, and evidence would be found to show that the bombing was to punish the U.S. for meddling in the Middle East and blaming Israel for every ill. Needless to say, the Al Qaeda operatives would inevitably show up dead. Ron's mysterious CIA friend gave the Feds the lead, but it was ignored. Finally, Kenneth's team located the address in suburban San Diego, but all they found were four dead Pakistani bodies and information implicating Al Qaeda. If they'd have found them alive, I bet we'd have had an information bonanza."

Palmer, too, put down his coffee. "If things would have gone as planned, the Muslim world would be even more enraged with the United States and would welcome the Chinese as their allies."

"While Israel became a friendless pariah in the new world order," Sapir added. "Always lots of ifs in this game."

"The Borotins flew to Beijing, met with the head of Te-Wu, and explained Vasily's new plan. Within days, an additional five billion showed up in the Borotins bank. More bribery and blackmail greased the way for them in the U.S. There's a certain senior senator about to resign for reasons of ill health today, a missing high-level congressman who's been implicated and a very senior FBI man under interrogation now. It wouldn't surprise me if there were more throughout government and their agencies. All signs point to someone high up in the Secret Service being implicated. They'll weed him out sooner or later." Palmer looked at five stunned faces. "You see how simple it was? Only they ran into one Matthew Dirksen."

"No wonder Netski settled the class action suit so readily," Rolfe said. "What's one-and-a-half-billion bucks compared to fifteen."

Momo took her husband's hand. "I suppose the stakes had become so high that it triggered Vasily's decision to take over the company himself."

Palmer looked into his old friend's eyes. "Rolfe, there's one thing you should know. According to Battini, Borotin wanted you out of the way so he'd have a legitimate reason to take over the company. Momo's cancer gave Blenheim the excuse to announce your resignation, knowing you'd be too preoccupied to make trouble. Without that, they'd have killed you."

Rolfe slumped back in his chair, eyes closed, as a lifetime of painful memories flashed through his mind.

"From bad things come good," Momo whispered to her husband.

"How are you feeling, Momo?" Sapir asked.

Momo grinned. "Chemo's finished and—knock on wood—there are no lingering cancer cells anywhere." She pulled off her turban to reveal a stubble of black hair. "It'll grow in soon, and then I intend to get some new boobs; this time . . ."

"Thank you for sharing that crucial information," Rolfe interrupted, revived by Momo's comment and joining in the general laughter. Beth brought them back to seriousness. "What happened to Jimmy Lee? Something terrible, I hope."

"Mr. Lee, a.k.a. Tang Shen-ming, fled to the Chinese Consulate in Los Angeles where he spent the night," Sapir explained. "The next day a Consulate car drove a single passenger to the Van Nuys Airport, where a man armed with a diplomatic passport and answering Jimmy Lee's description boarded a Challenger 604, bound for Beijing. We assume Lee was that passenger."

"Damn! damn!" Beth exclaimed.

"What did the Chinese government say?" Rolfe asked Palmer. "I presume you contacted them."

"Naturally. They claimed to be unaware that a Summit was taking place, had never heard of Blenheim or the Borotins or Tang Shen-ming, and announced officially that if there's ever a hint of an accusation, there will be—and I quote—'serious diplomatic and economic repercussions.'"

"You mean they're getting away with it?"

"Remember, I said 'officially.' Thanks to our own people in Beijing, and the CIA's humint—spies on the ground—we've learned there's been a purge in the senior ranks of government and the Te-Wu. For 'purge' read firing squad. We haven't been able to confirm it, but it's believed that Tang Shen-ming was one of the first to be shot."

"A quick death," Beth murmured. "Too bad."

"And the Borotins?" Falkman asked.

"The Russian government claims they're looking for Yuri, so far with no success. This may actually be true. Yuri has enough assets to live like an emperor anywhere in the world. And Vasily's officially dead, though when the FBI recover the body in that plane crash, I'll bet its DNA doesn't match Netski's."

"What about Vasily's girlfriend, Olga Petrova?" Momo queried.

"Gone to ground, as her father. With the Borotins subject to a worldwide manhunt, and old man Petrova linked to Yuri, my guess is it'll be a month of Sundays before that pair surface," Palmer answered.

"What was in the bombs?" Matt croaked. Exhaustion had overtaken him and he could barely speak.

"You want to know if they contained nuclear material."

"Fortunately not. That's the good news. The bad news is that there were enough explosives to obliterate the Resort and everything around it. Our CIA colleagues are crowing because they found out the Borotins got hold of enough Russian-manufactured RDX, otherwise known as Hexogen, to create the weapons, and sent it to China to place inside the boilers. Clever. If the bomb had exploded, there'd be no link to the Chinese."

"German boiler, Russian fissionable material, Russian installation team. If the operation went wrong, then it would look like the Russian government was involved," Sapir added. "Complete Chinese deniability and a win-win for them under all circumstances. The Borotins are brilliant."

"They came so close," Matt said, covering his face with his hand. "If only I'd . . ."

"Listen, Matt." Rolfe's voice sliced through the room. "No more 'ifs.' I've got a longer list than you do, starting with if I hadn't sold to Treadway and if Momo didn't have cancer."

"What about if the U.S. or British government had listened to us and cancelled the Summit?" Palmer said.

"What if people in the FBI and Secret Service hadn't been bribed?" Sapir complained.

"What if the CIA had officially become involved?" Falkman added.

"Speculation's useless," Rolfe went on. "In fact, you and Beth are heroes. That's the only 'if' that matters. If you two hadn't been around, the world would be one huge bonfire. I can't begin to imagine the chaos."

Matt thought it over. He felt as heroic as a soggy dish rag. Suddenly he wanted them all gone—his mentor, Momo, the intelligence men, even Beth. He had to work his own role through, and he could only do it in private. Mustering up his last iota of strength he said, "Rolfe, one last question. Are you sure the Resort can't recover?"

Chapter 120
Manhattan

Rolfe Ritter surveyed Falkman's conference room with disgust. The table was strewn with half-eaten sandwiches on paper plates, empty Starbucks coffee cups, shards of chocolate-chip cookies, and crumpled cans of coke and Red Bull, while the credenza hosted remnants of a platter of California rolls and opened packets of soy sauce from a neighboring restaurant named Sushi, Sushi and Sushi.

Those seated around the table, mostly young lawyers with bloodshot eyes, were equally unkempt—the men with ties askew, the women with uncombed hair—cell phones perched in ears, thumbs busily working Blackberries and iPhones with furious intensity, fingers pounding on laptop keyboards. It must have been, Rolfe thought, one hell of an all-nighter.

"They're not quite ready," Falkman told his visitor, ushering him quickly from the fetid room.

"Shit, Ron, it's fucking chaos," Rolfe said. "Not quite ready? This bunch doesn't look like they could arrange a one-car funeral."

"Relax." Falkman led Rolfe to his office. "I told them you'd be leaving for London in a couple of hours, and if the papers weren't ready, they could kiss their Christmas bonuses goodbye. You'll be signing the contract in a few minutes."

"Seeing's believing," Rolfe said, sitting in an easy-chair to the side of Ron's desk.

Falkman sat at his desk, facing him. "This is a big day. You're about to pull off an amazing deal. What I have to know is how you swung it?"

"Come on, Ron, you know most of it, and I'm damn sure you guessed the rest."

"I know the terms. Explain the how part."

The hotelier leaned back, patently enjoying himself. "When we left young Dirksen lying in that hospital bed, I couldn't stop thinking about the Resort. It would've been criminal to let it languish, but there was no one left at Kestrel to make a decision about anything, let alone how to handle the aftermath of the near disaster. It was my hotel, my brainchild, built with my sweat and blood. I knew private equity vultures would quickly start circling around, wanting to buy Kestrel from Blenheim, break it up and sell off the pieces—my company, my creation, my life's work." He grimaced. "I couldn't stand it."

"Don't forget, others sweated and bled beside you. Me, for example. Start believing in your own bullshit and it's the beginning of the end."

"You're right. Sorry. Anyway, the next morning I called Palmer and we had breakfast at his hotel."

"Sir Kenneth! How was he involved with Kestrel?"

"He wasn't. But he'd been resurrected by his prime minister after both our State Department and the FBI admitted they should've listened to his warnings. Anyway, we worked out a plan."

Ron leaned forward. He was enjoying himself too. "Which was what?"

"Kenneth called the number two person at State and told her he'd learned that I was so angry about their bungling that I was about to sell the entire story to the media—that I'd hired the William Morris Agency to effect the sale, and that a bidding war had already started."

Falkman was horrified. "I hope you'd never do such a thing."

Rolfe grinned. "You know me better than that."

"That's the problem. I do know you, all too well."

"Palmer warned that if the story were disclosed, there'd be devastating consequences. It wasn't merely a question of Rolfe's story exposing a coverup, the bigger issue would be the public realizations that the U.S. couldn't even handle security at a single hotel. The FBI and Secret Service would be ridiculed, just when they were most needed to combat terrorism. Too, despite Chinese denials of participation, there'd inevitably be a rift with them with serious political implications. As for the Russians . . ."

"Okay, Okay, I get it. He scared the shit out of them. Then what happened?"

"He explained that he'd known me for years, having replaced my late godfather, his predecessor at MI6, in my affections. Maybe he could persuade me to keep quiet. But it wouldn't be easy. He'd have to offer me something more valuable than the fortune I'd make by selling the story."

Falkman roared. "I can't believe you're still these playing games at your age!"

"I learned from the most Machiavellian of them all," Rolfe shrugged. "You."

Falkman smiled at the younger man with his trademark 'butter wouldn't melt in my mouth' look. Rolfe continued, "What could State offer for my silence? Kenneth was at a loss. They talked for an hour. Then—inspiration! Kenneth had an idea that might work, and it wouldn't cost State a penny."

"Let me guess," Ron said, wiping tears of laughter from his eyes. "The very proper Sir Kenneth Palmer suggested the U.S. government persuade Blenheim to sell its Kestrel holdings to its former owner at a fraction of what it was worth. In exchange, Mr. Ritter would agree to sign the strictest confidentiality agreement ever penned."

"Give that man a prize! State called their cooperation a reward for my services."

"And persuaded Battini to agree to the sale so that he'd escape a death sentence. So what if he runs Blenheim from a prison cell? He's still its chairman and can sign papers on the company's behalf."

"And as I said to Palmer when we were making this up, who's going to complain? The Chinese government, who denied the incident ever took place? The Borotins, who've disappeared? Netski who has his life back as Vasily Borotin? Not a chance. The State Department's going to use my money to pay for their Summit costs—and yes, before you ask, some of it's actually going back into Kestrel. The State Department still has a valid contract with the hotel for the Summit and is going to pay Kestrel every last penny of what it owes. So in a way, I'm paying myself. I can use the money to relaunch the Resort and profit from the publicity. It'll be the best known and most demanded resort in the world. I can promise you one thing, it won't be my last resort."

"Absolutely incredible," Falkman said, awestruck. "The deal's the closest thing to legalized theft I've ever encountered."

"Glad you approve, Maestro." Rolfe pulled a piece of paper from his jacket pocket and handed it to his lawyer. "This is a list of members of my old gang who are still in the company or rejoining it now that the bad guys have gone. The percentages next to each name are how much of the company I want them to own. Also some is going to the families of Bertrand, Gidon, Sammi and Yossi Bar El."

"A regular Robin Hood," said Ron.

Tears suddenly sprang to Rolfe's eyes. "It's the way to give to the living and my thanks to those who died."

"I've worked out the financing," Ron said quietly. "The little you have to pay for Kestrel you'll receive by way of a bridge loan from your friendly Wall Street bankers. You won't have to put in a penny from your own pocket. The security is the company itself. The interest rates your banker buddies are charging are piggishly high, but it doesn't matter. You're playing with their dough.

"Within a few months, assuming the stock market holds up, you'll be launching an initial public offering and will sell 70 percent of the stock in a company called Metropolitan Hotels, currently a division of Kestrel. By segregating it from the rest of Kestrel Hotels and Resorts, you'll have created a stand-alone, very large and substantial midmarket hotel franchising business. I believe it'll be a hot stock and its shares will soar after the IPO on the New York Stock Exchange."

Rolfe knew both the melody and the lyrics. "Of course it will. The bankers have priced the deal cheaply enough to make sure it sells quickly, so they get their bridge loan back and pocket their outrageous fees for engineering the deal. Bonuses all round, new houses in the Hamptons galore."

"And they won't be finished with you. Since you retained 30 percent of its stock, you'll be the Metropolitan chairman. They'll besiege you with new opportunities. You'll either agree to some of the deals, or, more likely—knowing how much you dislike the franchising business—you'll auction off Metropolitan to one of the public hotel chains and make a fortune. Whatever happens won't matter. You haven't laid out a penny for this part of the company. It's what my grandfather called *geffininer geld*."

"Meaning?"

"It's Yiddish for found money."

"I just want to be clear. Once Metropolitan goes public, I'll have paid back the money I borrowed and won't owe anyone anything?"

"Not a nickel."

"So when the dust settles, I'll own Kestrel Hotels and Resorts debt free without having put up a single penny?"

"Bingo! It's truly the deal of your life." Falkman looked squarely at his overjoyed friend. "This time, please don't screw it up."

"I won't. Promise."

Ron shook his head. "I know you better than you know yourself. Something will happen and you'll be in deep shit all over again."

"Me?" Rolfe feigned surprise. Already his mind was leaping into the years ahead. "I'll be Kestrel's chairman and CEO, but I'm much too old to be its president—that job takes real work, and I intend to be with Momo on some tropical isle watching the sunset."

"You have a candidate for the job, of course?"

"My initial idea had been that Kestrel's first press release would announce the appointment of Matthew Dirksen as its new president and COO. God knows, he's shown his loyalty."

"You said, 'initial idea.' Does that mean it won't be Matt?"

"The more I thought about it, the more I realized that he'd want to put the Resort back on the map. He's so closely identified with the place now that it would be crazy for him to do anything else. Besides, he loves the place. After he found out that Beth was safe, the first words out of his mouth in the hospital were about his property. I looked around the company and concluded I wanted a young, ambitious, energetic, self-starter who could grow into the job, who I would enjoy training and could ultimately be a candidate for CEO when I retire."

Falkman shrieked with laughter. "You? Retire? Who's kidding who? The only way you'll retire is when they nail the lid down on your coffin! Enough already—who's your new president?"

"Beth Taylor, the press release will be on the wire as soon as your geniuses give me the contracts to sign."

Ron grinned from ear to ear "At least you're true to form—you've always had an eye for beautiful women. Promise me you'll keep your pants zipped up with this one."

"Yeah, Yeah! Momo said the same thing. Besides, Matt's a big guy and I'm too old to outrun him. If Beth and he marry, as I suspect they will, it'll be out-and-out nepotism, but who gives a damn? It'll be my company and I sure as hell don't!"

One of Falkman's junior partners poked his head around the door. "We're ready for Mr. Ritter. All you need to bring is your pen."

"Just in time," Rolfe said. "Ron, can you arrange for a limo? I've got to be at the airport in an hour."

Falkman took his arm. "Of course. Sign the papers and start a new chapter in your life. God help us both!"

Chapter 121
London / Monaco

EUF corporate headquarters hadn't changed in two years. A life-size picture of its chairman, Sir Martin Treadway, still dominated the reception area; watercolors by Miro, Chagall and Cecil Beaton still graced the hallways. Rolfe had been fired the last time he visited. Now . . .

Treadway, impeccably dressed in a grey suit, tailored shirt, and blood-red tie, stood as Rolfe entered and extended his hand.

"Rolfe, dear boy, how wonderful to see you again. Do sit down."

Rolfe sat on the large brocade-covered sofa while Sir Martin chose a matching armchair at right angles to him.

"I understand congratulations are in order," the Englishman said. "Your press release crossed the wire last night."

"Thanks," Rolfe replied without a hint of sincerity.

"Not come to sell me Kestrel a second time, have you?" Treadway smiled at his joke.

Rolfe didn't. "No. I've come to talk to you about my stock in EUF."

"What stock? I don't understand."

"I still own a substantial number of shares, remember. Part of my payment for selling you the company. Too, I had outstanding stock options when you booted me out. Over a million options, I believe."

"I didn't exactly 'boot' you," Treadway sputtered.

"It doesn't matter. I have five years to vest those options and the share price today is less than it was when they were granted."

Treadway scowled. "What's that got to do with anything?"

He's getting angry, Rolfe thought. Good. "You lived like royalty off this company after you bought Kestrel, and Blenheim paid you a fortune for it. But during that time EUF stock had underperformed its peers. I want you to make the stock price higher."

"Take it up with your broker." Treadway stood. "Don't waste my time."

"Sit down, Martin. I haven't even started yet."

Sir Martin Treadway sat.

"Let me tell you an irrefutable fact," Rolfe went on, his tone dry ice. "Your greed and ambition were the root cause of what could have been a major disaster. As it is, your sale of Kestrel to Blenheim, without the requisite due-diligence on the buyers, has contributed to a substantial number of deaths. Do you want me to list them?"

Color drained from Treadway's face. "So what?" he spat. "Selling your hotel business for a high price isn't illegal. In our world, as we both know, it's commendable. The fact that some people died is of no consequence legally. This conversation is finished. Be so good as to leave my office."

Rolfe smiled, opened his briefcase, and extracted a file. "This is a private investigator's report I'd had prepared on you when you bought my company. It was updated a year later and then again two weeks ago. You can read it at your leisure. I think you know what it says."

The Englishman picked up the file as though it contained anthrax. He blanched.

"What do you want?" he whispered.

"Your resignation from EUF and all the corporate and charitable boards you sit on."

"Never!"

"Then the report goes public. Every rule you broke, every law you circumvented, every financial regulation you disregarded, every perquisite you somehow forgot to divulge, the political contributions the company made that bought you your precious knighthood. They're all documented. You might just avoid jail, but you'll be fighting lawsuits for the rest of your life. As to your reputation . . ."

He rose, turned, walked swiftly from the office. Only when he reached the street did his emotions erupt. Passersby gave him wide berth. Why come anywhere near a well-dressed madman howling with laughter at the wind?

*

Rolfe concluded his account. “It was fun. Fun!”

He sipped the vintage pink Tattinger he and Momo were sharing on the balcony of their penthouse apartment overlooking Monte Carlo’s marina.

His wife settled next to him on the chaise. “I wish I’d been there.”

“You were. In my heart. I did it for you, for both of us. After all, we’ll need to be secure in our old age.” He caressed her hair, almost fully regrown, shining in the golden sunset. On his lap lay the day’s edition of the *Financial Times*.

“SIR MARTIN TREADWAY RETIRES. EUF STOCK SOARS,” the headline read.

Momo kissed him. A long-unused phrase came into his mind: Information is key. Knowledge is power.

Chapter 122
The Côte d'Azur

High in the hills above Eze, in the heart of France's southern Riviera, two men sat watching the same sunset as Rolfe and Momo Ritter. Surrounded by heavily-armed guards, they had not moved from their heavily-fortified compound since their arrival weeks before.

The older man signaled for a fresh bottle of vodka. A servant brought it within seconds. He filled two glasses; both men drained them.

"We came close, Little Brother. Very close." He poured again.

"I understand the mistakes I made," Vasily Borotin said. "I won't make them the next time."

Yuri raised his glass high. "Lift your glass. We're going to drink a toast."

Vasily did as commanded. "What to?"

Yuri Borotin's laughter rose to the heavens. "To the next time."

EPILOGUE

Century City, Los Angeles

"How was the trip?" Ron Falkman asked.

"Terrific. Momo and I just got back to L.A. last night. You should see the new Audley Resort in Bora Bora. Bloody fantastic! It's the best in the Pacific. The opening party was amazing. The owner really went to town, even flew over the French prime minister." Rolfe Ritter leaned back in his leather desk-chair, feet up on the desk, ankles crossed, phone comfortably cradled in his ear, contentedly sipping on Starbucks double espresso cappuccino. "I've just walked into the office. What's up?"

"I assume you've been following this damned financial crisis?"

"Sure. Business slipped fast but we implemented cost-cutting measures at all the hotels, and things are slowly picking up. Beth is terrific, working 24/7 and executing our contingency plans perfectly. Business will come back; it always does."

"It's not business that's the issue right now. You've got bigger problems than that."

Falkman's comments doused Rolfe's mood with the speed of a tsunami. "What the hell are you talking about?"

"Listen to me very carefully for once Rolfe, this is serious. Your initial public offering for Metropolitan Hotels is off. The markets are too volatile, business went down too far during the pits of the recession, the banks have their own troubles and are skittish. There is no investment banker interested in taking on an IPO like this now or in the foreseeable future. Most still have egg on their faces over failed offerings and are hunkered down in their own Wall Street bunkers."

"You warned me that was a risk when we were signing the contracts. It's no big deal. Even if business keeps going down the toilet, there's plenty of money to keep paying interest on the debt. When the economy gets better we'll try again."

"I told you to listen. Please do just that."

His lawyer's coldness jolted Rolfe back in his chair. He pulled his legs off his desk and leaned forward, a familiar hollow feeling growing like cancer in his stomach. "I'm sorry, Ron, go on."

"Your friendly Wall Street banks that lent you the money are in deep trouble. The Feds put in dough to keep it alive, but the price was heavy government oversight. All your buddies are out. The new gang are cleaning shop and showing the regulators how tough they are."

"And . . .?"

"And they've called your loan."

"What? How can they do that?" Rolfe shouted.

"Calm down. Your screeching doesn't impress me. In order to buy the company from Blenheim, you borrowed the money from your investment banks on a bridge loan, repayable upon the IPO."

"Sure. When the economy turns, I'll do an IPO and pay them back. What's the problem?"

"The problem is that the terms of the loan are very clear—you have to pay it back on an IPO or within a year. It's been eleven months and they're notifying you they want their money back in exactly one month from yesterday."

"So we'll find a bank that will lend us the money and pay those bloodsuckers back. Their interest rates are usurious anyway."

"In case you haven't noticed, the banks are all in deep shit; they've shut up shop, Europe is in financial chaos, and governments everywhere throughout the world are having to step in. You've got more chance of being struck by lightning on a sunny day than getting a loan right now."

Rolfe slumped in his chair, stunned by the implications of Falkman's words. "If I can't pay the bank back, then what?" he whispered.

"They'll take the company. You're gone."

"Never! Not again! I'm never giving Kestrel up again. I'd rather put the company in bankruptcy and give myself time to work it out. Give it to those greedy bloodsuckers. Not a fucking chance!"

"Bankruptcy's not an option," Falkman said in measured words.

"Bullshit! Of course it is."

"Not in this case. Your loan documents say that if you put the company into bankruptcy you personally are liable for the money. It's called a 'bad boy' guarantee. You've given your personal guarantee to the bank. As I said, bankruptcy isn't an option."

"I'll sell some of our properties. People are always trying to buy them. We'd get a fortune from some Middle East fund for Vence alone."

"Only the bottom-fishermen are out there right now. If you sold all your real estate to them, you wouldn't have enough to pay off your debt. Besides, all your properties are mortgaged to the banks to secure your debt."

"What other options do I have that don't force me to lose some or all of the company?"

"None that I can see," Falkman said—a solemn judge delivering a death sentence.

"I'm fucked. What am I going to do?" Rolfe Ritter whispered, vainly seeking a straw to clutch.

"You'll do what you always do; scramble around, turn every leaf over in the forest and something will come up. It'll work out for you, it always has."

"How?"

Ron Falkman chuckled, "I have no idea, it's a mystery."